CHILDREN OF RHANNA

D1628479

CHILDREN OF RHANNA

Christine Marion Fraser

CORONET BOOKS

Hodder & Stoughton

Copyright © 1983 Christine Marion Fraser

First published in 1983 by Fontana
A division of HarperCollins*Publishers*
This edition published in 2000 by Hodder and Stoughton
A division of Hodder Headline

The right of Christine Marion Fraser to be identified as the Author of
the Work has been asserted by her in accordance with the Copyright,
Designs and Patents Act 1988.

10 9 8 7 6 5 4 3 2 1

All rights reserved. No part of this publication may be
reproduced, stored in a retrieval system, or transmitted,
in any form or by any means without the prior written
permission of the publisher, nor be otherwise circulated
in any form of binding or cover other than that in which
it is published and without a similar condition being
imposed on the subsequent purchaser.

All characters in this publication are fictitious and any resemblance to
real persons, living or dead, is purely coincidental.

A CIP catalogue record for this title is available from the British Library

ISBN 0 340 76569 0

Typeset in 11/13pt Garamond by
Phoenix Typesetting, Ilkley, West Yorkshire

Printed and bound in Great Britain by
Mackays of Chatham plc, Chatham, Kent

Hodder and Stoughton
A division of Hodder Headline
338 Euston Road
London NW1 3BH

To Tracy, for her timely reminder about the
S.S. *Politician*

Part One

Winter 1941

Chapter One

Fergus paced the kitchen at Laigmhor, his footsteps eerily enhanced by the silence that enshrouded him. The black cavern of the window with its drab covering of blackout blinds, gaped at him like the blank eye of a dead fish and added to his sense of desolation. Going over, he pulled the blind back a fraction. The mist lay over the moors and he could see nothing but dismal swirling wraiths floating and billowing over the landscape. The night sounds of Portcull came to him as in a dream; the echoes of a dog's bark from Murdy's house by the bridge that spanned the Fallan; faint sounds of merriment from one of the village cottages; the hoot of the steamer's horn from Portcull harbour; a wail from the siren. Captain Mac was certainly making the most of his enforced stay at safe anchorage. He had told Fergus he would ceilidh the night away with the help of Tam McKinnon's home-brewed malt whisky. From the sound of it one half of the ceilidh was on board ship, the other half no doubt in Tam McKinnon's cottage. A light flashed out at sea, filtering uncertainly through the hazy curtains of haar that warped everything that was normal and real. It all added to Fergus's own sense of unreality and he hunched his broad shoulders wearily and dug his hand into his jacket pocket, reassured for a moment as his fingers curled round the familiar stem of his pipe.

His thoughts were sluggish, mixed, taking him back over the strange events of that long exhausting day. It seemed years since they had boarded the steamer at Portcull harbour: At 6 a.m. the village was hushed and peaceful, the sea dark and calm, the ship's crew subdued and heavy-eyed after a night of ceilidhing with relatives on the island. Kirsteen was pale and drawn, heavy and awkward in the advanced stages of her pregnancy. Lachlan McLachlan, the doctor who tended the population of Rhanna, had advised Fergus to take Kirsteen to a mainland hospital because she was expecting twins and it was safer for her to be under constant medical supervision. She hadn't wanted to go. 'I want to have my babies at Laigmhor,' she had told Fergus somewhat defiantly. 'It seems right that they should be born here. I'll hate it in hospital.'

But something deep inside Fergus had rebelled at the idea. A flash of cowardice perhaps, a knowledge that in a hospital he would be divorced somewhat from the stark drama of birth. He hadn't wanted to go through that again. Far better a hospital, away from Laigmhor, away from Rhanna.

In the cabin she snuggled into him, fragile despite the swollen bulk of her belly, resentment and rebellion making her silent and uncharacteristically sullen. Her hands were cold but her face was warm against his and she smelt of fresh air and freshly laundered underwear. The faint fragrance of lavender clung to her and the smell reminded him vividly of Mirabelle, so much a part of Laigmhor for so many years, so much a part of everyone she had tended in her selfless years as housekeeper. Though she was gone now, she still lived in his memory and he had found himself wishing at that moment that she was still there with them all, fussing, comforting, scolding, safe, so safe.

He nuzzled Kirsteen's wheat-coloured curls and in a rush of protectiveness crushed her to him in a fierce embrace.

'I love your strength, you great brute of a man.' She laughed and he thought, 'I'm not strong, not now, not strong enough – for this.'

She lay in his arms, quietly, no resistance left in her, hardly even a smile for Kate McKinnon who came breezing into the cabin, her strong homely face full of sympathy as she surveyed first Kirsteen's stomach then her face. 'Ach, my poor lassie, just about well done they are from the look of the oven – ready to pop out any time, I'd say from the look of you – are you feeling all right, mo ghaoil? You look a wee bit tired.'

'I'm fine, Kate, I never was a good sailor, that's all.'

'Well at the rate we're going, we might as well get out and walk,' Kate said vigorously. 'Would you listen to that damnty siren! It's worse than Tam's snoring when he's had a bellyful of whisky.'

It wasn't till then that Fergus became fully aware that the ship's siren was blaring out at regular intervals and he stared at Kate. 'What's wrong?' he demanded. 'Don't tell me the mist has come down?'

'Ay, as thick as my head feels this morning,' Kate imparted cheerily. 'It will be tonight before I get to Barra at the rate we're going now.'

'You're going over to Barra then?' Kirsteen smiled, already feeling better in Kate's boisterous company.

'I am right enough, I thought I might go and visit some of my relatives there – and o' course to see how is the *Politician* doing. These damt salvors have made a fine mess o' things.' Kate's cheery face became sad. 'Fancy the likes – blowin' up a boat and all that good whisky still in her hold – but ach we might get a bit o' peace then and have no more o' thon officials sniffin' about the islands to see if we have been hidin' whisky and foreign money.'

Kate had every reason to sound huffed. Up until recently she and her husband, Tam, had been making a tidy little profit from the produce of his illicit whisky still, which was safely tucked away in a 'secret room' in old Annack Gow's blackhouse. The whisky had been bottled in small brown medicine containers and, in the guise of cough mixture, had found its way all over the island and spilt over into neighbouring islands. Tam and Kate had kith and kin living the length and breadth of the Hebrides and his superb-tasting malt whisky had found a ready market. Annack and a few of Tam's contemporaries had shared some of the 'takings', but it was to the crafty Tam that most of the profit had gone.

In February of that year the S.S. *Politician*, en route

from Mersey to Jamaica and the United States of America, had run aground on the rocks in Eriskay Sound. A large part of her cargo had consisted of twenty thousand cases of Scotch whisky, which the salvors had been unable to reach. The Hebrideans had heard the news with delight and from all over the islands, boat parties set forth, braving the dangerous waters of the Sound of Eriskay and the Minch. Bottles had bobbed in on the tide, crates full of whisky had been thrown onto sandy beaches, the whim of the wind deciding which island would be next to benefit from the water of life. Money had come in too, Jamaican ten-shilling notes, floating tantalisingly on the silken waves before being tossed ashore. It had been as if an Aladdin's cave had erupted under the sea to spew out its treasures. No one had known what to expect next; the chief occupation of the day was beachcombing. Bicycles and thousands of shirts had come from the *Politician*'s generous holds. It had been carnival time in the Hebrides, a spree of endless ceilidhs and uninhibited revelry. Jamaican money had circulated through the islands, as far north as Benbecula, and the Customs and the police, in a furore over the whole affair, had begun searching, finding a lot of the whisky but missing the bulk, recovering and destroying large amounts of Jamaican notes, though vast amounts had been left unaccounted for. A sweating Tam had closed down business for an indefinite period, being careful however to hide away a few casks of his malt 'for emergencies'.

At sight of Kate's soulful expression, Kirsteen burst out laughing. 'You're the limit, Kate. See how the *Politician* is doing indeed! Away to see what you can find more like! And I know fine that Tam's whisky is still popular despite the glut and folks are still willing to buy it.'

Kate looked suitably downcast. 'Ach well, times are hard so they are and Tam hasny the brains to be doin' much else but the odd job and brew a drop or two o' whisky on the side.' She sniffed dismally. 'Things was goin' fine for us till that damt boat hit those rocks and now my poor Tam has had to suspend his business for a whily. We might as well make the most o' things till the Customs have satisfied themselves that we are no' doin' them out o' anything . . .' A wide grin split her face. 'Fly they may be but no' as fly as us when it comes to hidin' things. Now – I'm away to see Mollie. She is needin' a shirt or two for Todd and is goin' to see will her sister in Uist slip her a few.'

She breezed away and the cabin was quiet again. Kirsteen smiled at Fergus and they settled down to read the magazines they had bought.

They were barely twelve miles out to sea when the first pain seized Kirsteen, so violently it took her breath away and made her tremble. But then the mist had crept thickly and insidiously over the water and the ship's engines had slowed till it seemed they had all but stopped.

Kirsteen lay back on the narrow bunk bed and tried not to let Fergus see that she was in pain but there was no fooling him and he stared at her, his eyes black with apprehension.

She forced a smile. 'Fergus, I'll be all right. These aren't proper pains, false I think they call them. It's too early for the babies to be born yet.'

'Lachlan says twins can be premature,' Fergus said tersely. 'What if they are coming? We're stuck out here and the mist is getting thicker. Dammit! It will take years to get to Oban at this rate.'

'We have to make a stop at Barra and then the Uists – if the worst happens we'll get a doctor there.'

'It's hours to Uist, we're only a few miles out from Rhanna. I can't let anything happen to you. I'm going to ask the Captain to turn back!'

'No, Fergus!' she cried, her face so white he felt his heart racing with dread. 'Stop it! I know what's on your mind! For heaven's sake, it's only a few wee twinges. Oh please don't be so afraid for me, darling, I'm perfectly healthy, I've had Grant; now I'm having twins, it's natural for me to have some pains now and then. Don't worry so.'

'I'm not worried!' he shouted at her.

'Oh yes you are! I've felt your worry for more than eight months now! You're terrified of birth, Fergus. I don't blame you, it's only natural after what happened to Helen – what Shona went through.'

'I am not terrified,' he gritted. 'What do you take me for? Some kind of damned cissy?' His jaw was tense with rage because he knew that she was right. He was terrified; memories were starting to engulf him, forcing him back over the years to Helen, his first wife, upstairs in the bedroom at Laigmhor in the throes of childbirth; the cold sharp light of a January dawn; a child's thin wailing cry – and Helen, dying, her fiery hair framing the delicate cameo of her face. Later came his torture of mind and soul, a heartrending grief that had made him turn away from his infant daughter Shona, rejecting everything that reminded him of Helen's death. He had thought it all forgotten, buried in the ashes of his past, but now it was all coming back. A cold prickle of foreboding touched his spine and made him shiver.

'I'll get you a cup of tea.' Anxiety clipped his tones. She lay back with a sigh and he went to fetch the tea which she drank gratefully.

'There, I'm fine now.' She smiled, her eyes a startling blue in her pale face. Briefly he clasped her hand then he got up. 'I'm going on deck for a smoke. Try and rest.'

He stood on deck and looked down at the grey water below. It was glassy, deceptively calm, the same kind of sea that had robbed him of one of his finest friends, Hamish Cameron, the big laughing Highlander who had been grieve at Laigmhor when Fergus was still an infant. Hamish had died in the sea by the treacherous Sgor Creags, jagged masses of rock near Port Rum Point. Fergus, too, had nearly died but in the end he had been saved, though his left arm had been amputated by Lachlan because it had been so badly crushed by those pinnacles of rock it was beyond repair.

Fergus looked again at the glossy swells rising and

splashing against the hull and he shuddered. He feared and hated the water and here he was, with Kirsteen, gliding slowly along on the steamer, cradled by his enemy, yet relying on it to carry the boat safely to land. The mist enveloped him and he could almost hear Canty Tam's voice saying, 'The Uisga hags love the mist, they can make things happen to people that never happen on land. See, their auld hag faces are smilin' for they like nothin' better than the mist to cast their evil spells.'

'Silly fool,' Fergus thought, but nevertheless he moved away from the rails and went down below to the cabin. Kirsteen was moaning in pain and she gasped, 'I – I think it's the real thing, Fergus. It's too soon – but you mustn't go losing your head over it – I'll keep till we get to Barra.'

Without a word Fergus turned on his heel and went to seek out the Captain. 'How long till Barra?' he asked curtly.

Captain Mac was a Lewis man with a shock of white hair, a bulbous red nose, and calm brown eyes. He blinked at Fergus sleepily and said with a wry grin, 'About the time it might take us to get to the moon. We canny go like the clappers o' hell in mist like this. What ails you, McKenzie?'

'Not me, it's Kirsteen. I think she's started to go into labour.'

Captain Mac's eyes twinkled and he slapped his knee. 'Bugger me, would that not be a fine thing for you? The first twins ever to be born on board the old girl and myself acting as chief midwife. I tell you it would give me something to tell my grandchildren and the lads would make a fine tale of it at the ceilidhs . . .'

He was brought to an abrupt halt as Fergus gripped his arm painfully. 'Bugger your grandchildren and your ceilidhs! My wife isn't some sort of object in a circus. I want you to turn back – to Rhanna – now.'

'Ach, get a hold of yourself, man,' Captain Mac said somewhat peevishly. 'If you must know I was just about to give the orders to turn back for I am no' daft enough to think we'll ever make anything o' it in this kind o' weather.' He glanced at Fergus reproachfully. 'By God, you're a de'il o' a man when you're fighting for your own – but . . .' he was remembering how Fergus had lost his first wife. 'I admire you for saying outright just what's in that stubborn buggering mind o' yours.'

He glanced at his abused and battered clock on the shelf. 'I tell you what, son, that old witch Behag should just be opening the Post Office by now. How would it be if I get a message through to her on that wireless contraption thing o' hers? The old bugger will spread the news about before you can undo your fly, but at least she can alert Lachlan that we are coming back and that bonny wee Kirsteen will get attention the minute we get to shore.'

Fergus gripped his shoulder. 'Thanks, Mac, that's a grand idea, we'll share a bottle next time you're in port – celebrate in style.'

Captain Mac chuckled heartily. 'Ach, I won't be

waiting for the next time. I'm for a good celebration tonight. If the mist holds I'll get along to Tam's for a taste o' his cough mixture. My first grandson was born last week and I have wet his head so much I doubt I've maybe drowned the poor wee mannie.'

When Fergus arrived back at his cabin, it was to wonder what sort of telepathy existed among women for there was Kate and Millie filling the air with sanguine utterances while they took turns at rubbing Kirsteen's back. Kate's big capable hands squeezed and pummelled till Kirsteen protested but Kate would have none of it. 'Weesht you now,' she ordered authoritatively. 'I'm an expert on matters like these, for haven't I went through it often enough, and the last time on my own wi' never so much as a pat on my bum to help me on – ach, Nancy was there right enough but she was only a bairn herself and could do little more than gape at my sufferings – near died I did, but the Lord pulled me through – wi' a good bit o' co-operation from myself o' course. Did I tell you how?'

'Yes, Kate, you did,' Kirsteen broke in hastily. She had heard Kate's story many times before and was in no mood just then to listen to gory details about birth. She felt sick and afraid and when Fergus came in she stared at him wordlessly.

'We're turning back,' he told her, his dark eyes lingering on her lovely face with its finely honed features and beautifully shaped mouth. 'Don't worry, there's no fuss, Mac was about to go back anyway.' His voice was soft, intimate and Kate's eyes flashed.

'Would you listen to him – makin' love to her wi' his voice!' She grinned at Kirsteen. 'It's no wonder you're lyin' there wi' a belly like a Christmas puddin'! If Tam had used that voice on me all our married life I'd have spent my days on my back doin' all the things we aren't supposed to like and churnin' out bairns like sausages!'

Everyone laughed, even Fergus, because it was impossible not to like Kate with her blunt tongue and earthy humour. She was reliably strong in difficult situations, never panicking, enjoying any challenge that chanced her way.

'Look you here,' said Mollie, wife of Todd the Shod, the village blacksmith. 'You won't get to see your relatives in Barra for a whily yet, Kate. It wouldny go amiss if you was to share a droppy o' your cough mixture wi' us.'

'But you don't drink, you just turn up your nose and sip at a glass of good whisky like a hen wi' a sore throat,' Kate accused firmly. Mollie's face grew red, but she persisted. 'Ach, it's no' for myself, Fergus here could be doing wi' a dram, I'm sure. It's no' every day a man is about to become the father o' twins and it's no' every day that Kirsteen here gives birth to them. A droppy would do her good.'

'Ach, you're right enough.' Kate delved into her bag. 'Tam won't mind a wee bottle or two going to his friends.'

As if on cue Captain Mac appeared at the door, his words for Fergus but his gentle brown eyes survey-ing with languid joy the bottle that Kate was pulling from her bag. 'Just to tell you, McKenzie, I got the message through to Behag and she has promised to have Lachlan standing by at the harbour.' His eyes roved slowly from the whisky bottle to Kate's ruddy fresh face. 'My, would you look at what this bonny woman has smuggled into the innocent-looking shopping bag o' hers.' His eyes twinkled. 'Cross my palm wi' a full bottle and I won't be telling the Customs mannie.'

'You haverin' de'il, Isaac MacIntosh!' an outraged Kate yelled. 'You blasphemin', twisted old sea dog! How could you say a thing like that, after all my Tam's given you in the way o' free whisky?'

'Oh, he's a good man all right, my bonny Kate, but a crafty bugger for all that. Last night he made me stump up a shilling for a half-pint of the malt. I've never had a free drink from him yet.'

Kate's eyes bulged with chagrin. 'Never!' she breathed. 'Wait till I get my hands on that lazy lying cheat . . . Just for that . . . here.' She thrust a bottle at Captain Mac. 'Drink it all and there's more where that came from. Now –' she said, turning to Kirsteen, 'you take a good swallock o' this, mo ghaoil, and then me and Mollie here will give you an arm and help you walk about for a bit. It's the best way to keep your muscles goin'. When he's fu' enough, Captain Mac will give you a song, that's another thing that helps when you're in labour.'

'A song?' Kirsteen asked rather dazedly.

'Ay, if the wee buggers are at all musical they will be in quite a hurry to come out and see what it's all about. When I was having Angus, Tam was in the kitchen, stupid wi' the drink and singin' his head off, and there Angus popped out so quick even auld Biddy was taken aback.'

Fergus threw back his head and roared with laughter. Putting his arm round Kate's shoulder he whispered in her ear, 'You're a wild wild woman, Kate McKinnon, but thank the Lord for you right this minute – and I wouldn't mind a good dram from that shopping bag of yours.'

When they arrived at the harbour Lachlan was waiting with his motor car, which he had managed to get started after much pushing from one or two stalwarts making their leisurely way down Glen Fallan. Captain Mac's predictions about Behag's ever-busy tongue had proved true enough.

As Kirsteen was helped down the gangplank and into the car curtains twitched all along the length of the harbour and Lachlan's thin face broke into a smile. 'Just think of yourself as royalty,' he told Kirsteen. 'They were all agog when they heard you were going to have your twins on Rhanna after all. I might add that Biddy, too, is delighted. She was quite peeved at the idea of another midwife bringing Rhanna babies into the world.'

All that had been hours ago, or it might have been yesterday to Fergus's confused mind. It seemed as if daylight had hardly broken at all during that drab misty day, which had merged into evening without much noticeable difference. Lachlan had gone away to take evening surgery, and now he was back upstairs with Biddy and Babbie, the young nurse who had come to Rhanna earlier that year for a holiday and had stayed to become Biddy's assistant.

Fergus knew he would only be in the way if he stayed in the house, so he busied himself around the farm, glad of the company of old Bob the Shepherd, and Matthew the grieve of Laigmhor. But he couldn't escape Kirsteen's cries of distress when he came in with Bob at teatime. Seven-year-old Grant had been all for coming home after school, delighted to know that his mother hadn't gone to Oban after all, but Fergus had chased him up the road to Slochmhor where he was staying till everything was over.

'Rotten babies,' the little boy had sniffed, his black eyes flashing scornfully. 'We don't need them, Father, it was fine the way it was. I want to come home. Fiona bullies me all the time. This morning she skelped my ear just because I went to see old Joe's new boat and was a wee bit late for school.'

'You needed a skelping then,' Fergus had told his young son firmly. 'You play on Mr Murdoch's good nature. Off you go now to Phebie's. She'll have your tea ready.'

Phebie, the doctor's wife, had prepared a meal for Fergus and Bob, which they ate in an uneasy silence while round them bustled Biddy, scuttling on spindly legs from sink to fire with pans of water. She was seventy-two now, age was showing in her lined face and knotted fingers but she wouldn't hear of retiring. 'I'll work till I drop,' she sharply informed those who dared to suggest she was past it. 'Auld Murn went on till she was eighty. I'll push up the daisies when *I* decide the time is ripe and not before.'

Everyone who knew and loved the kenspeckle old nurse fully believed that she was capable of dying when it suited her. 'She's as tough as cow's hide,' said Kate. 'She's seen that much o' life and death in her time I fine believe she has learnt the secrets o' both. It wouldny surprise me if she does just what she says. The day she knows she can work no more is the day she'll die.'

Bob's grizzled old face was serious as he tackled his meal. Across from him, Fergus went rigid as yet another agonised sound rent the air. 'Kirsteen, Kirsteen,' his heart cried out helplessly. 'I love you, my darling, yet I can't share your suffering.'

Bob looked at his ashen face and muttered, 'She's a strong lassie. Dinna fash yourself, lad. By God, it's a terrible struggle for the women right enough. I thank the Lord I'm a man and will never know the pain o' givin' life. It's times like these I'm glad I never married, though betimes I think what a grand comfort a wife and bairns must be. I'm used to livin' alone but I often wonder what it would be like to have a daughter lookin' after me in my auld age. At sixty-eight I'm still a bit of a spring chicken . . .' He chuckled, not because he didn't believe that he was indeed still in the prime of life, but at the spark of amusement in the other man's eyes. 'Ay, smile, lad, for at forty you are still that, but I'm tellin' you, in another twenty years or so you'll take bad at the idea o' folks thinkin' you're gettin' on, for you will still think much the same things you're thinkin' now. Forbye that you're a lucky man, you'll never know an auld age without your bairns around you, for you have provided yourself wi' plenty and enough to guarantee that one at least will look to you when you're nothin' but a heap o' dry bones.'

He rasped the back of a gnarled hand over his stubbly chin and scraped back his chair. 'I'm away down to Todd's to see if Conker has been shod yet. I might stay and have a game o' cards wi' Todd but I'll look in on you later.'

'I doubt it.' Fergus smiled faintly. 'Captain Mac and his crew will be ashore and there will be ceilidhs all over the place, so you'd better take your fiddle along with you.'

'Ay, right enough then.' Bob sounded apologetic. Quickly he pushed his feet into his wellingtons, waved his crook at Dot, who sprang up obediently and glided to his side, waved his stick in farewell to Fergus and plodded away over the cobbles of the yard. After that it was so quiet in the kitchen Fergus felt he might have been alone in the house except for the tread of feet in the room above and Kirsteen's muffled cries.

The flames from the fire gave the room a mellow hue; shadows danced on the ceiling and distorted everyday objects into strange shapes. Light spilt golden over the hearthrug, falling on a quivering little bundle of curling amber fur. The three-month-old spaniel was a new arrival at Laigmhor, yet was so familiar a sight lying there in the pool of warmth that Fergus's heart turned over. It might have been old Tot breathing gently in contented slumber. Tot had been Shona's dog, given to her by Hamish when Shona had been just five years old. Tot was dead now, but this little dog was one of her offspring. His master had offered him to Fergus just recently.

'I'm going off to stay with my sister in Australia,' the old man said rather sadly. 'I'm getting too old now to enjoy living on my own.' He had glanced down at the pup. 'Thought you might like this wee devil. You mind auld Tot had pups? Well this one sprung from one o' them. The bairnies will like him. Children should never grow up without a dog they can call their own. Farm dogs is all right in their place but they know better how to work than play, this one will play wi' a body till they are just about dropping.'

When Grant first saw the pup he immediately christened him Squint. It was an appropriate name as one of the limpid brown eyes was badly crossed, yet rather than detract from the dog's appearance, it added to it and endowed him with an irresistible appeal. Fergus could hardly wait to see Shona's face. She would be home for Christmas.

The thought made his heart bound with joy. He hadn't seen her since her marriage to Niall, the doctor's son, nearly two months ago. God, how he missed the child of his first marriage. Her departure from the island had left a void in his heart. They had spent so many of her eighteen years together at Laigmhor, comforting each other in the days of their loneliness when his heart had pined for Kirsteen and when Shona had been plunged into an abyss of despair on learning that Niall was thought to have been killed at Dunkirk. She had been expecting his child at the time, and in a state of shock had given birth to a little stillborn son. Fergus could still see the child in his mind's eye, the neat perfection of it, the small head covered in downy fair hair, the flesh waxen and cold as marble. It had taken her a long time to get over the trauma, but it was all behind her now. Niall had come back from the dead and they had married and gone to live in Glasgow where Niall was training to be a vet, and Shona a nurse. Fergus breathed deeply. Often he was so busy in the bustle of farming and family life that he had no time to miss his firstborn child, but sometimes he fancied he heard her light step on the stairs or her singing in the kitchen and he never quite got over the feeling that she still occupied her bedroom upstairs. He missed going to her door, whispering goodnight to her and hearing her whisper softly back, 'Goodnight, Father.'

He stopped pacing and sat down in the inglenook. Squint opened one eye, got up, stretched lazily, then on big, gangling puppy paws padded over to Fergus and climbed calmly onto his lap. His body was warm and soft. Fergus caressed the golden ears and felt again he was back in the past feeling Tot's fur under his fingers.

A light tap came on the door and it opened quietly. Phebie stood there, her sweet face smooth and rosy, her expression slightly defensive. 'I hope you don't mind, Fergus,' she said rather hesitantly. 'I have left Grant to Fiona's tender mercies.' She smiled. 'It's strange how these two snarl at each other so much. How unlike Shona and Niall at their age.'

'It would be asking too much for history to repeat itself,' Fergus said as he lifted Squint from his knee and got up. He looked at Phebie and the knot of tension in his belly uncoiled a little at the sight of her calm face. He knew of course the reason for her defensive attitude. Once, long ago, he had rejected Phebie's offer of help at a time such as this and he had lived to regret it sorely. He stretched out his arm to her. She was soft and warm, like a plump little rosebud that smelt of antiseptic, for she quite often helped Lachlan out in the surgery.

'I'm glad to see you, mo ghaoil,' he told her in his deep lilting voice. 'I've been sitting here feeling sorry for myself. I feel so strange, as if the clock was turned back and I'm re-living that hellish night of Shona's birth.'

'I know how you must feel.' She felt drawn to him in this moment. Often he was a dour, unapproachable creature, though she had learnt that underneath his hardness there lay a soft heart.

'I'm a coward, Phebie,' he continued, shamefaced. 'I wanted this to happen in hospital. To be near Kirsteen yet to be apart from her. I should go to her now but I can't. I don't want to see her pain because there's nothing I can do to help her.'

'Nonsense,' Phebie became brisk. 'Kirsteen knows you're down here and not miles away like some

husbands are when their bairns come into the world.
I'll make tea, a good strong brew; I could be doing
with a cup myself.'

In minutes the kettle was singing on the hob. She
poured two cups and handed him one and he was
annoyed when his trembling hand slopped some of
the liquid into the saucer. 'You are in a state,' she
said. 'Sit down for heaven's sake before you fall
down. I don't think I'm strong enough to catch hold
of a man your size – not that it wouldn't be nice, but
think of what Lachlan would say if he found us in
each other's arms . . .'

He glowered and she giggled. 'Och c'mon now,
let's see a smile. Would you like me to make you a
sandwich? No doubt you haven't eaten very much of
what I left earlier.'

'Ay, that would be fine.' His tones were brusque
in the effort to conceal his emotions. Babbie danced
into the kitchen, smiling smiles he felt she had no
right to in such a situation. Her red hair gleamed in
the lamplight, her green eyes sparkled.

'Relax, Mr McKenzie,' she said. 'Kirsteen is coping
beautifully, but these things take time. Labour isn't
known as such for nothing, you know – but of
course –' her eyes crinkled again – 'what would a
man know of that?'

There was no smile in response in the dark,
ruggedly handsome face looming above hers.
Instead, the well-shaped, sensual mouth tightened
with annoyance.

Babbie went to the fire and lifted the teapot, her

face glowing in the fire's light. In her pocket was a letter from Anton Büttger, the young German Commander who had crash-landed his plane on Rhanna in March of that year and who had been badly wounded in the process. She had nursed him back to health and during that time they had fallen in love. He was now in a prison camp in England and she longed to see him again. His letters to her were the one thing that illuminated her life. The present one had come on yesterday's boat and she had read it so often she knew every word by heart. The war could end next week or next year, whatever way it went she would wait for him to come back to her. Dreamily Babbie poured tea into large cups. 'I've been sent to fetch a cup for Biddy – laced with a drop of brandy if you've got any. She's grumbling like mad up there, even though she's so thrilled you would think she was having twins herself.'

She went off with a laden tray and the kitchen was quiet again. Phebie was not a demanding companion and Fergus found himself thankful for her presence. Each little night sound made his ears crackle with awareness. A strange mewing cry filtered through the silence but it was a sound outwith the sturdy walls of Laigmhor, a seabird's cry, a haunting, lost sound that melted away into the night.

Fergus could sit still no longer. 'I have to go out to the cowshed,' he told Phebie, and lifting a lamp from the dresser, he made his way outside, not to the cowshed but to the little garden at the back of the house. Mirabelle had planted roses here. Despite

24

storms and howling winter gales they somehow managed to survive and in the summer the air was filled with their fragrance. Carefully he set the lamp down on the mossy earth. Yesterday he had noticed a perfect red rosebud shining like a jewel amidst withering foliage. The light from the lamp picked it out, red as a ruby as it loomed out of the chilly mist. It was studded with droplets of moisture that lay on its satin-smooth petals like teardrops on a baby's cheek. He cut through the stem with his tobacco knife and the rosebud lay in his hand, marble-cold, an object of perfection. It was then he saw another bud on the same bush, a fragile-looking red blob, smaller than the first, drooping slightly on its stem as if cowering away from the threat of winter that ought to have killed it but hadn't. With a gentle finger Fergus touched it, a strange thought coming to him. It deserved to live; he couldn't leave it to die after such a game struggle for survival. It needed to be cherished, protected. Gently he plucked it and tucked it into his pocket along with the other.

Chapter Two

Just before midnight the first baby was born, and half
an hour later came the second, a feeble little mite,
with hardly a flicker of life in its tiny body.

'Get water,' Lachlan instructed Babbie. 'Two
basins, one hot, the other cold.'

Babbie flew downstairs, brushing aside Fergus's
questions, urging him instead to help her with the
water, which he did silently, not daring to ask for
further details from the young nurse who told him
quickly what was happening. Biddy busied herself
with Kirsteen, while Lachlan and Babbie between
them worked with the baby, bathing it alternately in
hot and cold water. For fifteen minutes it seemed as
if there was no life in the infant. A pall of eerie quiet
surrounded the doctor and the young nurse, broken
only by whimpers from the first arrival, Biddy's voice
soothing Kirsteen, the plop, plop of water, accompanied by splashes as the infant was plunged from
basin to basin.

'Come on, come on,' Lachlan rasped. 'Cry, for
God's sake, cry!' His face was shiny with sweat, his
brown eyes alive with desperation.

'The skin is turning pink. Look, Lachlan,' Babbie's
voice was jubilant. The baby jerked and trembled,

the tiny fists clenched, the chest heaved and filled the lungs with air, the pink mouth opened wide to give vent to a life-saving cry that was music to the ears of everyone in the room.

'The Lord be thanked,' Biddy beamed as the baby was wrapped in blankets and brought to Kirsteen's side. She stroked the young woman's hair tenderly and whispered, 'There, there, lass, have a good greet, it's all right now. My, my, are they not lovely just?'

It was nearly two o'clock when Lachlan came downstairs and into the kitchen. He stood for a moment, shoulders drooping with weariness, unruly locks of dark hair falling over his brow. The lamplight found every hollow in his thin boyish face, sweat gleamed on his upper lip but his eyes were luminous, the slow breaking of his smile like a summer dawn pouring sunlight over the dark earth.

Fergus leapt up at his entry, his muscular body taut with suspense, his strong brown right hand bunched into a knuckle of steel. 'Well?' His voice was breathless, strange to his own ears.

Lachlan held out his hand. 'Congratulations, Fergus, you have sons, identical twins. Kirsteen is naturally very exhausted, but she's fine, just fine, man.'

'Thank God – oh thank God!' Fergus's voice was husky with relief. In a few quick strides he was across the room, grabbing Lachlan's hand, pumping it so vigorously the doctor gave a little laughing yelp. Phebie, too, was on her feet, laughing, kissing Fergus, kissing Lachlan, waltzing him round and round.

'Hey, go easy,' Lachlan protested. 'I'm feeling a wee bitty fragile right now. It's not every day I deliver twins.' Fergus was making for the door but Lachlan put out a hand to stop him. 'Not yet, Fergus, there's something you should know first.' He was silent for some time and it seemed as if the house held its breath in suspense of what must follow. 'You know of course we had quite a fight to save the life of your second son . . .' He spoke slowly, almost unwillingly. 'Both babies are premature, and therefore small, but the youngest is well below what I consider to be a healthy weight. He – well – the next few days will be critical for him. His breathing may fail, by rights he should be in an incubator in hospital, but it's impossible to move him, he would never survive a journey of any length. Also –' Lachlan took a deep breath – 'I think I can detect a heart condition. It's difficult to tell at this stage how serious it is, only time will tell us that. Otherwise he seems normal enough, but he is very frail and there's no knowing if he'll survive. Kirsteen doesn't know any of this and it's best not to worry her just now.'

Babbie appeared in time to hear his last words. 'I'll stay for as long as I'm needed,' she said quietly. 'The babies will need constant supervision, and if an emergency arises I'll be nearby to cope.'

'Ay.' Fergus nodded dejectedly. 'The bairns are to have Mirabelle's old room so you can sleep there; the bed's made up. I lit the fire earlier, so the room should be warm.' He looked from one to the other. 'Thank you both – for everything,' he said briefly

29

but it was enough for Lachlan, who nodded.

'On you go up now,' he said. 'Don't let her see anything is wrong. We'll give you ten minutes and then we'll all have a dram together – I could be doing with it,' he finished with a weary sigh.

Fergus walked into the hall. All was hushed, even the ticking of the grandmother clock seemed more subdued than usual. It had ticked just as sweetly, just as steadily on that morning of Shona's birth more than eighteen years ago. No doubt it had been lazily swinging the time away when he and his younger brother, Alick, had been born, because he remembered as an infant gazing solemnly up at the round serene face of it. It had appeared a huge object to him then, and even now, when he loomed above it, it still seemed bigger than he, solid, reassuring.

The oak-panelled walls were rich yet mellow in lamplight, the pictures that hung on them were as familiar to him as his own name. He had known no other home, he had trodden these floors, these stairs, for more than forty years. He climbed up the wooden stairs as he had done countless times before. Routine was so much a part of life it often seemed to stagnate and it was easy to think that nothing could ever change. But changes, when they did come, were sometimes so dramatic they brought feelings of panic, a sensation of being unable to cope. Such things were happening to him now. He went on upwards but felt he was stepping back over years, living again things his mind had buried. Eighteen years had gone by, yet it was all so near, so real. The first stop in the mists of time came when he went into Mirabelle's old room to check the fire. This was to be the nursery. Everything that the babies needed was here. To one side of the fire stood the old family cradle, gleaming with a fresh coat of varnish. Beside it was an exact replica, beautifully fashioned by Wullie the Carpenter; the only things it lacked were the tiny cracks of age, the gnaw-marks made by babies cutting milk teeth. Fergus saw the cradles like someone looking at a scene from a dream, for more real to him was the feel of Mirabelle's presence in the room, the lingering perfume of lavender, the vision of her sitting on her rocking chair by the window, her snowy white mutch cap appearing like a beacon in the black oblong of the window when you looked up and saw her from the garden. So Shona had seen her the day she died, worn out from a lifetime of caring for others.

'Mirabelle, my dear old friend,' he whispered into the warm silence. 'Two bairnies are going to shatter your dreams with their cries, but you'll look to them like you looked to the rest of us.' An odd peace stole into his heart. Somehow he felt that the old lady was still here, watching over them all, all those she had called my bairnies.

He put more coal onto the fire then went out of the room and along the passage to the bedroom he shared with Kirsteen. When he opened the door he was transported back to a morning in January 1923. Peace lay over everything and everyone the room held; the shadows were full of secrets, kept yet

31

shared; by the fire Biddy was sound asleep in a deep comfortable chair, skinny black-clad legs spread wide to the heat, hands folded over her stomach, her head falling forward onto her scraggy bosom, the big pin in her felt hat glittering in the soft light.

Kirsteen lay depleted against the pillows of the big double bed, her ruffled curls damp with perspiration, her eyes closed, her face beautiful as the sculpture of a young girl whose innocence hadn't yet been violated. For a brief moment Fergus saw again a pure white bed, a girl still with the face of a child, blue-lidded eyes closing as death beckoned her away from the life she had so loved, a girl who had laughed, who had cried, who had adored him with all the exuberant passion of youth – and who had died at the age of twenty-one. In a blinding flash, filled with clarity of each small detail, Fergus saw it all, then in a dizzy sensation of whirling forward through time, he was back in the present, seeing not a bed of death but one filled with life, three lives.

Kirsteen opened her eyes and saw him standing motionless in the doorway. She lifted her hand and held it out to him. 'Fergus, my darling, come and see what we have made together.' Her voice was low, laden with an intimacy that made his heart turn over. He tip-toed over to the bed, not knowing if he did so to allow Biddy to sleep on undisturbed or because to break the tranquillity in the room would have been a violation. He stood tall above her, drinking in the sight of her lying there with the children of their love at her side.

'Kirsteen, my dearest,' he whispered huskily. 'How do you feel?' Though weary beyond measure, her face was alive with joy, tears of thankfulness drowning her eyes, a smile curving her soft lips. 'I feel – happiness. It was a sore struggle but it's over now, it's over, Fergus.'

No, he thought, it's only just begun, the heartache of the unknown. Pain, sharp and overpowering, filled his heart. Surely having gone through so much, her sweet happiness couldn't be shattered by the death of one of their newborn sons. It would be too cruel to give life only to have it taken away. Tears choked him and to hide them he bent his dark head to kiss her warm lips. Even though her body was racked by fatigue she was overwhelmed as always by his nearness. She caressed the black curls at the nape of his neck and in the passion of love he put his arm under her head to pull her up close so that she was lying against his powerful chest, hearing the dull steady throb of his heart. 'I love you, my Kirsteen,' he murmured, 'and I thank God for keeping you safe.'

'I promised I would give you more sons,' she smiled. 'Don't you want to see them?'

He straightened and gazed at the two bundles cocooned in white blankets and saw two thatches of jet-black silken hair, the indentation of the fontanelle on each little head making them look fragile and vulnerable. She pulled the blankets away from the puckered faces, identical faces, though one was smaller than the other, the skin so transparent he could see the delicate fretwork of veins. This was the one who might not live, and it looked to him to be already on the brink, but he couldn't let her see that anything was wrong.

'They're very small.' It was all he could find to say and he wished immediately he could take it back.

A frown crossed her face. 'I know Lachlan says it's natural for twins to be smaller than single babies but I never realised – how tiny – especially –' her slender fingers stroked the cheek of her youngest son – 'this one. He was all but dead when he was born. Lachlan and Babbie between them saved his life. She's a fine nurse and Lachlan's a wonderful doctor – but will this baby survive, I wonder.'

'Of course he will; he's a McKenzie, remember,' Fergus said, changing the subject quickly. 'Wait till Alick and Mary hear about this; now we have two sets of twins in the family. Grant might feel better when he knows he's got brothers. He was dreading the idea of sisters. There's only one girl in his life at the moment and that's Shona. He worships her, though he tries hard to let on he doesn't.'

'I wonder how he's getting on at Slochmhor. I hope he isn't fretting.'

'Not him! He's filling his time nicely. He made himself late for school this morning by going to see old Joe's new boat. He loves that old man with his stories of the sea.'

Her hand tightened over his. 'He will never be a farmer. He's not yet eight and already the sea is in his blood. I wonder will one – or both of these babes

grow up to love the earth – to till Laigmhor soil . . .
If not I'll have to give you the rest of those five sons
I promised.'

'Hell no! Never again! I couldn't go through another
day like this and you're not going through more hell
just to please me. I don't care if all my sons grow up
and go to sea – or to the moon for that matter – you're
more precious to me than a few acres of soil.'

Footsteps sounded on the stairs and Lachlan came
into the room with Phebie and Babbie at his heels.
Biddy grunted and groped among the cushions for
her specs. 'Where are the damty things?' she
demanded irritably. 'If it's no' them losin' themselves
it's my teeths playin' hide-and-seek wi' me.'

'If it's your specs you're looking for, they're on the
end of your nose, Biddy,' Babbie giggled.

'Ach, it's a cailleach I am indeed.' The old nurse
smiled sourly and sniffed the air. 'Here, is that whisky
I'm smellin' and no one ever offerin' me a drop!'

Lachlan handed her a well-filled glass and Biddy,
snuggling back contentedly into the chair, gazed into
the fire and began to croon a lullaby. Phebie was
over by the bed, utterly enchanted at her first glimpse
of the twins. One of them stirred and gave a weak
cry and Babbie moved quickly to pick him up. 'I'm
taking them through now, Kirsteen. The cradles have
been nicely warmed with hot bags and there's a fire
in the room.'

Anxiety creased Kirsteen's smooth brow. 'But –
they'll be hungry,' she protested. 'And I wanted to
feed them myself.'

'You will,' Babbie promised kindly but firmly. 'Just now they only need some boiled sweetened water and you must have a good night's rest. Don't worry, they'll be fine with me. I'll attend to their every need.' With a small bundle on each arm, she went to the door where Lachlan had a few quick words with her before she went along to Mirabelle's old room.

Kirsteen lay back and Lachlan went to put his hand over hers. 'It's for the best, mo ghaoil. You get a good night's rest and I'll be back in the morning to check up on the bairns and to make sure you're behaving.' He put his arm across Phebie's shoulders and was about to offer Biddy a lift in his trap when he saw that she was asleep once more, the empty whisky glass clutched against her bosom.

'Leave her,' Kirsteen said softly. 'It's been a long day for her. She can go through to Shona's room later.'

'I had a mind to sleep in there tonight,' Fergus protested.

Phebie laughed. 'Well, just think how nice it will be for you if you waken in the night feeling lonely and there's auld Biddy snoring beside you.'

Kirsteen gave a small tired smile. 'Use Grant's room, darling. There's room in the house for everybody – you can all stay if you like.' Her eyes were closing despite herself. Lachlan led Phebie away and their footsteps receded downstairs. From the room at the end of the corridor a thin little wail pierced the night, then all was silent once more. Fergus felt uneasy. He stood for a long time looking down at

Kirsteen. The firelight brushed her pale face with gold, her hands were relaxed and still on the coverlet. He felt alone and more than a little afraid of the thing that he knew but she didn't. She stirred and gave a sigh. 'Fergus, you're there, aren't you?'

'Yes, darling, I'm here.'

'Go to bed,' she murmured. 'You must be tired.'

'I am . . .' His fingers curled over the two rosebuds in his pocket and he took them out and placed them on the white pillow by her head. They looked like two drops of blood that had been preserved for all time.

She opened her eyes and saw them. Slowly she picked them up and holding them to her lips she kissed them. 'They're beautiful, one for each of our sons – but where on earth did you find roses in December?'

'In the garden, growing on the same bush. I wish I could give you an armful – I will yet, I want to get you something special for Christmas. I've a mind to go to Oban next week and do a bit of shopping.'

'You could buy me the world but nothing will be as precious to me as these; I shall keep them always. You know that big family Bible that belonged to your grandparents? I'm going to press your rosebuds into that.'

Biddy was snoring gently, her lips making little plopping noises as she sucked in and expelled air.

'Dear old Biddy.' Kirsteen's eyes were like leaded weights and in seconds she was asleep again, the rosebuds clasped to her breasts. Fergus tucked the blankets round her, and brushed her hair with his lips, then he padded soundlessly away to Grant's untidy room.

Glass net floats hung over the bed like bunches of gaily coloured balloons, crayoned pictures of boats were pinned askance on the walls; opposite the bed hung a big gilt-framed painting of the sea, the first thing the little boy saw each morning when he woke. But child of the waves and wind though he was, a floppy teddy bear was tucked carefully under the quilt. Fergus picked it up and looked at it. Quite unthinkingly he put it back in its place, undressed and got into the small narrow bed. In the darkness the rough fur of the bear brushed his face. The bed was cold and he thought longingly of Kirsteen's warm body beside his. How had he borne all those years alone in an empty bed? He had almost forgotten what it was like. Curling up into a tight ball he fell into a restless sleep, unaware that in the night he hugged his son's teddy bear to his chest like the little boy of long ago who had cuddled a battered cloth bear made by Mirabelle. Three doors from where he slept Babbie kept a lonely vigil on a helpless baby who barely appeared to be breathing. In the dark hours before dawn Biddy came through to relieve the young nurse, and there, by the fire, in Mirabelle's big chintz armchair, she held the tiny infant to her old bosom, smelt the fragrance of silken hair against her face, said silent prayers for the preservation of the youngest McKenzie son, and, as always, she felt so much love for the newly born it might have been her own babe cradled so lovingly in her arms.

Several critical days passed, days in which the fragile baby held to life by a thread. Lachlan was hardly away from Laigmhor, Biddy was in constant attendance, while her young assistant made the strenuous rounds of croft and cottage. She was exhausted, but insisted on spending her nights at Laigmhor. 'Ach, what did I ever do without you, lass?' Biddy said with misty eyes, pulling the girl to her and fondling her fiery red hair before pushing her away in embarrassment and toddling off on spindly legs.

Kirsteen cried when she heard that her smallest son was fighting for his life, but with the determination that Fergus knew and admired so much, she spent little time indulging in useless tears and instead set about positive action. She breast fed the babies, cuddled them, whiled away the long hours in bed doing everything she possibly could to help in the battle, and everyone was overjoyed when Lachlan finally announced the crisis was over.

'The bairnie will live,' he said simply. 'God and McKenzie between them put a spirit into the wee lad that wouldn't be beaten. He'll need a lot of care, mind you. His heart isn't strong; he might never be as big or as strong as his brother; but the chances are the older he gets, the stronger he'll be.'

After an extended stay at Slochmhor, Grant came home, utterly disgusted at the first sight of his baby brothers. 'They're ugly,' he stated with a toss of his black curls. 'I hope I didn't look like that when I was a baby.'

'Ach, you'll have looked worse!' Fiona scolded, her bright eyes flashing under her dark fringe of hair. 'And you're no better now – at least they'll likely get better looking by the time they get to your age.'

The little boy's dimpled chin jutted out in indignation. With his snappish black eyes and rosy cheeks he was the ultimate in childish beauty, though when he scowled he looked very much like his father in a rage. 'At least I don't look like a Robin with beady eyes and a funny wee beak.' He glared into Fiona's laughing face. 'I'm going down to the harbour,' he went on peevishly. 'Ranald is building a big new boatshed and I'm helping him,' he finished off proudly.

After that a steady stream of visitors came to Laigmhor, all bearing small gifts for the twins, whose arrival had caused a great stir of interest. For the sake of convenience the cradles were brought down to the kitchen where the womenfolk gathered to stare and admire. Knitting needles had been busy for months and very soon heaps of tiny garments lay everywhere.

'My, my, is it no' just like the stable from Bethlehem itself?' Mairi McKinnon observed, her round-eyed, rather vacant gaze absorbing the scene with quiet bliss.

Fergus had cut and brought in a small spruce tree. Shiny with baubles and tinsel, it sat in a corner of the room; a few stray hens clucked in the pantry; the women stood, shawled heads bowed over the cradles, their faces bronzed in the warm flicker of firelight. Mairi, in her unsophisticated way, had described the scene perfectly.

But it was Dodie, the island eccentric who lived in solitary existence in his tiny cottage on the slopes of Sgurr nan Ruadh, whose gift touched Kirsteen the most. She was in the kitchen drinking a well-earned cup of tea when she saw him standing by the gate looking with soulful eyes at the languid activities of the sheep that dotted Ben Machrie. Unlike the rest of the islanders to whom the business of visiting was a normal habit at any time of the day, he never entered a house unless specifically invited to do so. Kirsteen felt only in the mood for solitude but no one ever hurt the old man's feelings by ignoring his presence.

'Come on in, Dodie,' she called from the doorway. 'I have just made a strupak.' He loped up the path with agility, his large wellingtons making slapping sounds with every long step.

'I was just passing on my way over to Croynachan,' he stuttered in mournful apology. Shy of women in general, he was only just growing used to Fergus's comparatively new wife, and he stopped short at the doorstep, his stooped gangling figure blotting out the light. He was dressed in a threadbare raincoat and hairy tweed trousers that were tucked carelessly into the wellingtons. A greasy cloth cap was jammed on his head so tightly his ears stuck out on either side, giving him the appearance of an oversized gnome.

From the end of his carbuncled nose a large drip dangled precariously; his strange, inward-dreaming eyes were full of water from the bite of the December air; his calloused, ungloved hands were mottled with purple. If he had taken the charity the islanders were only too willing to give, he would have been well-off indeed, but simple though he was, he maintained a fierce pride and accepted without complaint the harshness of his own existence.

Kirsteen's heart swelled with pity even though she was somewhat repulsed by the smell that emanated from him in waves. 'Sit down, Dodie,' she invited kindly. 'Elspeth sent some fresh scones over from Slochmhor. They're still hot and delicious with butter melting over them.'

'That cailleach,' he sniffed, momentarily causing the drip to ascend in his disapproval of Elspeth Morrison, the sharp-tongued housekeeper of Sloch-mhor. He had never forgiven her for chasing him up the village street brandishing a broom just because he had accidentally stumbled into her clean white washing and pulled it to the ground. Despite his grievances however, he tucked heartily into the scones, a finger placed strategically under his chin to catch the rivulets of melted butter, which he expertly scoped back up to his mouth.

'Are you no' sittin' down yourself to have your strupak?' he asked Kirsteen politely.

'Er – no, I prefer to stand at the moment,' she told him with a faint smile.

'Ay.' He nodded wisely and his carbuncle wobbled

slightly. 'Your backside will be sore for a whily after havin' two bairnies.'

Taken aback, she stared at him, and he himself, utterly dismayed at the audacity of his statement, blushed crimson and choked so violently on a crumb she had to rush forward and thump his bent back. Though prim to the point of being prudish, the old eccentric was astonishingly frank about the facts of life, even though normally he reserved his observations for the animal kingdom. Animal matings and animal births filled him with joy and in this case he had simply forgotten which category Kirsteen came into.

'I'm sorry, Mistress McKenzie!' he wailed, getting to his feet so hurriedly the table tilted and the cups slid gently to the edge. 'I'll be goin' now, thankin' you for the strupak.' He babbled on unintelligibly. 'I have a potach in my pocket for Ealasaid so I have, and if I could find the bugger I might get some milk too. I left my pail down by your gate.'

He lurched to the door but Kirsteen stayed him by saying kindly, 'Don't you want to see the babies? They're asleep just now and you'll see them at their best – not like poor Mrs Gray. They roared their heads off when she came and she couldn't get a word in.'

'Ay, indeed just,' he gabbled. 'I have a wee somethin' for them – somethin' really special seein' they are doubles.'

The 'wee somethin'' proved to be two beautiful silver teaspoons, which he withdrew from some hidden pocket inside his coat. With reverence he placed a spoon at the foot of each cradle then stood with his hands folded over his chest, the big thumbs pointing upwards.

'Dodie,' Kirsteen gasped, picking up one of the spoons. 'These are beautiful but . . .' She left the question hanging in mid-air for she knew he would be offended if asked outright how he had come by such items.

'I paid for these myself,' he volunteered with pride. 'I took them as wages for some wee jobs I did to Burnbreddie. Her leddyship said your bairnies would not be born wi' silver spoons so I decided it would be a fine thing for the auld bitch to be proved wrong and . . .' he paused, stretching his lips to show tobacco-stained teeth, the nearest he ever got to a smile, 'herself providing the very things she said they would never have.'

'They're lovely, Dodie,' Kirsteen said, deeply touched not only by the gifts but by the thoughtfulness that lay behind them. Once before Dodie had bestowed a simple treasure on Fergus when he had lain at death's door after his accident. It had been a discarded horseshoe, polished over and over till it gleamed. 'It will make him get better,' the old eccentric had whispered tearfully but with deep conviction. Fergus had always maintained that the charm had helped to speed his recovery and to this day it hung above the fireplace in the bedroom.

'I am after hearin' that one of the bairnies is no' very strong, so these will maybe bring him luck and, of course,' he said, his lips stretched again, 'they will come in handy when they are breakin' their milk teeths and are learnin' to sup food.'

A tiny fist boxed the air and Dodie stared in awe as Kirsteen pulled the blankets back. 'My, would you look at that!' Dodie was completely enchanted. 'By God, they are beautiful just – I had two just like them myself a good few years back – like two wee peas in a pod they were. Even the black socks on their feets were all alike.' Kirsteen was rather taken aback but she had no time to utter a word because Dodie was racing on. 'Ay, lovely they were just. I had a hand in bringin' them out o' the yowe for they were her first and she was that grateful neither she nor the lambs ever let me out of their sight after it. Ach, they were buggers betimes, but my – I was that proud inside myself I could have burst wi' happiness.' His odd dreamy eyes filled with tears and into them he scrubbed a horny knuckle. 'I'm sorry, Mistress McKenzie – it's just –' He swallowed hard. 'I never got over havin' to sell my lambs – they were causin' a nuisance, you see, them bein' like pet dogs and runnin' into folks' houses lookin' for biscuits. Old Behag says she came home one day and there was one o' my sheeps at her fire and sharn all over the floor. The old hag nearly killed my bonny bairn wi' that witch's broom she keeps at her fireplace – ach – they were the nicest lambs you ever saw and these is the same, two bonny wee lambs.'

Kirsteen thought it was a beautiful comparison and she was minded afresh that there was more to Dodie than met the eye. He had a compassionate love for all of God's creatures and would literally never harm even a fly. He was a figure that invoked pity, yet his artless beliefs and philosophies lifted him high above the more sophisticated and materially well off.

'I'll be goin', then.' He shuffled to the door, nervously playing with a loose button on his coat.

'Wait a minute and I'll sew that on,' Kirsteen offered and he submitted to her swift repair work with surprisingly little objection.

'I like it fine here,' he enthused, gazing fondly round the homely kitchen. 'I never feel like bein' myself in other folks' houses but here it's different. I mind Mirabelle aye made me welcome though I never right understood what way she needed to cut an onion and place it beside my chair for I was never one for the smell of them – they make my eyes cry.'

Kirsteen hid a smile. Fergus had told her of Mirabelle's method of drowning out Dodie's offensive smell, her belief being that to cut an onion was to kill unpleasant odours as well as all 'living germs'.

'There.' Kirsteen gave the button a pat. 'That should keep for a while.' She went to the larder where she stuffed scones and cake into a bag. 'Here, take these for your tea,' she said, pushing the bag at him. She reached up to the mantelshelf. 'This, too. Merry Mary didn't have Fergus's favourite brand and he put it up there and forgot about it.'

'But – it's – baccy,' Dodie protested even while his eyes shone, for he liked nothing better than a good chew at 'thick black off the roll'.

'It is that,' Kirsteen agreed. 'Put it in your pocket.'

'Ach, it's kind you are just.'

'No more than yourself. These bonny spoons will be treasured always. By the way, it's Christmas soon. If you stop by you will get some turkey and plum pudding and there might just be a wee gift on the tree with your name on it.' On impulse she reached up and kissed his nut-brown cheek, vowing to herself that warm woolly gloves and socks would be waiting for him on Christmas day. His face immediately blazed a brilliant red and he turned away so quickly he tripped over the doorstep. Picking himself up, he galloped away up the glen in a daze of breathless joy.

Chapter Three

A week later Fergus left for his trip to Oban. During that time he had collected all the clothing coupons he could find. His own supply was barely depleted because he seldom had reason to buy new clothes. Many of the older men were delighted to sell him their coupons including Dodie who was overjoyed and somewhat bemused that the scraps of paper he had always regarded as useless could actually fetch him money.

'Ach, McKenzie will have cheated that poor simple cratur',' Behag Beag, the fault-finding postmistress of Portcull, stated sourly. 'Fancy having the cheek to offer money for things as scarce as clothing coupons. It's like this black market I am hearing goes on over yonder on the mainland. It's only villains do things like these.'

'McKenzie of the Glen is not a man to cheat anybody!' Kate McKinnon stoutly rose to Fergus's defence. 'Especially would he never cheat Dodie out o' a farthin'! He's kind to old Dodie – no' like some I could mention.' Kate leaned across the counter and gave Behag a conspiratorial wink. 'Am I no' after hearin' that you sold your own coupons to my Nancy and the poor soul payin' more than they were worth

– and her wi' all these bairns to clothe – ay.' Kate shook her head sorrowfully while Behag's wizened jowls fell in dismayed layers over her neck for she had sworn Nancy to secrecy.

'There's some would do anythin' for sillar,' Kate went on, thoroughly revelling in Behag's discomfiture, 'but my, you had better no' be throwin' your coupons about too much, Behag, or you'll end up with no' even a decent pair o' breeks to cover the cheeks o' your bum – now o' course that might have been all right in your younger days when you were maybe tryin' to tempt a man up your skirts but the only thing you'll get up there now is a chill in the bladder that will keep you runnin' to your wee hoosie for weeks!'

Kate went off, skirling with laughter, leaving Behag to fume and vow that one day she would report the McKinnons to the Customs mannie and rid the island once and for all of a sinful and illegal product. But Behag knew that her vow was just a shallow one and she prayed to the Lord to forgive her for being too weak to face up to the certain wrath of the islanders if she dared to expose the McKinnons, for they were a family beloved by many. Forbye that, she was not averse to a drop of McKinnon's brew herself, entirely for medicinal purposes, of course. The preservation of a person's bodily functions could in no way be construed as a sin and after Kate's triumphant exit Behag flounced to the back shop where she took a good swallock of the malt to help her get rid of the lump of rage that had risen in her throat.

'I'll only be away for a night or two,' Fergus told Kirsteen. She was going through a spell of depression and was inclined to be unusually irritable. He nuzzled her ear, feeling the softness of her breasts against his hard chest. He had been gentle with her since the babies' birth, contenting himself with just kissing and holding her though his desire for her was so strong he wanted to crush her to him and take her without constraint.

'Why do you have to be away at all?' she whispered sulkily, drawing away from him and lowering her face so that it was veiled by the shadows of early morning.

'Because I want to buy you something special for Christmas – I've never given you a proper present, so just for once let me do this.'

'But you won't be able to get anything! It's wartime – remember?' she told him rather resentfully, thinking of months of watered-down tea, of scrimping to save a little out of each week's rations so that they could all enjoy a real feast at Christmas.

'I'll get something,' he said with a conviction he was far from feeling. 'Don't you worry about a thing. Shona and Niall will be here within the next day or two and Matthew will see to things around the farm.'

'Oh – to hell with the farm,' she cried, throwing her head back in a fit of pique, an action that curved her neck into a slender arch. Her blue eyes were rather dull and weary-looking, for her days were filled from morning to night with the constant demands of two infants and a lively son. Phebie was a wonderful source of help but there were the nights of broken sleep to contend with and Fergus felt a pang of guilt.

'We're going to get someone in to help you here,' he said firmly. 'When I get back I'll see to it, and I don't want any of your refusals. Nancy's eldest daughter, Janet, is a good sensible girl and she's grand with bairns.'

'Yes,' Kirsteen said dully.

Fergus's black eyes snapped. 'Och to hell! I won't go and leave you like this! Dammit! You know how I've always hated leaving home even for a few days. It was for you! Just for you! I only want to make you happy.'

'Oh, Fergus, I'm sorry,' she said with a rush of remorse. 'I'm being childish and bad-tempered. Lachlan says it can happen like this but I don't like myself very much at the moment. When you come back I'll be a ray of sunshine, I promise.'

She straightened his jacket and pushed him towards the door, which she opened decisively. The morning was dark with pearly mist hanging over the fields and clinging to the hills. The chill breath of winter rushed into the warm kitchen. Putting her arms up she drew his head down and kissed him so deeply his heart quickened.

'Little seductress,' he murmured. 'If you want to stop me going that's the surest way. Why couldn't you have done that last night?'

'Too soon, my darling, but you wait, I'll give you

a Christmas present that won't cost anything but that you will never forget.'

'Promises, promises,' he chuckled, his breath condensing in the frosty air. 'I'll keep you to them but right now I must go if I'm to catch that boat.'

'Fergus.' He was halfway down the path when her voice stayed him. 'We haven't given our sons names yet. I want them to be special and I want them to come from you.'

Many hours later Fergus arrived at Oban. The mist hung in a purple pall over the fishing port, huddling the town into a clammy blanket. Ghost shapes of trees probed the dour sky and spread winter tracery over the wet slates of rooftops. In the bay the needles of masts pierced into the haar; pinpricks of guide lights shivered over the grey water, ending the subdued dance on the glistening cobblestones by the harbour. The remoteness of the night made him hurry through the near-deserted streets towards the small homely hotel run by Maggie and Murdy Travers. They had befriended him when he had come to Oban seven years before in a fruitless search for Kirsteen.

Maggie welcomed him with delight and led him into the cosy parlour where Murdy was snoring in the depths of an armchair with his feet atop the range. At their entry he opened an enquiring eye then rose with agility to pump Fergus's hand heartily. After that, it was like old times, with Maggie plying him with platefuls of food while she reminisced about the time of his exhaustive search for Kirsteen and his eventual travels to England to find both her and his little son.

'Ay, and now you have two more,' Murdy said, gazing thoughtfully into his whisky glass and gave a dignified hiccup. 'I tell you this now, lad, never show you have a favourite. My mother favoured my elder brother more than me and never took pains to hide the fact. To this day I have never got over the hurt of that. Maggie and me only had our lassie, so we had no problems there. It's easy to spoil a lassie and you can get away with doin' it to that bonny wee girl of yours – but treat the lads the same, son, and remember – the heart that hurts most least often shows it.' It was an unusually serious speech for the jovial Murdy. He hiccuped again and grinned. 'By God, I'm on my soap box tonight, I must be soberin' up – where's that whisky? . . .' He struggled out of his chair and Maggie rushed to hold him upright. 'You auld bodach,' she giggled. 'Drunk as a lord and sayin' things you'll regret come mornin' – but mercy on us! It is mornin', nearly one o'clock. Up to bed wi' you this very minute and if you think I'm goin' to help you off wi' your clothes you've another think comin' for I doubt it will take me all my time to get myself under the covers.'

Though he was fatigued Fergus slept only fitfully and wakened as dawn was creeping coldly over the sky. It was the habit of years that made him get up and dress quickly. The room was chilly but he was

used to that at Laigmhor. There was no sound of life
in the house and he guessed the Travers must still
be asleep. Noiselessly he crept downstairs and let
himself outside. The wind had freshened during the
night and swept the mist away, leaving the morning
bright and bitterly cold. He turned his steps in the
direction of McCaig's Folly, which reared up against
a turquoise sky washed over with gold. As he
climbed the steep deserted hill, the Folly became
more than just a giant landmark: the great circle of
weathered stone loomed above him, powerful in all
its Colosseum-like splendour. The deepening gold of
the dawn filtered through its double row of tall
windows and he couldn't help thinking that the
building was like some great Roman temple lit from
within by thousands of candles. With the slow
measured tread of the Hebridean he walked across
the unroofed inner gallery. Scrambling up to one
of the window apertures he perched himself on the
grey stonework and gazed out over the shimmering
landscape. Today the horizon was cloudless, the rich
hues of sunrise diffusing into a brilliant blue that
deepened to purple in the dome of the heavens
where stars still sparkled faintly. His gaze travelled
downwards to the dream-like splendour of the Mull
hills whose corries were erased by distance, though
a faint glimmer of snow was discernible on the high
sullen peak of Ben More. For a long time he looked
at the hazed island of Mull, thinking how much it
resembled Rhanna, though on a much grander scale.

He felt contented and very peaceful and had to

force his mind back to the reason he had come to this high place of solitude. Kirsteen had told him to think of names for their sons – and he had never been over-imaginative about things like that. It was easy enough to make up names for horses and cows – but boys! He smiled at his thoughts and watched as the sun rose higher to inject the water with shades of blue and silver. The nearer islands lay in shadows of damson and jade, though the long tawny shape of Kerrera was touched by fingers of golden light, which were reflected in the deep dark water of the Firth of Lorn. Lorn. Lorn! Fergus sat up straighter. Blue and languorous. That was how the Firth of Lorn looked this morning. The twins had the bluest eyes he had ever seen. Kirsteen said their eyes would change, grow dark like his, but he was convinced they would stay like hers.

'Lorn.' He murmured the name softly. One of his sons would be Lorn – and the other – he suddenly thought of Lewis. Shona and Niall had spent their honeymoon in Stornoway on the island of Lewis. Lachlan had relatives there . . . 'Lorn and Lewis.' He spoke the names aloud and they echoed round the cloisters of the Folly like a melody. 'Lorn and Lewis!' he cried again and gave a deep chuckle of satisfied laughter. Wait till he told Kirsteen. He wanted to go home right away but there were other matters to settle first.

Maggie came with him to help him with his shopping. 'You have no need to be buying toys now,' she told him as she pulled on her gloves. 'I doubt you would get them anyway but I have been busy this whily. I've made things for you all and look – come over here,' she said, and opened a drawer in the sideboard and proudly withdrew an exquisitely carved model of a fishing boat. 'For that wee rascal Grant,' she said, beaming. 'My Murdy made it. He's no' as green as he's cabbage lookin'. Took him months to do, mind, but och, he knows fine the wee laddie is mad on boats and will take care of it.'

Maggie had been right about the shortage of goods in the shops and here he was looking for fur jackets for Kirsteen and Shona. 'Fur jackets!' Maggie shook her head doubtfully. 'You will be lucky if you manage to find a fur purse! But wait you, I know the very place! Not much to look at mind but the wee mannie there has stuff in that shop you would never credit.'

The shop was situated in a back street and its appearance was so dilapidated it was hard to imagine that it was occupied at all. But the 'wee mannie' was there all right, shuffling from the back shop in answer to the rusty tinkle of the bell above the door. The interior of the shop was dismal and matched well the proprietor's gloomy expression and his greeting of, 'A bitter day is it not? I canny get my blood goin' in the right direction in weather like this.'

Fergus swallowed and wondered why on earth Maggie had dragged him here but his heart lifted somewhat when, having voiced his request, the little man's eyes lit with interest, though he hummed and hawed so much Maggie burst out, 'Ach, stop fooling around, Mr McDuff, you know fine what the laddie means. Have you got what he is wanting or haven't you?'

'Fur jackets,' Mr McDuff said thoughtfully. 'These are no' easy to come by, no' easy at all. Times are hard, hard indeed . . .' He looked over his specs at Fergus. 'You will need plenty money and plenty coupons.'

'I've got enough of both.' Fergus placed the coupons on the counter and taking out his wallet he fingered the contents provocatively.

Mr McDuff tapped the side of his long nose and whispered, 'I might have the very thing, though I wouldny say that to just anybody. Seein' I know Maggie here . . .' He shuffled away into his back shop and several minutes later re-emerged with two beautiful jackets over his arm, one the colour of dark honey, the other a rich grey that glowed silver in the feeble light from the window. 'These are all I have,' Mr McDuff said, laying them on the counter. 'They are not what you would call new, mind, but near as good as. I forgot I had them. There's no' many folks rushin' to buy fur jackets the now.'

Fergus could hardly believe his luck. 'I'll take them,' he said rather breathlessly, seeing in his mind's eye the look on Kirsteen's face when she beheld his gift to her.

'Plenty money, mind,' the old man said, rubbing his hands together gently, a nervous twitch lifting one corner of his mouth as Fergus counted his notes one by one and placed them on the counter.

Mr McDuff's fingers scrunched over the money quickly before he scooped it up and placed it with a show of nonchalance into a drawer. 'I will wrap the jackets up –' He paused. 'I have a nice bitty paper I was savin' for my special customers and by God! You're the most special I've had this year and I'm thinkin' you've maybe made my Christmas too.' Methodically he wrapped and tied the boxes. 'It's no' everybody gets string to put round things these days but I'm thinkin' these jackets must be for two special ladies so I'm makin' an exception in your case.'

'Very special ladies,' Fergus agreed soberly, though the minute he was outside the shop he grabbed Maggie's waist and pulled her to him. 'You're a witch, Maggie Travers! The most magical witch I've ever known I tell you, you beat all of Canty Tam's water witches for tricks and spells. Come on, I've got a few coupons left, your wee mannie was so excited he didn't take them all, and I'm going to get you something really grand for Christmas.'

Maggie giggled and protested but Fergus swept her along. 'Really, laddie,' she told him with a twinkle, 'that old bodach is known as McDuff the Bluff in these parts. He was a furrier before the war and I know fine he still has plenty of furs in that back shop of his even though he told you you got the last two.'

'No matter. I never thought I'd get anything so grand, so you and Murdy are getting presents whether you like it or no.'

The next morning Fergus left for Rhanna on the

mid-morning boat. Murdy and Maggie saw him off, the latter in tears as she pushed parcels into his grasp. 'You come over and visit us whenever you can now,' Fergus told them firmly. 'Let us repay you for all you've done for us. The doors of Laigmhor are always open to you.'

'Ay, we will that,' Maggie sniffed. 'Away you go now and don't forget to give all our friends on Rhanna our love.'

It was very late when the craggy drift of the Rhanna hills at last reared up on the horizon. The sea was like a crumpled piece of ebony paper, a shade darker than the vast reaches of the star-studded sky. The boat pushed its way through the Sound of Rhanna, lifting the waves to foam, cutting steadily along. The water in the harbour was velvet-smooth, the village so silent that the noise of the boat's engines was like a profanity, tearing the peace apart. Ropes were tied, the throbbing of the engines lessened, then ceased. The crew languidly saw the few passengers off. Niall was at the harbour with the pony and trap.

'You shouldn't have bothered,' Fergus protested, though he had been wondering how he was going to carry everything up to Laigmhor.

'Orders,' Niall said grinning, throwing parcels into the back of the trap. 'Shona is at Laigmhor waiting.' He laughed. 'Ay, and a fine time I've had with her all day – like a wee lass she is waiting for Father Christmas to come down the lum. Come on, in you get.'

In the darkness Fergus smiled and listened with pleasure to the slap of the sea beating against the shore. The little white houses of Portcull sat solid and serene against the black slopes of the night hills; scents of salt and peat smoke filled the air. The pony plodded up Glen Fallan and now there were other smells. The men had been spreading dung on the fields. The rich reek of it mingled with the sharp tang of frost. The air was cold against his face. From the hills a stag roared once then was silent. The burns frothed down into the river, shimmering in a glint of moonlight. In the distance he saw Laigmhor, a dim white blob against the slopes of Ben Machrie. Chinks of light shone from the windows and his heart leapt. No matter how short was his separation from his beloved home, he never failed to feel excitement and joy on his return.

They clattered into the cobbled yard and he turned to Niall. 'I'll take my cases in but leave these other things by the back door till I get settled.'

'Right, I'll just get Dusk into the stable and I'll be right with you.'

Fergus stepped over the threshold to see a sparkling-clean kitchen. A peat fire sang in the grate, throwing showers of sparks up the chimney. On the hearthrug, three cats were piled on top of the obliging and good-natured Squint, who appeared to be sound asleep, but at Fergus's entry he got up hastily and a shower of indignant felines landed on the floor. The little dog hurled himself at the dark man standing smiling in the doorway and Fergus threw up his arm to catch the ecstatic, quivering bundle of golden fur. A delicious savoury aroma filled the room. Shona was by the range, lifting a crusty brown steak pie from the oven. Her glorious curtain of auburn hair hid her face but at the opening of the door she pushed it back impatiently from her flushed face. 'Damned hair! I'll get it cut, I swear I will no matter what Niall says –' She stopped short in her tirade and a smile lit her elfin face. 'Father,' she said softly, rather shyly, 'it's so good to see you.' She rushed at him and Squint groaned in protest as the air was squeezed from his tubby little body. One of his floppy ears fell into Fergus's mouth together with a lock of Shona's hair.

'Hey, give me air! he shouted laughingly. 'I'm smothering.'

'Och, be quiet, it's not every day I get to coorie into you,' she scolded, nuzzling her face into his neck.

She was radiant in her youth and beauty. Her hair was silk under his fingers, the vibrant love she had for him pulsed into him and a lump came into his throat. Gently he pushed her away and studied her sparkling face. 'Married life suits you, mo ghaoil, you're bonnier than I've ever seen you.' Over Shona's head his eyes met Kirsteen's. She looked different. The weariness had gone from her eyes; there was an aura of quiet elation about her. And when she caught the message in his glance she blushed and was once again the young girl he had chanced upon in the woods by Loch Tenee where she had been swimming. She had been drying herself when he had come upon her. Shock had turned her into an immobile golden statue with droplets of water gleaming on her smooth skin and wet little tendrils of blonde hair clinging round her pink ears. Vividly he recalled the scene and his legs felt unsteady beneath him.

'Hello, Fergus.' Her voice was soft, her smile secretive, filled with gladness to have him back. 'This child has been spoiling me. I've done nothing since she came. She's fussed over me and coddled me and looked after the twins.'

'Ach, I've enjoyed it,' Shona broke in. 'Though if I have some of my own I think I'll start off with just one. Now, we're all starving to death waiting for you, Father. I want everyone seated at the table in five minutes and that's an order! Wash yourself first, Father, there's hot water in the pan . . .' She giggled and looked from one to the other. 'It's so lovely to be home,' she said, her blue eyes shining with the brilliance of a summer sea. 'I love being married to Niall and I'm very happy – but this . . .' she said, glancing round the room, 'this is where I belong – at Laigmhor – on Rhanna. I miss it so much, but one day we'll come back – though of course we'll have to find another house. It's crowded here, I can hardly believe I've got more brothers, when will it ever stop?' Her eyes travelled to the little golden spaniel draped once more by the fire. 'Dear wee dog,' her voice had grown husky. 'When I first saw him the years just rolled away – I thought Tot had come back, then this wee devil opened his eyes and instead of crying I laughed instead. I love him, he's so silly and

playful, the way Tot was when Hamish first gave her
to me.'

'You can take him back with you, I took him
knowing how much you missed Tot . . .'

She shook her head. 'No, Father, let the babies
grow up with a dog of their own. My childhood
would have been a less precious memory without
dear old Tot – besides, Grant loves Squint already,
he says he's going to take him to sea and he'll
become an old sea dog.' She choked with laughter.
'Grant puts me in mind of myself when I was his age.
Yesterday he dressed that poor wee pup in a scarf
and bonnet exactly like old Joe's. When I came in
and saw Squint lying at the fire I thought he was a
hobgoblin. Then to make matters worse, Grant leapt
out at me from the larder and near scared the wits
out of me. We had a job getting him off to bed
tonight. He was all for staying up till you came
home.'

Niall came in, his tanned face glowing from the
sting of the night air. He rubbed his hands together
and sniffed the savoury fragrances mingling together.
'Mmm, my mouth is watering. I'm starving. Do you
know, Fergus, this daft daughter of yours hasn't let
me eat a thing since this afternoon. Favouritism that's
what it is, pure neglect of her new husband in favour
of her father.'

There would have been a time when he would
never have uttered such things to dour, unapproachable Fergus, but things were different now. Fergus
was different, though he was still, and probably

always would be, a man of few words. He had a pride of bearing that many took for arrogance, but he was not nearly as formidable as of yore. He laughed more, and took things less seriously – though he protected those he loved with such fierce passion few dared to rile him openly. It was perhaps because of that, that 'McKenzie of the Glen' as he was now becoming known, was more talked about behind his back than anyone else on the island.

Shona giggled and clouted her husband playfully with the dish towel as he was drawing his chair into the table. After that everyone seemed to talk at once. Shona was immediately busy and so efficient that Fergus watched her in delight. She had always been a mercurial creature, a tomboy who rarely sat still, but now she glowed with an inner radiance, her movements swift and graceful. Marriage to Niall had certainly been her salvation, though Fergus knew that this daughter of his would never know complete contentment until circumstances allowed her to come back to live on the place she had loved since her first stirrings of awareness to the beauty and enchantment of her island home.

Proudly she set food on the table and smiled at Fergus. 'You see, Father, I've learned to cook now that I'm a sedate married woman.' She dimpled mischievously. 'No more awful dumplings or burnt porridge – well just sometimes. For did not Mirabelle say herself more than once that "no' a body in the whole wide world is perfect, even those that put themselves on a pedestal so that they can spit and do other nasty things on the lowly and imperfect".'

Fergus's deep laugh boomed out. 'A sedate married woman uttering profanities that would make Mirabelle turn in her grave . . . If I mind right she was quite prim and proper in her way!'

'Ach, she was right enough, but if things riled her enough she could come out with some surprising observations. She used to mutter a lot under her breath when she was harassed, and once, when she thought I was too young to understand, I heard her saying, "Ach, that Behag, she has a face on her like a threepenny bit in a cow's backside waiting for change."'

Everyone shrieked with laughter and the meal was a merry one with Fergus and Kirsteen giving the two young folk all the latest gossip and news about the island. When the table was being cleared Fergus went to the door and brought in his parcels, though he was careful to leave the huge bouquet of red roses he had brought for Kirsteen by the lobby door.

'Peenies off,' he ordered. 'I've got something for everybody to be opened on Christmas morning, but these,' he said, indicating the biggest packages, 'are for now, for the two women in my life. I hope to God you like them. I'm not very good at choosing things for females, but Maggie helped me. Anyway, see what you think.'

Kirsteen and Shona were like children in their eagerness to discover what the parcels contained, though they were careful to preserve the precious pieces of paper and string. In awe they stared at the contents of the boxes.

'Well!' Fergus's voice was frayed with anxiety, his cheekbones tinged red with embarrassment.

Kirsteen lifted up the silver-grey fur and looked at it in disbelief. 'Fergus, oh my darling, it's beautiful, the most beautiful jacket I've ever seen. How on earth . . . ?'

'Ask no questions. Presents should be accepted without question . . .' His face relaxed into a smile. 'All I can tell you is that we owe a lot to Maggie Travers not forgetting McDuff the Bluff of Oban.'

'I'll never get a chance to wear it,' Kirsteen said, her voice was low, 'but I shall treasure it always. Thank you, oh thank you, my dearest.' She kissed him on the cheek. Her lips were warm and he could sense the depth of her emotions.

Shona had said nothing, she just stood staring at the gift, stroking the soft honey-coloured fur with trembling fingers, her blue eyes swimming with tears. 'I don't know what to say,' she whispered shakily. 'Oh, I do know!' Impatiently she brushed her eyes. 'But I can't get my tongue to make the words come out properly!'

Niall put his arm round her slim waist and pulled her against him. 'You'll look so grand in that you'll be ashamed to walk down Sauchiehall Street beside your poor tattered husband.' He grinned at Fergus. 'And I thought I was doing well getting a rabbit's paw to put in the nylon stockings I managed to get her. Ach well, she can always put it in the pocket of her jacket – it will bring her luck.'

Later, when Niall and Shona were busy at the sink washing up, Fergus went to get the roses, and then, taking Kirsteen by the hand, he led her into the parlour where he made her sit down. Tentatively he presented the bouquet to her. She saw the discomfiture in the big ruggedly handsome Gael and her eyes filled with merriment, which made his own flash in chagrin.

'Oh don't,' she laughed. 'You looked so handsome holding them. You suit red roses, my darling. You should carry them more often.'

'Even when I'm mucking out the byre?' he hissed, and they both burst out laughing, though his eyes devoured the sight of her so vibrantly lovely in a blue wool dress, her corn-coloured curls clinging round her head, fine little tendrils crisping round the delicate shells of her ears. Her smooth skin was flushed, her eyes were very blue and she looked ten years younger than her thirty-five. They were acutely aware of each other. She put out a slender hand to him and his big work-hardened one closed over hers so tightly she gasped. 'I've missed you so,' she told him rather breathlessly. 'And yet – I don't know what to say to you.'

He fell on his knees beside her and enclosed her in his embrace, his lips caressing her hair. 'Then don't say anything,' he breathed. 'Just listen to me. I can't remember when I've felt so happy. You have given me two fine new sons, but most of all you have given me your love and that means everything to me. It's going to be a wonderful Christmas. I'm going to hold you and kiss you and love you. I want you all the time and never more than at this minute. You look like a wee lassie sitting there, your skin all pink and your nose like a shiny button off a Sunday dress.'

She lowered her head quickly to hide the tears that had sprung to her eyes. His two nights away from her had seemed like years and her heart beat swiftly at his nearness. She took his face in her hands and gazed deep into his eyes. 'I am going to be very wanton and let you do anything you want with me – and I'm so much in love with you I almost forgot to ask – names – did you think of names for the twins?'

'Ay, I did that. I couldn't sleep my first night with the Travers and I got up at dawn to walk up to the Folly. The view gave me inspiration and I thought of Lorn and Lewis.'

She stared at him, and he reddened. 'You don't like them,' he accused.

With a gentle finger she traced the curve of his rebellious mouth. 'Fergus, my Fergus, they're beautiful – perfect. Lorn and Lewis, they're poetical. There's more to my strong farmer than meets the eye. You have a romantic centre under that tough shell you show the world.'

'Och, get along with you,' he said uncomfortably, and she smiled and took his hand.

'Come on, let's go up and christen the babies. The poor wee souls are just numbers at the moment.'

He looked into the kitchen to bid goodnight to Niall and Shona and was astounded to see that the room was filled with rainbow-coloured soap bubbles. Squint was sitting entranced, one eye roving towards the ceiling, the other fixed on a large bubble that had landed on the tip of his nose. He snapped and the bubble burst, the look of comical surprise on his face sending Niall and Shona into shrieks of laughter. Fergus, too, laughed – though he asked rather sourly, 'Am I to believe there is a sudden glut of soap? According to Merry Mary it's more scarce than gold at the moment.'

Shona wiped her eyes. 'Ach, don't worry, Father. I gathered all the bits and pieces I had and made them into liquid soap. I brought a few jars with me, so we're having a bubble party.'

'Well, see and don't flood the place,' he warned, eyeing Squint who was joyfully skating about on the wet floor. 'We're having an early night, so see you two behave yourselves.'

'We'll get along over to Slochmhor the minute we're finished here,' said a rather flushed Niall, and Fergus nodded and went on upstairs.

Kirsteen had gone on ahead. The nursery was hushed and peaceful. The babies had cried a good deal that day but now, though awake, they were quiet, their huge blue eyes gazing in wonder at the dancing shadows on the ceiling. Kirsteen buried her face in the roses Fergus had brought her. They were exquisite, but not nearly as precious to her as the two rosebuds he had given her on the morning of the babies' birth. She went to the dresser and softly pulled out the drawer where lay the family Bible. It opened at the book of Job in the Old Testament where the pressed rosebuds nuzzled the yellowed pages. Reverently she touched the roses, which though faded still retained a whisper of colour.

'Lorn and Lewis,' she murmured. She held the lamp higher and a sentence on the page seemed to leap out at her. 'Though thy beginning was small, yet thy latter day should greatly increase.' She mouthed the words to herself then said aloud to the silent room, 'And so be it.'

'Talking to yourself – or to them?' Fergus came in and stood gazing down at the babies. 'They're awake, yet they're not crying,' he said in wonder. 'Have you bewitched them, little witch?' He put his arm out to her and drew her in close to him. 'Which will be which?'

The youngest baby had a tiny dimple on his chin, a replica of his father's. 'This shall be Lorn,' she said softly. 'He will grow up to be strong like you, strong and self-willed, stubborn and wonderful. Oh, I know Lachlan is worried for him just now but it won't always be so.' She picked the child up and propped his downy head under her chin, very aware of his frailty. His heart fluttered swiftly against the softness of her breasts but she vowed silently never to let him be aware that his was a lesser strength than his brother's.

Fergus scooped the other baby into the crook of his strong right arm, and in a mood of abandonment, danced with him round the room. 'Lewis!' he cried joyfully. 'Lewis Fraser McKenzie! How's that for a grand title, eh, my bonny wee man?'

Kirsteen watched him and felt that all the joy on earth belonged to them in those wonderful moments. Fergus's shadow pranced on the ceiling and she felt such an unbearable love for him rising in her breast she wanted to sing aloud in her happiness, knowing she would remember him like that, dancing with his son in his embrace, for the rest of her life. 'And I have here his bonny lordship, Lorn Lachlan McKenzie!' she said, her breath catching with the pain and passion of her emotions. 'Lachlan has a few namesakes on the island but none will bring him greater credit than this precious infant.'

Fergus caught her by the waist and they danced together, their laughter ringing out, the babies in their arms gurgling in keeping with their parents' mood.

Downstairs Niall grinned. 'Would you listen to them up there? Like a herd of elephants. If that's what babies do to people we must have what these two have.'

'Not twins!' Shona said, shocked.

'No, babies will do,' he yelled gleefully, and, pulling her to him, he kissed her deeply. She lay against him, cherishing the warm nearness of him. 'Babies can bring pain too,' she said eventually, and rather sadly. 'I didn't bring Father much joy when I came into the world, but things came all right for us in the end because ours was a mental rather than a physical battle. It won't be so for Morag Ruadh. I feel sorry for her, but more for the bairnie – so bonny but

72

for her poor wee leg. Other folk would just accept it
as a natural thing, but Morag will see it as a dam-
nation brought about by her throwing away all her
saintly scruples and giving herself up to the lusts of
the flesh I know fine what I'm talking about, for the
besom said the self-same things about me when I lost
our wee boy and me with no wedding ring on my
finger.'

Niall stroked her hair. 'Hush now, my babby, these
things are in the past now but I can well believe that
Caillich Ruadh made your life a hell at the time. I
can't feel sorry for her, all my sympathies are with
the bairnie and poor old Doug. Mark my words, she
will become a religious fanatic after this, and she'll
drag Doug down with her. His life will be hardly
worth living, though the bairn might bring him some
comfort – even though it might not be his.'

Even Niall couldn't know how apt his words were to
be. At that very moment at Dunbeag House,
Portvoynachan, Morag Ruadh held to her breast the
little daughter to whom she had given birth a few
days before. Moaning and crying in a paroxysm of
remorse and shame, she rocked the baby back and
forth, back and forth, then she laid it down and for
the hundredth time since its birth, she clasped her
long supple fingers to her lips as if in prayer. The
child was beautiful, perfect, so perfect – except . . .
Morag lifted up the skirt of the baby's flannelette
gown, and through a watery blur she gazed in disbelief at the skinny little legs; one completely normal,

the other as twisted and shrivelled as a piece of unravelled yarn. Morag's thoughts travelled back to the night of the manse ceilidh held by the Rev. John Gray for the Germans who had arrived so unexpectedly on Rhanna. For the first time in her life, saintly Morag had thrown caution to the winds and had seduced two Commando guards in the minister's fuel shed. Later, Dugald had also succumbed to her wild abandonment, and when she had discovered she was pregnant he had married her without question. But Morag didn't know who the father of her child was; all she knew in those dreadful despair-filled hours after her daughter's birth, was remorse so deep and tortuous she fully believed the child's deformity was a punishment sent to torment her for the rest of her days.

She held the infant high above her head and cried aloud in her grief, 'I did this to you, my babby, but I will make it up to you. From this day forth you are a daughter of God! As long as there is breath in my body no man will tarnish your purity! As sure as God is my Judge!' The hair of the child was golden. Morag stroked it with reverent fingers, tears flowing from her eyes. 'My bonny one, so bonny. Your name shall be Ruth. When words come to your lips you will say unto me, "Whither thou goest, I will go and thy God will be my God and nothing but death will part thee and me". Don't cry, my little one, no evil will ever befall you as long as I'm here to look to you. You will be a servant of God and the angels and I was aye a body who kept my word.' She muffled her sobs into the soft folds of the baby's neck. Dugald came into the room with a tray. Already he adored his tiny daughter. To him she was perfect and to him that was all that mattered.

Morag looked at her husband. His mop of silvery hair shone, his honest grey eyes regarded her with steady affection. She didn't love him; she never had. Oh, he was a good man and she was fond of him, but she had only married him to give the child a name. She would be a good wife to him, she would cook, clean, sew – but never again would she share the marriage bed with him and in sacrificing her lustful and ungodly urges she would perhaps allay in some small measure the dreadful sins that lay in her mind like festering sores.

But it wasn't due to sin that out of four babies born on Rhanna in the December of 1941 three of them had congenital defects. Lachlan suspected something other than coincidence when three days before Christmas in a cottage at Portcull he delivered Kate McKinnon's daughter, Annie, of a healthy eight-pound baby girl who, though rosy and sound of wind and limb, made not the slightest whimper in her entry into the world. Annie was Kate's youngest daughter and there were some who had said she should never have married Dokie Joe, a cousin twice removed. The child was their firstborn and Annie was thrilled at first sight of the chubby pink bundle, but her joy turned to dismay when several hours elapsed and no sound escaped the baby's rosy lips. 'She doesny cry, Doctor,' Annie told Lachlan in a frightened voice. 'She is bewitched an' no mistake. There are some who would think it a mercy to have a bairnie who doesny greet, but I'm thinkin' it's no' natural – I'm thinkin' that my bonny wee Rachel has maybe been struck dumb. These folks were maybe right when they said that Dokie an' me shouldny have wed. Even Mither said that close blood doesny make for wise bairns.'

But Lachlan dismissed this. If Annie and Dokie had been first cousins, there might have been something in what she said, though Rhanna was full of close blood marriages and one had yet to produce a defective child.

'It's early yet, give her time,' he advised gently.

'But she's struck dumb, I'm tellin' you, Doctor.'

He uttered words of comfort, though in his heart he knew that Annie had stumbled onto the truth. Lachlan thought about little Lorn with his weak heart and frail body, he thought of baby Ruth, beautiful but for her pathetic twisted leg, and he looked now at Rachel and knew that it wasn't just chance that had brought about such tragic malfunctions. Desperately he sought the answers from his personal store of medical knowledge, from medical textbooks, but at that time there were none. He didn't know the reason, and the knowledge of that brought him sleepless nights and frustrating days, for he was a man dedicated to his profession. In time, the answers would come, but not then, in the winter of 1941, when two sons and two daughters of Rhanna emerged from their mothers' wombs to breathe the sweet air of hill and sea; suckled at their mothers' breasts, fought their separate battles for survival in those first tender stirrings of life, in their dreamings and their awakenings as yet unaware that the delicate threads of their lives were even then being woven into a pattern binding them together in a tapestry already planned by fate.

Part Two

Spring 1950

Chapter Four

The last nine years had brought some changes to Portcull, the greatest being the conversion of the largest house, which was next door to the Smiddy, into an hotel. This innovation pleased all the menfolk, delighted Todd, but disgusted Mollie, who claimed the establishment not only brought the Smiddy down, but encouraged drunkenness.

Bed and breakfast signs had sprung up outside croft houses all over the island, many of which greatly puzzled and misled the tourists. One at Nigg grandly proclaimed 'Bed and Breakfast with all conveniences', the conveniences being the dry lavatory situated in the bushes at the back of the house and the rickety bus that shook and rattled its way over cliff roads only suitable for horse-drawn traffic. Another sign at Portcull laboriously extolled 'Mrs McKinnon invites you to bed'. Here Tam had run out of space and in tiny letters at the bottom had added, 'and breakfast with home-made mealy pudding and home-cured bacon.' Outside old Joe's cottage a large white notice screamed in red letters: 'Fresh lobsters and crabs for sail. If owner out, take crabs from coal bucket – carefully, they nip – leave money in tin marked nails.' Elspeth Morrison, though turning up her sharp nose at what she called money grubbing, nevertheless placed a minute notice on her gate, which read 'Eggs laid while U wait – duck, hen, goose – take your pick – hard boiled for picnics in peat creel'.

At the bottom of the hill road to Nigg was the most mystifying and tantalising notice of all. At Ranald's urging, Dodie had finally capitulated to the 'towrist boom', and Tam, who spoke English but thought in Gaelic with its grammatical charm, painted a sign that even he could hardly understand when it was finished. 'Is a head two miles,' the sign read, 'German swastika genuine – old relic from world war two. A hundred thousand welcomes all.'

Tourists had been baffled to follow the trail only to find an embarrassed Dodie working in his fort-ressed garden. Tempers had flared at the idea of him being the ancient relic they had laboured over hilly moor to find, but when it was discovered that the roof of his wee hoosie was indeed formed from the tail-piece of the Heinkel bomber that had crash-landed on the island, dismay turned to amazement and cameras soon began clicking. News of Dodie's swastika soon spread, and regular visitors to the island brought friends to look. Over heather hillocks they scrambled to get a better view, and the tin that Dodie had hitherto placed too discreetly on a window sill was now painted pink with a bold sign on it saying, 'Donations here, no buttons thank you. He breeah.'

Ranald had suggested to Dodie that he open up

his wee hoosie and charge folk to have a look inside, for here the old eccentric had brought bits and pieces from the bomber and had arranged them till the inside of the dark little hut resembled the cockpit of a plane.

'It would be to their advantage,' Ranald earnestly told Dodie. 'These folks is sometimes burstin' for a pee, and them bein' townpeople they're no' likely to go behind a bush like us. Charge them for the use o' your wee hoosie, and while they're in there havin' a pee they could put a collection into a tin for bein' allowed the privilege o' playin' wi' that control column thing and lookin' at all these instruments on the back o' the door – I tell you if it was me I wouldny hesitate,' Ranald finished rather enviously.

But Dodie drew the line at this. For one thing he couldn't imagine the sophisticated tourists clapping their hands with glee at the idea of using his large chamber pot, the only 'convenience' he had in the wee hoosie. For another thing, he was a creature who liked his privacy and wasn't entirely happy at the invasion of that peaceful spot drowsing amidst the heather. The task of clearing up picnic litter fell to him, and though not fussy about personal hygiene, he couldn't bear to see his environment violated.

All over the island a variety of home-made jams and heather honey was temptingly displayed to catch the visitors' eyes, and always there was the battered old money tin which so endearingly betrayed the trusting Hebridean nature that only the guilt-ridden few did not leave their coppers.

Because it was the Easter holidays the children, barefoot and free from the rigours of the classroom, went about their various tasks and pleasures without hurry yet with an intentness that ensured they made the most of every precious minute. In the yard at Laigmhor Lewis took his brother's hand and they ran to the big barn, which was cool and dim, full of slanting sunbeams and ancient cobwebs. Here were the growing posts, two massive uprights, fashioned from tree trunks. A jumble of dates and niches had been etched into them, an untidy scrawl of red paint on each spelling out the names Lorn and Lewis. The growing posts had been Lewis's idea, conceived at the tender age of five when he had just learned to write. 'One day you'll be as big as me,' he had earnestly told his brother. 'Every month we'll measure ourselves just to see how fast we're growing.'

Lorn had eagerly accepted the idea. His greatest ambition in life was to be as tall as his brother because the first five years of his existence had thwarted all attempts of his to be 'normal'. Childhood ailments that only temporarily affected Lewis had left his brother ill for weeks. One crisis had followed another, and Lorn's infant years had been severely restricted. Wullie the Carpenter had fashioned a little cart for him and he rode about in this, pulled by a tiny Shetland pony, all over the island roads. Wherever Lewis went, his brother went alongside in his miniature trap. When Lewis followed his father out to the fields, Lorn went too, sitting astride Fergus's strong shoulders, loving the feel of the wind in his face, the smells of the earth, the reassuring hardness of his father's body. Grant, too, carried him about in this fashion, striding with him down to the harbour to watch the boats, holding him in the water to teach him to swim. Fergus didn't know about that, or he would most certainly have forbidden his eldest son ever to take Lorn out again. Lewis and Grant between them let their brother do a lot of things that might otherwise have been forbidden because they sensed that their father was afraid for his youngest son and this had perhaps made him over-protective, a point brought home to him one day by Lachlan.

'You must let him do more, Fergus,' the doctor had advised quietly. 'If you don't, he'll be an invalid for the rest of his days.'

'I think I know what's best for my son!' Fergus had snapped defensively.

'And I think I know better,' Lachlan had said gravely. 'Be careful with him, yes, but for God's sake, man, don't pamper him; he won't thank you in later years.'

Fergus had said nothing more, but, as always, he took Lachlan's advice, with the result that Lorn now ran free beside his brother, and though his heart was still weak and he wasn't physically robust, his fierce fighting spirit continually urged him on.

Lewis, tall and straight for nine years, grabbed his brother and pushed him against a growing post where after a few seconds of silent concentration he made a new notch on the hard wood. 'Half an inch taller than three months ago,' he reported earnestly.

The look on Lorn's face was worth the lie. 'I knew I was growing, I could *feel* myself getting bigger – now, it's your turn.'

Lewis stood to attention beside his post, his broad shoulders straight, and Lorn stood on tip-toe to make a mark above his brother's curly head. 'Half an inch – we've both grown the same amount – you're still three inches taller than me, but I'll catch up with you all right.'

''Course you will,' Lewis said off-handedly. 'Now stop blethering and let's go. Old Conker will be fed up waiting for us but I'm going to get us a scone an' jam first – I'm starving.'

He dashed over the yard to the kitchen, leaving Lorn standing stroking the silken nose of Conker, a magnificent Clydesdale with not a grain of temperament in his sweet and placid nature.

Children adored Conker, whose time was divided between working in the fields beside Maple, his stablemate, and acting as companion to all the children who came and went from Laigmhor. Fergus now had a tractor and several other pieces of farm equipment, which made the hard business of farming a whole lot easier, but many of the older farmhands scorned the new-fangled stuff and adhered to the old ways, particularly Jock and Murdy who claimed that nothing but a Clydesdale could plough a true furrow. Likewise, the twins cared nothing for machinery. They were as much at home on the backs of horses as they were on the ground. Under Jock's guidance, Lewis was able already to handle a plough. Lorn could only stand by and watch, but Lewis swore to him that as soon as he was old enough to handle a plough on his own he would teach Lorn everything he knew. With the clearsightedness of youth, Lewis knew of the unspoken dreams in his brother's heart, and though Fergus trusted him to look after Lorn, Lewis did so up to a point but was determined that he wouldn't turn him into a cissy. With this in mind, he let his brother fight his own battles at school, and even though Lorn invariably emerged from them pale, shaken, and breathless, he was able to hold up his head with pride and in time he had shaken off the nickname, Tumshy, that had been bestowed on him when he had started school as a skinny little six-year-old.

Biddy was coming along the glen road, riding a bicycle she had acquired from the SS *Politician* back in the fateful year of 1941. Her green cape flapped behind her in the wind; her skinny black-clad legs ground the pedals round with jubilant energy; the hair that escaped her felt hat was now snowy white; her lined old face was serene even though she had left her 'teeths' steeping in a glass by her bedside. She was still the same teasing, grumbling, fun-loving Biddy, but age had cloaked her with a look of venerable dignity and everyone honoured her convictions. The medical authorities had officially retired her but she would have none of that. 'Damt officials!' she had snorted indignantly. 'They think they can just sign a bitty paper and put folks out to grass – well they can just bugger themselves! No one but God will ever stop me workin' and only then when He has a mind to take me.' So she still carried on with the work that was her life and no one dared to sway her from her path. Indeed, they were delighted at her decision: to them she was 'auld Biddy', a part of Rhanna, as much a feature of any sickroom as the very walls themselves.

'Hello, Biddy,' Lorn called, knowing that her almost-blind old eyes would never see him. She raised a hand to wave and had such a frantic struggle to regain her balance she wobbled the rest of the way down the glen.

Fergus came striding down from the fields and Lorn ran to him. 'We're going to meet the boat, Father, we're going on Conker.'

Fergus smiled at his son. 'Ay, there will be quite a crowd coming off. We'll be having a few visitors ourselves over the next week or so, plenty of folks to keep us busy. It's well seeing Easter is here.' He took Lorn in his strong right arm and swung him onto conker's broad bare back. Lorn wriggled and protested, 'I can manage up myself, Father, I'm not a baby.'

Fergus laughed, his black eyes crinkling in his weatherbeaten face, 'Ay, and you're not a man either.'

'But you never help Lewis the way you help me,' the little boy persisted, his blue eyes darkening with chagrin even while he remembered those early days sitting on his father's shoulders, the good solid feel of power beneath him making him feel safe, safe and wanted. These were times to be cherished in his heart for ever, but now he was feeling more and more that he had to make a stand for himself, to prove to his father that one day he would be strong enough to make a farmer.

Fergus ruffled his son's earth-brown curls and without answering went over to meet Lewis, who was emerging from the kitchen.

'See and be back in time for dinner,' Kirsteen's voice floated from within.

'Ay, Mother, don't worry.'

'You watch your brother now,' Fergus warned. 'Don't let him do anything daft, and see and help him on and off Conker.'

Lewis smiled up at the big man looming above him. 'Ach, Father, of course I will.' He grasped the hard brown hand briefly then raced over the yard and took a flying leap onto Conker's back. The horse was used to such wild behaviour, and with a flick of his ears he began to amble out of the yard.

Lewis had a love of life that bubbled out of eyes vibrantly alive with excitement and laughter – except when he went into one of his rare tempers. Then they grew black and crackled like a thunderstorm in full fury over lowering hills. He sat on Conker and ran an impatient hand through his tangle of curls, which, like Lorn's, gleamed chestnut in the sun. 'Ach, c'mon with you, Conker, get along now,' he urged the horse. 'Auld Todd's new limousine is coming on the boat and everybody's going to see it. Move your backside or I'll give you a good hiding!'

It was an idle threat. Both boys adored the animals of the farm as much as the soil itself.

'Born farmers,' Kirsteen told them with pride, though her heart cried out for her youngest son with the love of the land ingrained in him and the wistful, stubborn tilt of his chin trying so hard to show everyone he didn't care that he couldn't do the things he longed to do. And all the time she knew how much his bruised young heart hurt him. He held onto his brother's waist, delighting in the feel of Conker's strength under him. He was a slightly built child, full of a temperament that could raise him to the heights or plunge him to the very depths of despair. Dour and sullen with all but those he loved, he was not as popular as Lewis whose buoyant charm won many hearts. Physically, Lewis was his father's image, but it was a skin-deep resemblance. Lorn was the one who had inherited Fergus's mental and emotional make-up, and because of it his path through life was as rough as his brother's was smooth.

'Fancy auld Todd winning a limousine,' Lorn said, his voice full of awe for the news that had taken everyone's breath away. Todd openly scorned the 'rubbishy wimmen's papers' that his wife avidly devoured, but in the blissful privacy of his wee hoosie he secretly enjoyed many of the juicier items and he had tried a very tempting competition, never dreaming that he of all people would win the first prize of a silver limousine. Of course, the news had had to come out along with the fact that he was, in the words of the villagers, 'an auld pretender and a hypocrite just'. But in the excitement of the moment all the talk had gone over Todd's head as he and Mollie impatiently awaited their big moment. Now it was here. An important personage escorted by reporters from various newspapers was arriving with the car to ceremoniously hand over the keys. The whole of Portcull, together with spectators from other villages, would be at the harbour, trying to appear very nonchalant and not in the least interested in one of the greatest events to come to the island for many a long day.

'What will he do with it?' Lorn wondered. 'He canny drive a car, only horses.'

Lewis brushed the flies off Conker's mane and laughed. 'Him and Mollie will treat it like a baby. They'll clean it and pamper it and likely sit outside the Smiddy all day just admiring it.'

In the distance the Sound of Rhanna shimmered like a blue satin ribbon. As they reached the bridge by Murdy's house they could see a black knot of people gathered at the harbour. The boat would take some time to unload passengers and small pieces of cargo before dealing with the more ungainly items, but even so Lewis wriggled with impatience and tapped his heels on Conker's sides.

In the grassy yard of Annie McKinnon's house, two little girls sat on the old swing, locked into a small world of their own. 'I have some grand news for you, Rachel,' Ruth Donaldson said rapturously. 'You know Merry Mary's retiring soon – well my father is

going to take over the shop so we're moving here –
to Portcull, to a house near my grandparents . . .'
Ruth paused for a moment, remembering the look
on the faces of Jim Jim and Isabel McDonald on
hearing the news. They had been astonished and
apprehensive, certainly anything but pleased when
their daughter, Morag Ruadh, told them, 'You are
both getting a mite too auld to be managin' on your
own, so I will be on hand to look to you. The Lord
knows it will no' be easy but I was never a one to
shirk my duties and the more sacrifices we make in
this life, the more we will be rewarded in the next.'

Jim Jim's pink pleasant face had taken on an
agitated frown at her words, and in the trauma of the
moment he had made a faultlessly aimed spit into
the peats burning in the grate, much to Morag's
disapproval. Isabel had said not a word. For almost
ten years now, since Morag's marriage to Dugald, she
and her husband had led a life of unparalleled peace;
but now the bliss was about to be shattered, things
would be worse than they had ever been because of
their daughter's fanatical devotion to the church.

'I'll get back my old job as church organist,' Morag
had told them with prim happiness, 'Totie was never
much good at it and was more than pleased when I
told her I was coming back. We are all going to be
very happy together, wait you and see. Oh ay, family
worship will just be like it was in the old days when
I was here to keep an eye on you.'

Rachel absorbed her friend's news thoughtfully
and showed her approval by making the swing go

higher. The breeze ruffled her dark curls and she reached out a rapturous hand as if to touch the blue sky. The clip clop of hooves on the stony road made them both look up.

'Look, Rachel, there's Lorn and Lewis,' Ruth said, pointing excitedly, the violet of her eyes darkening and her solemn little face lighting up. 'They're going to Portcull. I'll have to go too. Mam will be out looking for me if I'm not down the road for dinner time.'

Rachel pushed her silken black hair back from her face and her brown eyes flashed. She was a stunningly beautiful child, tall and slim, brown as a gypsy, wild as the wind that blew down from the mountains, as mercurial as the sea that lapped the Rhanna shores. Strangers couldn't help staring at her nor could they resist speaking to her, but when she stared back wordlessly they took her silence for insolence, and told each other she was nothing but an impudent urchin.

Some of the older islanders said she was possessed of 'the power' and could take things away from folk just by willing it. She had taken Squint away from Lorn and Lewis. Some years ago he had simply deserted them in favour of her. All attempts to win him back had failed. He adored the little girl. Without uttering a single word she could make him do her will by a few simple gestures. He flopped beside her now with lolling tongue, his alert brown eyes gazing up at her, ready to obey the commands of her expressive hands.

Rachel knew that the only reason Ruth was allowed to play with her was because she could not communicate orally, and though she might hear evil she certainly could not speak it. Her assumption was unerringly correct. In committing herself to a sinless life, Morag Ruadh had sentenced her daughter to a rigorous existence bound by endless religious rules that, if broken, not only brought hell down on the head of the sinner, but misery to the entire household. 'You mustny mix with blasphemers,' she warned Ruth repeatedly. 'Folks these days is corrupt and take a delight in corrupting others. Oh ay, I know fine they talk abut me behind my back, but I am strong in the Lord, therefore I shall not falter.' Thus it was that when she came to visit her aged parents in Portcull she allowed Ruth to go and play with Rachel. 'But mind her now,' she never failed to warn. 'Thon wee lassie might be dumb but I am hearin' she has other powers that are no' natural. That can happen to folks wi' a faculty missing; another can take over and it might no' always be to the good.'

Rachel held Morag in contempt but suffered her because she loved little Ruth with her big languorous violet eyes and golden hair, glorious features in a child otherwise rather plain. Her callipered leg made her walk in an ungainly fashion and her mother dressed her in rough drab homespuns because vanity was sinful – all of which effectively hid the otherwise lithesome grace of the child's small-boned figure.

Ruth saw the expression in Rachel's eyes and she took her hand. 'Och, Rachel, c'mon now, you mustny be angry. Is it no' good news I am after tellin' you? When I come to live in Portcull we'll play together all the time and go to school together. But look you, come with me to the village now. The twins will give us a ride on Conker. We'll go and ask your mother. Quick now, I hear tell Todd the Shod is getting his new motor car today and if I give Mam the slip for a wee while I might see it arriving on the harbour.'

Annie nodded her acquiescence at the request. She was bathing the youngest of her three sons in the kitchen sink and was much too harassed to bother where Rachel went or what she did. She and Dokie Joe loved the little girl after a fashion, but had long ago given up trying to understand her, for she was clever to a degree that left them feeling bewildered and inadequate. Her gift for music made them proud, and they were able to boast that she had inherited it from her great-grandfather, whose violin, in its red velvet case, had been merely a toy for countless other McKinnon children. But to Rachel, finding it one day at the back of a cupboard, it was a dream come true. She had plucked fiddle strings since the age of four.

Old Andrew had recognized her talent and had taken her in hand, and now she could extract from her great-grandfather's scratched old fiddle tunes that amazed everyone who heard them. In music Rachel found expression for all her unspoken thoughts and fears, hopes and dreams.

Annie wiped her soapy hands on her apron and, reaching for the biscuit tin, gave each of the children a biscuit. Rachel held up two fingers and Annie said in exasperation, 'Two more! Is it made of money I am? Doesn't your poor father have to work his fingers to the bone out on that cold raw sea and sometimes no' enough fish to fill a sardine tin . . .' Through the window she saw Conker plodding up the road and her face broke into a smile. She pushed two more biscuits into Rachel's waiting hand. 'At least you're no' a selfish wee lassie. Away wi' you now before Dave catches his death in the sink. Mind now, Ruth, get along to your grandparents' double quick, for I won't be havin' that saintly mother of yours sayin' my lassie leads you astray.'

Rachel pushed half her biscuit into Squint's ready jaws and hurried with Ruth out onto the sunlit road. Boldly she stood in Conker's path and when the horse stopped she grabbed Squint, and without preliminary hoisted him up to Lorn, who took him without question. The boys had long ago forgiven him for his desertion. There was a wealth of animals at Laigmhor and they much preferred working dogs to any other.

'We're going to watch Todd's car coming off the boat,' volunteered Ruth while Rachel grabbed her to give her a leg up.

The boys regarded her steadily. She wasn't as well known to them as Rachel, but like everyone else they felt sympathy for her in the restricted life she led. Unlike Rachel, she was shy and awkward; she lisped and blushed easily and was self-conscious about her limp, she also wasn't easy to talk to. Lorn sensed in her the same feelings of inadequacy that were in him and he was, at nine years old, unable to help anyone else to cope with similar feelings. But Lewis had no such complications to hamper his spirit and he gave Ruth a friendly grin.

'Your mother will be keeping a lookout for you,' he predicted, 'so just you keep with us and she might not see you in the crowd.' She blushed crimson and stirred up in him a memory of Dugald standing red-faced and silent in the kitchen at Dunbeag while his wife lectured him for 'idling away the Lord's time in useless pursuits', these being an innocent visit to Portvoynachan harbour at sunrise to watch the fishing smacks coming in, and a quiet sojourn over the moors with jotters and pencils in the hope that the solitude would give him the inspiration he needed to write his beloved poetry.

Ruth didn't answer. She was having difficulty mounting Conker and Lewis was about to scramble down to help her when he spotted a figure proceeding up the glen. Though it was some distance away the children knew it was either a tinker or a tourist because of the forward-leaning gait, which suggested the burden of a rucksack or a poc, the name for a tinker's sack of wares.

'If it's Stink the Tink I mustny speak to him,' Ruth said nervously. 'Last time I did Mam made me stay in my room the whole of the Sabbath to learn by heart three of the Psalms.'

'Ach, it won't be a tink at all,' Lorn said. 'Most of them will be down at the harbour or up by Dunuaigh, and Stink was round the doors yesterday selling colanders so it won't be him back again.'

The figure came closer and proved to be a bearded young hiker dressed in shorts and thick wool stockings draped over stout walking boots. 'Good day to you,' he nodded pleasantly, his accent suggesting he was a foreigner who had picked up English well. Wriggling the pack from his back he laid it on the grassy bank and flopped down beside it.

'Good day, sir,' the children chorused in polite unison, though Lorn eyed the stranger with reserve, and Rachel, hands folded behind her back, stared at him openly. The young man stared back, unable for a moment to tear his gaze away from the untamed gypsy-like beauty of the golden-skinned child with her unruly black curls and unwavering brown eyes.

'I wonder if you could help me,' the young man said, drawing a map from his pocket and studying it intently. He was thin and boyish, his dark-rimmed glasses giving him a studious appearance. 'I am looking for a place called Croft na Ard. It isn't marked on this map and everyone at the harbour seemed so excited about something I couldn't quite understand the directions they gave.'

'Ach, they speak in Gaelic when they get het up,' Lewis said, grinning. 'Has the cargo been unloaded yet?' he added anxiously.

'No, there was bother with one of the Highland beasts, which caught its horns in the rails. There's quite a commotion down there at the moment and everything has been held up.'

'Good.' Lewis climbed down off Conker and went to look at the map, though there was no need as he knew fine where Croft na Ard was situated. But he loved people and enjoyed finding out about them. Lorn hid a smile as he watched his brother studying the map, tracing fields and roads with a grubby finger, which stopped suddenly. 'There it is, Anton Büttger's place. He came back here after the war and married Babbie, our district nurse. We have two nurses; the other is auld Biddy. She's past eighty but still sprachles about, delivering babies and drinking whisky.'

'Biddy.' The young man's eyes grew dreamy. He gazed round him, at the hills and the drowsing moors, and retreated into a trance. 'Ah, I remember Biddy all right and I'm so glad she's still alive. I've dreamed of this island for years and vowed I would come back one day. How is Mr and Mrs Gray and Tam McKinnon and that wonderful old man who played the fiddle like a dream – Andrew, his name was Andrew?'

'Old Andrew's fine, although he's the oldest man here. Old Madam Balfour of Burnbreddie swears the island people live long because they are pickled in drink. Mr and Mrs McKinnon are just grand – especially Tam. This,' Lewis said indicating Rachel, 'is their granddaughter, Rachel. She canny speak but she can hear and is the cleverest girl in the school. She's as tough as any boy and can fight with her fists.

She had to learn to do that because the others used to call her names but don't dare do it now. She's so good at everything she even teaches auld Murdoch, our teacher, how to teach. You don't have to be afraid of her though because she only gives black eyes to people her own size.'

His laughter rang out and the other children relaxed and smiled too. Lewis did that to people; to him strangers were just potential friends and he had the knack of putting them at ease.

The young man smiled at Rachel. 'Tam McKinnon's granddaughter. Tell me, does he still make whisky that slides down the throat like nectar?'

Still wary, Rachel tossed her dark head and her eyes fell on the violin case slung over the stranger's shoulder. Her face immediately lit up, and laying her head to one side, she made an action as if playing the fiddle.

The young man nodded eagerly. 'Yes, it's a fiddle. I carry it with me wherever I go. Do you play?'

Rachel nodded vigorously and Ruth spoke for the first time. 'She could play almost before she could walk. Old Andrew taught her.' Ruth's heart raced at her audacity and trepidation rose in her breast as she wondered what her mother would say if she knew her daughter had been conversing with a strange man.

'Lewis and me play too,' Lorn said, his deep blue eyes holding the young man's gaze. 'We practise with Bob and old Andrew in Ranald's boatshed and sometimes we have our own wee concerts there.'

The stranger's eyes were sparkling behind his glasses. 'That sounds wonderful. Perhaps you will allow me to come and practise with you in Ranald's shed. I am here for two weeks' holiday and would love to get together with people who play the fiddle. After the war I became a music teacher, but always I wanted to come back to Scotland and now I have a post in the high school of Oban.'

Rachel was enraptured. The stranger watched her expressive hands trying to convey her joy and he said casually, 'You do not speak with the language of those who cannot speak? I can teach you if you will let me. When I was in prison camp, there was a boy there so badly injured in the head he was deaf and dumb. He learned the language and taught it to me. Look, Rachel, this means the sun is shining and the day is beautiful.'

He made a few swift gestures with his long nimble fingers and Rachel followed them intently, her fingers fluttering as she copied the signs.

'Good girl, you learn swiftly. You will soon be able to speak without words and you can teach your friends to speak your tongue.'

This delighted the little girl. For the first time she showed her pearly teeth in a radiant smile, and the young man felt sadness in him for the absence of laughter in her, for a joyous sound that would never peal out from her soft child's mouth.

Something that might have been a tear gleamed in Rachel's eyes but she brushed it away. Lewis put an arm round her and gave her an affectionate hug, but he didn't speak. The stranger seemed to have enchanted them all. Then, the hooting of horns from the harbour brought Lewis to his senses. He made to walk away over to Conker but the young man put a hand on his arm. 'Please, I can see you are twin brothers,' he said, looking from one to the other and smiling.

When the twins were apart they were identical to the inexperienced eye; it was only when they were close together that the difference in them became apparent. 'Yes, but I'm the eldest,' Lewis told everyone, not to boast, but in his child's way, trying to save his brother the embarrassment of having to explain why he was so thin and small.

'Where do you live? What are your names?'

Lorn didn't answer, the stranger was being too inquisitive. But Lewis couldn't help saying with pride, 'We are Lorn and Lewis McKenzie. Our father is McKenzie of the Glen.'

'Fergus McKenzie, ah yes, the big proud man with eyes of steel and a heart of gold – he was the one who found me – on the moors. I remember his voice, soft, full of light and shade, like music. I knew he felt he should hate me but couldn't . . .'

The eyes of the young man were far away. The children watched him rather apprehensively, fascinated by him, yet something telling them to tread carefully.

The stranger came back from the past and came forward to gallantly lift Ruth onto Conker's back.

'And you, little golden-haired princess, what is your name?'

'Ruth Donaldson,' murmured the little girl hesitantly. 'My father helps Totie Little in the Post Office at Portvoynachan and my mother is Morag Ruadh. She is a spinner and everyone wants the things she makes.'

'Of course, Morag Ruadh. Does she not also play the piano? I remember the Reverend Gray had a great regard for her music . . .'

'Please, sir,' Lorn broke in rather rudely, 'who are you?'

This was received with a delighted laugh. 'At last you ask! No one at the harbour recognized me – perhaps the beard – I am Jon Jodl. I was one of the Germans who crash-landed on Rhanna almost ten years ago . . .'

'A Jerry!' Lewis exclaimed and pulled Conker's head up so sharply that the horse snickered and drew back. The four children sat on his broad back and stared rudely at the bemused young man.

Lorn's face was white. 'Have you got German measles?' he asked rather breathlessly. 'Have you brought them with you?'

Jon Jodl spread his arms in appeal. 'German measles! No – I don't understand – did I say something wrong?'

Annie came out to her door with a basket of washing under her arm. 'Rachel, you get along,' she called. 'You mustny idle your time away with the towrists. Get along or you can just come right back and do the dishes!'

'He breeah!' A familiar cry rent the air and Dodie came galloping down the hill path from Nigg, temporarily stopping the children in their flight. Now in his late fifties, he had grown more bent with the passing years but otherwise he was the same Dodie, travelling the island in all weathers, accepting the changes that tourism was bringing to Rhanna with a reluctant elation because though suspicious of the foreign invasion, he was not averse to the opportunities it brought to his life. 'I am just going down to the harbour,' he mournfully told the children. 'Torquil Andrew of Ballymhor was after tellin' me that Todd the Shod has a fine new motor car comin' on the boat. He got it in a magazine for nothing.' He pulled up short at sight of Jon, his wellingtons scrunching on the stones.

'Dodie,' Jon said, beaming. In his mind he had pictured many times the folk of Rhanna, their charm and hospitality, the simplicity of their uncluttered lives. To come back and hear all the names he had cherished in his memory was a dream come true.

Dodie rubbed his grizzled chin. 'Ay, that's me right enough, I'm Dodie.'

'Ealasaid – do you still have your Ealasaid?'

Dodie's eyes immediately swam and he gulped. 'My bonny cow died a few years back but I have a calf of hers, her name is Ealasaid too, for they are all alike – all from my first Ealasaid.'

'Rachel!' Annie's voice came again. 'Come you

back this minute and get the dishes done!'

Rachel gave Jon a last lingering look then tapped her heels into Conker's flanks. The horse began to amble away and Dodie was left to gaze at Jon with real liking Anyone who spoke to him about his cow was worth a few minutes of his time.

Lorn turned. 'Come on, Dodie! He's a Jerry! You'll get the measles!'

The old eccentric immediately took fright, but for different reasons than those of the children. 'A Jerry!' he threw back over his hunched shoulders. 'You've no' come to take the roof off my wee hoosie! You canny do that. The towrists pay to come and look at it!'

'No, Dodie, no!' Jon cried, and in an effort to convey his sincerity he shouted out the only Gaelic word he knew: 'Slainte! Slainte!'

His Gaelic 'health' echoed round the hill corries but except for Annie peeping curiously from her window it fell on deaf ears.

Chapter Five

By the time Conker had plodded on into the harbour, many of the visitors were making their way to the hotel, ably assisted by the children out to make an easy shilling by carrying luggage. The majority of people were watching the unloading of the boat's cargo. Up the shore came Grant, a brawny young man dressed in an old blue jersey. His arm was linked through that of his sister Shona and with them strode Niall holding two-year-old Helen in his arms. The twins scrambled off Conker, shouting for joy and raced forward. It was quite a reunion. Shona and Niall hadn't been expected for some days yet. Lorn buried his face into Shona's hair. She smelt of roses, and the little boy clung unashamedly to her for he loved his big sister with all his heart.

'You've grown, you wee wittrock,' she laughed, holding him at arm's length to look at him.

'Have I really, Shona? Lewis measured me on the growing post this morning and he says I've got half an inch taller than last time.'

Helen stirred in her father's arms and pointed a chubby finger at old Mo. 'Pwam!' she squealed in delight and they all went over to the crowd gathered by old Mo's pram. The ancient tinker was sitting up, a whisky bottle next to him, a bow in one hand, a beautiful violin in the other. From it he was extracting haunting melodies that soared above the general hubbub to merge with the soft wind hushing over hill and moor. Jon Jodl stopped on the road above to listen in wonder and Rachel saw him standing there looking rather lonely. On impulse she scrambled away from the crowd and raised her hand to him. He glanced down and saw her and waved back. 'I'll see you later, Rachel,' he called, though he knew she couldn't hear him. Shouldering his rucksack once more he plodded up the road to Croft na Ard, which lay south about a mile and a half from Portcull. Rachel went back to join the throng. The visitors were entranced by the old Irishman's playing, but none more than Rachel, who shut her eyes and concentrated on the ethereal strains. She loved and admired old Mo with all her heart and quite often she took her own old fiddle over to Dunuaigh to join the tinkers in their camp-fire gatherings.

'Delightful!' Rachel's reverie was broken by a high gushing voice. Coppers were raining into old Mo's pram as his long fingers, so out of keeping with the rest of his tough appearance, skilfully guided the bow over the strings, bringing to a finale the tear-jerking *Dark Lochnagar.*

'What's the old boy's name?' asked one man of a squinty-nosed youth.

'Mo.'

'Mo? – how strange. What does it mean?'

'Moses.'

'Moses? But surely not! How did he come by it?'

'Ah well, that is indeed a fine mystery, sir. We found him floating in the sea in a big wicker basket and we gave him the name of Moses. He knows not where he came from or where he's been, and might be a leprechaun for all we are knowing – but there you are, sir, strange things happen in Ireland that can't be explained away. We took old Mo into our family and will look after him till the angels think it's time he should be joining them.'

'But surely a leprechaun is a sort of Irish fairy?'

'Indeed that is right, me fine sir. You are lookin' at an old man who might have come from the land of the little folk itself.'

The glib-tongued young Irishman kept a straight face throughout this monologue. The tourist eyed him suspiciously then shifted his gaze to old Mo's battered countenance. 'Fairy indeed!' he said contemptuously and stalked away without putting a penny into the pram.

'Is he not a mean sod now, Grandfather?' The young man grinned at the leprechaun and began to count the takings.

Rachel clapped her hands in delight as old Mo took up his fiddle once more but his efforts were lost in the ripple of awed comments that heralded the appearance of Todd's car dangling from the wire hawsers of the ship's crane.

'Would you look at that now, Mollie,' whispered Todd in hushed tones, his mouth hanging open in his benign craggy face. 'Is she no' a beauty just? I never pictured the like.'

Mollie was momentarily speechless. It had never occurred to her that the motor car would be anything as grand as this. Rhanna boasted quite a few powered machines of one sort or another, but mostly they were dirty temperamental affairs that banged and rattled their way round the island roads. Everyone was speechless at sight of the sleek gleaming machine dangling against the blue sky.

Tam McKinnon was first to find his voice. 'By God, it's beautiful just! A body could live in a motor car like that. It's near as big as my house!'

'Ach, you'll be sellin' it,' the money-conscious Ranald told Todd. 'What good is a car like that to a cratur' who knows more about servicin' horses?'

'No, indeed I will never sell her,' Todd said with reverence. 'She is so beautiful she is like a – like a . . .' He fumbled for words to describe the car.

Old Joe, now ninety, his snow-white hair frisking out from his peaked cap, his sea-green eyes as serene as the sheltered waters of Loch Tenee, murmured gently, 'Like a mermaid, all shiny and silvery and as slender as a birch tree with a shape to her that makes you want to touch her.'

'You romantic old sea dog!' said Fiona McLachlan who was standing nearby. A slender, bright-eyed seventeen-year-old, her bobbed hair shining in the sun, she was now at university studying marine biology, but had arrived home for Easter two days before. She took the old man's arm and snuggled against him, remembering how as a child she had listened enthralled to his wondrous tales of the sea.

He squeezed her hand, smiling at sight of her fresh youthfulness. 'You're growing more bonny each time you come home, lassie. How many young men have you got dangling on the end of a fish hook?'

'None,' she stated emphatically. 'Well, none that matter anyway. I'm a career girl, Joe. Boys can be a nuisance and I'm not taking any of them seriously.'

The photographers and newspaper reporters were following the progress of the car from crane to terra firma. The hubbub rose to a crescendo mingling with the screams of the gulls and the strains of old Mo's fiddle. Fisherwives leaned ample arms from windows and watched the proceedings in comfort. Fishing boats began tooting their horns as two very distinguished-looking gentlemen joined the throng. It was difficult to make sense of the jumble of faces, but Grant had just spotted Fiona and he came pushing towards her.

At sixteen he had the face of a boy and the build of a twenty-year-old, with muscles that rippled from battling against the seas, for he had joined the fishing smacks at fourteen. His smooth skin was tanned by salt and wind; with his dimpled chin and black curls he was a young Fergus all over again. Often he was away from home for days at a time, and there was already about him a toughness that came from combat with the sea and from mixing with hardened sailors. A boy became a man quickly under those circumstances. He had just arrived home after a sojourn at sea and it was his first sight of Fiona for many months.

'Well, well, if it isn't cheeky wee Robin herself!' was his rather cutting greeting. 'Are you going to spend your holidays hunting for frogs and poking about in the water for things that normal folks canny see unless they are wearing microscopes instead of specs – or are you going to behave like a normal girl and be seen at a dance or two . . . wearing a dress?' he finished, eyeing the slacks that had sent shock waves of disapproval through the community of womenfolk when first they had sighted them as she came off the boat.

'Fiona McLachlan – wearing the trowser!' they had told one another in round-eyed dismay. 'Whatever next? That lassie! She was aye a wild one – peety her poor parents – they have a handful there.'

Fiona tossed her head and looked down her pert little nose. Every time she saw Grant McKenzie he seemed to grow bigger, broader, more handsome, more impertinent. From infancy they had bickered with each other, indulging in splendid verbal battles that made Phebie squirm and wonder if her daughter would ever become a lady – especially now she was 'wearing the trowser'.

'Ach, hold your tongue, lad!' spat old Joe. 'Is that any way to treat a lass with her feets no' long on the island!'

But Fiona was more than a match for Grant. He might tower above her but the look of dislike she threw him made him visibly shrink. 'As if you could tell a dress from a sack, Dimples McKenzie – or would know what to do with a girl if she was hanging naked in front of your nose! You should be in the pram with old Mo there! That's the right place for big babies who sook the bottle still – only now it's whisky instead of milk.'

Grant reddened, but hid his chagrin in a shout of derisive laughter. 'I wouldn't like you hanging naked in front of *my* nose! I doubt there would be anything to tell me you're a girl.'

'You McKenzies are all the same,' Fiona said, her voice cold, 'self-centred, hard, selfish – you should all go and live with Elspeth – you'd make a fine team.'

'Even Shona?' taunted Grant. 'You should go and tell her that – she's standing over there with Niall.'

Fiona walked away, very dignified, her eyes shiny. Disapproval flitted over old Joe's face as he looked at Grant. 'You shouldny be so hasty wi' that tongue o' yours, you young bugger. Fiona is too fine a young lady for you to be saying the things you do to her. The sea is making you hard already.'

'It never did you any harm,' answered Grant, sulky and abashed. 'And Fiona was never a young lady – she was always more like a boy than a girl.'

'Then you must be needin' specs! Stop gabblin' now and look at that old show-off Todd, gettin' his photos taken inside the motor car as if he was the lord o' the manor – ready to drive the damt thing away and him no' even knowin' where the petrol goes.'

Fiona ran towards Niall and Shona, the joy back in

her eyes. 'Niall! Shona!' she yelled, and threw herself at them in delight.

'I never thought I'd see the day you would look so elegant,' Shona said, smiling in welcome. 'And wearing trousers too. The cailleachs' tongues will have had a field day.'

'Red-hot!' giggled Fiona. 'You ought to wear them, give the old hags something to fuel their fires.'

'Where did you spring from?' laughed Niall. 'I didn't see a thing of you till this moment.'

'I was in the crowd. How did you come? I didn't see you getting off the boat.'

'We came with Grant in the *Magpie*. He was tied up at Campbeltown and the chance was too good to miss. It was a smelly journey but this wee devil loved it – the smellier the better,' Niall said, lifting his daughter up to the sky. She chuckled with glee, a rosy-cheeked bundle with deep brown eyes and fair hair touched with red.

Niall and Shona were now living in the Mull of Kintyre, a handy gateway for the islands. Until recently Niall had been assistant vet to his toothy senior, Mr Frank Finley, nicknamed 'Fang' by the mischievous Shona, but he had just been made a partner in the firm, and Fiona hugged him when she heard the news.

The ceremony of handing over the keys was over and Todd and Mollie now posed beside their benefactors, both in and out of the car. Their daughter, Mairi, together with her husband, Wullie McKinnon, was being asked to pose too.

'Any more relatives?' asked a beaky-nosed photographer rather sarcastically, and was immediately swamped by a deluge of the McKinnon clan. Tam and Kate rushed forward pulling with them numerous grandchildren. Reporters were jotting furiously, losing track of all the McKinnons who swarmed round them.

'Get a hold of that little gypsy girl and stick her on the bonnet!' cried one ambitious photographer, but Rachel was having none of it. She backed away and at a safe distance stretched her lips into a hideous grimace.

'Little brat!' cursed the photographer while the delighted crowd clapped and cheered. The scene was becoming shambolic. The reporters had spotted old Mo and they surrounded him, cameras clicking, tongues wagging, as old Mo lay blissfully in his pram swigging at his whisky. One of the tinker women rattled her stack of colanders amidst the reigning chaos, and then Dodie came into the scene, his fascination of the flashing cameras getting the better of his shyness.

'What's these?' he asked. 'They're no' like the ones the towrists use to take pictures of my wee hoosie.'

'Get that old boy!' yelled an excited voice and a flashbulb popped in Dodie's amazed countenance. The tinker woman rattled her colanders again and Dodie leaned over old Mo's pram to touch the shiny objects with joy. 'These is lovely just,' his broken teeth flashed. 'What are they?'

'A new kind of po!' shrieked the incorrigible Kate

joyfully, but Dodie took her seriously.

'Ach, they'd be no use at all.' He shook his head and his carbuncle wobbled. 'Everything would go straight through.'

Kate was bent double in a spasm of mirth but she managed to gasp, 'Ay, you couldny trap even a fart in a colander, Dodie.'

'Priceless, priceless,' mouthed one reporter, scribbling furiously. Todd, feeling neglected and outdone, had climbed onto the bonnet of his new car, and with arms folded stiffly over his chest, one leg crossed over the other, he shouted, 'Right, lads, here is the man himself, the fastest driver on the island. I tell you, I was driving cars afore any o' you cut your milk teeths! Am I no' worth a pop o' these flashes in your wee boxes?'

'The lying old cheat!' Grant gasped, laughing so much Lorn almost fell off his shoulders. 'If you asked him where to put the key he would stick it in a horse's backside!'

Portcull had never seen the likes of such a day. The noisy squabbling of the gulls along the harbour walls was lost in the din; the children danced about, making faces at the cameras, their peals of mirth ringing out.

Ruth had laughed till she was sore. She had forgotten everything but the complete and glorious joy of the moment. To laugh like that, with such careless abandon, was a new and totally wonderful experience for her. It was good to laugh; it was life; joyous, bursting, bubbling life. She wanted to know more of it, to become familiar with it, to feel that laughter was right and good and not sinful.

Ever since she could remember Ruth had felt as if she had been in mourning over something she didn't understand. The only times she came near to feeling like today were when she was with her father on his tramps over moor and shore. She loved him, the feel of her hand in his, his arms lifting her over rough or difficult ground, the gentleness of his fine ascetic face, the goodness burning in his grey eyes like the steady flame of a candle. His poems were beautiful, his stories, when he took her on his knee by the fire, so filled with sensitivity that often she cried quietly, the tears marking a slow course down her cheeks. She sensed the sadness in him, the loneliness brought about by visions lost, hopes long faded of a man who had dreamed of becoming a writer but hadn't. She knew that he was unhappy but that in some way she brought him joy because his eyes glowed when she came home from school. He was the only reason she liked going home. It wasn't a happy place. Other houses rang with laughter, with nagging and bickerings. There were no rows in her house, it was too quiet, too clean, too orderly. The atmosphere was oppressive, as if all the life the house had ever known was held down by an invisible force that had robbed it of light, shade, tears, joy, all the things that went on in normal homes. Her red-haired, quick-tongued mother did all the talking, she nagged, scolded, but in a strange quiet flat voice, as if she was afraid that someone, other than the occupants of the house, was listening. Once Ruth saw her on her knees in the bedroom, praying passionately, calling on God to cleanse her soul, to forgive her sins, vowing over and over to recompense for all the evil things she had done. She did all the things that other mothers did, like cooking, cleaning, sewing and weaving, often well into the small hours of morning, but she did it all mechanically. She didn't gossip like other women, yet with a mere tightening of her lips and a toss of her red head, she could say more than all the gossipmongers put together. She tended her husband and daughter devotedly, saw to their every need, yet somehow she couldn't give them the thing they needed most – her love. Occasionally she took Ruth to her bosom and stroked her hair, her long nimble fingers playing with the silken curls while she said over and over, 'My babby, my babby,' but the gesture, the words, conveyed no love, only a fearful sort of apology to someone unseen and Ruth always felt uneasy and knew there was something strange about her mother.

But these things were far from her mind that day at Portcull harbour and Lorn, sitting on Grant's strong shoulders, felt an echo of her emotions touching a chord in his heart. Without knowing why, his eyes sought out Ruth, standing with her golden head thrown back, her usually solemn little face transformed into beauty by the light of sparkling happiness. She looked round and caught him watching her and the violet of her eyes darkened to purple, the dimpled smile remained fixed on her face for an eternal moment. Then the familiar flush spread over her cheeks and her features composed themselves into wistful solemnity.

Lorn wanted suddenly to go over to her and take her hand. She looked guilty, as if to laugh was wrong. He felt compassion turning to anger, at Ruth, at her mother, at the strangeness of life. He didn't know why, but he was overwhelmed by the feeling and his heart pounded, the way it always did when strong emotions swamped him. He wanted to touch Ruth with some of his own joy, share some of the love he knew in his own life. His mother was so different from Ruth's. She was beautiful, but not in an obvious way. Hers was a subtle beauty, natural and sweet: she loved without fussing, more with her deeds than with her hands. She conveyed her love through her eyes so that there was no embarrassment, just a warm glow brought about by knowing how much she cared. From his elevated position on top of Grant's shoulders Lorn spotted Morag Ruadh emerging from her parents' house and watched her walk swiftly along. Lorn opened his mouth to give Ruth a warning but Morag had easily spied her daughter's bright head.

'Ruth!' she called imperiously. 'Come you up here this minute.' Ruth limped away up the shore, feeling that every eye was on her, when in fact the engrossed crowd hardly took notice of her, only those up by the bridge hearing Morag's voice and seeing the anger burning her cheeks to red.

Rachel took Ruth's hand in passing and both

children gazed at each other in understanding before Morag's arm shot out to pull Ruth away from the harbour. At a safe distance she whirled the child round so abruptly she stumbled and almost fell. 'So – this is how you spend your time,' Morag gritted, her lips a tight pale line in her ruddy face. 'The de'il is in you and no mistake. Have you been mixing with those tinkers again?'

'Ay, Mam,' Ruth whispered, her own face flaming to crimson.

'I thought as much! Well, I tell you now, my girl, it will be the last time. It's that Rachel! Leading you astray. It won't happen again – oh no – you've defied me once too often.' Her blazing eyes fell upon Rachel, who had come further along the shore. She stood, straight and tall against the backdrop of the sea, arms folded behind her back, her dark, turbulent eyes boldly staring at Morag.

'Ay, she's a queer one all right,' Morag said, her voice strangely breathless. 'She gives me the creeps just to look at her. She is wild that one – like – like as if she had sprung from the very well o' tinker blood. Knowing that Annie I wouldny be surprised . . .' Her voice tailed off and she seemed to jerk herself back to reality, if such a state existed in her narrow, religion-bound mind. 'You will never play with her again, Ruth, do you hear?'

Ruth slowly raised her golden head to look up into her mother's strange glittering eyes. The coldness in them made her draw in her breath, and she was unable to answer. Morag shook her. 'Do you hear me, girl?'

Rebellion, strong, deep, overpowering, flooded Ruth's gentle soul. To give up Rachel was more than a punishment, it was a shattering of the only happy companionship in her life other than her father's. Her mother's punishments seldom took physical form, always they were designed to test heart and soul to the limit of endurance. Ruth bit her lip. She couldn't promise to relinquish the warm, stimulating friendship of fearless, exciting, untamed Rachel.

'Defiance, eh?' Morag's face was pale now, her voice low and flat yet charged with seething rage.

'No, Mam,' Ruth cried. 'It wasn't Rachel, it was me. I wanted to come down to the harbour! I asked Rachel to come!'

'A fine story, lies above all else!'

'Ask Mrs McKinnon then!' Ruth stormed tearfully. 'I made Rachel go into the house and ask her mother.'

'So, the minute my back is turned you go dancing about after fun. I won't let the de'il take you, my lassie! 'Tis all the more reason you must promise me you won't see Rachel again. If you don't I will be forced to take your jotters and pencils away from you. You idle too much time away with your father, writing down all these foolish notions that are in your head. There will be no more walks with him unless you . . .'

'No, Mam!' It was the protest of a tortured soul. The little girl threw her head back in appeal, her eyes drowning in tears of pain. 'I promise, I promise.'

'As well for everyone's sake, I'm thinkin'.' Morag

felt no triumph, only a flooding of shame at the sight of her daughter's face twisted in agony, but she couldn't relent, to do so was a sign of weakness, the first crack in the shell she had built round herself against softening influences that could so easily penetrate the unwary heart, make a body do things they lived to regret for ever . . . She held Ruth's hand firmly and led her up the path to the house. 'Your grannie has had a bad turn,' she told the child unemotionally. 'It was lucky that auld Biddy was passing, for I could not leave the house and, of course – you never at hand to run and fetch the doctor. Your father was expecting me back for teatime, but I will have to stay here tonight. Folks have a duty to their parents, so they have. Erchy is going over to Portvoynachan with the mail and I want you to go with him. You must make your father's meals like a good lassie. As a penance you will go without your dinner and mustny eat a bite till teatime – also you will go to your room when you have washed the teatime dishes and learn the Commandments till they are burned into your head . . . away you go now – you mustny keep your elders waiting.'

Erchy was leaning against his red post van, avidly devouring the headlines on each bundle of newspapers he had dotted over the bonnet for convenience. He was never in a hurry but Morag gave Ruth an impatient little push. The child hesitated, looking through the door of her grandparents' cottage.

'Is – Grannie going to be all right?' she asked fearfully, wanting to run inside and put her arms round old Isabel, whom she adored.

Biddy appeared, her dim eyes kind behind her specs. 'Ay, my wee lamb, she'll be right enough. It's just her heart gave her a fright. Don't you worry your wee head about her.' Biddy knew it was more than likely that a morning of Morag's spicy tongue had caused Isabel to have the shakes, but she held her counsel though the sight of Ruth's white strained face made her fume inwardly at Morag.

'Here,' she said, and fumbled in her pocket. Withdrawing a crumpled paper bag, she offered it to Ruth. 'You take some Imperial mints, they will keep your jaws busy till you get home.'

Ruth felt the waves of disapproval tautening her mother's body. 'No, thank you, Biddy, I'm – I'm not very hungry.'

'Here, what's all this?' Jim Jim appeared beside Biddy and put his hands out to his little granddaughter. 'Come in my wee one and have your dinner before you go home. Your father will keep for a whily and I will not have you going away from *this* house with an empty belly.'

Morag quelled him with a stony stare, but Ruth settled the matter by limping hurriedly to the post van and climbing into the passenger seat.

'My, my, some folks are aye in a hurry,' Erchy said, gathering the bundles of papers and throwing them into the back of the van, covering two hares he had retrieved from his snares earlier. On the journey over the high cliff road he whistled, talked, and offered the little girl chocolate but she refused and didn't respond to any of his banter. He had often told his cronies, 'She's a sad, sad wee lassie that Ruth Donaldson,' but now he glanced at her pale, set, plain little face and sensed something more than sadness. They were hurtling over the firm emerald-green of the links – cunning Erchy avoided the bumpy road whenever he could and knew every diversive route – but soon they were climbing a sandy sheep track and were back on the road again, in time to see Jon Jodl turning up the grass-rutted road to Croft na Ard, The High Croft. Ruth sat up in her seat and gave a shy wave, which made Erchy's eyes gleam with interest. 'Are you knowing the mannie, then?' he asked nonchalantly, the words jolting in his throat as the wheels hit a rock.

'No,' Ruth answered guardedly. 'We met him on the road earlier and Lewis told him the way to Croft na Ard.'

'Oh ay, young Büttger's place, eh? Does the hiker laddie know him then? A fine lad is Anton – for a Jerry – he will likely know lots of folks from way back.'

Ruth was caught off her guard and for the first time a spark of enthusiasm flickered in her eyes. 'You're right enough, Erchy, he is a friend of Mr Büttger's – Jon something or other – a strange name. They fought in the war together and crashed their plane on Rhanna the year I was born.'

'Get away now!' Erchy received the news with

such enthusiasm he almost ran over a group of cud-chewing sheep reclining on the verge. 'Jon – let me think now – a clever-looking wee lad wi' specs? Ay, ay, it's coming back – he was at the Manse ceilidh – oh hell!' Erchy slapped his knee in delight. 'What a night that was, me playin' the pipes and old Andrew the fiddle. This chappie – Jon Yodel – something like that – by God! Was he no' a marvel on the fiddle! Even old Andrew had to admit he was good.'

'He *is* a fiddler! Rachel and him and all the other fiddlers are going to be playing together while he's here.' Ruth's misery was swamped by eagerness. 'He's going to teach Rachel the dumb language.'

'Bugger me!' Erchy slapped his knee again and slid Ruth a sidelong glance. 'Another Jerry, eh? Are you no' feart you'll catch a dose o' the German measles from him?'

Ruth giggled despite herself. 'I don't care! I don't care, Erchy!' she cried, and Erchy, as pleased by her smiles as he was excited by the news, fairly hurtled towards Portvoynachan, hardly able to wait to tell everyone about Jon's arrival.

Jon trudged along, gazing over the lush green pastures to the ocean beyond. The white sands in the bay shelved into the water, turning it to shades of kingfisher-blues and greens, and further out from the shallows purple merged to deepest ultramarine. Several small groups of crofters were down by the shore, filling their carts with banner-like tangles of seaweed brought in by the spring tides. The carts were in the water, the ponies waiting patiently in the splashing waves, while all around them, against the pale gleam of sky and sea, was a bustle of activity as the men and women gathered the harvest of the sea to fertilise the land. A tractor purred busily in a nearby field and Jon wondered if it was Anton who was at the wheel. He was near the farmhouse itself now, a sturdy whitewashed building surrounded by numerous outhouses. Round a corner came a tall, fair, bronzed young man, stripped to the waist, his muscles gleaming with the sweat of his morning's labour. At sight of Jon he stopped abruptly, his keen blue eyes enquiring.

Jon smiled in delight at sight of his former commander but said politely, 'Excuse me – I wonder if I am on the right track. I am looking for a fellow by the name of Anton Büttger. Perhaps you know him or can tell me where I can find him.'

'I am he,' Anton said carefully and with slight suspicion. After more than four years on the island he was as wary of tourists as the islanders themselves. He plunged his arms into the water barrel and threw glistening flurries over his shoulders and face, keeping one eye on the visitor. Jon could contain himself no longer.

'Anton,' he breathed, suppressing his jubilation with difficulty, 'don't you know me? Have I changed so much? Don't you remember poor nervous little Jon Jodl – spewing into a tin while we were up there flying in the clouds?'

'Jon!' Anton came forward a few paces to look in

disbelief at Jon's shining face. 'Good God, Jon!' he cried with a little yelp of laughter. He strode forward and embraced the young man to him and for several moments they laughed and slapped each other and stood back to gaze and smile, and say each other's names over and over.

'Come inside and explain all,' said Anton after a while. 'You can have dinner with us, Babbie will be in shortly.' He led Jon to a side door and they went into a large airy kitchen with a flagged floor scattered with rag rugs, on top of which sat smugly comfortable-looking chintz easy chairs. The deep window recesses gave splendid views over the Sound of Rhanna; on the ledges sat posies of wild primroses; the rich smell of newly turned earth filtered in through the windows, mingling with the delicious fragrance of home-made lentil broth; snowy muslin curtains billowed gently in the breezes; the strains of a Gaelic air wafted up from the bay. A dark-haired young girl was busy at the table but she paused and looked up as the men came in.

'This is Jean,' Anton said. 'She comes up from Portcull every day and keeps the house spic and span for us.'

Jean darted Jon a shy smile but went smartly about her business as the men sat down and became engrossed in newscatching.

'So, you are in Oban now, Jon,' said Anton at last. 'That is wonderful. You can spend all your holidays here – but perhaps I presume too much – perhaps you go back to Germany whenever you can.'

But Jon shook his head. 'Not so often as I used to. You see, my gentle little Papa is dead now and –' he spread his long fingers expressively, 'Mamma gives me no peace: Why did I go away? Why do I stay away? It may be wrong of me, but I cannot stand to be in her shadow. She destroys the character, ruins the personality. She was one of the reasons I left home – the other, well that is easy, since the day I left Rhanna I wanted to come back and make my home in Scotland.'

'You are not married?'

Jon shook his head ruefully and gave a funny laugh. 'No, I think Mamma put me off all that. I've had enough of pushing and bullying to last me a lifetime. Of course, not all women are like Mamma,' he hastened to add. 'You were lucky, Anton, you found the girl you love when you dropped in on Rhanna on a flying visit . . .' He laughed. 'But I make silly jokes – tell me about Babbie; it sounds like a fairy story with a very happy ending.'

Anton's blue eyes flashed. 'No endings, only lovely beginnings that are like chapters in a book. We are still getting to know one another though we have been married more than four years now. Ah, Jon, it was a long wait, Babbie here, me in the prison camp – but she waited. The war ended, I came back; all the lust for flying out of me and all the things my father taught me about farming unlocked from my head.'

'Did you marry here?' Jon asked eagerly.

'Where else? I went back to Germany after my

release but I felt only sadness. Babbie and I have no family; all her friends were here, and so now are mine. The Reverend John Gray married us in the church at Portcull – it was a wonderful wedding. Babbie's friend Shona was the matron of honour and McKenzie of the Glen gave Babbie away to me –' he said, his teeth flashing, 'the nicest gift I have ever had. The ceilidh went on for days afterwards, though the first one was at Laigmhor. At first we lived with dear old Biddy in Glen Fallan, but McKenzie of the Glen was all the time putting in good words for me in the ears of the Laird. Old Madam Balfour took a stroke soon after her son came back from the war and now cannot speak a word, or no doubt she would have put her spokes in the wheels. Burnbreddie himself is a good man and did not rebel too much at the idea of a German tenanting one of his farms.' He gazed round fondly at the white-painted walls. 'It was pretty run down when we took over. The two sons were killed in the war, and the old folk had not the heart to go on – we are still building it up, making the fields work again.'

'Burnbreddie is a man who does not hold grudges?' Jon said quietly.

Anton shook his head. 'No, he has the big heart and the hearts of all our friends are even bigger – after all, those boys, and many more, were sons of this island and we . . .'

'No – don't say it.' A flash of the old tension flitted over Jon's face. 'In my dreams I still remember and often I wake up shaking.'

Anton put a brown hand over Jon's. 'You are right, my friend – no sense in raking it up . . . Good God! I still cannot believe you are here! We have so much to talk about – but first you must eat!'

'Are there any little ones yet?' Jon asked with a smile, looking round in a way that suggested he might have missed something.

Anton laughed. 'No, you won't find any lurking in the corners, Jon. We don't have any yet and I am selfish enough to want to keep Babbie to myself for as long as I can. She is dedicated to her job, anyway, and I think she just might grow into another Biddy all over again . . .'

Wheels scrunched outside and Anton's eyes flooded with light. The next minute Babbie came flying in, her freckled skin glowing, her hat slightly awry.

'Liebling,' Anton greeted her, putting an arm round her waist and kissing her with unashamed love. It was then that Jon noticed his friend's right hand, three of the fingers missing, a reminder of the trauma he had endured after his nightmare landing on Rhanna. Jon swallowed but had no time for further thoughts. Anton was drawing Babbie forward. 'Look, liebling, see who we have here – my comrade, Jon Jodl. You remember one another, don't you?'

Jon had encountered Babbie only briefly on the night of the Manse ceilidh, but he had not forgotten the girl with the red curls and the odd, dreaming green eyes. Then he had sensed sadness in her, but there was no trace of that now in the radiant young woman standing before him.

'Jon,' she said, and held out her hand. 'Of course I remember you. You were pale and ill then, but behind that distinguished little beard you glow now with health.' She glanced at the rucksack lying on the floor. 'Where are you camping?'

'Nowhere yet,' laughed Jon. 'I have only just arrived.'

'Then you must stay here of course –' She held up her hand to ward off his protests. 'I insist – besides,' she said, her eyes sparkling mischievously, 'there are ulterior motives. Spring is Anton's busiest time – you will be called upon to work for your keep, young man, and while you're doing it you and Anton can catch up with all the lost years.'

Jon flushed with pleasure and Anton laughed deeply. 'You see, my friend, your papa was not the only one to marry a bossy woman – only one difference – I spank mine when she gets out of hand.'

Jean was hovering, waiting to serve the meal and Babbie pushed the men towards the sink. 'Wash!' she commanded. 'You smell of dung, Anton, and Jon looks nearly as bad as old Dodie.'

Jon paused with the soap in his hands. 'I met him today – in Glen Fallan – I also met some children, two of Mr McKenzie's sons and two little girls, one who was dumb and the other who limped badly.' He frowned. 'I was getting on well with them till they heard I was a German then they just took to their heels and ran, saying something about German measles.'

Babbie and Anton exchanged glances, the former remembering when Lachlan had found out that rubella, or German measles, could cause terrible defects in unborn children. There had been a mild epidemic of measles some weeks after the Germans' departure from Rhanna in the spring of 1941. Kirsteen, Annie, and Morag Ruadh had all succumbed to the rash in the early stages of their pregnancies and with the exception of Lewis, their babies had all been born with congenital defects. The illness had been discovered in Australia in 1940 and had gone under the microscope till eventually news of its effects on the unborn had filtered through to the medical world and Lachlan had had the answer to the thing that had puzzled him for so long. The islanders had soon heard about it, too, and the cry had gone up: 'German measles! The Jerries must have brought it thon time they were here!'

The belief had persisted for quite some time, during which an exasperated Lachlan had tried to reassure everyone that the illness was not specifically carried about by Germans. Gradually the indignation had died down till the whole thing became just a joke. On Anton's return he had been the butt for much teasing and leg-pulling and the islanders had taken an absolute delight in scuffling away to clear a path every time he appeared.

'But the children believe it still,' Jon said after hearing Babbie's explanation. 'They looked positively terrified.'

Babbie smiled. 'Children love to exaggerate, also

they love to scare themselves to death. They heard all the gossip in the beginning and are even more reluctant than the old folks to let it rest.' Her eyes fell on Jon's violin case and her smile widened. 'Mark my words, Jon, when next you see them you'll only have to start playing your fiddle to have them dancing behind you as if you were the Pied Piper himself.'

Jon lathered soap over his arms. The sound of the sea, the wind, wafted in through doors and windows. Jean was setting bowls of steaming broth on the table, the sunbeams pranced over the white walls and spilled blood-red over the ruddy flags on the floor. He smiled with quiet joy at the vision Babbie's words presented in his mind. How good, how very good to be back on Rhanna with people he had never forgotten.

Chapter Six

After the twins had made their departure on Conker, Fergus sank down into a chair in the kitchen and closed his eyes with a weary sigh. Janet Taylor, who lived at Croft na Beinn, but who came faithfully every day to Laigmhor as her mother had done before her, was hanging out teatowels in the washing green at the back of the house. She was an efficient worker though rather slow and dreamy and was often side-tracked in the midst of her chores. Now she left the washing to play with a kitten and in the interlude Kirsteen paused by Fergus's chair and stood looking down at him. The collar of his thin shirt lay open, showing where the mahogany brown of his neck merged with the pale smoothness of his shoulders. His firm mouth was relaxed and she longed as always to kiss it and to place her pinky into the deep cleft on his chin. His body was lean and lithe, the muscles in it so hard, not even repose relaxed them. There were more white hairs among the jet black of his curly thatch, but otherwise there was nothing to tell her that more than twenty years had passed since her first meeting with him in the woods by Loch Tenee. Her life with him had been turbulent, beautiful; full of problems and of joys; of soaring heights of ecstasy, of plunging depths of despair; but through it all, her love for him had grown and blossomed into a greatness beyond compare. He was often difficult to live with, quick-tongued and dour, but he tempered these things with the magnitude of his deep and abiding love for her. Often he goaded her to fury, but just as often he induced in her laughter, joy, pain, dear and tender adoration. He was the man he had been and always would be and she wouldn't have had him any other way.

Occasionally she invoked stark terror in herself by imagining what her life would be like without him, the kind of nameless fear she had experienced when he had been lost in the sea by the Sgor Creags, but quickly she pushed such thoughts aside and snuggled into the warm nearness of him in bed beside her.

She put out a finger and gently stroked the little white hairs above his ears. 'You're tired, darling, you should learn to ease up a bit.'

A smile curved his mouth but he didn't open his eyes. 'Havers, woman, are you hinting that I'm getting past it?'

She fell on her knees beside him, entwined her arms round his middle and put her head on his lap. 'Past it! After last night? No wonder you're weary, you passionate brute.'

Lazily he drew her up on his knee and cupping her face in his hand he drew her to him and nuzzled her lips with his. 'Mmm, you shouldn't have reminded me – couldn't you send Janet down the road on some pretext? We could always go upstairs and lie down for a wee while – seeing you think I need resting.'

She giggled and lay against him. 'I wouldn't put it past you – but seriously, you do work too hard. Never mind, though; in a few years' time you'll have the twins out in the fields with you. They can hardly wait to grow up and be farmers like their father.'

'Lewis perhaps,' he murmured into her hair, 'though he'll have to sow a few wild oats before he's ready to settle down. He's keen on the land, ay, but he's a restless lad. He canny seem to settle his backside for two minutes at a time.'

'Lorn will keep him steady, see he sows his oats in the right places. They'll both be a credit to you . . .'

'You set too much store on Lorn,' he said rather sharply. 'Don't do it, Kirsteen, you'll only end up getting hurt!'

'And you don't set enough store by him!' she said, equally sharply, pulling away from his enfolding arm to glare at him. 'Don't you know he worships you? Only wants to be like you . . . ?'

'Dammit! These are hardly the qualities that will make a farmer out of a lad like him! Kirsteen, don't let's go over it again! Time will tell but I warn you now, he hasn't the stamina for the land. The guts, ay, but the strength, no.'

Kirsteen's cheeks burned red. It was an argument they had had quite often in the past, but now that Lorn was getting older, more eager to follow the plough, the rows were growing more heated. *'That's* because you coddle him, Fergus. That was all right in the beginning, but not now. Oh, can't you see? He wants to grow, to expand, to have you show him how to do things the way you show Lewis.'

His eyes blazed like coals and he pushed her away. 'Are you asking me to kill my son? Are you, Kirsteen? Because in his condition it wouldny be hard . . .'

'Condition! Condition! You make him sound like a feeble baby! Oh, I know he's not strong, but he tries so hard and you never encourage him . . .'

'Kirsteen,' Fergus said, his voice softer now, 'I don't want to raise false hopes in him. Can't you see? It's because I love him I can't let him get hurt!'

'But he is being hurt,' she said bleakly. 'You hurt him almost every day of his life by refusing to let him do the simplest tasks around the farm – and I don't mean feeding the hens or – or patting butter into rounds . . .'

'You can be very stubborn when you want to be, Kirsteen,' he told her coldly. 'You are splitting hairs, talking about hurt feelings – I am talking about physical hurt. I'm afraid for him. Dammit all! Are you too stupid to see that!'

Her breath caught in her throat and her head went up proudly. '*I* can be stubborn! Well – if that isn't McKenzie cheek, I don't know what is. You're the most stubborn, pig-headed boor of a man anyone could possibly meet! How I've put up with your tempers and your sulks all these years I'll never know – and to think that only a few minutes ago I thought you were the most wonderful man on earth –' She laughed mirthlessly. 'The most thought-less would be more apt.'

'And what about you!' he lashed back, his jaw working furiously. 'The girl of my dreams – my night-mares more like! You never give me a minute's rest; you demand all the time – even in bed! Nag, nag, nag. You're getting to be like that auld yowe Elspeth Morrison and that's no mean feat.'

They stood glaring at each other, white-faced, nostrils aflare, in the heat of the moment having to exercise all their self-control not to lash out at each other physically. He had never raised a hand to her, but now she couldn't stop herself any more from striking out, dealing him such a crack the force of it spun his face to the side.

'So, I give you no peace in bed?' she gritted. 'And all these years I thought you were enjoying it. Well, if you're worried that I might keep you awake in future, you needn't fear. I'll move your things into Grant's room; I'm sure you can rake up some excuse. Why not tell him that at fifty you're past it!' She was horrified at the poison pouring from her lips, but she had lost control and raced on. 'Alick and Mary will be here in a few days – Alick always liked me, didn't he? Why don't we swop? You have Mary for a few nights and I'll have Alick – see what it was he was going to give me all these years ago.'

She had gone too far, and she knew it. The time when Alick had tried to seduce her – with all its terrible consequences – was almost too much to even think about and now she had brought it to the surface where it reared between them like an ugly monster, spewing its venom over them.

Fergus had turned so white she thought he was going to collapse. His eyes were livid black pools, full of disbelief, hurt, shock – and something that was almost hate. Roughly he gripped her wrist and jerked her towards him till her face was inches from his. With clenched teeth he ground out, 'Never, never mention that again to me or you'll be sorry you ever met me . . .'

'What makes you think I'm not sorry now?' Her throat was tight, she hated herself, but the words were out before she could stop them.

Something deep in his eyes made her reel with pain, a hurt so raw he couldn't stop it showing. She felt weak. She was immediately sorry for all the harsh things she had said, but it was hardly the time to utter a feeble apology, and nothing she had said could ever be taken back.

His grip on her wrist slackened and she saw all the fire go out of him. He turned his head from her and the rays of the sun caught and gleamed on the snow-white hairs among the jet black.

She pressed the back of her hand to her mouth and reached out to touch him, but he pulled his shoulder out of her grasp.

'Fergus,' she rasped, the unshed tears making her voice harsh. 'I'm . . .'

Janet came rather warily into the kitchen. She had heard the tail end of the row but was unusually excited about something and pointed out of the window. 'Would you look at who's coming up the road.'

Fergus remained immobile, but Kirsteen went to stand by Janet. Up the winding glen came quite a procession led by Lorn and Lewis astride Conker. 'It's Shona and Niall!' Kirsteen cried, hastily patting her crisp curls and wondering how she could act normally after what had gone before. Peeling off her apron she threw it on the draining board. 'The wittrocks that they are – they're several days too early – there won't be enough dinner to go round.'

Fergus had joined the two women by the sink, his hammering heart lightening a little at sight of his daughter, slim and lovely, her auburn hair shining in the sun. She was leading the way through the gate and Fergus couldn't help saying, 'Shona – we'll have smiles about the place again.'

Kirsteen reddened and hissed at him furiously, 'Maybe I should go away for a while – it might be worth the welcome home.'

His eyes snapped and he turned away. The kitchen was filling with Fiona and Grant, Shona and Niall, with clamouring children, with hens boldly strutting, together with two sheepdog pups eagerly sniffing for scraps. For several minutes chaos reigned. Lorn and Lewis were talking excitedly, describing the meeting with Jon, the events at the harbour.

'Rachel made faces at the camera,' Lewis chuckled gleefully.

'Och, that Rachel,' Janet said in exasperated admiration for the little cousin who laughed at all the conventions Janet herself hated but was too fearful to contravene.

Helen was wobbling on chubby legs, chasing the hens round the table before dropping on all fours to join the pups in their quest for crumbs. Grant watched her antics and his deep laugh boomed. 'Just as mad as her mother,' he quipped, giving Shona a brotherly squeeze that left her gasping. Kirsteen put her hands over her ears and shrieked, 'We didn't expect you two for some days yet! How on earth will I feed you all?'

Bob appeared and proceeded to remove his mud-caked wellingtons, which he clumped heartily against the outside wall. His dog, Meg, was immediately pounced on by her pups who proceeded to feed there and then, eyes blissfully closed as they clung to her teats, squeezing her belly with their fat puppy paws. Bob stopped his beating to gaze into the crowded kitchen with surprise. 'My, my, the gathering o' the clans right enough. I'm thinkin' I'll just get along home and have a sup o' milk and a bite o' bread and cheese.'

'No, no, Bob, wait!' Kirsteen cried rather dazedly, automatically picking Helen up from the floor to cuddle her. 'I'm sure we can sort something out.'

'Don't worry, Kirsteen,' Fiona said. 'Shona and Niall can come home with me.' She threw a meaningful glance in Grant's direction. 'You have your hands full here – all these helpless men to see to.'

'Away you go then, Shona. If you're lucky you

might get frog's legs for dinner,' flashed Grant, glaring at Fiona.

'Agree bairns, agree; for I hate to see peace,' smiled Fergus dourly, not deigning to notice the resentful look thrown at him by Kirsteen.

Shona hugged him. 'We only dropped in to say hello; we'll get away with Fiona. I'll be along later this afternoon while Helen's having a nap – come on, you wee devil,' she said, and scooped her daughter out of the big wickerwork dog basket and made for the door.

'Enjoy yourselves,' grinned Niall and went rather thankfully to join Shona and Fiona by the gate. The glen was peaceful with the hills drowsing in the heat and great shaggy Highland cows browsing among the lush grasses by the river. In the blue sky above an eagle planed lazily on the air currents.

'Phew,' Niall took a deep breath as he took his little daughter into the crook of his arm. 'To think Laigmhor used to be so quiet!'

Shona laughed. 'Och, it still is, we just disrupted everything, that's all.' She glanced around her with delight, her blue eyes brilliant with joy. 'It's so good to be back, to be home – oh, Kintyre is bonny but this,' she said, spreading her arms and skipping along, 'this is *me* somehow! Wild, peaceful, restless, dreamy – I feel like a daft wee lassie again when I'm back on Rhanna.'

'You *behave* like one!' giggled Fiona, taking the older girl's arm and skipping with her.

*

Phebie was in a chair by the table, napping in the rays of the sun pouring through the window of Slochmhor. She opened her eyes to see Niall standing grinning at her from the doorway and immediately she scrambled to her feet. 'What on earth – what may I ask are you doing here? You should have phoned – are you forgetting we have the phone in now?'

'Indeed no. I know you like surprises and we're about the nicest you could get. Fang let me away early; we came with Grant on the *Magpie*.' He advanced and Phebie made a clumsy scramble away from him. 'Don't you dare, my lad – I'm too auld for your capers now.'

'Havers, you're just a spring chicken, a nice plump one ready for the catching.' Niall's brown eyes were gleaming with devilment and Shona and Fiona smiled from the door, knowing what was coming. Round the table Niall chased his mother, the way he always did when he came home. Phebie shrieked, laughed, panted, and begged for mercy while Helen clung to her mother's skirts and observed joyfully, 'Gwannie's daft! Gwannie's daft!'

A chair was knocked flying and Niall caught his mother to lift her high in his strong young arms. Phebie had grown plumper with the years, but that didn't stop her son from running with her a few yards before he set her down, for good measure giving her a smack on her well-rounded bottom. Her round face was flushed pink and though she was breathless with laughter, she grabbed the dishcloth from the sink and swiped him over the face with it.

'Enough, enough,' he gasped. 'You win, I'm beaten, I give up.'

Lachlan came clattering downstairs, his thin face alight with enquiry. 'What is all this?' he grinned. 'I thought it was an invasion.'

'It is,' Phebie said fervently, sinking into a chair to fan her hot face with a corner of her apron. Lachlan swept his little granddaughter into his arms and danced with her round the room. 'My bonny wee Ellie,' he sang and the child crooned with him and grabbed a fistful of his unruly hair.

Phebie stopped fanning herself to say thoughtfully, 'How strange, I just remembered; when Niall was a baby he used to call Shona's mother Ellie.'

'It's nice,' murmured Shona, tucking away a wilful strand of her long hair. 'Not as formal as Helen.' She stroked the baby's satin-smooth cheeks. 'How would you like to be called Ellie, you daft wee thing?'

'Ellie, Ellie,' the child repeated the name happily.

Fiona sniffed. 'The only thing is, Ellie could be short for Elspeth and who in their right mind would want to be called after . . .'

'I heard that, miss.' Elspeth appeared, cabbages clutched to her bosom, a streak of earth lying over her gaunt cheeks. She went over to the sink and laid the cabbages down, her shoulders sagging slightly.

Fiona saw that her one-time dragon was now just a very lonely and rapidly ageing old lady and she was immediately repentant. Going over, she put her arm round Elspeth's shoulders and gave her a hug. 'I'm sorry, Elspeth, I'm a wee bitch to you, but you have to admit you've been an old one to me. I think Elspeth is a lovely name and to prove it I'm going to call my new white mouse after you . . .' She darted away as Elspeth turned on her. 'No really, it's a compliment. My mice are very special to me. Please smile, you look really nice when you smile, which isn't often.'

'I think I've come to the wrong house,' Niall said, shaking his head. 'This is all very undignified for me, you know. After all, it's not every day the son of this house becomes a junior partner in a thriving veterinary practice with his name just newly on the brass nameplate by the door.'

'Niall!' Phebie's face was glowing with pride. 'When? You never told us!'

'I'm telling you now – and since I'm such an important personage – isn't it high time I had my dinner? I'm starving.'

He picked up a buttered scone and proceeded to eat it, earning himself a smart rap on the knuckles from his mother.

'Just like old times,' smiled Lachlan, sitting down at the table and scraping in his chair. He caught Niall's eye and a glow of pride filled his heart. The tears and the laughter of his children's growing years echoed in his mind, a distant yet an ever-present melody that reached into the present to bring him joy.

*

Ruth let herself into the house. All was silent in the rather dingy, low-beamed, green-painted room, which, because half the things were packed in readiness for the move to Portcull, was even more spartan than usual. The air reeked of disinfectant. Twice weekly, Morag washed down the walls and floors with strong carbolic. The floor was bare wood, scrubbed white with only a rug at the fire to relieve the starkness. The mahogany sideboard, the bureau, and hard wooden chairs smelled strongly of polish, yet there was no shine on them. The house looked unlived in, there were no homely touches to add atmosphere, no cat or dog to give a welcome, as Morag had forbidden them in the house. The only ornaments on the walls were Bible markers, which were liberally scattered throughout the house.

A quick check revealed that her father was not in, and Ruth reasoned that he had most likely gone to share Totie's midday meal rather than have a solitary repast in that bare room. Ruth decided that a walk over to Totie's cottage would be lovely on such a day, and she stepped into the sunshine gladly. The cockerel was crowing loudly in the grassy run, as if proclaiming his relief at being released from his Sabbath prison, an upturned peat creel from which he could see the activities of the outside world without being able to join in. This practice of confining the cockerel on the Sabbath was by no means restricted to religious beings like Morag Ruadh. On crofts all over Rhanna, and indeed on islands throughout the Hebrides, it was considered immoral to have a cockerel roaming loose amongst the hens, so into creels, lobster pots, baskets, and fish boxes they went.

Despite everything, Ruth couldn't help feeling happy as she limped along to Totie's cottage perched high on the cliffs some distance from the village. The sun slanted over land and sea, making a bright mosaic of gold, green and blue; puffins, razorbills, and herring-gulls swooped, dived, and cried from the steep crags of the cliffs and rose up in thick clouds from the sea; the scents of wild flag and blue-bells mingled with the dank salt smell of the tangle left by the tide to dry in the sun. Ruth lifted her head and felt life bubbling into her until she shivered. It had been a wonderful morning; she was looking forward to going to live at Portcull – and she would still see Rachel despite her mother, because they would meet at school. She would have at least one friend there – perhaps the twins would speak to her as well. She liked them, especially Lewis; he didn't make her feel uncomfortable the way Lorn did. He was shy, like her; two shy people rarely invoked confidence in each other.

The skirt of Ruth's brown wool pinafore lifted in the wind. It was a hot, uncomfortable garment and the rough material made her knees itch. She wished she could wear a pretty cotton gingham dress like the one Rachel had been wearing that morning but she knew it was useless to ask her mother to make her anything that she considered to be flimsy and provocative. She hardly knew what that big word meant, but had an idea it was something to do with tempting boys – though she couldn't see how any girl of nine years old could do that. Still, Rachel had looked lovely in the simple pink frock; it showed off her suntanned limbs and black curls to perfection.

As Ruth hurried her calliper creaked slightly. She was to get a new one fitted soon, but even so she knew she would never be graceful or pretty enough to provoke boys.

The merriment of the morning came back to her; a smile lit her solemn little face, and she skipped as she approached Totie's cottage. As long as no one was watching she could skip quite well – and dance, too. Rachel had taught her how to do that in the shed behind her house and Ruth had forgotten her limp in the excitement of dancing with Rachel.

Totie's cottage, though windswept and bare of protective trees, was nevertheless well cared for and tidy, with its dazzling white walls and small patches of cultivated land. Totie was a capable woman who, despite all odds, grew all her own vegetables. The potato patch was in the process of being planted in a sandy soil sustained by great quantities of seaweed. A heap of seaweed and a barrowload of dung had been piled onto the earth, waiting to be dug in. Ruth walked over the unfenced springy turf to the door and was about to knock on it when her father's voice froze her action. His was a quiet voice but strong and deep and she heard plainly the words, 'Dear God, Totie, sometimes I don't think I can bear another day in that house with that woman. My times with you are the only things that keep me sane. If it wasn't for Ruth I swear I wouldn't stand another day of Morag.'

Ruth's heart hammered into her throat. That wasn't her father speaking, it couldn't be. But it was – his voice came again from a window at the side – from Totie's bedroom. 'I love that bairnie. The day she was born was the happiest in my life. She's the only joy in that godforsaken house. It's been hell for her since she was a babe and I'd give anything to see laughter in that sad wee face. If hitting Morag was a means of getting happiness for Ruth it would give me the greatest pleasure to do it – but she's stone that woman! A damned statue without a heart! How I rue the day I married her . . .' He gave a short bitter laugh. 'If only I'd known I didn't have to – from what I hear, Ruth could be any man's bairn – oh ay, the first and last time Morag let herself go she made a right proper job of it – and all those who have to live in her shadow have suffered for her sins ever since!'

'Ach, you should confront the pious bitch!' Totie said scornfully. 'Tell her you're not going to be punished for the things she did all these years ago.'

'I can't.' Dugald's voice was full of despair. 'Hell would be a nicer refuge afterwards – forbye, I must think of my wee Ruthie – I don't know why but I'm almost convinced she *is* mine. Yet, I'll never know for sure – that's the hell of it. Morag has damned us all.'

Ruth felt faint, so sick and giddy she leaned back against the doorpost and pressed the palms of her hands against the rough wall of the porch. She fought to control herself. It wasn't real – none of it was real – but she had to know more, had to find out if she was imagining it all – her father in Totie's bedroom, discussing things that made a mockery of her life. With her heart in her throat she crept over the springy grass till she was standing to the side of the bedroom window. There was silence now and she hardly dared to breathe. The green of the machair stretched before her staring eyes; far below, the blue sea eddied into bays of shimmering golden sands. It was such a beautiful world, such a beautiful sun-kissed day, but it was all crashing about her ears like a flimsy matchbox tower. She sucked in her breath and held it, hot unshed tears pricked her eyelids, her legs trembled till she thought she would fall. She leaned hard against the wall for support and threw back her head, her violet eyes staring up at the blue vault of the sky. Was God up there? Who was this God that her mother feared rather than revered? Where was He? If He existed how could He allow so much unhappiness? Her mother had turned Him into an invisible force that haunted them all.

Her grandparents spoke about God in a different way from her mother. Their simple faith had a beauty about it, and it was a joy listening to them reading from the Bible. Yet as soon as her mother intruded, God became different, a stranger without mercy for the smallest lapse from grace.

Standing alone on that sunlit day, Ruth's gentle soul became diffused with feelings of loathing – for her mother? For God? She didn't know. She only knew that her being was so flooded with the powerful emotion she felt ill.

Her father's voice came again. 'Thank God for you, Totie. What I would have done without you all these years, I'll never know. It won't be easy seeing you when we move to Portcull, but I'll find a way – even if it means creeping out of the house in the middle of the night.' He was thanking the God who ruled his life – and he spoke of years with Totie . . .

With her heart in her mouth Ruth turned her head slightly and, raising herself on tip-toes, she glanced quickly in through the window. Her father lay in bed with Totie in his arms, his white head shining like a beacon in the shadows of the room. Ruth turned away and rammed her fist into her mouth to stop from crying out. She moved slightly and her calliper creaked quite loudly.

'What was that?' Dugald's voice sounded strange – faraway yet anxious.

Totie's voice came softly. 'Only the bedsprings – relax – we only have a wee while together.'

Ruth's heart fluttered and her face burned. Inch by inch she edged away from the window and at a safe distance from the cottage she began to run, a clumsy, halting gait that carried her back to the empty house and her own bleak thoughts. The one dear person she had thought was hers wasn't after all. She planted her small hands on the table and her breath rasped in her throat as the harsh sobs shook her body.

After a while the tears were followed by the dull ache of hurt, and then by anger, then rebellion. She wasn't hungry but she limped to the larder and cut a hunk of bread and a slice of cheese. Her mother had said she wasn't to eat a bite till teatime – who was her mother to tell her what to do? Tell her she mustn't play with Rachel, talk to boys? She was only nine years old but in her mother's mind she was already a Jezebel. Conflicting emotions raged through her. She stared at the bread and cheese lying on the plate and, picking it up, she crammed it into her mouth but the tightness in her throat wouldn't allow her to swallow. Coughing and choking she rushed outside and was violently sick. Going back to the kitchen she sat with her elbows on the table, her smarting eyes staring ahead of her without seeing anything.

She felt drained of all strength, all feeling. With her head in her arms she slept for a while and awakened with a start. Four o'clock and no sign of her father. He must have gone out in his van to deliver groceries from Totie's shop. She rose and automatically began to prepare a meal, and when her father's footsteps finally sounded on the path, the potatoes were boiling over the fire and the cold chicken left over from Sunday was neatly sliced on the plates.

Dugald came into the kitchen, his silvery hair slightly windblown. Ruth didn't look up but went on mashing turnips in a bowl with such vigour her arms ached.

'Where's your mother?' Dugald asked, putting his arms round the little girl and kissing her hot cheeks.

'Grannie took a bad turn so Mam had to stay – she won't be back till tomorrow. Erchy brought me home in his van.' Ruth was surprised at how normal she sounded.

'So it's just you and me tonight, my wee lamb?' His voice was light, relieved.

'Ay, Father. Wash your hands and sit down before the dinner gets cold.'

'Anything you say, madam.' He laughed, his steps light as he went into the scullery and poured water from a bucket into a bowl. 'You're a clever wee lassie getting the meal ready all by yourself,' he called over his shoulder. 'Have you been here all day, Ruthie?'

She hesitated only fractionally. 'Ay, Father. It was nice so I played outside for a while.'

By common, unspoken agreement they omitted to say Grace, a usual practice when Morag was in the house. During the meal Ruth was silent, toying with her food.

'Are you all right, Ruthie? Aren't you hungry?' Dugald asked.

She looked straight into his steady grey eyes. 'Not very, Father – I'm – I'm a wee bit worried about Grannie.'

'Ach, she'll be fine,' he reassured. 'She's getting on and gets flusters a bit. Your Grannie was never one to flap, but maybe she's getting a wee bit excited at the idea of us coming to live beside her.'

Ruth remembered the look on old Isabel's face when Morag had first told her the news. 'Ay, that will likely be it,' she said quietly and got up to clear the table and wash the dishes. Dugald grabbed a dish-towel and began to wipe the plates. Ruth moved

away. 'I'll go to my room now,' she said and went to
the door leading into the hall.

'But, it's only six o'clock, Ruthie – you don't have
to go to bed yet. You and me could have a nice cosy
evening together. I thought we might go for a walk
by Aosdana Bay. We could watch the sunset from
the top of the cliffs then come home and maybe write
a poem about all the things we see. Over supper I
had a mind to snuggle you on my knee and read you
a wee story I wrote about the fairies that live over by
Caonteach Cave.'

Ruth hung her head. How lovely to walk beside
that tall dear man in the gloaming; to watch the fishing
boats sailing in; to hear the sea lapping the shore,
making the pebbles and shells sound as if they were
chuckling; to perhaps gather some and bring them
home to wash them in readiness to be laid into the
little jewel box he was carving for her – but best of
all – to sit on his lap by the fire and hear his voice
weaving tales of the wee folk who, it was reputed,
lived in the rock pools near the caves.

'I can't, Father,' she said, her voice low, 'I was bad
today – I stopped at Portcull harbour to watch Todd's
new car coming and Mam was so mad she said I
was to go to my room after tea and learn the
Commandments.'

His heart twisted. She was so vulnerable-looking,
so sad and lost, so pathetic with her small body
encased in the drab frock and her fair head bowed
as if in shame of some momentous crime.

'Ruthie, my wee lassie.' He went to her and

stooped down to cuddle her to him. 'You have never done a bad thing in the whole of your little life. Bugger the Commandments! I'm sure you know enough of them to last you a lifetime. You get your jacket and come out with me.'

She raised her head in wonderment. 'But – what if Mam asks . . . ?'

'Let her,' he said firmly. 'I'll take the consequences. Now – put on your jacket and let's go.'

With her hand firmly in his they wandered silently over the white sands of Aosdana Bay, listening to the haunting song of the curlew, the whispering of the sea, the mating croon of the groups of scaup, drakes, with the purple-green gloss of their plumage making bright patterns in the translucent blue pools among the rocks. Then they climbed to the clifftop and sat side by side watching the sky turn from gold to pink and finally to a blaze of crimson that turned the Sound into a sea of blood stretching to the infinity of the horizon.

When they finally came home they shut the henhouses for the night, then went indoors where he made steaming mugs of milky cocoa, which they drank together by the fire's light. She went to rinse the mugs and came back to see him sitting on the old rocking chair by the range. In firelight and lamp-light the bare room looked homely and welcoming, the feeling of oppression was gone and in its place was love – pure and real. He held out his arms. 'Come here, Ruthie,' he said softly and she climbed onto the lap she loved. He stroked her hair, curled a silken strand round his fingers. 'You have the bonniest hair of all the wee lassies on the island – it's like the hair on the heads of the fairy folk. I once saw a fairy who looked just like you – beautiful as a princess with hair as fine as gossamer, the shine to it brighter than fairy gold. But she wasn't a princess – oh no – she was a queen, the queen of all the fairies who live in the shiny rock pools by Caonteach Cave . . .'

Ruth lay back and listened, her heart touched with a joy that was almost pain. The arms of her beloved father were round her, holding her close to his heart and she knew that he *was* her father. Whatever her mother had done, whichever way she tried to atone for it, she could never, in all the days and years that stretched ahead, take away the beauty of this night, this now, this sweet ecstasy of a little girl's knowing that the arms that held her close were the arms of the father who loved her when perhaps no one else in the world did.

Lorn lay in bed thinking over the events of the day. So many people had been in it, but best of all were Shona and Niall. They were downstairs now with Phebie and Lachlan. Laughter drifted from the parlour. He wished Shona was staying at Laigmhor, but with Uncle Alick and Aunt Mary arriving soon, all the rooms were needed. The only room that was left was a tiny box room at the end of the passage and nobody ever used it except to store things. The scene at the harbour came to him and he smiled, then quite unbidden Ruth's face floated into his mind. She was a strange girl, gentle and shy, yet he sensed something great in her, something squashed so deep inside she probably wasn't aware that she had it. Someday it might get a chance to come out – someday . . . His child's mind grappled with the notion but couldn't quite make sense of it.

'Lewis – do you like Ruth Donaldson?' he asked suddenly.

Lewis's tousled head emerged from the blankets. 'Ach, she's all right – a bit soft, but, of course, she's a girl.'

'So's Rachel.'

'She's different, she's tough for a girl. She doesn't bother about being dumb the way Ruth cares about her funny leg.'

Lorn was silent for a few moments, then he observed slowly, 'Ay, but that Morag Ruadh is an awful mother to have – praying and scraping all the time – and I've heard her telling Ruth no' to drag her leg – as if she could help it. Rachel's mother is no' ashamed that Rachel's dumb – but she's queer in other ways. She lets Rachel run wild – as if she canny be bothered with her.'

'Och well, they're just girls,' Lewis said rather impatiently. Unlike his brother he rarely delved into the deeper issues of life.

'Still, I feel it's a shame for Ruth,' Lorn persisted, frowning in the darkness. 'Nobody bothers with her much.' He was silent again then said in a rush, 'I wonder if Father's ashamed of me. Sometimes I think he is.'

'Ach, you're daft then.' Lewis's tones were scornful. 'He's only feart you'll hurt yourself because of your heart.'

'I suppose in a way I'm like Ruth and Rachel.'

Lewis punched his pillows in disgust. 'Stop blethering and talk sense! I'm lying here thinking about Todd's new car. I don't like cars as a rule, but someday I'd like a car like Todd's – I'd like a fiddle like old Mo's as well – it's no' just any old tink's fiddle. I heard tell he got it from a man on Barra for a few shillings. The missionary made the man feel so ashamed for playin' on the Sabbath he sold it and has wanted it back ever since, but old Mo wouldny give it back for all the tea in China.'

'Maybe he would for all the whisky that's left over from the *Politician*. Todd's brother-in-law from Uist found a case a whily back when he was mending the thatch on his hut roof and everyone left what they were doing to have a big ceilidh.'

'Well, we'll be having a big ceilidh at Portcull next week for Merry Mary's retiral. We'll get to play our fiddles with old Andrew and Rachel and maybe that Jerry hiker we met today.'

'I wonder if Merry Mary's wart might drop off in the hall with all the dancing and hooching,' Lorn pondered.

'I hope not,' Lewis returned fervently. 'Everyone would see it happening and none of us would get paid for it – and *I'm* going to be the one that will. When she retires she's going to try and grow a lot of vegetables to sell to the towrists and I've promised to help her to fetch seaweed and dung. That way I'll be able to keep an eye on her wart and if she knocks it off while she's digging I'll get to collect all the pennies from children all over the island who placed bets on it.'

'You would,' Lorn sniffed peevishly. 'You always get what you want.'

'I'll share the money with you,' promised Lewis sleepily.

'Would you?' enthused Lorn. 'In that case I'll come over to Merry Mary's with you and supervise – make sure you help her properly and don't knock her wart off with the shovel.'

Both boys collapsed in giggles at the absurdity and soon fell to discussing the fishing expedition their father had promised them during the Easter holidays.

Chapter Seven

While Lorn chatted happily with his brother, his parents were at that moment discussing his future with Lachlan, who had asked them to forsake the gathering in the parlour for a quiet talk in the kitchen. Kirsteen and Fergus had put a good face on things for the benefit of the company, but now, sitting together on the couch, they were both acutely aware of the barriers between them. Lachlan twisted his thumbs together for a few thoughtful seconds, then he looked from Fergus to Kirsteen and smiled wryly. 'I thought I was word-perfect in what I have to say to you, but now the time has come all the bonny rehearsals have gone out of my head. I'll have to be blunt – it's about Lorn – I've been keeping a close eye on him and have noticed how much he has improved this last year or two. When he was an infant he was too weak for me to even consider that something could be done for his heart – but now . . .'

Fergus had been sitting at the edge of the couch staring at his shoes but at those words his dark head jerked up and he stared at Lachlan enquiringly. A pink flush had spread over Kirsteen's face and she said tentatively, 'Now?'

Lachlan shifted, playing for time by filling his pipe and taking some time to light it.

'Och, c'mon, man, out with it!' Fergus said tensely.

'Well, I've been discussing your son's case with a colleague of mine, a chap I became acquainted with when I was away on one of my refresher courses. He's a heart specialist, a gifted man who's been doing some pretty wonderful things in his field. New techniques are being tried all the time in open heart surgery – and from what I've told Jack, he feels he would like to have a look at Lorn, see if surgery could possibly improve his condition.'

Hope and fear churned Kirsteen's stomach into a tight coil. 'What kind of surgery?' she asked.

'It's very difficult for me to assess without the proper tests, but I would imagine there might be some misplaced connections between the heart and the blood vessels – Jack would have to see Lorn to really know for sure what is wrong. On the one hand it might only mean one spell of surgery; on the other hand it could be a long, involved affair – perhaps several operations over a period of time, but in my opinion your son deserves this opportunity to improve the quality of his life. If all went well he could end up as sound as any other lad.'

'And if it didn't work, he could go through hell and end up the same – or worse than he is now,' Fergus stated flatly.

Lachlan spread his long fingers and shrugged. 'I can't promise miracles at this stage, nor at any stage for that matter. It's a chance I feel you ought to take, though – I cannot say more than that.' He leaned forward and tapped out his pipe on the grate then he swivelled round and looked them both straight in the eye. 'Don't feel you have to rush into any decisions now – talk it over between you; really thrash it out.' He put his hand over Kirsteen's and said gently, 'Believe me, I know how difficult this is. Take your time to discuss the matter thoroughly. However, I know you will both want to do the right thing for the wee lad's future – and surgery might provide an answer to what sort of future he'll have.'

Grant came into the room on a quest for food. 'Our visitors are starving,' he grinned cheekily, 'especially Phebie, who's fading away. I thought I saw scones being baked earlier and they smelled delicious.'

Phebie stood quietly in the background, knowing what the talk had been about. She caught Kirsteen's eye and her sweet face was full of sympathy. Later, when everyone was leaving and the kitchen was filled with chatter, she took Kirsteen aside and put a comforting arm round her shoulders. 'I know how you feel, Kirsteen,' she said quietly. 'Och, it's hard, so it is, so very very hard to try and think what's best for the bairnies we bring into the world. Sometimes it seems they bring us nothing but sorrow – but ach – what joy they give too – and they deserve to get the best deal possible.'

Kirsteen hugged her. 'Thank you, Phebie, you have been a wonderful friend and a comfort to me from the first day I set foot on Rhanna. Whoever gives you comfort, I wonder?'

'Lachlan and God,' said Phebie simply. 'If one fails me the other is aye to hand.'

Kirsteen gazed thoughtfully into Phebie's bonny face and thought, 'This woman is good, truly good. She has been through a lot herself, yet her belief in God has never wavered.' Kirsteen held her breath. When had she last communed with God in earnest? Not the automatic ritual of Sunday worship, but really and truly talked, asked, confided? She couldn't remember and as she bent to kiss Phebie's warm soft cheek she felt ashamed.

Everyone was moving out into a night of velvet sprinkled with stars. Fergus remained at the door, but Kirsteen went to the gate. The cool night air brushed her hot face, the dark moor stretched away, felt rather than seen; in the distance the sea was a subdued silver streak. Grant was walking the visitors up the road, but as the men moved away Shona paused at the gate and murmured into Kirsteen's ear, 'Next time I see the pair of you I hope you will have made it up.'

Kirsteen let out an audible gasp. 'How on earth –?'

'Ach, I'm not the daft wee lassie I once was; I've been married long enough to know the signs. Babbie taught me a thing or two a whily back when I could never see the obvious for looking – forbye,' she smiled in the darkness, 'Father always gives himself away. When you're not watching, he's watching you under his eyebrows and he's just a bit *too* nice to everyone, if you know what I mean.'

'Oh, but, Shona,' Kirsteen burst out, 'it's worse,

much worse than just a silly row!' She checked herself, wanting to pour her heart out, but knowing that to do so would be to betray others, to rake up things that were long buried. Also, she was hating herself for slapping Fergus, for hurling such cruel abuse at him. To have Shona hate her too was too terrible to contemplate. 'Thanks for the advice,' she said lightly then added, 'How very strange life is – to think I once taught you when you were just an infant, now you're teaching me.'

'I know.' Shona sounded rather sad. 'Life passes so quickly. 'When I was just a baby you were a young woman and there was no way we could bridge the gap – now we're both women and can speak to one another on the same level.'

'And you make me sound an absolute relic!' Kirsteen laughed. 'Get along now before I fold up and crumble away before your eyes.'

Shona giggled and sped away up the glen to catch up with the menfolk. Kirsteen felt exhausted, so drained she felt she would drop off the minute her head touched the pillow, but once in bed she didn't lie down. She hadn't carried out her threat of moving Fergus's things into Grant's room and she sat up, hugging her knees, waiting for Fergus to come up. The sound of his step on the stairs set her heart racing madly, but he didn't look at her when he came in. Instead, he went to the linen chest and took out a couple of blankets and a pillow.

'Fergus – we – we must talk – about Lorn.' Her voice sounded feeble, strange even to her own ears.

'Ay – we must,' he said shortly, the deep voice cold and distant. They might have been standing at either end of a long bridge – so far apart they seemed in those moments, as if all the years of their intimate loving had been wiped out like chalk marks on a blackboard. He said nothing more and walked with measured step out of the room and along the passage to the tiny box room at the end. It was a jumble of odds and ends, bits of unused furniture, discarded toys, the two wooden cradles that had rocked his baby daughter and his infant sons. The sight of them caught him unawares and he was whisked back to a long ago night of love, of laughter, of dancing with a baby in the crook of his arm, of Kirsteen standing with bowed head gazing tenderly at their smallest son. Now that infant was a boy – a boy whose future rested on an operating table under bright lights, surgeons' knives cutting . . . Fergus gave a little cry and threw an old rug over the cradles but he couldn't shut out the thoughts, the fears, the misery that engulfed him as he lay on the uncomfortable old horsehair sofa that had stood in the parlour in his father's day. His head ached slightly, but overriding all was the ache in his heart. Kirsteen had been cruel, so cruel – vicious almost. Why? Why? Why? The question banged around in his head. They had had rows before, some more heated than that of the morning, but never before had she said such venomous things – things he had thought buried. He had goaded her, of course, but hardly enough to make her rake up that thing about Alick, an incident

166

that had cost him his arm, cost Hamish his life, caused him to lose Kirsteen for six long, heart-breaking years.

He tossed and turned. The sofa was full of lumps, draughts seeped in through the sparse coverings – he should have brought a quilt . . . Lorn, what about Lorn? The decision was too great, a burden of responsibility that crushed into him like a ton weight. Perhaps Kirsteen was right: maybe he had tried to shield the boy too much. He should have been harder with him, made him tougher – prepared him better for the harsher things in life and in that way he himself might have been better prepared for the enormity of what lay ahead. Help me, God, he prayed in despair. Help me – us – to do the right thing for our son.

Kirsteen remained sitting up long after Fergus had left the room. Her limbs felt so rigid they might have been locked. She heard Grant letting himself in and coming upstairs. There was a bump followed by a muffled curse. She smiled mechanically. Fiona infuriated him by putting all sorts of silly comparisons against his adolescent clumsiness: one day he was the boy with frog's feet, another his hands were likened to bunches of bananas.

A tremor passed through Kirsteen, and she shivered. Slowly she unwound from her cramped position and, throwing back the covers, she got up and padded to the wardrobe. Inside, hanging under layers of tissue paper, was the silver fox fur Fergus had given her after the twins were born. The joy and love of that night came back to her. She thought of how he had gathered clothing coupons together and had gone off to Oban on his Christmas shopping spree. He had brought back something for everyone, his eyes shining with the pleasure of giving – giving her red roses . . . She lifted the paper away from the jacket and buried her face in the soft fur. She hadn't worn it very often, at christenings, weddings – on a wonderful holiday with Shona and Niall on the Mull of Kintyre when they had all dined out and gone to several dances.

'Oh, my darling.' She bit her lip and threw back her head but she couldn't stop the tears spilling. It would be no use going to him in his present state of mind. It would only serve to make things worse. She went back to bed and in her despair she cried silently to God for help and drifted into a fitful sleep, waking before dawn to hear Fergus come quietly along the passage and downstairs. He had risen earlier than need be, so that none of the family would know that he and Kirsteen had quarrelled, that he had slept in a separate room.

Alick and Mary arrived a few days later, minus their fourteen-year-old twin sons who were now spreading their wings and had gone off with the Scouts to Easter camp. Mary immediately changed from her elegant town clothes into garments more suited for a farming holiday, while Alick and Fergus caught up with all the news. Alick was slim and distinguished-looking with his grey hair fashionably styled, his moustache and small beard neatly clipped: except for the dark eyes there was nothing in his appearance to connect him with tall, dark, hard-muscled Fergus.

The following day all the menfolk from Slochmhor and Laigmhor went off on a day's fishing expedition. The women had gathered at Slochmhor and Shona stood at the window, watching the men trudging away, wishing that she was going with them. Although Alick was wearing an old jersey and tweed trousers tucked into wellingtons he still managed to look sophisti-cated, but the illusion was shattered as, with his arms slung round the twins' shoulders, he let out a wild whoop of delight. It was a mild day with the hilltops shrouded in mist. It had rained in the morning but now a stiff breeze was breaking the clouds apart to reveal patches of blue.

'A grand day for a spot of fishing,' Alick observed. 'Even if we don't catch any it will be nice to sit at the lochside and eat all that lovely food we have in the baskets – and, just picture it – a whole day without a single woman's tongue flapping away in our eardrums.'

Lewis looked up at the sky. 'Look, it's a fluffy cloud day!' he yelled, pointing at the big clouds racing along. 'I can see a dragon's face in that one with a big pink tongue spitting out fire.'

Alick laughed. 'Shh! Maybe it's Elspeth sitting on a cloud watching us.'

Lorn held onto his father's hand and couldn't help giving a little skip of joy. He was with his father, he was one of the men, and it was a 'fluffy cloud day'. He loved his brother's fantasies about such days, often they spent ages watching the wind sculpting the clouds into fantastic shapes and human faces.

Shona, still watching from the windows as the men receded into the distance, said, sighing, 'Sometimes I wish I was a wee lassie again, running around doing things like guddling and fishing. It seems unfair, so it does. Men grow up, yet they never look out of place doing the things they did as boys. I feel like an old grannie left behind with my knitting.'

'Well, I'm glad Lachy's getting a break,' Phebie said. 'And that *I'm* getting one with him and Niall out from under my feet – besides,' she said, her eyes twinkling, 'they don't know it yet but they're taking us all for a picnic on Monday and we're all going to roll our Easter eggs.' She went into the pantry and came back with a basket piled high with big brown eggs. 'I boiled these last night – more than two dozen of them – enough for two each, and we are going to take chairs and sit outside to paint faces on them. I found a box of Fiona's paints at the back of a cupboard, and since tomorrow is Sunday they will all have to be painted today – so get your peenies on everybody.'

Shona chuckled with delight and immediately began carrying kitchen chairs outside to set them on the grass. Mary rushed to gather all the aprons she could find. 'What a marvellous idea, Phebie,' she approved as she went to the door with an armful of Elspeth's spotless linen aprons. 'I haven't rolled an

Easter egg in years.' She was a well groomed and elegantly coiffed woman, but after half an hour her hair had fallen down and streaks of paint covered her face and hands.

The sun was breaking through the clouds and Shona glanced appreciatively round, feeling it very good to sit there with the windbreak of green pines releasing a rain-fresh fragrance, the nearby sheep chopping away at the rich, sappy green turf, the hens strutting and clucking; shrieks of merriment from Fiona, who was having a wonderful time trying to make Grant's eggs' faces as disagreeable looking as possible. On one she had painted deep black frowns between eyes screwing up into a squiggle of black curls, on the other he was grinning foolishly above a ridiculously exaggerated dimple. On the back of each egg she had dared to write 'Dimples' in bold red letters.

'He'll throw them to the gulls,' Kirsteen predicted.

'Or he'll skite you round the lugs with them,' Shona said, giggling, deftly removing Helen's chubby fingers from the gooey paint box. 'Look,' she said, holding up an egg painted with big brown eyes and golden-red hair. 'Ellie's egg.'

'Ellie's eggle.' The little girl clapped with glee, lost her balance and landed on the grass with a soft thump.

On the face of it they were a jolly company, but Shona glanced at Kirsteen's face and knew that she hadn't yet made up with Fergus. She was laughing and talking as happily as the rest, but her blue eyes were weary and Shona guessed that she had been losing sleep over the matter.

A little black car came meandering along the glen road from Downie's Pass. It groaned to a halt at the gate and Babbie got out, her expression one of amusement as she observed the gathering outside Slochmhor. 'What on earth are you lot up to?' she asked, eyeing the heap of gaily painted eggs. 'Would I be right in thinking you are quite literally having a hen's party?'

'Ay, indeed you would,' Shona said, laughing. 'We're just getting a picnic prepared for Monday – why don't you and Anton come? You never seem to have time off these days – I've hardly seen you since I arrived. A break would do you both the world of good.'

'Sorry, I can't,' Babbie said and sighed ruefully, pushing a hand through her red curls. 'I have too much on my plate at the moment. Biddy helps all she can but even at that . . .' she smiled rather wearily, 'it's a bit like working on the Forth Bridge – when you get to the end you have to start all over again, and with me being off part of Saturday and all day Sunday, Monday is my busiest day really.'

Shona sprang to her feet and began to peel off her apron. 'Are you forgetting I'm a nurse – I'll come with you today and between us we'll get through your patients like a dose of salts.'

'Really – would you? But you're here for a holiday . . .'

'Am I? With Phebie making me work my fingers to

the bone painting eggs and forcing me to get up out of my bed in the morning in order to drag Fiona and Niall from theirs?'

'But . . .'

'Away you go, lass,' Phebie ordered kindly. 'I'll look to wee Helen though I can't promise you'll find me all in one piece when you get back. I thought Fiona was wild as an infant but this one beats all.'

'You see, no "buts",' Shona said, linking her arm through Babbie's and pulling her away. 'I'm quite looking forward to coming with you, it will be like old times, we can have a rare old blether and I'll get to see a lot of folk I haven't seen in ages.'

Mary had already endowed an egg with a squiggle of red loops and enormous green eyes and was starting to streak yellow locks over another.. Babbie turned back. 'I wonder – do you think you could do one with dark hair and specs and the name Jon, spelt J-O-N. I've a feeling Anton's friend would love to come on an island picnic.'

Fiona delved into the egg basket. 'Say no more,' she intoned authoritatively, and with fiendish delight swirled her brush into black paint and began drawing two black circles on Jon's egg.

Elspeth appeared with a brush in her hand. She had been upstairs tidying the bedrooms with such energy she had lost some pins from her severe grey bun, which Fiona had likened to a 'mouldering cow pat'. 'What's this, madam?' Elspeth asked tightly, eyeing Fiona's apron, which was patterned with livid splashes of red and blue. 'Is these my aprons? My beautiful aprons, just fresh from the wash line and newly starched?'

Phebie's lips twitched. 'We'll wash them, Elspeth,' she said soothingly. 'It will come out easily – it's only watercolour.'

'Only! Only!' Elspeth repeated menacingly.

Fiona's bright eyes glittered. 'Ach, you shouldny bother, Mother,' she advised mischievously. 'I think they look better with a bit colour in them, it makes them look artistic – like Elspeth herself – and . . .' she spluttered with mirth, 'she's got her brush all ready – only she looks more like a house painter than an artist.'

Elspeth screeched and, raising her brush, waved it threateningly at Fiona, who vacated her chair with agility to prance away over the turf, Elspeth on her heels, scattering sheep and hens in all directions, her hair falling in lanky grey loops down her back. Behind her wobbled little Helen, falling into sheep's sharn, picking herself up, waving her hands and screaming with joy, as she followed hot on Elspeth's heels. Mary clutched her stomach and shrieked so heartily her chair flew out from under her, and while Phebie and Kirsteen rushed to help her up, Shona took Babbie's hand and they flew to the car in fits of giggles.

Monday dawned in a haze of ethereal light that bathed the hilltops in gold and brushed the sea with bronze. By eleven o'clock, the world was awash with sunlight and on the journey over to Croy, with the

company divided into three traps, each keeping pace
with the other, everyone began to sing – all except
Kirsteen and Fergus, who, making the excuse of
being polite to their guests, sat on opposite seats,
Fergus with Mary, Alick with Kirsteen. 'You can't say
I'm not giving you the opportunity to get close to my
brother,' Fergus had muttered to Kirsteen as they left
Laigmhor. Kirsteen was still smarting with hurt at the
remark, and now, to add insult to injury, Fergus was
giving every appearance of enjoying himself, laughing
readily at Mary's witticisms – and he had thrown his
arm lightly round Mary's shoulders and was
murmuring things the others couldn't hear but that
were making her laugh. Kirsteen's cheeks burned
and she felt panic rising in her. How long could this
go on? The rift between her and Fergus was growing
wider with each passing day. She had tried to talk to
him, to tell him she was sorry, but always he had
some excuse for walking away from her. Things
weren't made easier by having to carry on normally
in front of the visitors, but each night Fergus was
careful to ensure that he was last to go upstairs and
first to rise in the morning so that no one was aware
that he was sleeping in the box room. Kirsteen
wanted to stop the trap and run away – anywhere to
hide her humiliation. Grant was driving the horses at
a spanking pace as he happily bawled out a tune.

Alick glanced questioningly at Kirsteen. He was
looking very handsome that day in a dark blazer and
light grey flannels. 'Hey, what's wrong?' he enquired
quizzically. 'Has the cat got your tongue? This is a

picnic, not a funeral.' His voice was soft, well-modulated and rather pleasing to the ears. He grinned teasingly. 'What's the matter, Kirsteen, don't you like sitting beside me or is it just that you can't bear to let big brother away from your side for a single minute?'

Kirsteen gave herself a shake – she couldn't – she wouldn't – let Fergus see how much he was hurting her, and she forced herself to smile at Alick, her blue eyes very bright in her smooth-skinned face.

'*That's* better.' Alick looked at her appreciatively. She still had the figure of a girl – with breasts that were soft yet firm, skin that was smooth and golden, blonde hair a ruffle of curls in the breeze. Her white dress was simple, loose-topped, with a soft flowing skirt belted at the waist. It draped over the curves of her body, revealing without flaunting. A gust of wind at Downie's Pass made Mary yell and hold onto her hat, and without warning Kirsteen's skirt billowed in the air, briefly exposing her long shapely legs before she grabbed at the folds and tucked them firmly under her. Alick's eyes gleamed at the sight, and Fergus's mask of jollity fell away. A thundery shadow fell over his dark face and he glowered at his brother. A bemused Alick interpreted the message. 'This woman is mine,' it said more plainly than words. 'I know every plane of her body, the secrets of it are mine alone. I know how she looks in sleep, how she responds to me when she is awake.'

Alick sensed the tension and shifted uneasily. He realised for the first time since the start of the holiday that Fergus and Kirsteen were not on speaking terms.

'Big brother is watching us,' he mouthed in Kirsteen's ear. 'For God's sake, I don't want any trouble. Come on, sing – we're on a picnic and I, for one, am going to enjoy it.'

And sing Kirsteen did, in a rather shaky voice, and she kept on singing desperately till they arrived at Tràigh Mor Bay, Bay of the Great Sands. Here, on the cliffs above the bay, rising up from the machair, was a towering mass of soft rock, which rose up to a height of seven hundred feet, studded with hazel bushes and innumerable starlike primroses. Jagged cliffs of a harder rock divided Tràigh Mor Bay from An Coire Srùb Bay, Bay of the Spouting Kettle, where at high tide the sea thundered into vast underground caverns to gush spurting and foaming, fifty feet and more, from a spout-shaped vent above the splintered crags. The tide was in now and it was an awesome experience to hear the sea roaring into the vast subterranean caverns and to watch it spuming out of the blow hole, sending millions of glistening droplets high into the air.

'We'll have to wait till the tide goes out before we go down,' said Phebie, who was as jubilant as an excited child. It wasn't often that she and Lachlan had time to spend together, and they went off, arm in arm over the emerald-green clifftops, which were studded with numerous wildflowers. Grant was hoisting Lorn onto his shoulders and he held out a hand to Lewis. They ran laughing to watch the spout at close quarters, followed by Shona and Niall skipping like small children. Babbie and Anton followed more sedately, hands entwined, lost in a world of their own. 'Do you remember, liebling,' he whispered into her ear, 'that day we made love in the sands at Aosdana Bay?'

'As if I could ever forget,' she murmured dreamily.

His hand tightened over hers and he said tenderly, 'We had so little time to love then . . . now,' he said, gazing at the panorama of sea and sky, 'now we have it all – all the years of our lives to love.'

Babbie laid her curly red head against his fair one and they walked on, lovers even after four years of marriage.

Jon and Fiona were finding they had a good deal in common, for he, like she, was interested in flora and fauna, and they strolled away, pouncing every so often on unusual plant specimens.

Mary stood at the end of the cliffs in raptures. 'How perfectly wonderful!' she exclaimed in her high light voice. 'I've never been to this side of Rhanna before.'

The wind buffeted Kirsteen, tossing her curls, moulding her dress to her body, whipping up her skirt to once more reveal her long brown legs. She was unaware of the effect that the sight of her was having on Fergus. God, she was desirable, a creature that could tempt any man to – to – the muscle of his jaw tightened. If only they were alone in this place where passion had carried them heavenwards on effortless wings. Surrounded by such memories they could perhaps have made up – made love on the sands as they had done so often in the past . . .

Kirsteen staggered and stumbled on a rock. Alick

gallantly caught her arm, and without being able to help it, she found herself leaning against him. She felt awkward and unsure. Alick might go off with Mary, leaving her alone with Fergus and she didn't know how to handle him in his present frame of mind.

But then Fergus solved the problem for her. He was calling on Mary, his lilting voice snatched by the breeze: 'Mary! I'll show you round the place! I know it well. Come on.'

'What did you say?' Holding onto her hat, Mary bent into the wind towards him and he took her arm to pull her close, the wind giving him the excuse to shout louder than was necessary.

'I know how to get along Coire Srùb Bay without getting wet feet – even at high tide. I'll take you along by the reefs where you can see the Bodach Beag – when the tide recedes we'll go over.'

He was turning the knife in a wound already tender. Kirsteen swayed and closed her eyes. Coire Srùb Bay was *theirs*, where they had come in the wonderful days of their courtship; made love on the hot white sands – but most of all, Bodach Beag had belonged to them alone: they had laid claim to it on their first picnic in the bays of Croy. It was a tidal island, cut off from Rhanna at high water, a picturesque haven inhabited only by sheep who cropped the turf till it resembled a bowling green. The surrounding sea was broken by high craggy rocks and reefs bounded by pink shell sands. At the eastern end, abutting into the sea, was a round tower of rock shearing up to a tattered pinnacle fifty feet high. Its name, Bodach Beag, meant Little Old Man, and from certain angles it did indeed appear as a bent old man gazing broodingly into the frothing sea far below. Kirsteen and Fergus had gone to Bodach Beag on their first picnic together, they had been cut off by the tide but it hadn't mattered. They hadn't cared about time on that sunlit summer's day with the sea foaming at their feet and the great crags enfolding them as they made love on the sands with the water caressing them as tenderly as they caressed one another . . . Kirsteen gave a little sob and clamped her fist to her mouth.

Fergus and Mary had disappeared and Alick reached out to touch her. 'Hey, c'mon now,' he said soothingly. 'It can't be that bad.'

She passed a hand wearily over her eyes. 'Oh but it is, Alick, it is.'

'Everyone has rows in marriage,' he told her. 'Hell, I had enough of them myself at the start of mine.'

'This is more than just a row, Alick – it's – oh, I don't know what it is – I only know it's all my fault!' she cried despairingly.

'Nonsense, there's always two sides.' Alick glanced round. The clifftops were deserted, everyone having dispersed about their various pursuits. 'I tell you what,' he said, and taking her by the shoulders, he gently pushed her down on the grass and sat down beside her. 'We're going to sit here, in full view of everyone who isn't here, and you are going to use my shoulder – oh yes, I insist.' His dark eyes were compassionate. 'You can trust me now, really. I'm not the silly young goat I once was – in fact I'd say I've grown into a rather dignified and somewhat respectable gentleman – in case you haven't noticed.'

Kirsteen gave him a watery smile. He had always been able to make her laugh, to forget things – that had been the root of the trouble all these years ago.

'But – you'll hate me when you hear – it's – it's about you.' She clasped her knees and avoided his eyes though she couldn't avoid hearing his startled intake of breath.

'About me? I don't see . . .'

'Oh, it wasn't about you really, it was about Lorn when it started. I wanted Fergus to stop shielding him and let him do more about the farm. He got angry – you know how afraid he is for Lorn – one word borrowed another and – and it ended up with me casting up the past – raking up that time when you – when you . . .'

'Oh hell, no,' Alick protested, 'not that! No wonder Fergus was looking daggers at me earlier. Oh, Lord!' He drew up his knees and gazed broodingly at the swirling sea below. There was silence between them for some time before he burst out, 'But why, Kirsteen? It's not like you to be so petty.'

Her face burned crimson and she shook her head. 'I don't really know. Well, perhaps I do – at least I think I do – I felt as if history was repeating itself. Lewis being made to feel he always had to play the protector, fighting Lorn's battles – like – like . . .'

'Like Fergus and me,' Alick finished bitterly. 'Have

no fear of that, Kirsteen. The twins are entirely different from me and the big brother who did all my fighting for me. Lewis is the strong one physically, ay, but Lorn is the one with the backbone. Oh, don't get me wrong. Lewis is a grand little chap – a bit devil-may-care, but he'll settle down. He's too wise to ever let himself be leaned on by Lorn or by anyone else.'

'I'm sorry, Alick,' she murmured, 'I shouldn't have burdened you with this, and you on holiday.'

He smiled crookedly. 'Isn't that what brothers-in-law are for? To confide in now and then? I've always had the feeling that I owed you something, Kirsteen, and if a bit of advice from me helps you, then it is also salving my conscience to some extent. And I'll tell you something for nothing. Fergus is crazy about you – why else do you think he's gone off with my wife? Certainly not because he's ever been overly fond of her – I can assure you. He's behaving like a spoilt brat and the best thing you can do is ignore his behaviour. He'll be the first to come to his senses, believe me. He didn't search for you for six long years just because you happen to be a very lovely lady.'

'But I slapped him!' Kirsteen almost wailed.

'Really?' Alick grinned. 'Then no wonder he's sulking, I doubt anyone has ever hit him before. No doubt he deserved it, so stop worrying and let's go and enjoy ourselves. The tide's on the turn.'

They found the others on the beach, swimming or paddling, and without more ado Alick rolled up his immaculate trousers and went into the fray, leaving Kirsteen to go behind a rock and peel off her dress to emerge wearing a yellow swimsuit that made even Lachlan whistle in teasing admiration.

Fergus walked with Mary along Coire Srùb Bay. Now that he was out of Kirsteen's sight, his mask of jollity had fallen away, leaving his face dark and brooding.

In a way, Mary was glad to be free of his attentions, for while she had always enjoyed flirting with men, she had always instinctively known that Fergus wasn't the flirtatious type and she had felt somewhat uneasy when he had made such unusually friendly overtures towards her. She had never fully understood him, though she liked him a lot better than she had done in the beginning. 'Fergus, let's go back,' she suggested. 'I can see your Bodach Beag another time. I'm getting a bit peckish.' Hiding a smile at the alacrity with which he accepted her decision, she ran to keep up with him. She wasn't going to get her feet wet if she could help it, and she needed his help to negotiate the slippery reefs and rock pools.

Everyone was enjoying themselves at Tràigh Mor Bay. Fergus's eyes flashed at sight of Kirsteen in the yellow swimsuit, her limbs golden, her head thrown back in an agony of laughter as Niall and Shona splashed her with great handfuls of freezing sea. His absence hadn't affected her at all, and his frown deepened further when he spotted Lorn swimming happily, flanked by Lewis and Grant. A sharp protest rose to his lips but he quelled it.

Grant saw Fergus and unease clouded his young face in anticipation of the expected admonishment, but relief made him smile again as Fergus took off his shoes and socks and waded out to the shallows.

Lorn scrambled onto a rock, his breath coming fast but his blue eyes triumphant. 'I can swim quite well now, Father,' he said rather defiantly.

'So I see,' said Fergus dryly. 'You have obviously been practising.'

'I taught him, Father,' Grant said gruffly. 'I think everyone should learn how to swim. You never know when you might have to – do you?' There was a message in the words. Grant held his father's look boldly.

'Ay, you're right, lad,' Fergus conceded at last and understanding passed between father and son.

Rachel appeared over the cliffs. She had been to the tinkers' camp at Dunuaigh, which had been deserted except for old Mo lying in the sun in his pram. The old man and the little girl had spent a wonderful hour playing their fiddles, and Rachel was in a jubilant mood when she came to Tràigh Mor Bay and saw the frolics in the sea below. Without hesitation she raced with Squint down to the beach to stand for a moment curling her bare feet into the warm sand, savouring the feel of it trickling between her toes. She was wearing grubby blue shorts and one of her brothers' white cotton shirts and she looked like a beautiful boy with the wind tossing her short raven curls over her brow. Her eyes were turbulent, filled with a great restlessness, an enquiring love of life that could find no expression in speech. Carefully she laid her beloved fiddle on a rocky cradle, then ran straight into the sea to splash joyfully over to Jon. Her fingers told him the blithe message. 'The sun is shining and it is a beautiful day.'

'You remembered!' Jon cried in delight. 'You will learn more of your special language, Rachel. I will teach you many words before I have to go back to Oban.'

Squint barked and threw his body into a curving golden arch as he leapt like a dolphin over the waves. He was a lovable clown of a dog, as much in love with life as his small mistress, and the children rolled him onto his back in which position he remained quite contentedly, trusting implicitly the human hands that held him as the sea cradled him and swirled his floppy ears back and forth. His tongue lolled from the side of his mouth and he seemed to be grinning as one eye gazed thoughtfully at the sky and the other kept guard on Rachel. Later, when the eggs were being rolled over the hillocks, he chased after them, pouncing on them, tossing them into the air before fetching them back uncracked to their owners. Everyone was in a state of high spirits. For once Grant and Fiona were agreeable to one another, and when he saw the eggs she had painted for him, he let out a burst of laughter.

Rachel stood with her arms folded behind her back watching everyone rolling their eggs.

'What a pity we don't have one with her name on it,' Kirsteen murmured.

'Oh yes we do,' Grant said, and with a flourish presented Rachel with one of his eggs. She gazed at the loops of black hair, the grinning face and finally turned the egg round to see the word 'Dimples'. The ruse couldn't have been more successful. The dimples on her cheeks deepened, and brandishing the egg above her head she took to her heels, her brown legs a blur as she careered down the slope with Squint prancing beside her.

When the picnic was over everyone sat on the sands in replete contentment listening to Jon and Rachel, who sat side by side on the rocks playing their violins to the accompaniment of sea and wind. The melodies soared and blended with the sounds of nature, for nothing was more natural than to hear the music of instruments that were meant to be played in the open air. Terns, razorbills, and shearwaters cried from the cliffs and plummeted into the blue water as the strains of the fiddles filled the bay with sweet refrains. Jon's touch was sure, the bow silk against gossamer, the notes fine yet full of a liquid resonance that were one moment like the gentle waves lapping the shore, the next like the wild seas crashing, racing before the wind. Jon and Rachel were lost in the magic of music. The young man was enchanted by the untamed child, in his mind he likened her beauty to that of the wild harebells fluttering in the wind, fragile yet strong, a wildflower at one with the solitude and grandeur of nature.

Everyone had gathered into pairs. Lorn and Lewis sat side by side on the flat smooth stones over the rock pools, dangling their feet in the warm water; Shona's glowing auburn head was on Niall's shoulder, and little Helen was asleep in her arms; Babbie and Anton were perched at the entrance to a cave, his blond head close to her red one, her green eyes sparkling as he murmured things for her ears alone; Alick was with Mary; Fiona and Grant sat companionably side by side; Lachlan, his unruly hair blowing over his eyes, his thin face solemn as he listened to the music, had his arm protectively round Phebie's shoulders.

Only Fergus and Kirsteen remained apart from each other. Idly he played with the shells at his feet, picking them up, poking them back into the sand. He gave the impression of nonchalance, but every fibre in him longed to go over and crush Kirsteen to his heart, to feel her warm sweet nearness, to kiss her lips, caress her, tell her that he was sorry, for now that unreasoning anger had left him, he *was* sorry and longed to tell her so. He glanced at her from lowered brows. She was sitting against the shimmering blue-green backdrop of the sea, her hands clasped round her knees, the white dress blurring her curves to a softness that made her look not only gorgeous but strangely spiritual. Her fair head was thrown back, her chin proudly tilted; the symmetry of her profile was of the stuff that made poets pick up their pens; her skin was smooth and tanned, the tiny hairs on her arms bleached almost white after just a day in the sun. She was gazing straight ahead as if absorbed in the music. Fergus pulled in his breath – she was a million miles away from him, so aloof she appeared not to be aware of his existence. She had tried to speak to him, to tell him she was sorry – but he hadn't listened. Once more he had made the mistake of thinking he alone had the power to call the tune, but he had underestimated her own power, the strength of will that had once made her turn her back on all that she loved, to leave him knowing that she was carrying his child. The pain of his love for her ripped him apart. They had to talk – about Lorn – about everything, but she seemed now to be beyond his reach . . .

Jon was playing Rabbie Burns's *My Love is Like a Red Red Rose*. The beautiful evocative strains spilled into the air, liquid, haunting, accompanied by the pure, bubbling song of a nearby curlew. Kirsteen felt as if her heart was bursting with pent-up emotions. Red roses – Fergus – red rosebuds – the twins – laughing, crying – Fergus dancing on a night of love and laughter . . . Everything was a jumble in her mind. She felt Fergus's propinquity overwhelming her, sapping her of so much strength it took all her willpower to hold onto her mask of indifference. The exquisite notes flowed from Jon's violin and the words of the song beat into her, washing into her veins, swelling deep into her breast: 'And I will love thee still my dear till a' the seas gang dry.' She dug her nails into her knees in the agony of believing that the man she would love till the end of time seemed not to love her enough to forgive her for words spoken in the heat of anger.

Chapter Eight

The imminence of Merry Mary's retiral party was now uppermost in everyone's minds, and the day crept round at last, heralded by the arrival of slate-blue storm clouds building up on the horizon. An ominous calm lay over the glassy swell of the waves and old Joe rubbed his chin thoughtfully as he gazed out over the Sound of Rhanna.

'There will be a bugger o' a storm come nightfall,' he forecast with assurance, and one of the fisher-wives looked at him anxiously.

'The smacks were due in the day,' she said worriedly. 'And my man went out with them.'

'Ach, it will be all right,' Joe reassured. 'They'll maybe lie up at Mallaig for a while.'

'And maybe they won't,' the fisherwife said doubt-fully.

'Ach well, they know what they're doin',' old Joe soothed, though he looked again at the clouds and felt uneasy. If the men had indeed left the port of Mallaig they would be caught in the teeth of the storm long before they reached Rhanna . . .

Lewis squirmed as Kirsteen pulled the comb through his thick crop of curls but Kirsteen didn't prolong the agony and stood back to survey her twin sons with pride. Their faces were glowing from a brisk wash, auburn lights shone in their newly washed hair, and their blue eyes were big with excitement. Tonight they were playing with Rachel, old Andrew, old Mo, Jon, and one or two others who went to make up the 'Portcull Fiddlers'. They stood fidgeting in their white shirts and McKenzie kilts while Kirsteen gave them a thorough inspection. 'Right, you'll do,' she told them with a laugh. 'Take your jackets and go downstairs to wait for me.'

'I wish Grant was here,' Lorn said before he turned and followed Lewis downstairs. Kirsteen wished so too. Outside the rain slanted in horizontal sheets across the hills and battered against the window panes; the wind had keened over the moors and whined down the chimneys all day, sending so many blasts of smoke into the rooms that earlier Kirsteen had had to open doors and windows to allow the fresh air to swoop in and disperse the choking clouds. Out in the yard something clattered and Kirsteen prayed that it wasn't a part of the dairy roof, which had been mended during the winter gales. Fergus was out at the sheds now with Matthew, securing doors and windows against the fury of the gale. He had sent a message via Lewis that she was to go on ahead of him to the hall and he would be along later. She was dressed and ready but went along to her bedroom to pull back the curtains at the window. Rivers of rain gushed down the panes, interspersed with smatterings of hail and it was difficult to believe that only days before the weather had been so warm and springlike. She pressed the tips of her fingers to her lips and thought about Grant out with the smacks. His parting shot of four days ago came to her. 'Don't worry, Mother, I'll be back in time for Merry Mary's ceilidh – I wouldny miss it for the world. Press my navy suit and leave it ready on the bed – I must look my best for all those lassies waiting to pounce on me.' He had laughed, his dark eyes crinkling with mischief before he gave her a hurried kiss and went off.

'He'll be fine,' Alick had reassured her earlier. 'That lad could take on the Atlantic single-handed. He's got seafaring blood in him, with a few exceptions it runs in the family. I often wish I'd made a career out of the sea myself, though my view of it is maybe just a romantic one.'

Kirsteen could hear Alick talking with Mary in Shona's room as they prepared themselves for going out. Everyone was looking forward to the evening ahead. Part of Kirsteen didn't want to go: she wanted to stay behind and wait to see if Grant would come home; also – if she were here in the room when Fergus came in to get ready, they could perhaps at last make things up with no one but themselves in the house.

Absently she pulled a comb through her shining hair and almost without thinking went to open the door of the wardrobe to touch the wrappings on the fur jacket, wondering if she should wear it or if it was perhaps too grand for a village ceilidh . . . No – it wasn't just any ceilidh, this was a momentous night for little Merry Mary and it was only right that everyone should turn up looking their best. She took down the jacket and wrapped herself in its warm luxury. The fur collar nestled against her cheeks, she wished Fergus were with her to give her his approval, but they were still worlds apart, speaking without really communicating, and every night they went their separate ways to bed. It was such a strange situation. Kirsteen knew that it had to end, but at the same time she wondered just how long such a ridiculous state of affairs could go on. She buried her face into the collar of the jacket. Oh God! She missed him so: cuddled next to her in bed, talking over the events of each day, laughing over the little intimacies that only they shared . . .

The door burst open and Shona came in, her glorious mane of hair framing her sparkling face, the collar of her fur jacket pulled up cosily over her ears. 'Kirsteen, aren't you ready yet?' she chided. 'Lachlan's outside waiting with the car and Biddy's grumbling about the smell of it. She says she would rather have the smell of a horse's bum in front of her nose. You've to come with us though you'll be squeezed against Biddy. I'll have to sit on Niall's knee. The Johnstons are taking the twins and Mary and Alick –' She stopped in her outburst and her blue eyes shone. 'Oh, you're wearing your jacket, too! I brought mine hoping for a chance to wear it, but thinking it was a bit too showy for tonight. I'm looking forward to Merry Mary's ceilidh. Janet is looking after Ellie so I can stay out as long as I want. Isn't Father coming?'

'He'll be along later, he's securing things in the sheds.'

'You're still not talking, are you?' Shona sounded accusing.

'No-o.'

'I thought so.' Shona's face was serious as she faced Kirsteen. 'Now listen to me, Kirsteen. Niall and me only have a day or two left of our holiday, and before I go I want to see you and that stubborn father of mine on speaking terms. You're behaving like a couple of bairns, so you are! You both need a good skelping – and – and the cheek of you going all motherly on me and giving me advice about Niall a few years back. I haven't forgotten, in case you think it. You ought to be ashamed, the pair of you. Promise me you'll make it up tonight.'

Kirsteen's eyes sparkled suddenly. 'Yes, Grannie, I promise,' she said and giggled.

Little black specks were scurrying along the harbour, bending into a wind that was lashing the sea into white-veined rollers that churned round the reefs of Port Rum Point before throwing themselves violently against the Sgor Creags to roar and curl into the air in creamy plumes forty feet high. The fierce blasts of the sou'westerly shrieked low over the water, pushing the sea into the mouth of the harbour so that even in this normally sheltered anchorage, there was a violence in the waves lashing over the walls. The tops of the waves were being hurled onto the road, spattering over the hurrying figures making for the hall, but everyone was in a cheery mood and the stinging drops only made them shriek with surprise and scuttle along faster before another onslaught caught them out.

The village hall was no more than a converted barn, the term converted relating only to the addition of a new floor, some windows, and a mobile platform, a simple framework structure laid over with stout wooden planks. The hayloft still remained, much to the delight of courting couples who made full use of it when amorous feelings got the better of the desire to sing and dance.

Jon had spent a good part of the day helping the languid menfolk of the village to prepare the hall during the course of which there had been more discussion and banter than actual work, but with much tactful persuasion the young German had succeeded in accomplishing the task, and the hall looked splendid. It was hung with coloured lanterns and paper festoons, which, though made from newspaper strips coated with various hues of distemper, still looked very impressive – though here and there an odd item of news popped out.

Canty Tam, who revelled in gory details, leered at them and announced, 'I can see the headlines about thon murder where the mannie chopped his wife in wee pieces and fed her to the dog.' He leaned so far sideways in order to devour the exposed newsprint that he fell into a pile of chairs ably aided by Robbie, who clipped him on the ear for good measure.

Bundles of net floats hung round the platform together with bunches of balloons, and at the front was stretched a red banner on which Ranald had splashed in whitewash, A MERRY FAREWELL TO MERRY MARY. HASTE YE BACK.

'Here, what way are you putting that?' Tam asked with a derisive snort of mirth. 'The wifie is no' goin' anywhere; she's just givin' up the shop.'

But Ranald remained unruffled. 'Ach, it sounds fine, it's a poetic way o' sayin' things – though of course you wouldny know much about poetry. I read a lot and know fine there's more ways o' sayin' the obvious than just sayin' what is obvious.'

'Ay well, if that's what poetry does to the brain I'll stick to things that makes sense,' the grinning Tam returned.

But the crowd that poured into the hall that evening did not see the little flaws in the decor, and nods of appreciation followed the first swift appraisals. Merry Mary blushed with pleasure when she saw the efforts on her behalf and was amazed at the sight of the swelling ranks, but everyone who knew and loved the little Englishwoman with her limp ginger hair and big happy smile, was determined to give her a rousing send-off. She had served behind the counter of the village general store for more than fifty years, and as some of the older ones put it, 'was more native than the natives'. During her fifty years of service she had thoroughly enjoyed gathering and dispensing gossip, but had never done it in a malicious manner. For every bad word she had to say about anyone she had a dozen good ones to compensate, and everyone knew they would sorely miss the cheery smile they had grown so used to seeing whenever the bell tinkled above her door.

Merry Mary was radiant that evening despite a dress patterned with livid orange and purple flowers and, when Scott Balfour, resplendent in kilt and tweed jacket, came in accompanied by his attractive wife, Rena, a murmur went round the room. 'The Laird himself – Merry Mary is indeed honoured. He'll be here to make the presentations later.'

Elspeth, who herself had caused quite a stir appearing in a black dress with white ruffles at the throat and wrists, her grey hair attractively arranged round her gaunt face, her thin lips bearing a discreet smudge of lipstick, whispered to Merry Mary, 'It is a popular woman you are indeed, Merry Mary. I doubt there's naught but a handful here would turn up to see me off – no, not even for my own funeral.'

'Ach, I'll come anyway, Elspeth, never you fear,' the little Englishwoman said kindly. 'But it is talking of funerals you are and you lookin' so grand you might be goin' to your own wedding. Your hair is a treat, that it is.'

Elspeth blushed in confused appreciation of the compliment, but she said off-handedly, 'Ach, that rascal Fiona bullied me into letting her do it – she's a modern miss if ever there was one, though I'm glad to see she is no' wearin' the trowser tonight. I'm thinkin', though, that she's overdone things wi' my person, for I was never a one for fancy ways. But och, it's no' every day I get the chance to see one o' my friends off in style – mainly because there's precious few bodies I can call my friends,' she sniffed. 'I canny help but think o' Mirabelle betimes. She would aye listen to my troubles whether she felt like it or no.'

Merry Mary patted her scrawny arm. 'Well, you know you're always welcome at my cottage for a crack and a cuppy and you can bring me a bit o' gossip for I'll no' be gettin' so much of that now.'

Anton, looking exceedingly handsome with his fair hair brushed back and his blue eyes shining, approached and with a little click of his heels he first kissed Merry Mary's hand and then turned to Elspeth and made a similar gesture. 'Ladies, may I say how charming you look tonight and I am hoping that you will do me the honour of dancing with me later.' He looked Elspeth straight in the eye and she hastily composed her features into stern lines as he went on in his charming broken English: 'Frau Elspeth, I have never forgotten your kindness to me when I was ill and how you put the strength back in my "feets" with your home-made tablet. And though I don't see you often, I think of you and the times you came up to my room and fed me the Benger's Food – so tonight we will do the Highland Fling together, eh?'

'Ach, get away wi' you, your tongue is smoother than silk,' scolded Elspeth, acutely aware of Merry Mary's smile, though she was secretly thrilled at having been singled out by the young German for whom she had a soft spot (though never for one moment would she let the fact be known).

Anton turned away and Merry Mary nodded meaningfully and said, 'So, you were up in his room thon
time he was laid up and near dyin' – and all the time
you were puttin' it about you had no time at all for
Jerries. Well, well, 'tis learnin' we are all the time,
but –' she said, her eyes twinkling while Elspeth
snorted, 'don't worry, Elspeth; I will no' be tellin' a
soul about you and your wee secret sojourns in Mr
Büttger's sickroom.'

'You are a silly woman, Merry Mary!' Elspeth blustered. 'That was years ago, and anyways, I have no
intention of discussing it with you or anyone else.'
She stomped away in high dudgeon.

Babbie watched her retreat and her green eyes positively danced. Grabbing her husband's arm, she
smothered her giggles into his sleeve and hissed, 'You
impudent young bugger, Mr Büttger! That was positively brazen. I've always known you had a certain
charm, but that was bare-faced and calculated.'

Anton was unrepentant. 'Nonsense, liebling, I have
made the night for a lonely old lady and I have also
given Mistress Beag something to talk about – see
how she scowls thunder at me.'

He was right. Behag had witnessed the exchanges
and her jowls sagged over her neck as she told Kate,
'Hmph, did you see that? These two lettin' a German
kiss them – ay, that Elspeth never did fool me. She
is smoulderin' wi' passion under that sour face o'
hers and of course, wi' her bein' a widow woman
things will be worse for her – what I mean is, a pure

body like myself has no knowledge of the lusts o' the flesh and has no need to hanker after them.'

'Ay, right enough,' Kate said, nodding in mock sympathy. 'Though wi' all that enchantment you hide so well 'tis a miracle you escaped intact.'

Behag affected not to notice the sarcasm and gazed round the crowded hall. 'A fine turnout I must say. I wonder will I get the same when I retire. I've missed hardly a day behind the counter o' the Post Office and I am a native of the island, after all – Merry Mary is just an incomer.'

'You'll maybe get a send-off you never bargained for,' Kate said, and dimpled. 'Right off that damty island if you don't learn to smile a bit more instead o' grumpin' your head off. Folks only get what they deserve in this life, and if you go on moanin' like an old hag you'll get no more than a box o' matches and a rocket when your time comes.'

'My, my, but you're a spiteful woman, Kate McKinnon,' Behag blustered and flounced away to seek out her brother Robbie on whom she continually vented her wrath.

Jon had been passing the time with the Rev. John Gray who had been delighted at the young German's return to the island and had given him a very cordial welcome. Everyone had been glad to see Jon and his popularity was proven when he had affectionately been bestowed with the nickname 'Jock'. The men didn't resent his intrusion into the life of the village – rather, they were glad to off-load the responsibility of organising Merry Mary's ceilidh onto his willing shoulders, and when he climbed onto the platform to arrange the children into their places, a cheer went up and cries of 'Good old Jock!' went round the room.

Jon had already taught Rachel much of the deaf and dumb language and the two now carried on an animated conversation with their hands. Annie felt a rush of pride as she beheld her raven-haired daughter on the platform. She wished Dokie Joe was here to see his beautiful, clever child. His weather-beaten face would have given little away, but Annie knew that while he was too slow to keep up with Rachel's mercurial brain, he was nevertheless so proud of her that often, when he'd had a bit too much to drink, he boasted about her to his mates. Annie sighed. She often wished that her husband didn't have to make his living from the sea. Forbye being a financially uncertain existence, it was a lonely one for her with him being away for days on end. He should have been due in with the smacks tonight but there was little hope of that with the storm blowing up.

Torquil Andrew, a tall strapping man with Norse colouring and looks that set female hearts fluttering, came up to Annie. 'I'll be keeping you company tonight, Annie,' he stated softly.

Her dark eyes glittered. 'Ay,' was all she said, and her thoughts turned away from the cold dark wastes of the sea and back to the pleasant realities contained within the big, softly lit barn.

Lewis saw Torquil's hand briefly touching Annie's

and he thought about the time he had chanced upon them standing very close together in an abandoned fuel shed – too close – the kind of nearness that made grown men tremble and caused women to make funny little sighing noises. The ruffled Annie had jumped away from Torquil like a scalded cat and had hissed at Lewis, 'Never you be tellin' a soul about this, Lewis McKenzie! Do you hear?' Until the tirade, Lewis in his youth and innocence had not realised there was anything for him to tell, but at Annie's words he had sensed there was an opportunity going to make a little money. 'Not if you give me sixpence every week till the day you die,' he had told Annie with a smile, and though she had raged at him, she had from that day paid him silence money.

Lewis smiled to himself and drew his bow over his fiddle with a gay little flip. He loved crowds. He enjoyed gaining their attention, and he liked to be liked; but if the occasion demanded otherwise, that was the way of life and he accepted the good with the bad, without fuss.

Lorn was nervous and sat quietly beside old Bob, who was helping him to tune his fiddle. His heart was beating rapidly and he tried to will himself into a state of tranquillity. From the side of his eye he saw Ruth sitting in a corner in the darkest recess on the other side of the platform. Although her mother had made her a new dress it had certainly been created by the hands of an inexpert seamstress. It was shapeless and ill-fitting and made Ruth look more ungainly than ever. She was sitting very still, her hands folded serenely in her lap, but her violet eyes were huge with unease, and Lorn knew she was, like him, uncertain of herself, terrified of crowds. The sight of her made him feel more uncomfortable than ever, and he turned his head and looked up, catching his mother's eye. He smiled, a radiant smile that belied his racing pulse, and Kirsteen smiled back though she sensed his fears, and her heart twisted with the knowing that soon he could be facing hazards and pain that might prove too much for his sensitive spirit to bear. But the love of life was in his eyes: it leapt out like a living thing and she knew deep inside herself that he would bravely face anything the future might hold for him.

Old Mo was being lifted in his pram up onto the platform while his fellow tinkers were making good use of the opportunity to sell sprigs of dried white heather to the assembly. A smiling damsel, looking extremely pretty despite the fact that she was wearing dirty white sandshoes beneath a tartan dress, followed old Mo onto the platform and accosted Bob.

'Ach, get away wi' you, lass!' he told her irritably. 'We can get any amount o' that ourselves on the moors. It's the towrists you should be takin' in wi' your fancy talk, no' the folk who live wi' the damty stuff!'

'Ah, but you weren't thinkin' to be bringin' any with you,' returned the girl quick as a flash. 'Is it too mean you are to be buyin' a bit o' good luck for the old lass who has served you well all these long years?'

'You make her sound like a bloody cow,' grumbled Bob, but nevertheless he dug in his pocket for his coppers. Those standing nearby followed suit because the tinker girl was renowned for putting vicious curses on those unwise enough to reject her wares.

Up until then the majority of the gathering had consisted mainly of womenfolk but now the men, having fortified themselves in the Portcull Hotel, breezed in, merry and windblown, bringing with them the usual whisky fumes, though on this occasion the strong palpable smell of mothballs overpowered all else. Everyone wrinkled their noses though it was naturally assumed that the odour was just a stronger version of that which was experienced every Sabbath in kirk when Sunday best was brought out from wardrobes perpetually tainted by naphthalene. But there was another reason for the smell and it arrived when Dodie catapulted into the room, his aversion to social gatherings having been overcome by his desire to witness Merry Mary's official retirement. His entry caused all heads to turn and all murmurings to cease because, except for one other memorable ceilidh at Laigmhor, no one had ever seen the old eccentric so well turned out.

Although he still wore his greasy cloth cap, he was otherwise attired in a thin but well cut sports jacket with vented sides; his grey flannel trousers were immaculate, his white shirt spotless. He was obviously stunned with embarrassment at the sensation he was causing, and he stood red-faced, enveloped in mothball fumes, his lips stretched nervously in an attempted smile. The Laird, though startled, turned discreetly away, having noticed that Dodie's stout brogues were the very pair he had thrown into the dustbin some time ago and Rena whispered to him, 'Poor dear old Dodie, he wouldn't have taken them if I had offered them to him.'

'Mercy on us,' muttered a round-eyed Isabel. 'Would you look at that, Jim Jim. I'm thinkin' old Dodie has maybe come into some money.'

'Ay, ay, it's only towrists and gentry wear clothes like these,' said Jim Jim thoughtfully. 'But I'm thinkin' there's something gey queer goin' on, for he's reekin' o' mothballs like these other chiels that have just come in.'

Morag Ruadh tossed her red head and her lips tightened. Memories were stirring fires in her she had thought buried, invoked by the sound of Erchy and Todd tuning the pipes, a procedure that entailed much puffing and blowing in order to produce squeaks and groans and several other sounds that bordered on the unseemly. Morag felt a pang of excitement, which in turn made her feel uneasy. She had not had such feelings since that other night of the Manse ceilidh – a night she didn't want to remember. She had only put in an appearance tonight because Dugald was having the shop handed over and he had insisted that Morag be there. 'We are members of this community now, Morag,' he had told her quietly enough, though determination had edged his tones to sharpness. 'As my wife you will

accompany me to this function and you will bring
Ruthie. See she has a new dress, by the way. I will
not have my daughter looking like a sack of potatoes
in front of everyone, particularly the bairnies who
will be her schoolmates after Easter is over.'

The fiddlers were practising now and the strains of
a Strathspey filled the air. Morag's blood pulsed and
she tried not to think of the minister's words to her
recently. 'You must stop using the Lord as a vessel
for guilt, Morag,' he had told her sternly. 'You can
only be absolved if you treat God as a friend, not
some sort of enemy who spits fire and vengeance. If
you think like that, you are worshipping the Devil,
and the Lord himself will have difficulty finding a
door in your heart.' Morag glanced balefully at the
Rev. John Gray standing at the foot of the platform
talking animatedly to Jon Jodl; his hair was now
silvery-white, his face full of a serenity that the last
few years had brought him; contentment cloaked
him like a mantle.

Anger swamped Morag. What gave him the right
to be so smug and self-righteous? It had taken him
long enough to come to terms with the islanders and
in so doing coming to terms with God. His contentment had sprung from the night of the Manse ceilidh,
while hers had been robbed from her – it was all Mr
Gray's fault, really. She wasn't to blame, yet every
waking day was a punishment for her.

'Here now, man, where are you gettin' things like
these?' asked round-faced Robbie of the abashed
Dodie. 'These is towrists' clothes.'

'Ay, and that shirt?' put in Tam, gazing round at a display of shirts the same as Dodie's, both in quality and naphthalene saturation.

'Did you get them from that mannie who's been goin' round the island sellin' things out o' suitcases?' enquired Torquil Andrew, whose deep chest strained against the fine material of his own shirt.

Dodie nodded eagerly and his carbuncle wobbled. 'Ay, that's right enough. He came by my door a day or two back.'

Ranald eyed Dodie's jacket and trousers. 'But these things cost a lot of money. Have you won the pools, Dodie?'

Dodie glowered at the money-conscious Ranald. 'Indeed no. I am not a one to gallop my money away on such things,' he said primly.

'But what you get in your towrist tin wouldny even pay for that bonny tie you're wearin',' Ranald persisted.

But Dodie wouldn't be drawn. He was not going to give away the secret he had kept since the *Politician* had been doomed on the rocks in Eriskay Sound. On one of his frequent beachcombing sojourns he had chanced upon a treasure trove of shirts floating in with the tide like disembodied ghosts. He had collected more than five dozen of them, and, stuffing them into his peat creel, he had hastened home to wash them in the purling burn near his cottage. With the sea water out of them, and the sun and wind endowing them with a dazzling whiteness, Dodie had felt rich indeed and had visualised the look on the faces of those who would receive the gifts. But news of the police and Customs searching the islands for contraband had reached his ears and in a panic he had stowed the garments away in an ancient bride's kist, together with a generous amount of mothballs. He had almost forgotten his treasure chest till the persistent rapping on his door had heralded a visit from a travelling salesman burdened down with cases which, despite Dodie's protests, he had opened to reveal garments the likes of which the old eccentric had only seen on the backs of the gentry. The salesman hadn't appeared to hear Dodie's refusals to buy nor had he seemed to believe that he was poorer than a kirk mouse just. Perhaps tales of country folk owning treasures they believed to be worthless had reached the salesman's ears, for he had craned his neck and gazed past Dodie to the dim interior of the house. 'Surely we can do a deal,' he had purred coaxingly. 'You look as though you could be doing with some new clothes. You must have some sort of valuables lying about gathering dust.'

'I tell you, I haveny anything, only my shells and stones fro the seashore,' Dodie had wailed and was about to shut the door when he remembered the shirts. 'Wait you here,' he had instructed, and closing the door in the man's face, he had plodded up the passage to the kist in the bedroom. The shirts were as perfect as the day he had packed them away and he had presented the naphthalene-smelling bundles to the salesman, who, holding his breath, had flipped through them quickly, almost immediately recognising their quality, though he had said off-handedly, 'From the guff off them they must have been lying about for years. I'll give you three pounds for the lot.'

'Indeed you will no'. These is good shirts, and if you can't be doin' better than that I'll just be havin' them back.' But the man had quickly evaded Dodie's outstretched hands and for the next half hour the pair had bartered till in the end the exasperated salesman, realising that the old eccentric wasn't as simple as he had first imagined, had handed over a complete rig-out in exchange for the shirts. 'And I'll be keepin' one o' these to wear wi' my jacket,' Dodie had smirked, snatching a shirt back from the pile.

'No flies on you, old boy,' the man had said, grinning, and went off jauntily to make a good profit selling the shirts at croft and cottage, his smooth tongue gliding out explanations for the naphthalene odour.

Thus it was that the men, each believing they had secured a bargain, turned up at the ceilidh wearing identical shirts, and for once in his life Dodie felt like laughing himself into a fit as fishermen and farmers, crofters and shepherds, eyed one another in some discomfort.

Dodie galloped away from the scene to seek out Merry Mary to whom he presented a bottle of spray perfume. 'It's just a wee thing,' he told her with a gloomy smile. 'I know leddies need scent to make them smell nice.' From anyone else this would have been the ultimate insult, but from guileless Dodie it was a compliment, and Merry Mary accepted the gift with due appreciation, time dulling her memory to the fact that the spray bottle was identical to those given up by the *Politician* years before. Dodie had a tidy supply of the bottles which he kept for 'special leddies'.

Despite the fiercely competing aromas of whisky, naphthalene, and perfume, the evening was proving to be an unprecedented success. Outside the wind howled and the hail rattled against the windows but everyone inside gave themselves up to the gay tunes of pipes, accordions, and fiddles. Jon was in his element. He itched to play old Mo's violin, a beautiful creation of gold with deeper undertones of rich dark red. The old man obviously cherished the instrument, because it was in perfect condition. He looked rather worried by Jon's request to play a solo on it, but with a nod of consent he allowed the young German to pick it up. Jon was enthralled. He knew at once that this was no ordinary violin and as he guided the bow and touched the strings with his long intelligent fingers, evoking sounds hauntingly human yet that might have been the language of spirits, Jon knew that he held in his arms an instrument that could easily be 250 years old, probably a Cremonese, created by a great craftsman of northern Italy. Jon had seen a similar one owned by a well-known musician, but no two violins were alike; each had its own distinctive appearance and unique tone of voice. Jon closed his eyes and gave himself up to the ecstasy of being privileged enough to actually handle such a violin.

The minister was enthralled. Leaning his silvery thatch against the wall he closed his eyes, hugged one knee and breathed deeply. 'The boy is brilliant,' he murmured to his wife, Hannah. 'Ah, he makes me feel I am soaring on the wings of angels. What control, what sensitivity – and the tone of that violin – perfection.'

Rachel, too, was lost in enchanted admiration for the young man who had been so patient with her and taught her so much during the short time he had been on the island. Her eyes were dark with rapture as she watched his masterful fingers, listened to the notes spilling powerfully and evocatively, touching chords in her soul that pushed tears of pure joy from her eyes.

The last notes died away and the applause shook the rafters. Jon handed the violin back to old Mo. 'Thank you for letting me play it. It was a wonderful experience.'

The old man nodded and tucked his precious violin in at his side as if it were a baby. Jon realised he probably knew nothing of its value. An instrument like that could fetch a vast sum of money, but Jon wasn't going to tell old Mo that because he knew by doing so he would take away the only thing left to the old man, the deep contentment and joy he experienced every time he picked up his violin. He cherished it for that and to violate anyone's contentment would have been to Jon a sin. If the other tinkers found out its worth they would sell it, the money would be frittered away on useless modern trivia, and old Mo, already saturated in liquor, would just drink himself to death very speedily, his life joyless without his fiddle. At the moment he was quite happy; the violin brought him happiness as well as a fairly good profit and that, to Jon, was that, though as he parted with the instrument he felt that he was parting with a tiny part of his soul, for what musician would not yearn to own such a treasure as that owned by the old tinker.

The hall was now very warm and Phebie flopped beside Kirsteen on a bench to fan her face, laughing at the sight of Niall and Shona dancing a jig while everyone else did an eightsome reel. Fiona was a sparkling-eyed nymph in a pretty red dress, her long legs carrying her with ease over the floor. Captain Mac and his crew were present that night, having arrived into port before the full fury of the storm got under way, and Fiona wasn't short of partners.

'Thank the Lord she discarded her trousers in favour of a dress,' said Phebie. 'The besom wasn't going to, you know. She was all for coming in the trowser just to see the effect it would have on the cailleachs, but for once Lachy put his foot down and told her she could stay at home if she insisted on looking like a laddie.'

Biddy, who was comfortably ensconced nearby, sipping at a glass of rum, smiled sourly, showing her 'teeths', which she had remembered to wear for the occasion. 'Ach, you should leave the lass alone,' she scolded mildly. 'The bairnie has the right idea I'm tellin' you. Skirts are just a temptation to a man, but the trowser makes it easier for a lass to keep a finger on her halfpenny – and they must be cosy too. If I wasny such a cailleach, I'd wear them myself. They'd be fine for keeping out the wind when I'm on my bike.'

Phebie's eyes twinkled. 'Surely you aren't needing protection from men at your age, Biddy.'

'Ach, you daft lassie,' Biddy said, her old eyes crinkling. 'It's more like them needin' protection from the sight o' my auld legs. That bugger Todd told me the other day I looked like a bowly-legged hen wi' the gout – an' him wi' the most godforsaken knees I've ever clapped eyes on! Would you look at him up on that stage, wearin' the kilt and smilin' like he was proud o' knees like cow's knuckles.'

Todd was beyond caring about his knees or any other part of his anatomy. He and his cronies had made frequent trips outside where several bottles of whisky had been buried earlier. Bedraggled by rain and wind the men were now in stages ranging from merry to hilarious and turned deaf ears on nagging spouses. Old Mo, too, had quite a few bottles hidden in his pram and he, together with old Bob and Andrew, was decidedly under the influence. Even Jon was looking slightly flushed, and Anton murmured in Babbie's ear, 'I suspect our friend has had a drop of Tinker's Brew. His fingers are moving so fast, it's taking me all my time to keep up. I think we will go and sit by Frau Kirsteen – McKenzie is taking his time in turning up.'

Kirsteen was glad of their company. She had taken

part in one dance after another but still she felt lonely, waiting for the one person without whom her life seemed empty. The door opened and she couldn't keep the expectancy out of her eyes, but it wasn't Fergus and her face flamed.

Anton and Babbie both sensed her loneliness and the latter said with a laugh, 'Dance with Anton, will you, Kirsteen? He's got far too much energy for a tired old nurse like me.'

Anton was panting for breath but gallantly extended his arm. 'I would be honoured, Frau Kirsteen. You have grace, and I have a feeling you will not tread on my toes like my Babbie – her "feets" are growing more like Biddy's every day.'

Amidst skirls of laughter he whirled Kirsteen away and Babbie said to Shona, 'You know, if it was any of my business I'd give your father a good talking to, keeping Kirsteen waiting for him like this. He could easily have left the sheds to Matthew and Donald. It isn't often Kirsteen gets a night out. It will serve him right if, when he does arrive, she gives him the cold shoulder. He deserves it.'

Shona didn't say anything because Babbie had just voiced her own sentiments. Shona's deep blue eyes flashed. She thought of her own marriage with Niall. There had been a lot of rough patches but they were far outweighed by the smooth. Niall was an easy and wonderful person to live with, though often he had his hands full trying to deal with the frequent temper tantrums she threw. Shona sighed. Life would never be easy for someone living with a McKenzie, and she realised how lucky she was to have Niall and how fortunate her father was to have Kirsteen.

Alick shivered a little as he stood in the shelter of the porch where he had come to puff his pipe and get a breath of air – and to wait for Fergus. The wind tore in from the Sound, bringing blasts of salt-tainted rain in its freezing breath. Through the darkness Alick saw the sea, tossing and heaving, a white swirl of rollers that boomed and crashed into the harbour where they lost some power but were still vicious enough to heave themselves over the road and plosh against the sturdy walls of the cottages, some of the droplets showering Alick as he stood watching, awed and fascinated by the might of the elements. Voices floated and he stiffened – one of them belonged to Fergus. Matthew and his son, Donald, now a tall, fine-featured young man, went past Alick into the hall but Alick intercepted his brother with the accusing words, 'So, you've finally made it. What did you have to do? Re-build the dairy?'

Fergus was immediately on the defensive, his misery over his row with Kirsteen having resulted in a slow build-up of wrath against Alick. 'Just supposing I was! If I had to rely on you for help the damned place would be around my ears by now!'

'Oh, c'mon, big brother, Matthew and Donald would have managed fine between them,' Alick's voice was cool and controlled. 'Why don't you come right out and admit you were playing for time? Piling the punishment onto Kirsteen, making her suffer just a little bit more, nursing your grievances like a bloody baby! Well, sulking bairns don't make men big or turn them into all-conquering heroes . . .'

'You've a damned nerve!' exploded Fergus. 'Mind your own bloody business and get out of my way or you'll be sorry you interfered. I don't intend to get soaked to the skin while I stand here listening to you whining.'

'Me, whining? Well at least I say what's in my mind instead of putting the cork in and letting my grievances fester away like rotting sores! You'd better watch out, Fergus, don't push Kirsteen too far. If you think she's in there moping you've another think coming. She's a lovely and rather special lady, the men are queuing up to dance with her. One of these days you'll waken out of your petty little stupor and find she's not so willing to come running back at your high and mighty command – there's other fish in the sea you know.'

'Ay, and by God, wouldn't you like to be one of them!' cried Fergus harshly. 'We've already had a taste of you and your ill-controlled lust! It's strange how you invite trouble, from the day you walked, you lunged from one buggering mess into another. It's because of you we're in the damned state we're in now – but of course,' he said, laughing mirthlessly, 'you must know that already! It seems you and Kirsteen have been chatting cosily behind my back.'

'Too bloody true, but hardly cosily! That day of the picnic – when you were fawning over my wife

– your own was so flaming miserable I made her tell me what was wrong. By Christ! What she had to say made me feel uneasy all right. It all came back, all the things I tried to forget but never quite managed.'

A blast of wind hurled Fergus against Alick. The rain whirled and lashed about them, they were so close each could feel the other's heavy breath; in the darkness the brothers glared at each other, the pale blurring blobs of their faces only inches apart. Fergus felt dark bubbling rage overwhelming him. The truth of Alick's words had hit him like a sledgehammer, then, suddenly, Alick's fist shot out to land Fergus a blow on the face that sent him reeling backwards, away from the shelter of the porch, into the wind and the sleety rain that stung his eyes, blinding him for a minute. But Fergus's reactions were only momentarily suspended. Springing forward he caught Alick by the collars of his jacket and hauled him round the side of the building. The raging of a nearby burn was as nothing to the all-consuming rage that sped through his veins, charging him with a power that rendered the slightly-built Alick help-less. With a snarl Fergus pushed his brother into a rickety hayshed and threw him against the piled-up bales of hay. Then Fergus advanced, his black eyes throwing sparks in his deathly white face. 'You asked for this, little brother,' he gritted, and his knuckle of bunched steel smashed into flesh and bone.

Alick shook his head to clear it but he didn't cower

away as he might have done in days gone by. Fear
ripped through him but instead of making him
submissive it bolstered him into action. Dancing to
the middle of the floor he faced the towering mass
of bone and muscle that was his brother. 'Right,' he
said quietly, 'all's fair in love and war, so the
misguided saying goes. And with that in mind we'll
do this fairly.' Tucking his left arm behind his back
he went on tauntingly, 'I was the cause of you losing
your arm, as you've just reminded me – and I
wouldn't like to have an unfair advantage over a one-
armed hero – so – come and get me.'

The soft light from the hall windows filtered in
through the door of the shed allowing Fergus to see
the dim figure of his brother standing watching him
mockingly. In a blind fury Fergus lunged, but Alick
intercepted the blow with an upward toss of his hand
and before Fergus could regain his balance he was
catapulted across the shed by an expertly-placed
punch, which made his head spin. Surprise lowered
Fergus's defences and he wasn't prepared for the
next crack that sent him sprawling among the hay
bales. Rage boiled in his blood, but as well as anger
there was something else, something that reached
down, plucking at the churning cauldron of his
emotions: this was his brother fighting him, the one-
time blubbering, apron-tied boy for whom he had
fought endless battles, who was now fighting back –
at last he was fighting back. Briefly, Fergus
wondered when the change had come about.
Certainly Alick had seemed different after the hellish

nightmare all these years ago: the man in him had begun to creep out. But this – when had this happened? With little physique behind him, he was holding his own, winning by tactics that made Fergus look blundering and inexpert. Admiration flooded Fergus's being even as he went into the fray with his brother. They sparred, punched, hurt each other, while outside the wind howled, and the music spilled from the hall. Then, almost simultaneously they called a truce and collapsed onto the hay, panting, half-laughing, half-ashamed, wordlessly gathering breath from heaving lungs. Alick took out his hanky and dabbed a split lip tenderly before he said apologetically, 'We're even now for those years ago when you beat the hell out of me and I went scampering away with my cowardly tail between my legs.' He took a deep breath and in the darkness he smiled though it made him wince. 'God! I feel hellish – I'll ache for days – yet, I've never felt better in my life! We've never spoken about things – just locked it all away, now I feel I've crawled out of my hole to see daylight for the first time in years – and – it's a bloody marvellous experience, if you see what I mean?'

Fergus gulped a lungful of air. 'I know what you mean all right – what I don't see is how – how –'

'How I learned to use my fists? The Army taught me a few tricks, Fergus. I took up boxing for a giggle – well, I was always one for a giggle, as fine you know. But I became quite good at it – so much so I earned myself a bit of respect from the other lads. A good feeling that – to be respected – to feel self-respect.'

'You kept it dark enough.'

'Saw no point in boasting – I did too much of that in my time and found I kept getting smaller instead of bigger . . . Anyway, tonight you dug up my well-kept secret.' He passed Fergus a cigarette and they sat on the hay bale puffing companionably for a few silent moments then Alick said deliberately, 'I just had to get a poke at you back there. You're so bloody stubborn, you'd never have listened to me otherwise. You feel pretty peeved because Kirsteen threw me in your face – right? Do you know why she said the things she did? It was a kind of chain reaction. She was terrified the twins were going to turn out like you and me – one being made to lean, the other to be leaned on – history repeating itself, if you like.'

'Hell no! I never saw it like that,' Fergus groaned.

'Neither did Mother, but sometimes love can be blind and very blinding.'

Fergus gripped his brother's arm roughly. 'Thanks – for helping me to see,' he said awkwardly.

Alick laughed. 'Think nothing of it, big brother. I owe you some favours – and now, it's time you and Kirsteen got down to brass tacks and decide what you're going to do about Lorn's future. Oh, don't start! I got it out of Kirsteen yesterday. She's beside herself with worry and had to tell someone.'

'Ay, no doubt.' Fergus stood up. 'I think – we'd better show our faces at the ceilidh,' he said sheepishly.

'Do you think they're worth showing?' chuckled Alick. 'I feel as if an elephant has pushed me into a door. Here – take my hanky and clean yourself up a bit.'

'I suppose we could always say we just bumped into each other.' Fergus's deep laugh boomed out, and with arms thrown around each other's shoulders, the brothers went to join the ceilidh in a jubilant mood and were able to slip into the softly lit hall virtually unnoticed. Everyone was intent on enjoying themselves. Bruised faces and cut lips weren't uncommon at the height of a good ceilidh. Tam and one or two of his cronies had already come to good-natured blows over the location and owner-ship of the hidden whisky, and they were now ensconced in a corner re-creating the scuffles with avid enjoyment.

Across the crowded room Kirsteen's blue eyes met Fergus's dark gaze. Although she was apart from him she saw the hungry yearning in the burning glance he threw at her. Her heart skipped a beat, her cheeks reddened. The notes from Jon's fiddle poured into her and made her tremble. It was as if she was hearing the music for the first time since the start of the ceilidh. Warmth flooded her being. It was going to be a perfect evening, nothing could go wrong now – now that she had interpreted the messages of love, desire – forgiveness – flowing out of the beautiful black eyes of the man she loved with such intensity it was an ache in her heart.

Chapter Nine

Out on the Sound of Rhanna lightning forked into
the wind-crazed surface of the water. All day long the
smacks had battled against the raging seas and the
men were haggard with exhaustion. They had left
Mallaig early, when the sky had given no hint of the
brewing fury sweeping with insidious speed from
the south-west. The sea had been calm, deceptively
so, and it had remained like silk till the menacing
banks of purple-black cloud had started rolling over
the sky, blotting out the gold and the blue, spurring
the waves to restlessness. By the time the men had
realised a storm was in the offing, they were far out
in the Atlantic and it was too late to turn back.
Howling winds attacked the small boats, pushing
them through endless successions of deep troughs.
Smatterings of hail and snow whirled and eddied,
blotting out the horizon, confining visibility to a few
yards. The *Magpie* rolled and pitched and Grant staggered up from the fo'c'sle, feeling too sick to join the
rest of the crew in the hearty meal of bacon, eggs
and beans the cook had just prepared. He had
managed to gulp down some hot black tea sweetened with condensed milk, but even that lay heavy
in a belly delicate from a heavy bout of drinking the

night before. He had matched dram for dram to keep up with the rest of the men, but now he told himself it was the last time – he wasn't a man yet and no amount of hard liquor would ever make him one.

The mate was at the wheel and he threw Grant an amused smile as the boy brushed past him and out of the wheelhouse. The wind caught and bullied him, spicules of ice froze his lips to numbness and he gasped for air. His belly heaved and he was catapulted across the sopping deck to be hurled against the rails with such force he felt as if he had been punched by a giant hand. He retched and his vomit was thrown back at him by the wind, making him shiver in disgust and recall vividly but too late Skipper Joe's warning, 'Never spew into the wind, she'll just throw it back at you like confetti.' Grant coughed and spluttered. He had thought he knew it all, but every fresh trip out at sea warned him he was a mere novice . . . A vision of his mother flashed into his swimming head. Thank God she couldn't see him now – grey, splattered with vomit – his father wouldn't much like the sight of him either. Fergus was a man who could hold a good dram. Vaguely Grant wondered if such a man had ever been foolish, had ever taken too much to drink – been sick with it . . .

A thirty-foot wall of water crashed over the stern, sucking it down into a trough as deep as a ravine. For a heart-stopping eternity Grant choked in a watery world, his knuckles white as his hands clamped round the rail like a vice. Gasping for air

Grant slithered down the slanting deck – straight into the arms of Dokie Joe, whose tight black curls and grey-flecked black beard made him look older than his thirty-five years.

Dokie's eyes were narrowed to slits in his sea-drenched face as he glared into Grant's salt-reddened eyes. 'What the hell do you think this is?' he yelled above the wind. 'A bloody joy ride? Get into the wheelhouse and give Dan a hand. I'll be back in a minute.'

'Ay, ay, Skipper!' shouted Grant and fought his way to the shelter of the wheelhouse.

Dokie Joe was soon back inside the wheelhouse as well, smiling now, his white teeth startling in a face whipped to mahogany-brown from years of fishing in all weathers. Through the whirling hail and snow – now turning to sleet – he had caught a glimpse of land. 'Port ahead, lads. Old Righ's light is shining like a bloody great star on top of a Christmas tree. I've never seen such a beautiful sight.' His mask of toughness fell. 'I tell you this – out there in that cruel bugger o' a sea I had my doubts, ay, I had my doubts – but,' he said, taking the wheel from Dan, 'the old girl got us home. She's all right, is old *Magpie*. I mind when I bought her and my mother saw the name on her: "Paint it out, Dokie", she told me, "call her something else. *Magpie* is unlucky, it will bring sorrow." Ay, but the superstitious cailleach was wrong, for I aye knew the old girl had a reason to her name – magpies pick up anything that's worth something, and on every trip my old girl gets to the herring shoals first.'

Dokie Joe was thinking about Annie even as he peered through the blizzard for a sign of the markers at the mouth of the harbour. Dokie thought of her warm curvaceous body pressed close to his in bed. Tonight he would lie with her after all, make love to her . . . Back there he had had his doubts about ever seeing his family again, but now he could almost feel the silk of Annie's breasts against his hard hairy chest . . . a pulse beat in his groin . . .

Dokie Joe's hand tightened on the wheel. The *Magpie* was bucking wildly in the tide race swirling into the harbour. He revved up the engine in an effort to pull the boat further back into the open sea so that he could make a wider turn into the harbour, but the *Magpie* didn't respond. Instead, she submitted to the pushing, bullying wind at her stern and pitched headlong towards the long dark finger of Port Rum Point. Dokie felt fear crawling over his skin, and despite the freezing cold deep in his very bones he felt sweat breaking over his body. His rough voice bawled out orders, which the crew scurried to obey. They trusted their skipper – he knew the sea, its moods, its wiles. In his fight with it he often behaved like a ferocious tiger; and in his admiration of its delusive beauty he became soft, resilient, relaxed as an alert cat; it was as if it transferred its moods to him like a lovely temperamental mistress might induce love, hate, respect, anger, admiration in a besotted lover. Dokie knew the sea all right, and that was why now his heart thudded up into his ears and his brusque comments were laced with oaths. His lips were pulled back in a snarl over his teeth as he held tightly to the wheel. The boat leapt and plunged like a mad dog and Dokie knew – he knew where the *Magpie* was taking him. The Sgor Creags! They were waiting for him and his men, always they were waiting, like grey, patient vultures waiting for prey. He stopped cursing and cried in a muffled voice, 'Oh God, help us!'

Quite suddenly Rachel's face bounced into his terrified mind. He felt her presence very strongly, as if she was standing beside him in the wheelhouse of the *Magpie* . . . He shivered and moaned slightly. Strange – she was a strange wee lass . . . he didn't understand her, but God! he was proud of her . . .

The *Magpie* bounced before a mountainous wave which caught her and smothered her in a wall of grey water. When it receded the men saw the Sgor Creags in front of them. Dokie Joe wrenched at the wheel but nothing happened. The boat was like a paper toy being sucked into the whirlpools that raged round the reefs. Dokie Joe's reddened eyes widened in horror. Those bloody rocks! They were reaching for the *Magpie*, pulling her towards them as if they were magnets and she were held in a vice-like grip from which there was no escape. The cruel grey pinnacles of rock reared up, gnarled, racked, twisted by time and wind into grotesque shapes; they towered like spectres over the frail little boat, while the churning fury of the dark rolling sea battered her hull.

Grant felt awe ripping through him. For the first

time in his young life he smelt and tasted real fear.

The crash as the *Magpie* hit the reefs threw the men to the floor. Grant heard the propellers racing uselessly, heard Skipper Joe's terrified curses as he realised the *Magpie* was caught amidships by two massive fragments of jagged rock. The deck tilted and swayed. Grant was thrown to his knees. Through the thudding of his heart he heard the sea snarling over the rocks; heard the groaning screams of the *Magpie* as the Sgor Creags began ripping her apart; felt the cold finger of death hovering over him, eager to reach out and carry him off in its pitiless clutches.

Todd was now holding the stage, his cheeks puffed into red pouches. The skirl of the pipes set everyone hooching and they whirled gaily round the floor, stirring up the chalky dust from the floorboards. The children climbed down off the platform and went to sit in the corner beside Ruth. The bench was immediately under the platform, hidden from the rest of the hall, and the children giggled as they received an unparalleled view of Todd's hairy legs under his swinging kilt. Ruth felt happier. Her mother couldn't see her from this angle and she was able to chatter to Rachel in peace of mind. Lorn was beside Ruth and all at once he grasped her arm and choked in a strangled whisper, 'Look, Ruth, Todd's drawers are coming down.'

Sure enough Todd's knees were being obliterated inch by inch by folds of wind-bleached cotton. The children clutched each other and gave themselves up to ecstasy.

Lewis leaned across to his brother and hissed, 'I bet you twopence they've got his initials on. Mollie puts initials on all her washing when the tinks are on the island.'

'I'm not betting,' Lorn stated with a grin. 'I *know* they've got his initials on – I saw them on the washing line yesterday!'

Old Mo spluttered into his whisky as he too espied the slow unfurling of Todd's underpants. 'Bejabers and bejasus, the bloody lyin' cheat,' he mumbled to Bob. 'Was he not after tellin' me just two minutes ago he never wears knickers under his kilt!' Todd was stomping his sturdy legs, keeping time to the music, obliviously abetting the descent of his drawers.

'Mercy on us, no!' stuttered a red-faced Mollie. 'He could never bring such shame to our good name. I told him, I told him this very mornin' he was needin' the elastic mended, but would he listen to me? No, oh no! I am just his wife! It's shamed I am just.'

A deadly hush had fallen over the floor as word spread like wildfire. The Laird had been discussing farming with Fergus and his was the last voice to die down, tailing off with a cultured if explosive, 'Poor old chap, I don't think he's aware of what's happening.'

Todd wasn't. In an inebriated haze he was blasting away merrily, stamping his feet, his eyes closed in his perspiring face.

'And there's a hole in them too!' Mollie almost

sobbed. 'Right where I patched them on the seam!'

With a triumphal flourish the underpants slid down to lie in dazzling folds at Todd's thick ankles.

'Ach God!' Kate clutched her stomach. 'He's unfurling his banners in style is our Todd! I wish I had a pair o' bellows. That would put the wind up him right enough!'

Todd was now aware of his imprisoned feet. With a drunken grin splitting his face he shouted, 'Ach, the hell wi' them!' and calmly stepping out of the cotton layers he stooped down and, picking them up, threw them with a flourish over his shoulder, intending in a burst of showmanship to catch them on the tasselled drones of his pipes. Instead they sailed over his head to land gracefully on the golden head of Squint, who was lying peacefully at Rachel's feet. The little dog looked with comical cross-eyed surprise through one of the wide legs before he shook the garment from his head and got to his feet to sniff blissfully, his inquisitive nose poking into the torn patch. For a moment the drawers hung suspended on the end of his muzzle then he went wild with delight. Although he had all the points of a good gun dog there was also something of the terrier in his nature. Holding the cloth firmly with his front paws he began pulling it up and down like strings of gum before gathering the lot in his soft jaws to go racing round the hall, throwing the drawers into the air, catching them, exposing to the hysterical gathering the initials T. McD. emblazoned red on white.

The hall went into an uproar with everyone clutching each other for support. Dodie's screeching wail of a laugh rang out; Biddy cackled so heartily her glasses slid to the end of her nose; the minister leaned helplessly against his dumpy little wife, who was wiping her streaming eyes with the first thing that came to hand – a corner of Merry Mary's new dress.

'Pour auld Todd,' Niall sobbed. 'He'll never live this down as long as he lives!'

In the corner the children were rendered speechless. Lewis had fallen against Rachel; and Lorn's earth-brown curls were touching Ruth's golden locks – in the sheer ecstasy of their mirth they had both forgotten their shyness and were now in harmony with each other, as was every other laughter-racked person in the room.

Alick was standing beside Kirsteen. 'Only on Rhanna could this happen,' he commented breathlessly. 'I always seem to get more laughs when I come home here.'

'You get other things as well – such as a bruised face and a split lip.' She looked him straight in the eye and he returned her gaze, his heart quickening slightly. 'Thank you, Alick,' she said quietly. 'I'm not going to ask what it was all about – I think I know. And I think you're a really special person – I just want you to know that. You're quite a man, Alick McKenzie.'

Alick flushed and turned away. Her words made him feel ten feet tall. Quite a man – at last – quite a man. He felt complete and proud to be a McKenzie.

Fergus looked over at his wife. They hadn't spoken a single word to each other yet; they were like shy children not quite knowing where or how to begin. Kirsteen felt excitement beating into her as she looked ahead to when they were alone, anticipated the first tentative kisses, the first gentle caresses . . .

Then Scott Balfour was climbing onto the platform followed by the minister, the doctor, their respective wives. The band re-assembled and Squint took up his position by Rachel's side, Merry Mary blushingly arranged herself between Phebie and Lachlan and the presentation speeches began. Plaudits were showered on the little Englishwoman from each of the menfolk in turn, and then the Laird made the presentations. The village had done Merry Mary right well: face afire with embarrassment, she received an elegant carriage clock to grace her mantelpiece; with trembling lips she stared in speechless gratitude at the silver tray complete with tea service, a personal gift from the Laird and his wife for 'keeping the Burnbreddie larder stocked through war and weather' – and when she was presented with a discreet plain envelope containing 'a wee thing from every man, woman, and child on the island', a sob caught at the back of her throat. Finally, when a tiny tot stumbled onto the platform bearing a huge bouquet, which she handed to Merry Mary with a big shy grin, the tears spilled over.

'Thank you, thank you everyone,' Merry Mary said and fumbled for her hanky. 'I meant to be very grand

and to say things that were light-hearted and funny
– but now I find – I can say nothing except thank
you to every one of my dear friends on Rhanna.' In
confusion she melted into the background and
resumed her seat. A rousing cheer went up then the
Laird went on to the business of officially handing
over the shop to Dugald, who, with his tall straight
figure and mop of shining white hair, made a dignified figure on the platform.

Dugald wished Totie could have been there with
him, but she had decided it might not be a wise thing.
'I'm jealous, Doug,' she had said bluntly, 'and I don't
think I could bear to be in the same room with Morag
and not show her my claws.' Dugald's eyes fell on
Ruth sitting on the bench in the corner, and his heart
twisted. Poor lonely wee lassie. She was gazing at
him with pride in her huge violet eyes. For her sake
he had to stick by Morag; a child as sensitive as Ruth
might never get over the scandal of a divorce . . .

Morag listened while Dugald made a short but
appropriate speech. Something tugged at her heart.
She felt pride and something else, an affection that
bordered on love – he was such a good man. They
could have been happy together – if only – if only
her soul wasn't so tortured by guilt . . . Morag shook
herself angrily. He was a man like any other, men
wanted things from a woman that made a mockery
of so-called love. Always on the female scent they
were – like – like dogs sniffing after bitches in heat.
It wasn't clean – nor decent . . .

The Laird was holding up his hand, asking once

more for attention. To everyone's surprise Biddy was being invited up onto the platform.

Hearing her name Biddy grunted and stirred out of a rum-induced stupor but had no time to gather her senses. Babbie was beside her, helping her to her feet, escorting her up to the platform, placing her in a chair beside the minister.

'My damty specs, I canny *hear* without them!' hissed the old nurse, and with a smile Babbie retrieved the glasses and placed them on the end of Biddy's nose.

'It isn't my intention to steal Merry Mary's thunder,' the Laird began in his well-modulated, rather nasal voice, 'but I have a very special presentation to make, and while we are all gathered here tonight I can think of no better opportunity to carry out a duty that has fallen to me and that I am particularly honoured to fulfil.' He went on to explain that some time ago Lachlan had written to the Prime Minister recommending that Biddy, in view of her long and faithful service to Rhanna, be considered for an award.

The gathering in the hall gasped when the Laird read out the letter that Biddy had received from the Prime Minister's Principal Private Secretary, which ended by saying that His Majesty would be graciously pleased to approve that Biddy be appointed a Member of the Order of the British Empire.

The Laird cleared his throat. 'Biddy replied saying that she would be pleased to accept this mark of His

Majesty's favour, but she explained that she was too old and – hm – somewhat infirm to personally attend an investiture – and,' he said smiling, 'I have an idea that she thought that was that and promptly forgot all about the matter.'

Biddy glowered at Burnbreddie through the spikes of silver-white hair that escaped her hat. She was rigid with embarrassment. Had not the doctor coaxed her to write that damty letter of acceptance? It had all been just a lot of palaver that she didn't understand, and she had forgotten about it. She sucked in her lips with annoyance as a ripple of amazed comment bounced round the hall. She knew that for ever more she would be teased and tormented because she had omitted to tell anyone about the letter.

Her eye fell on Behag's sagging jowls and popping eyes. If it had been that cailleach, she would have told everyone: boasted, strutted, preened like a constipated peacock . . . Biddy sat up straighter and, puffing out her scrawny chest, peered haughtily down her nose. She was going to enjoy this after all, make the most of it, show old Behag she was somebody, an important personage of the island, a mother figure . . . After all, she had delivered three generations of Rhanna children . . . Ay indeed, she smiled and nodded, was she not nurse, mother, grandmother, to just about everyone present there that night? She folded her hands on her lap and settled herself back in her seat.

The Laird was continuing. 'Doctor McLachlan and

myself contrived between us to make sure that Biddy would receive her award, and I now have the honour, in place of the Lord Lieutenant of the county, who could not be here at this time, to carry out His Majesty's command . . .' He turned to Lachlan, who handed him a scroll and a small box, and then he went to stand by Biddy, his hand on her shoulder. 'It is with a feeling of great privilege and pleasure that I bestow upon Biddy the emblem and warrant of a Member of the Order of the British Empire as a token of His Majesty's awareness and gratitude for the many, many years of service our beloved nurse and friend has given to this island. She was just a slip of a lass when she took on her slim shoulders the great responsibility of nursing a community single-handed. She has through the years proven her worth, and has devoted her life to caring for others. Now she is an old lady –'

'Like a good whisky, the older the better,' Biddy interposed sourly, and a giggle went up.

'– she is now an old lady,' the Laird went on un-perturbed, and with a smile, 'and as she says, like a good whisky she has improved with time. I know that all of you here share my hope that she has got many a good year left in her yet. She has assisted many here tonight into this world – she has watched us come – and – yes – she has known the heartache as deep as the mothers themselves of watching the sons of Rhanna go marching into two world wars – many of them never to return.'

Biddy's eyes were filling and Babbie squeezed her arm comfortingly.

The Laird turned, and with genuine affection, he said softly, 'Ay, indeed, she has watched us come and she has watched us go, she has burped us and she has blessed us and – as if all that wasn't enough – she has now brought great honour to our island community.' Leaning forward he pinned the insignia on the old nurse's jacket and, handing her the warrant, he took her rough old hand in his and shook it firmly.

Biddy stared down at the silver medal mounted by a crown attached to a red ribbon. A swelling pride surged in her breast. 'A damty fine brooch,' she said huskily and sniffed loudly while the Laird helped her to unroll the ornately inscribed warrant and then held it up for everyone to see. There were gasps of awe followed by thunderous applause. Babbie hugged the old nurse and whispered, 'I'm proud of you, you dear old cailleach – and – if I serve this place half as well as you have done, I will be well pleased.'

'Ach, wait you, I'm no' finished yet; I still have a few bairns to deliver before I go out.' Biddy tried to sound firm but her voice came out in a wobble, and as she was surrounded by people, hugging her, shaking her hand, patting her shoulders, the tears finally spilled over and she wept copiously into Babbie's hanky.

'Wonderful, wonderful,' beamed Mrs Gray. 'Now

I'm sure you could do justice to a nice cuppy.'

Biddy scrubbed her red eyes. 'Ay, indeed, a cuppy is just what I need, all this fuss just because I have done a job I have loved. The good Lord knows it hasny been easy, and betimes I could fine have seen it all far enough, but ach! It's my life, what I was put here to do, and there is no need to go giving me medallions for it.'

The minister was giving the vote of thanks, and Mrs Gray stepped discreetly from the platform. She had spent a good part of the morning baking delicious scones and pastries, which had been added to the batches prepared by the village womenfolk. These delicacies had been put to heat in the ovens of nearby houses and several of the women had already bustled away to fetch them, leaving Mrs Gray and her helpers to preside over the ancient but efficient tea urn. A lull followed during which everyone juggled with piping hot sausage rolls and mugs of strong steaming tea, discussing between mouthfuls the events of the evening. Quite a crowd was gathered round both Merry Mary and Biddy to admire the respective awards; old Mo was announcing in a loud voice that he had to pee or burst, and there was a scramble to get him down from the platform and outside; several children were gathered in the alcove by the platform, giggling as they dared one another to dart out and grab extra helpings from the trays; the courting couples had sneaked into the loft, and through the general buzz Rachel's keen ears heard the rafters creaking. She smiled and, nudging Ruth, she pointed above her head.

'I know, I saw them go up,' Ruth said, and laughed. 'Jean and that skinny-ma-link Harry the Bus – *and* I saw Colin McKinnon go up with Betty Alexander. He's only fourteen and she's just twelve, yet Mary told me that Betty lets Colin put his hands inside her –' Ruth lowered her voice to a shocked whisper – 'inside her blouse. Her bosoms began to grow when she was only eleven.' Ruth was thoroughly enjoying herself. She was a naturally outgoing little girl who had been unnaturally stifled, and normally she kept a tight rein on her tongue. Only with Rachel could she unwind and reveal in some measure her true self. Morag Ruadh had hovered around earlier but now she was helping dispense tea and Ruth felt unfettered.

Rachel listened to her friend with avid enjoyment. It had been a wonderful evening, one she would remember: Jon's playing, Merry Mary's tears of joy, the dancing and singing, Biddy's old eyes filling as she looked with pride at her brooch. Rachel loved the old nurse with her whimsical ways, her snowy hair, her grumbling good nature, her continual search for her specs and her teeths – Rachel stiffened – her father had burst into her thoughts, so real and near she could see his brown skin, his grey-flecked beard, his brown eyes wildly staring. The little girl felt a strange, cold premonition of danger touching her, pulling her down into a chasm of dread. She had

had these feelings before, things she didn't under-stand, but never before had she experienced such force in a vision, such powerful intensity of trans-ferred thought it was as if her father was inside herself, hammering at her brain, clenched fists screaming at her to let him out – no – no – get him out – get help. She trembled and put her hand down quickly to Squint's soft head, reassured herself of reality by touching his cold nose, stroking his muzzle. He gave a little whimper, and she knew that she had conveyed her unease to him.

'Dad.' The word she had never been able to speak beat inside her head. She loved him, more than her mother, more than her brothers. He was tough, dour, silent, ignorant about many things, but often she sensed his love for her reaching out of his aggressive spirit to caress her, without words, without touch. When he was away at sea she ran wild; when he was home she became calmer, stayed nearer to home to cherish each minute he spent there. Sometimes he lifted her up in his swarthy arms and his beard scuffed the smooth bloom of her cheeks. Once, his dark, strangely gentle eyes had regarded her for a long time before he said in his gruff voice, 'My lassie – if only you could speak, tell me your thoughts. Those bonny eyes o' yours say things but I canny understand everything that's in them – I – you're my special bairnie.' She had laid her small hand on his arm and nodded, and from that day she had known what she meant to him. Now – now he was in danger – trying to reach her – to let her know . . .

She felt ice-cold: her dark eyes were wide and big as if she was watching some terrible disaster unfolding before her.

'Rachel, what's wrong? Are you all right? You – you look as though you'd seen a ghost.'

Ruth's voice came from a long way. Rachel shook herself and started to her feet just as the door burst open and Hugh McDonald, the young assistant lighthouse keeper, stood there, wind-tossed, rivers of rain and sea running from his mackintosh to lie in puddles on the floor. 'The smacks are in!' he shouted. 'All safe but for one – the *Magpie*'s on the rocks!'

In minutes the hall was empty but for old Mo lying in his pram, Biddy dozing in her chair, and Mrs Gray rushing to fill the urn in readiness for the men coming in from the smacks.

Chapter Ten

Grant thrashed in the freezing water, almost paralysed with cold and exhaustion, his brain so numb with shock he barely remembered being pitched from the *Magpie* into the black fury seething round the Sgor Creags. The spikes of rock had smashed a gaping hole in the *Magpie*'s hull and she had keeled over to lie half-submerged. With her bow impaled on a shaft of rock, she looked like a dying whale raising her snout above the waves in a desperate bid to resist the relentless pull of the churning depths. Everything had happened so quickly there had been no time to make sense of the jumbled impressions of men shouting, the boat tilting, the fleeting glimpse of Skipper Joe in the wheelhouse, his face twisted in disbelief as he struggled up from the deck, blood oozing from a gash on his cheek. He had thrown his arms round the wheel as if it were a baby and had cried out in protest, 'Christ, no! Oh, dear Jesus, no!'

'Leave her, Skipper! She's breaking up.' The warning roar had come from Grant, in a voice that didn't seem to be his, so unreal was the screaming pitch of it. The timbers had groaned, squealing in the agony of dying, as the little boat had been torn apart by the pitiless sea smashing over the deck. Grant had staggered, slithered, screamed as the snarling water reached for him and pulled him down. His flaying hands had caught and clutched at the capping, and for a moment he had lain gasping before he was torn away, lifted by a giant wave, which hurled him relentlessly into the waiting sea. The roar of it filled his head, the embrace of its icy clutches seemed to reach right into his heart and squeeze it, so that it seemed to stop beating. Dan's white face bobbed near him. Grant reached out but was lifted and tossed towards the rocks. Adrenalin pumped through him, spurring him into frantic activity. Kicking frenziedly he swam for his life. Something black loomed. The *Magpie*. The water was swirling round her, fighting to claim what was left of her from the teeth of the rocks. Grant knew that he was trapped. Behind him reared the stark treachery of the Sgor Creags, in front of him was the *Magpie*, no longer a friend but an enemy blocking the way to safety, seducing the sea to rage as it sucked and roared, sucked and roared, into the yawning hole amidships. He stopped struggling and allowed himself to be pounded by the waves. His limbs were growing numb, he couldn't feel his legs . . . He closed his eyes, waiting for oblivion to release him from a watery hell.

Something rammed itself against Grant's rib cage and lifted him up. It was a piece of wreckage as big as a raft. His frozen fingers clawed at it and he heaved himself up to lie, gasping, on it. Deep in his consciousness, a jumbled prayer of thankfulness took form. From somewhere close at hand he heard something like a groan. He looked up and though his eyes were burning with pain he saw through a watery blur the black outline of what remained of the *Magpie*; the mast wavered for what seemed eternity then with a shuddering crack it crashed through the wheelhouse. A trembling scream rose above the snarl of the storm. The sound of it filled him with horror and he moaned softly and whispered, 'You shouldn't have stayed, Skipper; you should have let her go.'

The crowd that spilled from the hall surged onto the little strip of shore laid bare by the ebbing tide, some of the womenfolk running to meet the bedraggled fishermen coming from the smacks. Captain Mac and his crew made straight for the boathouse where the Rhanna lifeboat was kept. Righ nan Dul, Keeper of the Light, was an old man now, but tougher and wirier than many a man half his age. He welcomed the solid, cool presence of Captain Mac. They were old friends of many years' standing, and when it came to dealing with the sea, action rather than words was their keynote. Hurriedly they plotted a course of action, with Righ suggesting that they take the boat to the harbour mouth to see if they could pick up any of the *Magpie*'s crew.

Captain Mac nodded his bushy white head. 'Ay, the tide's on the turn, and I'd say the worst o' the storm is over – the bugger has blown itself out.'

There were many willing hands to man the lifeboat, which was no more than a long rowing boat.

The men piled in, the shed doors were opened, old Joe released the mechanism and the boat slid gracefully down the slip and into the water.

Kirsteen stood a little way back, watching, her heart in her throat, her icy fingers nervously winding together. The wind had abated a good deal, but it still moaned deep in its throat, a sound of menace that struck dread into her heart. The waves were silken, greeny-blue troughs of satin in the light from storm lanterns held aloft all along the shoreline. It was frightening to be standing so close to the pounding sea, seeing the litter of debris held in the clutch of the green swell thrashing against the land; seeing the foam spuming high into the air, carelessly tossing out seaweed and pebbles; hearing the thundering roar like a lion defiantly proclaiming its might, untamed, unconquered no matter how submissive it might sometimes appear. In the excitement everyone had left coats and jackets in the hall. Kirsteen shivered a little in the bite of the wind. Everything, everyone seemed to be in confusion. She felt panic rising in her. Her son was out in that godforsaken sea – out by the Sgor Creags – the rocks that had killed Hamish – been the means of Fergus losing his arm . . . Fergus – where was he? Where was everyone who meant everything in the world to her?

She turned blindly and fell into Shona's steadying arms. Niall, too, was there; calm, comforting Niall with his strong arms and his soft reassuring voice.

Shona held Kirsteen and murmured soothing words, but her thoughts were far away – in that relent-

less sea with the half-brother she cared for more than
she would ever admit. Shona drew in her breath and
closed her eyes. Niall led them to a spur of rock away
from the wind – none of them saw the tall dark figure
of Fergus running towards the base of Port Rum
Point, scrambling over the slimy rocks to the tiny
strip of land that lay exposed along the length of the
rocky finger.

'Come back, Fergus!' Alick's voice bounced over
the bay. 'You'll get swept away on that damt Point!
The boat will pick the lads up.'

'For God's sake! It's my son out there!' Fergus
threw back, and plunged on, slipping, falling,
picking himself up, squeezing himself round
barnacle-encrusted outcrops that dropped down into
blackness. Time and again the sea reached out to
him, drenching him, plucking at his feet with icy
fingers. At one point the water roared into the dank
black hole of an enormous cavern. He had to swim
in order to bridge the gap and he felt himself spinning like a cork in the mêlée. Terror momentarily
engulfed him, but concern for Grant imbued him
with power and he lashed out with his legs. His hand
brushed a rock and he hauled himself onto dry land
once more. Soaked to the skin, his breath ragged, his
throat raw and tight, he ran on. It seemed to him he
had been running for ever with the wind tearing him
and the sea lashing him. His eyes were so filled with
salt he barely saw where he was going – only the
thin irregular ribbon of silver sand kept him from
plunging headlong into the water. The black holes

of caves loomed like the wide mocking mouths of giants; his world was one of thunderous boomings; of dark towering crags; of searing, biting cold. The wind strengthened and he knew he had reached the tip of the Point. He was whipped and bullied by the elements, and he staggered as he strained his stinging eyes into the heaving blackness.

His eyes adjusted and new shapes emerged out of the wall of water facing him, causing him to tremble with a mixture of dread and hatred of those menacing splinters rising sheer out of the sea. The last time he had seen them at such close quarters was years ago – yet in those moments it might have been yesterday: the horrendous nightmare loomed like a spectre: Hamish's face floated beside him, his sightless eyes seeing nothing, the blood bubbling from the hole in his skull, the sea all around lathering to a pink froth . . . Fergus shuddered. Never had he thought to face these rocks again. He loathed them with a passion that terrified him.

He stared wildly and saw another shape – a great black snout rearing up to the sky looking for all the world like a giant whale rising for air . . . the bow of the *Magpie* . . .

'Grant!' His voice came out in a rasping bawl. Over and over he called his son's name, and over and over it was thrown back at him. Rage filled him. The sea would not get his son! Not if he could help it.

'Father.' He thought he imagined the sound but it came again faintly and without hesitation he plunged into the element he feared more than any other. A spike of rock bit into the flesh of his hip but his mind was so preoccupied he felt no pain. It seemed a miracle to him when, in that freezing hostile world, he came upon his son clinging to a great plank of wood that had wedged itself between two rocks.

'Hold onto me!' Fergus ordered.

Grant let go of the wood and Fergus felt himself sinking under the weight of him. Naked fear ripped through him and his limbs went rigid. A pinpoint of light pricked into the darkness then disappeared, but in that split second Fergus had seen a small familiar figure standing on the Point. Lorn or Lewis? He didn't know which . . . he felt himself spinning in a void as waves of faintness washed over him. The water swirled round his legs, sucking, pulling, Grant was a dead weight against him and they both went under . . . Fergus kicked and wildly flayed the water with his arm . . . water flooded his lungs . . . he and his son were caught in a whirling underwater current that wouldn't let go. Grant thrashed wildly and they both bobbed to the surface . . . and miraculously a lifejacket was there within their reach.

'It's all right – Father, I'm here – hold onto this.' It was the voice of a child, a breathless, weak voice.

Lorn! How could it be Lorn! That tiny boy with the weak heart and skinny body. 'Go back, for God's sake go back!' Fergus rasped. The child was gasping, struggling for air, but his thin little arms were reaching out, holding on, keeping his father's chin above water . . .

'Hold on!'

Alick's voice! Cool, calm Alick who had always been quite at home in the sea . . . Now other arms were there, too, carrying Grant and Lorn to safety, and now it was just Fergus and Alick, Alick uttering soothing words of encouragement, cradling his brother, taking him to the haven of dry land. Fergus was aware of figures moving, familiar voices tossing hither and thither. His chest heaved and he choked out the sea from his lungs.

'This – this is getting to be a habit – you pulling me out of the Sound,' Fergus joked feebly.

Alick laughed, but it was a trembling, weak attempt. With frantic fingers he loosened the collar at his throat. 'It – wasn't me this time – it – was Lorn who saved you – foolhardly – brave wee brat – I couldn't stop him.' The pain reached up to his neck and seared through his jaws. He had never known such agony, it was crushing the breath from his body, forcing him to lie down near his brother. All around him was blackness, blacker than the darkest night. Only the blob of Fergus's face above him was grey.

'Alick! Are you all right?' Fergus, barely recovered from his own hellish experience, looked at his brother lying gasping on the sands and felt he was caught up in a nightmare without end. He forgot himself, his chattering teeth and numb limbs. 'Alick!' he cried again harshly. 'What's wrong?'

'I – think – big brother – I've come to the end of my holiday. Us city gents are – too soft for midnight swims – can't breathe – I think – my heart.'

Fergus raised himself onto his knees. 'I'll get help

– hold on –' But Alick's trembling hand reached out to stay him. 'No – no – stay – stay with me. I've always been afraid – of the – dark. I need you – big brother.'

Fergus gathered his brother to his breast. The wet hair beneath his fingers was plastered with sand and gently he stroked it clean. Alick's breathing was more laboured, his head heavier than it had been a moment before . . . Fergus's thoughts flashed back to boyhood days, of Alick relying on him, leaning on him – worshipping him . . . and tonight, the two of them fighting, Alick proving that he was quite a man – had been for years without Fergus being aware of the fact. And now – Alick was dying – dear God! He was dying! The pain of love, for someone he had always taken for granted and who was now about to leave him, shot through him like a knife. He caught his brother's head to him and touched the wet hair with his lips. 'You don't need me – I need you,' he sobbed harshly.

'An unusual way to end – an unusual holiday – but then – I was always a one for anything – different . . .' gasped Alick painfully. The last of his strength went into the hand clasped round Fergus's arm. 'You know – even when I hated you – I loved you – I never quite grew up, you see – big – brother . . .' His hands relaxed and fell away, his head lolled to one side, and with a little sigh he died peacefully in his brother's embrace.

Fergus gathered him up and cradled him as if he was a baby. All around him the wind moaned, the black night closed in like a mourning blanket. A sob caught at his throat. He wanted to shout his hatred at the sea, which had robbed him of so much, to scream, to give vent to useless wrath. Instead, he sobbed quietly.

'We'll take him, lad.' Bob's voice came softly, gentle hands drew him up and led him away, and as he stumbled along he saw not where he was going for his tears.

Some distance away everyone waited anxiously for the life boat to come back. The lanterns picked it out, bucking towards the shore, the keel grounded, and an army of willing helpers plunged into the water to pull her up. Annie stood a little way back, her shawl clutched over her head, her limbs immobile and stiff.

'We got them all but one.' Captain Mac's voice was gruff as he jumped from the boat.

'Which one?' Old Joe's voice was tense. 'It – isn't young Grant?'

'No, he was rescued from the Point – it's Dokie Joe. He's trapped in the *Magpie*, a goner from all accounts.'

Righ shook his head. 'Ay, and there is no way we can reach him until the old girl breaks up – even then . . .' The remainder of his words went unsaid, but everyone knew what he meant. The Sgor Creags had been known to hold onto a body till it was no more than a skeleton picked clean by seabirds.

Torquil Andrew turned on his heel and trod heavily over the shingle to Annie. Without words he put his arms round her and drew her close.

'Oh no, oh dear God no,' she said, leaning against him and sobbing. 'It's a punishment – a punishment, I'm tellin' you, Torquil.'

'Weesht now, mo ghaoil, you mustny think like that. Dokie stayed wi' the boat – he could have got out but he stayed wi' her – it's the way o' things.'

Rachel stood alone in the cold dark embrace of night. She watched Torquil leading her mother away. In that moment she knew that her father was dead. Her great brown eyes stared wildly into space. Her big, dour, adored father had been taken by the sea. She felt her world crashing round her. He had been her security, the only person she had ever really trusted. She loved her mother, but she had always been aware of her mother's weaknesses, her inability to cope with loneliness. Her father hadn't been weak; he had been strong, strong, strong; he had been faithful – and he was gone from her. Her lips trembled and formed the word 'Dad'. She wanted to shout it aloud but her voice was locked inside for ever . . . Arms were enclosing her, Jon's strong young arms, holding her close, reaching out and soothing her in her moment of greatest need. He said nothing, just knelt beside her and held her. She laid her head on his shoulders and his long sensitive fingers stroked her hair. Then she felt herself being lifted up and carried away through the night, and as he strode with her he murmured, 'I'm here, jungfräulich, I will stay with you as long as you need me.'

Ruth watched and squirmed against her mother's painful hold on her shoulders, every fibre in her longing to run to her friend to give her comfort, but Morag Ruadh's hold grew stronger, her voice when she spoke was without emotion. 'No, Ruth, you will come home with me and pray to the Lord to give Rachel strength – her mother too.' Her lips twisted as she thought of gay, vivacious Annie with her lust for life and her discontent when her husband was away at sea. 'The Lord works in mysterious ways, mark my words. Sinners must be punished one way or another –'

'Rachel has done nothing wrong!' Ruth cried passionately. 'Why should she be punished! You're afraid of her – that's why you try to keep me away from her! She's strong and good and beautiful and she's my friend – and – and I won't keep away from her when she needs me most. I won't! I won't!'

Morag's face flamed red, her hand shot out to crack her daughter hard on the face. 'You learn to get your facts right my girl! I wasny meanin' Rachel, though she is just her mother all over again. Never – never speak like that to me again. You will obey me, you will obey the Lord's word. You are a daughter of God, do you hear me, child?'

'I am my father's daughter,' sobbed Ruth, but even as her mother yanked her away she wondered, as she had wondered so many times lately, just whose daughter she really was – it might be better to think of herself as God's daughter after all.

The men carrying Grant stepped out of the shadow

of Port Rum Point and Kirsteen ran forward, so full of relief at seeing her son alive she couldn't speak.

'It's all right, Mother,' he said through chattering teeth. 'I'm not planning to leave any of you for a while yet – I never managed back for the ceilidh, but at least I'm home.'

Kirsteen looked up and saw Lachlan running towards the Point. Lewis, who had been watching the unloading of the lifeboat with interest, was running too, as if drawn by some sort of telepathy towards the little group some distance away.

'It's Lorn,' Grant murmured, the impact of recent events only now starting to come home to him. 'Would you credit it – the spunky wee bugger dived into the sea and kept Father afloat . . .'

Kirsteen was gone, racing with pounding heart to her youngest son. Grant looked up to see Fiona staring down at him, the soft curves of her slender body outlined against a watery light breaking through the clouds. She felt strange, light-headed, filled with something she could put no name to. Before she could say anything he said, as teasingly as his frozen lips would allow, 'Well, well, if it isn't wee Robin – all dressed up in a frock like a *real* girl. Are you disappointed to see I'm still alive and kicking?'

Anger rose up in her. She tossed her head. 'I might have known it would take more than a drop of the sea to kill a McKenzie!' she spat vindictively.

'Ay, we're a tough lot,' he retaliated without spirit. Without another word Fiona turned on her heel and walked over to join Mary, who was enquiring of a group of fisherwives if they had seen anything of her husband . . .

It was almost three a.m. when Kirsteen eventually made her weary way upstairs. Lachlan, concerned for Fergus because of the weak lung he had had since his accident, had ordered him up to bed an hour before. He had gone with surprisingly little objection, his shoulders bent, his steps dragging. But he wasn't asleep. He lay very still, staring at the ceiling, his eyes hollow in his white face. Kirsteen went over to the dressing table, and, planting her hands on its smooth surface, she stood with her fair head bowed, every muscle in her body sagging with tiredness.

'How is everyone?'

She whirled round to look at him. 'Fergus – I – I thought you'd be asleep.'

'Sleep! How can I sleep after what's happened? I wonder if I'll ever sleep again.'

She clasped her hands and stared down at them. 'You mustn't worry about the boys – Grant is sound asleep, he's young and strong and is only very badly shaken up. Lorn – well – I can hardly believe he's all right after what happened, but he is – oh, naturally drained of course. Lachlan has told me to keep him in bed for a couple of days. Mary – she – Lachlan gave her a sedative. I don't think she's really taken in what's happened yet. She kept saying she didn't know how she was going to tell her sons.'

'Oh, dear God,' Fergus said, his voice full of disbelief, 'I've been lying here feeling I've imagined it all – I can't believe he's really dead.'

Kirsteen felt sorrow engulfing her and she put her hands to her face. 'I know. Oh poor dear Alick! He'd been so good to me this holiday – so patient and kind, I don't know what I would have done without him.'

'Don't rub it in,' Fergus said, his voice heavy with grief, 'I feel hellish enough as it is – as if everything is my fault. We had a fight earlier and he beat the hell out of me! My little brother turned the tables and fought back. He laughed about it – said how good he felt that everything we had buried for so long was at last out in the open.' He bunched his knuckle. 'And just when we might have made a go of things he died pulling me out of the sea. What does it mean, Kirsteen? It all seems so senseless – he was only forty-seven.'

Kirsteen said nothing. It seemed there was nothing she could say to ease her husband's torment of mind. He turned his head to look at her, noting her stillness, the feminine fragility that gave her such grace and beauty, the strength that emanated from her.

'Kirsteen,' he said, speaking her name softly, savouring the sound of it, 'Alick had a great respect for you – also I think he'd always been a little bit in love with you. Perhaps he was never really aware of it himself, but he loved you enough to face up to me tonight – to tell me things I was too damned stubborn to admit. My darling, darling Kirsteen, I'm so sorry for everything – I've missed you so – I need you –'

She raised her head and saw his dark eyes burning into her. The room was in lamplight, shadows danced and played, everything was soft and dim. His trembling hand reached out to her. 'I love you, oh God how I love you. I need you more than I've ever needed you in my life – you're part of me, Kirsteen.'

She had no recollection of crossing the room, she was only aware of his nearness, his lips kissing her hair, kissing away the tears from her eyes, caressing her ears, her neck, her breasts. The power of their love for each other reared up out of grief and misery. His body was hard against hers. Slowly she undressed and got into bed to lie down beside him. They spoke no words; there was no need for them. His arm came round to draw her in close to him, his lips touched her hair, her face, her mouth. They lay quite still in one another's embrace, savouring the close, warm comfort of being together again. They were enclosed in a sphere of their own, worlds removed from reality, each so aware of the other they were lost in the exquisite joy of their reunion. The grief and uncertainty of tomorrow would wait; tonight was theirs – fleeting, intangible, unforgettable. The dawn would bring renewed awareness of the world outside their love, but it could wait – it must wait . . .

Rachel stood very still, her hands immobile by her sides, her eyes seeing yet barely believing that the crumpled broken body thrown so carelessly by the tide onto the sands was really her father, her big, hard-bodied father who had strode so tall through life. The tide had carried him round Portcull Point to Mara Òran Bay, Bay of the Sea Song. She saw him as he had been, tough, sullen, his surprisingly gentle brown eyes lighting up at sight of her and her small brothers waiting for him at the harbour. She saw him striding homewards through Glen Fallan, mock severity in his glance at sight of her grubby knees and dirty face; then one huge hand would reach out to her while the other felt in his pocket, pretending not to find the sweets and toys till with a show of amazement he allowed the bulging pocket to give up its treasures. How could that man now be this poor pitiful sodden lump? The men had covered him quickly, but not quickly enough. She had seen his crushed chest; the congealed blood clogging his mouth, matting into his beard.

The morning was gentle and warm; the sea shimmered blue; the sky was wide and boundless; seabirds were making a noisy fuss as they poked for molluscs among the seaweed left by high tide. It was all as it had been, as if there never had been a storm – as if the world could never be anything else but serene and warm and bright – as if her father had never lived – or died. Rachel saw, she heard, her eyes remained dry, but silent screams thrust up inside her skull like shock waves inside a subterranean cave: booming, reverberating, pounding – yet unheard in the world outside. Everything that could be released by the human voice was locked away inside. She was a small cauldron of seething emotions that could find no outlet.

Her mother was standing by Dokie Joe's body, her hands over her face, her shoulders shaking. She looked small and young and vulnerable. Torquil Andrew appeared round Portcull Point and soon his arms were protectively round Annie. When he glanced up and saw Rachel, he held out a hand to her, but she stared past him into nothingness.

From the clifftops Ruth looked down and saw her friend standing alone and her heart brimmed over with pain for the little girl who had always run free but who now stood as if held by invisible fetters, a tiny statue, silent and unmoving. Ruth drew in her breath and began to limp towards the cliff track, but her mother emerged from the house and saw her. 'Ruth!' Her tone was imperative. 'Wait you there, your grannie needs you to run a message.'

Ruth lifted her head defiantly and kept on going down but her mother's hand on her shoulder stayed her abruptly, and she swung round. Her heart was beating very fast. She feared her mother's wrath more than anything else in the world because it was such unreasoning, unthinking anger.

For a few moments, Morag said nothing. Her green gaze travelled down to where Rachel stood on the beach. Morag shivered. The little girl always made her feel uneasy – she dreaded the open frankness of the big expressive eyes, she couldn't take the accusation in them. Rachel couldn't utter a single word yet those eyes of hers said it all. 'You must leave

Rachel alone, Ruth.' Morag's voice was strange and far away. 'She has something in her that's gey strange – she's no' a normal wee lass – she has – the power.'

Ruth's heart bumped, but she cried, 'Leave me be, Mam. Rachel has God in her, *really* in her – and she's just lost her father. Let me go to her, *please*, Mam . . .'

The blood had rushed to Morag's face and she began to shake her daughter till her golden head became a wobbling blur. 'You wee bitch! If I'm no' mistaken the de'il has got at you. What is it that's changed you, Ruth? You were aye such an obedient wee lassie before.'

Old Isabel came out of her cottage, anger in her kindly old face. 'Ach, will you leave the bairn alone, Morag?' she implored. 'What is ailing you now I'd like to know? Go on the way you're doing and I warn you – the bairn will grow up to hate the sight of you.'

Morag whirled round to face her mother, 'If it's any o' your business, Mother, I will no' be havin' my lassie mixin' wi' that wee – that wee witch down there! She's a wild one. She has a funny look to her, I've seen that look before – she has the de'il in her and no mistake.'

'And where have you seen it, Morag?' asked old Isabel ominously. 'In the mirror? If I didny know better I wouldny be wrong in thinkin' *you* have become the daughter of the de'il. I canny believe betimes that you are the same lassie I bore from my own body, for through the years you have changed, Morag, and that's a fact – ay, and fine your poor auld father and myself know it for you have led us a fine dance in hell for more years than I like to think.'

The grip on Ruth's shoulder had lessened and she hurried away, hating herself for leaving her beloved grannie to Morag's fury, yet unable to stop herself from doing so. She reached the beach and Rachel raised her eyes, for the first time recognising someone outside her private hell. The two little girls clung together. Ruth felt the tension in Rachel's body and her heart brimmed over with compassion. What if it had been her father lying crumpled and dead on the cold lonely sands? The idea was unbearable. He was her whole life. She couldn't imagine an existence without him.

Old Joe came over and pushed some things into Rachel's hands. 'These were in his pocket, lass,' he said kindly. 'They will have been meant for you and your wee brothers.' Rachel stared down at the toy cars and the flute. Before he had gone away, her father had promised to bring her back a flute 'so that you can play fairy music to me when I'm tired, lass'. Rachel felt that she was going to fall down and never get up again, so much did her legs shake beneath her.

People were crowding the beach, a few tourists but mainly villagers who stood in sad-eyed little groups discussing quietly the tragedies wreaked by the storm. Canty Tam's voice floated loudly and clearly. He was proclaiming to all and sundry, 'I was after knowin' last night that the Uisga Hags would have a Rhanna man; it was a night just perfect for all the witches of sea and land to get themselves up.' His eyes gleamed as he leered vacantly in Rachel's direction. 'Ay, and the evil caillichs were no' content wi' just one – oh no – they had to have another – a McKenzie, too.' He leaned further sideways. 'Of course, there are some who have the power to call the witches, ay indeed. Witches know their own all right – a fine job they made o' Dokie Joe –'

Ruth leapt at him like an enraged animal and he was thrown to the ground, terror in his pale blue eyes. 'Shut up! Shut up!' she sobbed passionately and began violently to tear at his hair. Dugald ran down the path with Jon at his heels, the former to pull his daughter away from Canty Tam, the latter to run to where Rachel stood immobile. Jon fell on his knees beside her and pulled her to him, his arms strong and comforting. 'Cry, cry, jungfräulich,' he implored her, his own eyes wet at the feel of her slender small body bending trustingly to him. 'Cry, my dear little maiden,' he whispered soothingly. 'It is the only thing that will help to wash away your pain.'

Rachel responded to his impassioned plea. She lay against him, her eyes wide and big and staring, and from them the tears rolled, spilling faster and faster, and all the while Jon soothed her with words of comfort and reassurance.

Among the rock pools some distance away, Lewis sat watching the scene in Mara Òran Bay. There was a strange look in his eyes. He knew that he ought to go and say something kind to Rachel, but he couldn't face any more grief and suffering. He had come here to get away from Laigmhor and all those shocked, dull-eyed people bowed down with the burden of grief. He couldn't bear to see the pain in his father's eyes, the numb shock on Aunt Mary's face, the sadness in his mother's glance. Laigmhor was filled with the presence of death and the strange sickly feeling of illness – Lorn's illness. His brother was in bed, weak and breathless, his flying pulse bringing a frown of concern to Doctor McLachlan's face. Lewis loved his brother but couldn't bear it when he was ill. He hated and feared illness and unhappiness, and when Lorn was ill he felt ill, too. Lewis shuddered. His thoughts strayed back to Lorn – Lorn who was soon to go away from Rhanna to the uncertainty of a big town hospital where he would lie on an operating table while doctors did things to his heart that might make him better – or might kill him. Shona had told Lewis that morning, and he had backed away from her shaking his head and saying, 'Don't tell me any more, I don't want to know.' She had looked at him strangely. She always gave him the impression that she knew what he was thinking. Those beautiful blue eyes of hers had regarded him with frightening perception on several occasions and this morning she had said, 'Och, come on now, Lewis, you have to be told. Father asked me to tell you. I only found out myself yesterday from – from Uncle Alick. Lorn will be going away soon and Father and Kirsteen will need our help. Lorn will need all the support we can give him.'

But Lewis was angry with Shona for telling him – there was enough unhappiness to cope with. He was angry at Lorn, too. Lorn's weakness had always made him uncomfortable. All along he'd had to appease him and reassure him about things, more for his own sake than Lorn's because in appeasing his brother Lewis was in some measure comforted himself. By rights they should have had wonderful times as twin brothers – they could have had a lot of fun – if only . . . Lorn's dark eyes floated into Lewis's mind, rebellion and impatience fighting up out of them. Lorn wouldn't be afraid of hospitals – he would go through anything to be as fit as any other boy . . . Lewis felt suddenly ashamed, yet his shame didn't lend him any strength.

He glowered over lowered brows to Mara Òran Bay: more death, more unhappiness. He threw a pebble in the air and, reaching up to catch it, he saw that it was a 'fluffy cloud day'. The cheerful face of a clown grinned over the sky. Lewis's heart lightened. Wait till he told Lorn about that – but the face of the clown was changing, the big lips were slowly turning down – even the clouds were in mourning.

Lewis felt unease shivering through him. He put his chin in his hands and gazed far away over the shimmering sea. One day he would be a farmer like his father, but first he was going to enjoy himself. The world was big and wide and wonderful . . . Rachel was looking towards him, and though she was some distance away he felt her wild turbulence reaching him, touching him. Rachel was dumb, but she was so full of vibrant life she didn't need words to convey how she felt. She was like him, thirsty for all life had to offer, taking happiness where and how she could get it – yet, there was something in her that wasn't in him, only he didn't know what it was. He looked up. The clown was smiling again. That was how a clown ought to look.

The clear notes of a flute were borne to him on the breeze. Jon was walking with Rachel and she was playing the flute – not a sad tune, either – one that was light and gay.

Lewis stood up, his earth-brown curls tossing in the breeze, his blue eyes brilliant. It was all right to go to Rachel now; she had turned her back on the pathetic bundle that had been her father and she was playing the flute.

Lewis ran, his sturdy tanned limbs carrying him swiftly to Rachel's side. She didn't look up at his approach, but kept on playing, her fingers moving nimbly. Her black curls were dancing in the breeze, he noticed, and there was a sheen of blue in them where they were touched by the sun. Her body seemed totally relaxed; the curve of her lashes swept the rounded bloom of her golden cheeks; she looked as she had always looked – a sun-kissed waif, a child of the sea, the sky, the sun. She was like him – death was something she turned her back on in her search for the sunshine. She raised her eyes to look at him, and the expression in the deep dark pools made him draw in his breath; they were pain-racked, filled with pathos, torture, despair. Her naked soul was in her eyes, and Lewis knew that carefree little Rachel would never be the same again, that part of her – her vitality, her childhood – had died the moment her father had taken his last shuddering breath out there in the sea that swirled ceaselessly round the stark pinnacles of the Sgor Creags.

Part Three

Summer 1956

Chapter Eleven

Lorn opened his eyes to see fingers of sunlight pouring through the window to make a golden pool on the mellow varnished wood of the floor. Lazily he stretched and drew a deep satisfying breath. How good to breathe like that, to feel life and strength surging through his veins. How good not to feel breathless or faint any more. He stared for a few moments at his upstretched arms and frowned a little – they were too skinny; he would have to get some muscles in them, to work and work till they were hard and strong. From where he lay he could see the rugged thrust of the peaks of Ben Machrie – he would work till he was as strong as a mountain – well, he grinned – as strong as dear old Conker anyway.

He swung his legs over the bed and put his feet on the soft rag rug that had been made by Mirabelle. As he dressed he looked at Lewis's side of the room: it was tidy now, but tomorrow it would resemble a midden because tonight Lewis would be home from school for the summer holidays. All the children of Lewis's age had gone away to complete their education at mainland schools – all except Lorn who had spent much of his teenage years in hospital.

Time had often hung heavy for him, especially during his earlier years when his stays in hospital stretched into months and his visits home were brief, worrying affairs for his parents. When he had become stronger Kirsteen had taught him at home. Often she had looked very tired, but determinedly she had set time aside each day to sit with him and a hard taskmaster she had been, too, never allowing him to fob her off with excuses. From Shona he had learned that his mother had been called a Tartar in the classroom.

'I could never understand that,' Shona had said, her blue eyes lit with amusement. 'Oh, she was strict all right and made us all sit up like pokers, but the bairns respected her for it and half the older boys were in love with her and used to sneak flowers to her when they thought no one was looking.'

Mr Murdoch, too, had given freely of his spare time, and Lorn had developed a real liking for the fussy little man with the worried frown and twinkling eyes. But best of all had been Ruth, though at first they had barely been able to communicate because of mutual shyness. His bed had been in the parlour then and Morag Ruadh had only allowed her daughter to visit him on the condition she read to him from the Bible. 'Only the passages that will benefit his soul most, poor wee cratur',' Morag had stipulated. 'Later, when he's stronger, you may read Kings to him, Solomon has a lot to say that might make young folks sit up and take notice – you mustny go near his bed, mind, it's no' decent for a wee lass to be in a boy's room, but seein' he's lyin' in the parlour, it will no' be so bad.'

'Ay, Mam,' Ruth had promised obediently, but on her first few visits to Laigmhor, struggling with her own self-consciousness, trying to break through Lorn's, she had barely been able to see a word, let alone read passages from the Bible. Long silences had passed between them during which he had fidgeted and wished she would go; and she had sat very still in the chair by the window with her hands folded in her lap, her great violet eyes gazing longingly at the long ribbon of the Glen Fallan road winding to the harbour. The first time she hadn't been able to bear it and she had risen and hobbled away, leaving behind her Bible, which had slid from her lap. But gradually each had glimpsed something of the other's true nature, and Kings was abandoned for stories from Ruth's jotters, for card games, Scrabble, mischievous chatter.

Every time Ruth returned from a visit to Laigmhor her mother never failed to ask, 'Well Ruth, have you and Lorn enjoyed reading the Lord's word?'

'Ay, that we have, Mam,' Ruth always answered soberly. Her visits to Lorn had eased her first months at Portcull school. In the beginning the children had christened her 'Saint Ruth', and she had held her golden head high and borne the gibes; but one day, riled beyond bearing, she had flown at her tormentor like an enraged wildcat. Some of the children had witnessed her attack on Canty Tam the day Dokie Joe's body had been washed up on the beach. Others had only heard about it, but now they were all made aware that gentle, shy Ruth was possessed of a courageous fighting spirit that had to be reckoned with. Rachel had watched till Ruth had reduced her tormentor to a snivelling bundle, and then she had pulled her friend away and with shining eyes had spelled out a message in the sign language: 'Good for you, Ruth, I knew one day you would fight back. They'll never call you names again.'

But primary school days were in the past now for Ruth, Rachel and Lewis, and Lorn no longer had their company except in the holidays. He wasn't strong enough for a secondary education that involved fatiguing trips from home. And there were also the spells in hospital to contend with, so he had to make do with tuition at home. But he was strong enough to be able to get up and about more. No longer were his days spent in the parlour waving to people passing up and down Glen Fallan. He was able to ride, fish and swim in moderation, and, best of all, he was able to help his father around the farm, though these were light tasks to begin with. Oh, what joy to work beside that tall giant of a man in the morning fields! In the gloaming at harvest time, when all the world smelled of earth and rain and warm ripe hay, his heart glowed with quiet appreciation as he worked with the other men. He would never forget the day he climbed to the top of Ben Machrie with his father, or the heady euphoria of sitting in the heather on that high, windblown place, drinking the sweet water of the hill. It was as if he had climbed to the roof of the world to look at a panorama of patchwork fields and amber moors, and all around the blue, blue sea stretched to infinite horizons, studded with the green and purple jewels that were the islands – Barra, Eriskay, the Uists – and far in the misted distance the craggy ethereal peaks of the inner Hebrides – Skye and Mull, Rum, Jura, Eigg. His father was a man of few words, especially when he was outdoors working, but Lorn was glad of that as he himself hated superfluity of speech. As the years passed he chattered less and less, expanded mentally, physically and emotionally, and in so doing grew to understand his father. Mentally they had become very close: they worked in harmony, attuned to each other, communicating by instinct rather than utterance.

But everything changed when Lewis came home. He brought excitement, laughter, nonsense – and had so much to catch up on he was never still for a moment and talked from morning to night. He had hated having to go away to school without Lorn, but had felt better when the Travers, retired now and living close to Oban harbour, had insisted that he stay with them rather than in a hostel. Lewis had suffered a good deal during the years of his brother's fight for survival. He had experienced phantom chest pains and knew exactly when Lorn was on the operating table. When the surgeons' knives had been at work, Lewis had felt genuinely ill and often had had to be excused from school. But now all that was over. Lorn had undergone his last operation some months ago, and in his uphill climb to good health, his brother climbed with him.

Lorn met him at the pier that evening. He was tall and broad-shouldered in his fifteenth year. With his white teeth flashing, his suntanned face and his blue eyes sparkling, he was dashingly handsome. His manner was confident and assured, his charm of manner and speech very arresting. When he spoke to females of any age, his lilting voice became soft and silken and was so obviously irresistible to the fair sex that one or two young tourists with whom he had become acquainted on the boat stood gazing at him with fluttering lashes before walking reluctantly away. Lorn felt dwarfed by him and was overwhelmingly conscious of his own pale face and skinny arms.

'Hey, hello there, little brother!' Lewis cried in delighted greeting.

Lorn flinched. 'Ach, I'm not so little,' he growled. 'It's just that you're so big –' He broke off as he saw over his brother's head Ruth and Rachel coming down the gangplank with Jon at their heels. Rachel had changed, that much was obvious from her newly sophisticated dress. She was tall, slender and wind-blown, her face was vibrant with life. Beside her Ruth looked small, dainty, and rather delicate. But there was a change in her too, Lorn noticed instantly: she was less ungainly, her once plain little face was sweeter, almost pretty in its youthful serenity. Her hair, which had grown even lighter, was a startling halo of pale gold next to Rachel's raven curls. Both of them had blossomed from flat-chested little girls into shapely young maidens, though there was still an uneasiness about the way Ruth carried herself, as if to stand too straight and show off too much was something to be ashamed of. Rachel, on the other hand, walked tall and straight, so that her firm young breasts were thrust out. There was also a sensuality in the way she moved: it was graceful yet provocative, and the directness of her gaze obviously tantalised men. One of the young deckhands was being very attentive to her.

Lewis grinned at the look on his brother's face. 'Ay, they've changed. Imagine, even you noticing that! I always had the feeling you saw girls as boys with frocks on . . .' He threw his arm round Lorn's shoulders and they walked along the harbour towards Glen Fallan. 'I'll tell you a secret, Lorn my boy, girls are made different from us . . .' His voice was bubbling with mischief and Lorn shook his head and laughed. 'Ach, wait till you hear the rest,' Lewis instructed. 'And don't interrupt. Before I left Rhanna, while I was still with old Murdoch and feeling a bit wild about having to go to Oban, I chased Mary Anderson through the fields and rolled her around in the grass for a wee bit of fun – but something happened – she had bosoms – she was more than two years older than me – and I touched them. She let me do it and after a while she let me make love to her.'

'You – you mean you kissed her.'

'Ay, that too and all the rest.'

'But – hell, Lewis! You must only have been twelve!' Lorn exploded in disbelief.

'I could have done it at eleven.' Lewis sounded very confident. 'Don't you tell me you never had funny things happening to you when you were eleven.'

'I was too busy being ill,' Lorn answered faintly.

Lewis laughed, a hearty booming laugh. He hugged his brother closer as they trudged up Glen Fallan. 'Well, you're not eleven or ill now and I'm telling you this, it was grand with Mary, but too quick and silly – it's much much better the more you practise, so start practising – it's what girls are here for.'

Laigmhor seemed to come alive that evening. Lewis's delight at being home was infectious and he carried everyone along on an exuberant tide so that his buoyancy filled every room in the house. Kirsteen skelped him on the ear for swearing, and in retaliation he got up and waltzed her round the kitchen. Fergus leaned back in his chair and roared with delight at the look of exaggerated outrage on her face, and Lorn watched his father and wondered why it was he never laughed like that with him – but Lorn knew – he was too reserved, too like his father, and opposites made the best companions – his father and Lewis were opposites. Kirsteen pushed Lewis away. Her curls were ruffled, her face flushed. 'Bed, young man,' she said firmly. 'You too, Lorn, you must be tired, you've been up since dawn.'

Lewis turned at the door. 'When will Grant be home?'

'Next week sometime.'

'Good, I'm dying to hear all his adventures. Sometimes I think I might join the Merchant Navy. He promised to bring me back a native girl – I hope he doesn't forget.'

'A what?'

'Ach, dinna fash, as Dodie would say – a carved one, for my bookcase – though a real one would be better,' he ended with a chuckle and dodged quickly upstairs.

Fergus looked at Kirsteen. 'Lorn is still a boy but Lewis is already a man of the world.'

A shadow passed over her blue eyes and she went to stand behind her husband to gently massage his shoulders. 'I know – were you at his age?' He pulled her hand towards his lips and kissed it. 'In some ways, ay, I would be lying if I said otherwise . . . In other ways I was still a lad till the day I wed.'

She bent and kissed the top of his silvered dark head. 'You always said he would sow some wild oats before he settled down – we can only hope he'll have the sense not to scatter them too liberally.'

'Ay,' Fergus said off-handedly, and she couldn't see the frown that darkened his brows.

Lewis was up first next morning, punching his brother into wakefulness with a pillow.

'Hey, get off!' Lorn emerged tousleheaded. 'What time is it?'

'Six-thirty. C'mon, get up, it's a grand morning, just right for a paddle in Brodie's Burn.'

In minutes they were dressed and running down to the kitchen where the rays of the sun patterned the brick-red floors. Lewis gulped creamy milk from the big jug on the table and stuffed his pockets with scones from the larder. He was like a small boy, eager to explore old familiar haunts. The gentle heat of the sun probed into field hollows, coaxing the steam to rise and billow out over the landscape. Wreaths of mist encircled the blue hill peaks; down by the harbour, peat smoke curled lazily from the chimneys. The warm smell of heather was sweet in the air; the pure haunting call of the curlew rose out of the moors where greens and ambers blended harmoniously together; the path to Brodie's Burn was a blue and lavender carpet of harebells and wild thyme. Long before they reached the burn the boys removed socks and shoes to walk barefoot through the scented wildflowers. Lewis threw out his arms. 'What a morning to welcome me back.' He grinned wickedly. 'Of course, the sun always shines on the good and pure – hey, little brother,' he said, and threw his arm round Lorn's shoulders, 'this is how it should have been from the start, you and me together doing all the things we're doing now. But we'll make up for it – only good times from now on. Promise me – only good times. I don't know what it is about twins, but it's true they share everything. It must be something to do with coming from the same egg, but I was pretty damned sick every time you went into hospital. I hated it.'

'I didn't like it too well myself.' Lorn's young face

was dark. 'And I didn't exactly have hysterics laughing when the doctors were cutting me up.'

Lewis was serious for a minute. He looked into his brother's deep, steadfast eyes and said slowly, 'I know I'm the selfish half of the egg. When it split up it didn't make an even job of it – all the goodness went to you.'

'Ach, get away! I'm no simpering goody-goody!' Lorn protested awkwardly. 'I want things, the same kind of things you want – only I'm too damned afraid to go after them.'

'Not afraid,' Lewis said softly. 'Canny's the word for you, my lad. You're like Father – canny, dour, and as stubborn as a mule's arse. You can wait for the things you want from life – I can't, that's the difference; I want it all and I want it now.'

Lorn glanced all around him. 'You've got it all now, you daft ass. Stop gabbling and let's get on.'

Ruth was sitting on a low shelf of the Seanachaidh's Stone, her feet in the bracing waters of Brodie's Burn. She had divested herself of shoes and stockings, her calliper lay by her side. She was absorbed, her golden head bowed over the notepad in her lap, the tip of her tongue protruding from the side of her mouth as her pencil flew over the pages. This was one of her favourite haunts, a place of solitude seldom visited by anyone. She often came here before breakfast, before her mother arose to begin another day of religious ritual. The sound of feet swishing through grass made her start up in fright: her violet eyes darkened with the awareness that she wasn't alone, and she had the look of a young deer ready to take flight. At sight of the twins her cheeks blazed and she hastily removed her feet from the water and tucked them under her dress.

Lewis plunked himself down on the bank and plunged his feet straight into the water, teasing her with his roguish grin, enjoying the blushes spreading over her fair skin. 'A fine mornin', Ruth, mo ghaoil.'

'Ay, it is that,' Ruth stuttered. She felt naked, so conscious of the calliper lying on the light grey stone she tried to cover it with the hem of her dress.

'Och, don't be so worried about that silly old calliper,' Lewis scolded, ducking his head to watch his toes wiggling in the peaty brown water. 'No use trying to hide it – you've got a bad leg, and that's that. Get your feet out from under your frock and put them back in the burn.'

Ruth felt better. She relaxed slightly. Lewis had always been able to ease her self-consciousness, make light of her disability – but Lorn couldn't – he was trying very very hard to simulate his brother's indifference, not looking at her, letting his fingers dabble in the umber trout pool some distance away, but she could sense his awareness of her feelings, and she felt miserable with embarrassment. She glanced at the top of his head. His earth-brown curls were tinged with chestnut lights, his shoulder blades stuck out through his jersey, the arm that hung downwards was thin and void of sunburn. She saw the reflection of his face in the pool, an ascetic sensitive face – like her father's. The thought startled her.

He said without looking up, 'You suit that stone, Ruthie, it might have been made for you – after all, it's the stone of the storyteller.'

Ruthie! Only her father called her that. She felt the heat go out of her face. 'I know the legend of this place,' she volunteered shyly.

'Tell it,' Lewis said absently. He had little time for things of the past – the present was far more exciting to him – but he felt that as Ruth was here, she might as well entertain him.

'It was told to old Andrew by Neil the Seanachaidh, and old Andrew told it to me before he died last year,' Ruth began, hesitantly. 'Brodie was a hill climber who got lost climbing the Rhanna hills one stormy night. He lay hurt and dying, crying for help, but no one came. He wept so many tears of anguish they flowed down the hillside, and a spring welled up at the spot where his body was found. There was a great landslide on the night of the storm: the boulders and rocks that rolled down crashed through heather and bracken and came to rest in the fields and moors far below – all but one – this one I'm sitting on now. It came to rest a few inches from Brodie's body.' Ruth's purpled gaze was faraway and very bright. 'Later, in the dark nights of winter, the seanachaidhs gathered round the peat fires to tell how Brodie's Burn came to be, and in the quiet gloamings of summer nights, at the end of the day's work, they came to sit on this stone to rest and to tell the tales of the old days to the young shepherd boys. That's how this stone got its name, and how the story of Brodie got handed down – and that is why to this day the folk of Rhanna come up here and bathe their feet in Brodie's Burn. The old folks say the water is his tears, and that it has healing properties – that is why I bathe my feet in it when no one in the world is looking.'

She uttered the last words without a hint of self-consciousness, so lost was she in the tale she told with such sincerity in her sweet voice. Both boys were completely entranced. Lewis's eyes were on her face, drinking in the almost ethereal quality of beauty the last few minutes had brought to it. Lorn looked down at his hands and murmured softly, 'You're a fine storyteller, Ruthie – just like your father. One day, I think, you might be famous.'

Ruth started out of her reverie and the crimson flooded her cheeks once more. In confusion she said, 'Oh, I must go, Mam will be waiting for me to help her with breakfast – I – I'm late as it is . . .'

Lorn saw her dilemma. She was in a panic at being late, yet if need be she would stay where she was for ever. Under no circumstances would she put on her calliper in front of them, and without it she couldn't walk. Lorn stood up and gave his brother a little push. 'Come on, big brother, Mother will have breakfast ready, and I for one am starving.'

'Me too!' Lewis was like an eager hungry young puppy. He began to run. 'We'll be seeing you, Ruth,' he called over his shoulder, 'goodbye for now.'

'Goodbye,' Ruth returned, and waited till they were just mere specks in the heather before she uncurled her legs stiffly from under her. For a moment she stared with dislike at her small wasted foot, then hastily she pulled on stockings and shoes and fitted the calliper in place. Lachlan had told her mother that exercises and physiotherapy might do a lot to improve the leg, but Morag Ruadh had scoffed at the idea and had told Lachlan it was the will of the Lord. When Ruth had told Rachel this, her eyes flashed and she had promised that during these summer holidays she was going to massage Ruth's leg for her and make her do all sorts of exercises. Ruth smiled as she recalled the glitter of determination in her friend's dark eyes, and, gathering up her notepad and pencils, she hobbled away over the fields to Portcull. She stood on the hilltop looking down at the village. A thin banner of smoke rose from the chimney of her cottage. Her mother was up and had most likely already scrubbed the kitchen floor with carbolic. She would be making the porridge about now, stirring, stirring, rhythmically banging the wooden spoon against the pan sides. Ruth was fascinated by the ritual. She often fancied that her mother was a red-haired witch standing tight-lipped over the fire, brewing some sort of evil potion, using the wooden spoon as an instrument to rid her of all the emotions she bottled up inside.

Sure enough, when Ruth opened the door her mother was at the fire pounding the sluggish porridge viciously. She barely turned at Ruth's entry yet the sideways sweep of her hooded green eyes took in everything. 'You're late, Ruth, and you've got dirt on the hem of your dress.'

'Ay, Mam, I know, but it's awful hard to keep clean in a white dress.'

She stood waiting for the usual questions, a vision of summer in her pure white dress, the rays of the morning sun at her back making her look slightly insubstantial, a being not of this world with her violet dreaming eyes and the fluffy curling hair turned to threads of palest gold in the sun. For over a year now, except when she was away at school, her mother had insisted she wear nothing but white. The change from drab browns and greys had come about one rainy cold morning just after her thirteenth birthday. She would never forget the terror of that morning, or the lonely stark imaginings of a little girl who had been told nothing of the facts of life. She remembered the aching cramp deep in her belly, the misery of nursing her pain in silence, hoping it would go away. But it hadn't gone away, it had got worse and she had gone to her bed to lie down. Then had come the terror – of seeing blood seeping through her clothes – *her* blood – coming from some wound deep inside her body. In her ignorance that was what she had imagined, and, pale and shaking, her eyes huge with fear, she had limped through to her mother to cry out pathetically, 'Mam! Mam! I'm bleeding to death! Could you – would you help me, please.'

Morag Ruadh had turned round very slowly, her own face white and strained. It had been bad enough for her to watch Ruth's thin little body blossoming out – but this – this moment of truth was what Morag had dreaded more than any other. She had shut her mind to the inevitability of it, had refused to face the fact that one day it would happen. Her heart had gone queer within her and she had felt faint.

'Mam,' Ruth's voice had come again, appalled, shaken, fearful.

Morag had gazed at her child and the pathos and strain on the pale small face had twisted her heart. For the first time since the night of her baby's birth, all her motherly instincts were unleashed in one mighty upsurge of pure love. She had sat down in the rocking chair, had taken Ruth into her arms, and for the first time in many years had experienced the earthly joy of kissing and touching smooth skin and silken hair. 'My babby,' she had whispered huskily. 'You mustny be afraid, these things that are happening to you are natural – you've grown, Ruth, from a wee lassie into a wee woman. Weesht now, I will take you and bathe you and tell you what to do.'

Later, when Ruth was calm, her mother had held her at arm's length to gaze down on her and say, 'You mustny ever let boys come near you, Ruth, for they want nothing but to take away the purity of a young lass. From now on you will be dressed in virgin white, for nothing is cleaner that the white o' the driven snow. Heed what I say, my lassie, and remember – when the de'il tempts you, as indeed he will, you must remember my words and be mindful never to violate the purity o' the garments that clothe your body.'

Ruth never had forgotten that day or her mother's words, for each morning she was minded of them afresh when she arose to don white underwear and white outerwear. Boys whispered behind her back and christened her 'the white virgin', yet their glances were admiring, for with her fair skin and hair she was a vision of sweetness. The older folk had always pitied her in her drab frocks but now they called her 'the wee white angel' and their hearts warmed to her and grew colder to Morag Ruadh for stamping her daughter in ways that were enough to turn the lass to sin.

'And where did you go this mornin'?' Morag asked as Ruth busied herself laying the table.

'For a walk. It's a bonny morning.'

'And did you meet anybody at all?'

'Ay, the twins. Lorn is looking much better than he did,' Ruth answered carefully.

Morag glanced at her quickly and said meaningfully, 'Both lads are growing to be young men. You watch out, my girl, I don't take much to these ways you have o' goin' off first thing in the mornin' by yourself.' Ruth was saved further questioning by the arrival of her father. He gave her a quick wink and she winked back, enjoying the intimacy of one of several little habits that had sprung up between them over the years.

During Grace, Ruth sat with her eyes closed, thinking about many things, her mind drifting to

Rachel and the plans they had made for the long summer holidays. They would be aided and abetted in these by Ruth's grandparents, who, though now in their eighties, were still sound of wind and limb and had become adept at thwarting Morag's attempts to run their lives for them. They took a wicked delight in trying to outwit her, and Ruth dreaded the day when she would have them no more. She was far more at home in their cosy cottage than she ever was in the clinical confines of the place both she and her father referred to in private as 'the temple'. Here, all savoury smells were perpetually drowned in the ever-present fumes of carbolic and even the food itself seemed to be tainted by disinfectant.

'You're fidgeting, Ruth,' Morag inserted the reprimand into her own extended version of morning Grace.

Ruth folded her hands in her lap and prayed for patience. She was unusually restless that morning and in between polishing the furniture and black-leading the grate she kept going to the window to gaze with anxious eyes in the direction of the Post Office.

'Ach, what's wi' you, Ruth?' Morag demanded sharply. 'You're like a hen on a hot girdle.'

Ruth turned quickly back to her tasks but breathed a sigh of relief when Morag at last went into the scullery to fetch the meal basin and then took it out to the sunlit yard where she was at once surrounded by an eager army of hens. Ruth looked once more through the window and her heart leapt. Erchy was emerging from the Post Office and her grandparents' house was one of the first on his rounds. Throwing down her duster she limped to the side gate to burst shining-eyed upon Isabel and Jim Jim. She had only visited them briefly the evening before but it had been enough for them to slip her a letter that had arrived at their cottage more than a month ago. In wonder she had devoured the contents of it by the light of a torch in the privacy of the wee hoosie at the back of the temple. So exciting was the news contained in the letter that she had barely slept all night and had risen early to go and tell her grandparents her news before making her journey to Brodie's Burn. Her news had resulted in Isabel spending a feverish morning glued to the window. She had even supped her porridge there so that she would miss nothing of the comings and goings from the Post Office. Jim Jim had remained stolidly by the fire, smoking his pipe and spitting into the peats, but excitement had gained the upper hand in the end and the fire had been abandoned in favour of the window where he jostled with Isabel for the best viewpoint.

'Erchy's coming,' Ruth burst out breathlessly.

'Ay, ay, here he is now.' Jim Jim was at the door, grabbing eagerly at a package from the bemused Erchy's hands. He cocked a bright eye at Ruth who had grown pink. 'Love letters, is it? It's gey lucky havin' grandparents you can put things like these in care of.'

Ruth glanced nervously outside. Her mother had

fed the hens and had gone over a hillock to inspect
her washing. Only her red head showed, and Ruth
took the package from a disappointed-looking Jim
Jim and said breathlessly, 'I'll have to be going now,
but I'll come over at dinner time and show it to you.
Quick, Mam's coming back, I don't want her finding
out yet.'

Erchy scratched his balding sandy head and
grinned after Ruth's disappearing back. 'Family
secrets, eh? You haveny won a competition like our
Todd did a whily back? My, I could fine picture a
brand new motor car sitting at your door, Jim Jim.'
He pulled up a chair and took the cup of tea proffered by Isabel. 'Were you after hearin' that a rich
American lady has hired Todd's car for a fortnight?'

'Indeed no.' Isabel folded her ample arms on the
table and comfortably settled down to listen to the
latest gossip about Todd's car. He had never driven
it since the day it arrived, and for years it had sat
outside the Smiddy with a large 'For Hire' sign on the
window. Tourists were amazed to come upon the
incongruous sight of Todd and Mollie sitting outside
on kitchen chairs beside the gleaming car, smiling
benignly at the passing world, Mollie in her apron,
Todd in shirt sleeves, hairy tweed trousers and cloth
bonnet. So startling was the contrast between the
sturdy whitewashed cottage, the homely old couple,
and the sleek car, that the majority of visitors thought
the whole thing was a joke and the 'For Hire' sign
wasn't to be taken seriously. The car was popular for
island weddings and funerals but was seldom used

for anything else, therefore Erchy made much of the latest piece of news.

That day, Ruth spent so much time in the wee hoosie that Morag enquired sharply if her bowels were in good order. The minute Dugald came home he was accosted in the kitchen by his sparkling-eyed daughter. Morag had gone next door with a pot of broth for her parents, giving Ruth the opportunity to be alone with her father. She took him by the hands, propelled him to the rocking chair and made him sit down.

'What on earth's going on, Ruthie?' Dugald said, smiling, his eyes on his daughter's pink cheeks.

Ruth clasped her hands, and, putting the tips of her fingers to her lips, regarded him for a long silent moment. Then from the pocket of her apron she drew out her letter and handed it to him.

'Read it, Father,' she burst out in a strangely controlled voice. Slowly Dugald put on his glasses and glanced through the letter. It was from the editor of a well-known Scottish magazine informing Ruth that the short story she had submitted for consideration had been accepted for publication and would be appearing in the following month's issue. Ruth extracted the magazine from the breast fold of her apron, where it had been all day, and, spreading it open, she laid it on her father's knee. His eyes had grown misty and he had to remove his glasses to wipe the steam from them before he could commence reading. His voice was husky as he read out, '*Hebridean Dream* by Ruth Naomi Donaldson.'

He raised his head slowly and there was such a depth of pride in his grey eyes that Ruth drew in her breath.

'Well, Father, are you pleased?' she asked somewhat shyly.

'Pleased?' His tones were tight, charged with so many emotions he could hardly go on. 'My lassie, you've done it – you've done it, Ruthie. In bringing your own dreams to fruition you've made all my own come true. I'll bask in your reflected glory and by God! I'll bask in it till it dazzles me. I'm proud of you, my lassie – so proud I – I think I'm going to cry.' The mist in his eyes brimmed over, and, fumbling for his hanky, he buried his face into it and could say nothing further.

Ruth looked down at his thin shoulders, his bowed silvery head. She remembered the days of childhood rambles when all her world had revolved round him, when his slow pleasant voice had woven one story, one magical tale after another. She remembered sitting on his knee by firelight, listening enchanted as his fables lifted her and carried her up and out of harsh reality into lands full of beauty and wonder. He had been her guiding light, her teacher and mentor. All his own dreams had been shattered by a loveless marriage, but unselfishly he had encouraged her, nurtured her talent, nourished her mind with his vast store of knowledge, and in giving of himself, he had given her treasures far greater than any worldly goods. Love for him poured through every fibre of her being, throbbed in each pulsebeat. She laid her hand on his shoulder, and without looking up, he took it and held it and shook his head, too full yet for words.

'You gave me my gift,' she said, her musical voice soft. 'I am your daughter – that's the truth, isn't it, Father?'

Slowly he lifted his head. His eyes were full of tears, the pupils of them black and wide with the pain and the pleasure of minutes he would treasure for the rest of his days. Her violet gaze was on him, calm, assured. Understanding passed between them and he knew what she meant. He nodded. 'Ay, Ruthie, you are indeed my daughter, and I thank God for bringing you into my life. You have been more than a blessing to me – you have been my salvation.' He reached up and touched her hair. 'The bonniest hair of all the lassies on the island. When I was a laddie my hair was the colour yours is now – ay, indeed, you are mine, Ruth Naomi Donaldson.'

She took something else from her pocket and held it up. 'This was in with the letter, a cheque for five pounds – it isn't much but it's a start . . .'

Morag came in, muttering about the cantankerous ways of her parents, but she stopped short in her tirade to look suspiciously from Ruth to Dugald. 'What's wi' the pair o' you – and why isn't the table set, Ruth? I turn my back for five minutes and –'

'Morag, will you be quiet for once in your life and listen to *us* for a change . . .'

Morag stared at her husband. His voice had been pleasant but firm, and in the same tones he went on to tell her the news. As she listened, Morag's expression grew strange; something that was indefinable crept into her green eyes.

'We should be very proud of our lassie,' Dugald finished softly. 'She is a daughter any parents would be glad to own.'

Morag turned away. Her shoulders sagged, and she put out her hands quickly to steady herself on the white scrubbed table. 'And why is it you had your mail addressed to your grandparents' house?' she said finally, not looking up but keeping her gaze glued on the table top.

'I was afraid you would open it, Mam,' Ruth said quietly.

Morag threw up her head as an angry retort sprang to her lips, but a glimpse of Ruth's steady frank gaze made her bite back the words. That look – had she not seen the same look in her husband's eyes every day of her life for the last fifteen years? No matter what she had done to him, no matter how much she had denied him, the steadfast honesty in his deep eyes had never faltered. The same look was there in Ruth, growing stronger with each passing year – and now, the thing that Morag had always scorned as 'fanciful nonsense' had taken root to become reality – the dreams, the fables had come out of the clouds and were there, spread out in black and white, on Dugald's knee. Ruth had been born with a gift – she was a gifted child . . . born of a gifted father. Morag's heart beat fast – was it possible? Oh God, that it were so . . .

Ruth was beside her, placing the cheque on the

table. 'This will maybe help with my keep, Mam. I know fine things are dear these days and with me growing so fast it canny make it any easier – get a wee thing for Grannie and Granda – some baccy and maybe a wee sweetie.'

There was no hint of condescension in Ruth's voice; it was tinged only with the pleasure of giving. Love for her child flooded Morag's heart. In a rush of impulse her long fingers clasped round Ruth's hand and she said awkwardly, 'You're a good, good lassie, Ruth – and the Lord knows I'm proud o' you this day.'

'I'll set the table, Mam,' Ruth said. Turning away she winked at her father as she passed his chair on the way to the big oak sideboard.

That night Dugald went early to bed and lay entranced as he read *Hebridean Dream*. It was an enchanting tale, written in such a simple, moving style, that long before he had finished it his eyes had grown misty. He leaned back on his pillows to gaze unseeingly through the window. Ruth had written this, his Ruthie had woven this tale of such enchantment it had been judged good enough to be actually published. Good enough! It was wonderful! Wonderful! Wonderful! And his daughter had done it, *his* daughter! His flesh and blood. She had known all along of the doubts surrounding her identity and she had never uttered a word of them to another soul. Dear God! She must have gone through hell in her mind-searchings, yet her love for him and her loyalty to Morag had never wavered.

'You gave me the gift, I am truly your daughter.' Her words rang in his ears and he turned his face to the pillow. He felt comforted and fulfilled beyond measure and for the first time in years the rigours of his existence faded into insignificance. He forgot the cold, sparse emptiness of his lonely bedroom and fell asleep with the glow of love and pride filling every corner of his heart.

Chapter Twelve

The news of Ruth's success spread round the island like wildfire. When it reached Rachel's ears she went racing down to the village, her long bare legs carrying her swiftly. Ruth was in the henhouses gathering eggs, but she got up quickly to see who could by flying down the stony road in such a hurry. At sight of Rachel she put down the egg basket. The two girls stood regarding each other with warm joy, then Rachel covered the short distance that bridged them and took her friend into a strong, congratulatory embrace. In those precious breathless moments of swift heartbeats, both girls felt that everything they had ever dreamed of was coming true. The world was at their feet, the fire and energy of youth pulsed rapidly in their veins.

Rachel herself was on the crest of a wave. After her father's death she had felt her place would be at home with her widowed mother, but just a year ago Annie had told her daughter that she and Torquil Andrew were to be married. Now, a tiny baby girl with blonde hair and brown eyes had arrived, and the couple were very happy. Rachel wasn't impressed by the new arrival. She had never been the sort of girl to fawn with wide-eyed adulation over babies, she had had enough of them with her young brothers – for whom she had been expected to fetch and carry. The thing that was important to her was that her mother now had someone to lean on, and Rachel had dared to hope that she could pursue a career of music. Jon, who had visited Rhanna as often as he could, had encouraged her all the way, and her ambition was to stay on at school to study hard and perhaps go on to the Atheneum in Glasgow. To her joy her mother had raised no objection – 'Ay, your father would have wanted that,' Annie had said without a great deal of interest – the girl's euphoria was threaded with the dark knowledge that her mother was too wrapped up in her new-found happiness to care very much about that of her daughter.

Torquil Andrew, though kind, was never quite at ease with Rachel. He sensed that she had always known about him and Annie. Although he was a sensible man, he was also a superstitious one, and somehow, in Rachel's company, he felt that the spirit of Dokie Joe was very much alive and would never be allowed to die. Rachel didn't need words to tell him that or the fact that, though he was now man of the house, in Rachel's eyes he would always be an intruder. Yet he knew that he had been the means of freeing her from her ingrained sense of duty to her family, and he knew that she was grateful to him for that.

Old Isabel came out of her cottage and saw her granddaughter with Rachel. Morag Ruadh had gone away up the Hillock to the Kirk to supervise the tuning of the ancient organ, and now a sense of freedom cloaked the temple and its policies.

'Go you away and enjoy yourselves,' Isabel instructed as she came through the gate. 'You don't get out enough, Ruth.'

'But I've still to peel the tatties and prepare the mackerel that old Joe handed in this morning . . .'

'Ach, get away wi' you; I'll do these in no time! Your mother might think Jim Jim and myself are hapless, but there she is far wrong, lassie.' She held up a plump hand. 'Don't argue – when your mother comes back (and the Lord knows when that will be, for she'll have thon poor wee mannie sweatin' over that damt music box for hours), I'll just tell her I sent you over to Nigg wi' a knitting pattern for auld Aggie. A trip like that should keep you away for a few hours, eh?' She beamed mischievously, and Ruth hugged her and peeled off her apron.

The girls went off arm in arm hugging each other with glee at the rather awed looks thrown at Ruth from people she had known all her life. Lorn and Lewis had been dispatched from Laigmhor to fetch some groceries from Portcull and they came along the glen road, Lewis swinging the empty shopping bag in the air. He immediately set about teasing Ruth. 'Is it permitted for a humble peasant like myself to speak to one so grand?' he grinned. 'You're a sensation – do you know that, Ruth Naomi Donaldson? Old Behag nearly had apoplexy when she saw your name in print. They have called out the fire brigade to put out her tongue.'

'And to think just yesterday I was gabbling on about you maybe being famous one day,' Lorn said, 'and all the time you already were.' He bent forward and dropped a kiss on her hot cheek. 'Congratulations, Ruthie.' His voice was soft and rather intimate in her ear. 'You deserve all the success you get, you'll make this island proud of you.'

Ruth was confused. The kiss had been brief, yet she had the oddest feeling that his warm lips were still there against her face. His blue eyes gazed into hers and something that neither of them could understand passed between them, a short sharp little shock of tingling awareness.

Lewis's hearty laugh carried them over the moment. 'Would you look at that, Rachel! At last! Little brother is finding out what girls are for. Go on, Lorn, she won't bite, will you, Ruth? She might be a writer but she's still flesh and blood.'

'It's strange,' Lorn said, his face red, but his voice thoughtful, 'one day a person that everyone takes for granted suddenly does something that changes them in the eyes of the world. They're still the same but everyone starts to see them in a new light. If they really get famous the world puts them on a pedestal. It becomes an honour to get close to famous people, to get their signature – to touch them.'

'I've only written one little story,' Ruth protested awkwardly, rather taken aback at Lorn's deep-thinking philosophies.

Rachel was nodding her agreement at the words, though she couldn't suppress a smile as Lewis gave

Ruth a ridiculous curtsey and said in a high voice, 'Please, may I touch the hem of your dress, my lady, or will I dare to kiss your hand?'

Dodie came galloping down the hill path from Nigg. Grinding to a halt he cried in tones more mournful than usual, 'He breeah.'

The young people returned the greeting and Lewis added, 'Fine the day may be, but you don't look too pleased with yourself, Dodie. What ails you?'

'Ach, it's these damty towrists,' Dodie moaned. 'I'm gettin' fair scunnered wi' them swarmin' up the hill to look at the pattern on my wee hoosie.'

'Why don't you take the sign down?' Lorn suggested. 'You'll get peace then.'

But Dodie's countenance became more sorrowful than ever. 'Ach, it would be no use at all, they all know about the pattern now. Like flies round a lump o' dung they are, an' it's no' worth the coppers they put in my tin – there was two foreign coins there this mornin',' he ended with a sniff.

'Well, paint over it then,' Lorn said patiently.

Dodie's eyes filled. 'But I wouldny like to lose my pattern – it's a fine pattern, so it is.'

'But you could still have it,' Lewis pointed out. 'On the inside of the roof where only you can see it.'

Dodie brightened. 'Ay, that would be just the thing – only I used the last o' my paint on the door o' Ealasaid's byre – she'll be havin' her calf soon and I wanted to make the place nice for it comin'.'

'We'll bring some over and do it for you,' Lorn offered. 'Grant will be home in a few days and will be looking for something to keep him busy.'

'Ach, it's kind you are just, just like your father.' He was about to take off, but stopped in his tracks to rub his grizzled chin and stare in rather stupefied awe at Ruth. He couldn't read a word of English and had scant idea of anything that went on in the outside world, but he had heard about Ruth's story appearing in print, and was greatly impressed by the fact. His gaze travelled slowly from Ruth's face to her feet then travelled back again as if he was trying to convince himself that she was real and not some kind of transient apparition.

Ruth shifted her feet in some embarrassment but managed to smile and say, 'I'm just the same as I ever was, Dodie, you don't have to look at me as if I was a ghost.'

'Ay, but you will never be the same as you ever was,' Dodie returned cryptically. 'Everybody will be readin' your story and seein' your name. You will no' just belong to the island any more, you will belong to other folks – folks like the towrists who come and gawp at my wee hoosie and at myself as if I was different. If folk like these found out you were a writer they would come and look at you for you are different – like my wee hoosie.'

For all his unworldly ways Dodie had an uncanny insight into more sophisticated minds, and it was perhaps this that made the islanders pause occasionally and say, 'Auld Dodie's no' as daft as folks make out. He has his head screwed on even though the Lord never fixed it into the right threads.'

Ruth felt uncomfortable and was glad when a diversion appeared in the shape of Todd's car slowly purring down the glen road. In the passenger seat was Biddy who, despite her aversion to cars, had been delighted at being offered a lift into Portcull. She beamed toothlessly at the little group by the roadside, and gave a coy little wave such as she had seen practised by members of the royal family. Behind the driving wheel sat the rich American lady, and she too raised a hand in salute.

Dodie, perhaps hoping for a lift in the car himself, galloped off after it, followed by the twins who had been given strict instructions to get to the shops before they closed. The girls went off to the moors to spend a pleasant afternoon, though Rachel kept her promise and made Ruth remove her calliper so that she could massage the twisted little leg. Ruth sat in the heather and watched her friend's long slim fingers patiently working away. Only with Rachel could she allow herself to be truly free, and she felt no embarrassment in exposing the limb that had caused her such distress all her life. Rather, she experienced a strange sense of relaxation as she felt the blood coursing under Rachel's sure touch, and when she finally put back the calliper, she was sure that it wasn't just imagination that made her feel a strength in her leg that hadn't been there before. She looked at Rachel's lovely face, noted the proud tilt of her head. If only Rachel could speak. Ruth was certain that her voice would have been as sweet as the music she made. It seemed such a sad thing that a beautiful girl like Rachel could never express all those deep thoughts and emotions that crowded into her eyes.

Rachel read her thoughts and with her hands she spelled out quickly, 'You mustn't feel sorry for me, Ruth. I don't for you.'

'I know, I know!' Ruth cried. 'I don't feel sorry, it's just – how I would have loved to hear the voice that might have been yours – just once, so that I could have a memory of it inside my head!'

Rachel's hands said slowly, 'And I would love to see you running like a deer – just once – but we are as we are. If we had been different we might never have been friends.'

Ruth nodded wonderingly. 'I never thought of that. You can't speak but you think out things that other folks wouldn't dream of. I'm too busy imagining things to sometimes see the truth, I think I'm what's known as a romantic, while you have your two feet firmly planted on the ground.' She giggled suddenly. 'I have an excuse – only one of mine is firmly planted. Isn't that a fine picture for you – one leg on the ground like a flamingo and my head lost in the clouds? No wonder Dodie was looking for me back there.'

Laughing they ran over the heather and parted at the bridge by Murdy's house. In the distance Rachel saw Stink the Tink and she ran to him. The tinkers had learned to understand her sign language and Stink watched as her expressive hands asked, 'Why haven't you got old Mo with you today?'

Stink leaned against his laden wheelbarrow and rubbing a tattered sleeve over his sweaty brow he said sorrowfully, 'The old man is not at all well, miss. His chest is rattlin' like a bundle o' dry hay. He has not been outside his tent since we came last week and we are afraid for him, miss. He has not eaten a bit for days and is only able to sup hot toddy – we are all thinkin' the good Lord has set His finger upon the old man.'

Rachel drew back in horror, her smooth brow furrowed. Her beloved old rogue of an Irishman couldn't be dying – her visits to the tinker encampment to see him were one of the highlights of her life. But old Mo was indeed very ill. That evening, when the sun was low in the western sky, Rachel ran over the heat-hazed moors to the hollow near Dunuaigh. The smoke from the tinkers' fires curled lazily into the gold-washed sky and in the little burn that purled through the heather the tinker children paddled their feet, while nearby the women washed clothes. The small round framework tents with their weathered coverings of grey canvas were dotted together in companionable closeness. It was a familiar scene to Rachel. She of all the people on Rhanna knew the tinkers as well as they knew each other, and as her long brown legs carried her swiftly through the tough moor grasses, the children glanced up and waved to her in greeting. She found old Mo lying on a tattered pile of bedding. His pram lay outside, abandoned and forgotten-looking – as if the old man who had occupied it for so long would never again ride upon its creaking chassis.

The sound of old Mo's rapid breathing filled the dark confined space. Rachel knelt beside him and put her hand on his damp brow. His mottled face was grey and gaunt, and he didn't stir at her touch. Beside him lay an almost full bottle of whisky, and to Rachel that in itself was a sign that the old man was not long for the world. In a panic she started up. She had to get help. He couldn't, he mustn't, be allowed to die. She ran outside and without preliminary, began hitching a cart to a fly-tormented pony who was searching the heather for clover.

'It is no use, miss,' Stink cried. 'There is no help for him. Leave the old man to die in peace.'

But Rachel paid no heed. She jumped on the cart and, grabbing the reins, coaxed the pony into a trot. One thought beat in Rachel's head: Help, she had to get help. The doctor was too far away; the nearest person with medical knowledge was Biddy – and it was to the sturdy grey stone house in Glen Fallan that Rachel guided the horse. Biddy was preparing for bed. The remains of her supper of oatcakes and creamy milk lay on the table. Halfway through eating it, she had fallen asleep and sat by the embers of the fire, her cat Woody ensconced on her knee, her white head nodding onto her breast. Rachel opened the door and went inside to shake the old woman gently by the shoulder. Biddy jumped and Woody clawed her knee in fright before leaping down to scamper under a chair.

'Ach, what on earth!' grumbled Biddy. 'Can't a

body have a snooze at the fireside without bein'
shaken to bits?' She screwed up her eyes at the
intruder, but without her glasses she was blind. 'Has
the cat got your tongue?' she cried sharply. 'Get me
my damty specs till I see who you are.'

She grabbed the proffered glasses and stuck them
on the end of her nose. The vision of Rachel was a
hazy one. 'Are you a spook or are you real?' Biddy
demanded. 'What is it you're tryin' to tell me?'

But Rachel had no time to waste. She knew the old
nurse could make little sense of her sign language
and gently she began pulling Biddy to her feet.
'Please, oh, please,' the girl cried silently. 'Come with
me. Make her come, God.'

Biddy sensed the girl's urgency. The dazzling child
with her untamed quality and great expressive eyes
had always been a particular favourite of hers. Stiffly
she got to her feet. 'Go away ben the lobby and get
me my cloak and my bag,' she ordered. 'I'm no' a
mind reader but I'm thinkin' somebody must be ill.'

A few minutes later, they departed from the house
and Rachel goaded the horse into a trot. The sun had
set, diffusing the sky with fire. The cliffs of Croy were
red in the glow, the sea a sheet of flame; the peace
of night lay over the moors like an invisible cloak.

'It's as I thought,' Biddy said softly when the tink
camp came into view. 'Yon auld Irish de'il I haveny
a doubt.'

A tinker woman was bathing old Mo's brow; when
she saw Biddy she shook her red head. 'It's no use
me old woman, he's nearly a goner. Come mornin'

he'll be wi' the fairies. You have had a wasted journey.' Biddy puffed out her scraggy chest. 'I'll be the judge o' that, my bonny woman. Bring me some clean cold water and dinna waste too much time about it.'

With difficulty she eased herself over to the old man and examined him quickly, screwing up her nose as odours of all kinds were released from his clothing. She shook her head and turned to Rachel. 'Pneumonia. Too far gone to help. The bodach is burning up. The only thing we can do for him is make him as comfortable as it's possible to make a dying body.'

Rachel recoiled as if she had been struck. Gently the old nurse took her hand. 'My bairnie, you are young and strong wi' life tumbling through your veins so fast it's like a burnie rushin' after rain – this is an auld man, the stream o' his life is dryin' up. Look at him, Rachel, he is very very tired. He wants to die; he needs to rest. When a body gets old and feeble, the dawn of each new day can sometimes be more a curse than a blessing.' She shook her head sadly and sighed. 'Fine I know it too, some mornin's I feel like closin' my eyes like old Mo here and givin' up the ghost.'

Rachel felt the sobs tearing at her throat. She looked at the old man's grey, sunken face. Biddy was right, he did look tired and very old; the stubble that sprouted from his sweat-lathered face looked like snow lying on grey earth.

As the hours wore on, Mo's breathing became

harsher. And when Biddy grew weary of bathing him, Rachel took over, gently washing the perspiration from his face and chest. The only sounds in the ghostly hours before dawn were Mo's laboured breaths and the resigned moans from a nearby tent where a young woman lay in childbirth. Sometime before dawn the old man stirred and opened his eyes. They were dazed, and he seemed to struggle out from a far distant place, but awareness came into them at sight of Rachel. He struggled to speak, but no sound came and Rachel bathed his cracked lips and lifted his head to allow him to drink some water. He spluttered and said in a strong voice. 'Water! Water bejasus! It's the water o' life I'm needin'! Where's me whisky?'

The mouthful of burning spirits revived him and Rachel spun round to Biddy with hope in her tempestuous eyes, a look that said, 'He's going to get well, I knew he couldn't die.'

The old man reached out to her, and his damp horny hand closed over her wrist. 'Mavourneen,' he whispered, and there were tears in his eyes. 'Did not we make good music with our fiddles? The finest ever heard in any tink camp.' He gripped her wrist tighter, his other hand scrabbled frantically under the blankets and he withdrew his treasured violin. 'Here she is, me beauty.' He pushed it at Rachel. 'She's yours now. Take her and look after her as I have done – and I tell you this, me lass, she played well for me, but she'll play even better for you. Give me a tune now – "Danny boy" – ay – no finer tune to play an old timer off the stage. Go on now, mavourneen.'

With tears flowing down her face Rachel took the beautiful instrument, and the strains of the haunting melody filled the tent. It was like some sort of signal to the other tinkers. In minutes a crowd had gathered outside to pay their respects to old Mo.

His eyes were closing. Rachel put down the violin and laid her cool hands on his brow. A smile touched the corners of his mouth, and the fear that had engulfed him some minutes before dissipated like mist. A strange peace stole over him. 'You have the touch of the angels in those hands, mavourneen. Indeed you have more gifts than you know of yourself – many of them at your fingertips.'

One of the women came in and whispered in Biddy's ear, and the old nurse rose stiffly. There was nothing now to be done for old Mo and she followed the woman to a nearby tent where a young girl, awash with the sweat of childbirth, was in the last stages of labour. Biddy hastened to wash her hands and deal with the delivery while just a few yards away old Mo was breathing his last. His hands were still at his sides but a twinkle lit the dullness of his gaze as he instructed Rachel, 'Be playin' me out in style now – only – the best is good enough for – an Irish leprechaun . . .'

Rachel took up the violin once more. The old man's respiration was shallow and irregular, and as he died peacefully to the strains of 'The Londonderry Air' the rising sun burst brilliantly over the sea, and the lusty cries of a newborn baby boy filled the air with life.

Stink moved into old Mo's tent and pulled the blankets over the craggy old face. There was about it a serenity that had rarely touched it during the course of his tough life. The struggle for survival was over.

Rachel stumbled outside blinded with tears. The morning was filled with the glories of summer; the scents of the moor were sweet and strong; the languorous sounds of land and sea broke through the silence like a melody.

'I'll be havin' that! It might fetch a few bob.' A rough-looking tinker was stretching out his big fist for the violin.

Rachel's nostrils flared and she held the violin to her breast, enfolding it protectively with both arms.

'C'mon now, me fine lass, let's be havin' it.' The Irishman made to grab at the girl to forcibly take the violin away from her, but Biddy intervened with a sharp, 'Leave the bairn alone! The fiddle belongs to her now. The bodach told her so wi' his very own dyin' breath and I was there to bear witness. Get away from her, Paddy McPhie, or it's the police I'll be havin' on you. A fine disgrace that would be to all of you, and you wouldny be welcome on this island again.' She stood at the door of the tent, her lined old face yellow in the morning light, her white hair straggling over her eyes, her toothless mouth pulled in so that her nose almost touched her chin. She looked very old and very tired, but such an authoritative air emanated from her that Paddy's meaty fists fell to his sides and he shuffled away in shame. 'And I'll be havin' a good strong cuppy and a chair by the fire,' Biddy told the other tinkers firmly.

'You'll be havin' more than that, me fine old lass,' beamed the young father of the new baby. 'You brought my firstborn into the world, and helped old Mo go out of it in dignity.' He escorted Biddy to the fire, then sent the children scurrying to fetch blankets and a torn but well-upholstered car seat. In minutes Biddy was comfortably ensconced, wrapped in a tartan blanket, drinking tea laced with whisky while she waited for breakfast to cook over the flames.

Rachel wasn't hungry. She wandered away from the camp and sat with her back to a rock to gaze out over the moors to the golden sea. For over two hours she sat lost in thought while Biddy ate, drank tea, and dozed by the fire. Then she got up and went back to the camp. Biddy looked at the girl's sad face, and, rising, she put her arms round Rachel's shoulders.

'Come on, my lassie, we'll go home now. Don't bother wi' the cart, I could be doing wi' a walk to ease my bones.' Her face glowed suddenly. ''Tis glad I am you came for me last night. It's no' often I feel needed these days – ay – it's a wonderful way the Lord has – an old life goes out and a new one comes in, and I was there to deliver the bairnie.'

It was well after nine when they arrived at Biddy's house. Woody was at the door, mewing a rather reproachful welcome. Biddy paused, her rheumaticky hand on the gate, her shoulders stooped. On an impulse Rachel took the old woman in her arms.

'Ay, ay, go away now and get some rest,' Biddy's voice was husky. 'You'll greet for the bodach in days to come, my lamb, but remember – he was ready to go, that he was.'

Rachel turned, and walking quickly away, crossed a bridge over the river Fallan so that she could walk home over the moors. Skirting a heather knoll she paused for a moment to run her fingers over the smooth red-gold wood of the violin. The screeching of brakes on the road far below made her whirl round in horror. There, just outside Biddy's house, Todd's car had ground to a halt, from it ran an agitated figure – and lying on the road, like a tiny broken doll, lay the figure of Biddy.

Rachel's flying feet hardly touched the ground. She heard her ragged breath deep in her throat, her heartbeat rushed in her ears. The American visitor was kneeling beside Biddy, her volatile cries of distress reeling through the air. She rose at Rachel's approach and ran forward, a haggard, nervous-looking woman of about forty-five with sad eyes and suspiciously black hair. Her clothes were beautifully cut, yet looked untidy on her. The immaculate slacks had brought forth the usual nods of disapproval from the island women though the younger ones were reserved in their judgement as many of them had a hankering after the trowser themselves.

Rachel paused briefly in her flight to stare at the scene in disbelief before she turned the full fury of her gaze on the American. 'Hey, don't look at me like that, kid!' cried the woman in near-hysteria. 'It wasn't my fault. The old lady just ran straight into my path – I wasn't even doing thirty – she went after her cat . . .'

Rachel pushed past her and fell on her knees by Biddy, whose eyes were closed, and who was a ghastly grey colour, but other than some cuts and bruises there was no outward physical damage. Rachel felt the hills closing in on her. Frustration boiled in her belly. She had pretended to Ruth that she accepted the fact that she couldn't speak but she had lied. She wanted to scream, to talk, to ask Biddy if she was all right. Gently she reached out to stroke the hair from the lined brow. Biddy's lips fluttered and her eyes opened. She didn't appear to be in any kind of pain, but her skin was cold and moist, her breathing shallow. The American woman came running with a coat, which she tucked round Biddy's prone figure.

'Rachel,' Biddy murmured. 'Lay your hands on my brow like you did wi' the bodach.' Rachel did as she was bid and a sigh came from Biddy's pale lips. 'The bodach was right – you have the gift in your hands to ease a body's fears. Hold my hand, lassie, and don't let go.'

There was another squealing of brakes as the island bus came to a halt at Downie's Pass. Erchy had driven the vehicle at a spanking pace over the narrow roads and now, despite the sudden halt, not a single word of enquiry came from the tourists. They sat rigid, the white blobs of their faces peering from the bus windows. Erchy ran from the bus, followed by Jon, who often rode with Erchy on his tours round the island. Close on their heels ran Kate, who had been spending the night with her daughter at Croft na Beinn. Erchy was removing his jacket as he ran, and in seconds he was tucking it under Biddy's head. Her lips moved again. 'Is that Kate McKinnon's voice I hear? Are you there, Kate?'

'The very one.' Kate knelt and took the old woman's frail hand in her big capable one. Kate was of an exuberant, earthy, boisterous nature, but she was also cool-headed, efficient, and calm in an emergency, and Biddy was grateful for her presence in those strange unreal minutes. She held Kate's hand and gazing up at the green hills she murmured, 'Oft, oft have I walked these purpled hills and watched the sun go down.'

The American woman wrung her hands. 'Gee, she's delirious, she's going on about all the things she loves . . .'

'Ach, it's you who's delirious,' Biddy said with a touch of her old asperity, 'I'm sick walkin' the damty hills and watchin' suns go down when all I wanted was my bed – I'm just tryin' to pass my time on this hard road while somebody goes to fetch Lachlan.'

But Erchy was already away, turning Todd's car at Biddy's gate and setting it on the road to Slochmhor.

'It will no' be Lachlan who will come,' Kate reminded her. 'He's away on holiday and won't be back for a few days yet – but thon nice young doctor who's doin' for him will soon see you right.'

'I don't want him – he has hands like putty – I want Lachlan . . .' She tried to raise her head. 'Where's my cat? The bugger ran out on me when I opened the gate . . .'

Jon came from the riverbank with the cat in his arms and placed him in his mistress's trembling arms.

Rachel turned away. The pallor on Biddy's face was the same as she had seen on old Mo as death had drawn near. She bit her lip and walked unsteadily to stand some distance from the scene of the accident. Suddenly Jon was beside her, taking her hands, making her sit down on the grassy bank. She looked at his honest brown eyes and the little beard flecked now with grey, like her father's. It seemed the young German was always there when she needed comfort. He had also been with her the day she found Squint dead in his basket. Gently Jon had lifted up the little dog, and the glint of tears had been in his eyes as he had taken Rachel's hand and said, 'Come, jungfräulich, we will bury him in a quiet place on the moors and I will make a cross to mark his resting place.'

She remembered her hand in his as they walked over the Muir of Rhanna to bury the dog who had been such a wise and faithful companion to a little dumb girl. Out there on the open moors, with the wind sighing and ruffling the bracken, Rachel saw again a small golden spaniel, his floppy ears flying in the breezes as he raced towards her over the heather, the expression of joy in his gloriously comical face making her laugh as he flopped by her feet to look up at her in cross-eyed adulation. Jon had given her strength then, and she often went to sit by the simple elm cross that he had carved.

Now, here was Jon again, his words of comfort, spoken in his charming broken English, reaching out to ease her sorrow. Todd's car appeared in a cloud of dust, and Rachel went back to Biddy's side as the young locum jumped out. In a short while Biddy was being carried into her house, hurling abuse in the doctor's ears and moaning for a cuppy. But her voice was weak and Kate's face was grim as she set about helping to get the old woman into bed. The doctor took Kate aside and told her, 'She is suffering badly from shock, which has affected her heart. I'm afraid it's rather serious, but I'll do what I can.'

Rachel crept away from the bedroom door and went slowly downstairs where Jon was waiting for her. He led her outside. 'Come, jungfräulich, I will walk home with you.' He glanced at the violin that she was hugging like a baby. 'Your old friend has gone?' he asked quietly.

She nodded and her head fell forward onto her chest. He felt her pain and misery and lifted a tentative finger as if to stroke the satin black of her hair, but then he thought better of it and his hand fell back to his side. 'I told you once before, Rachel, cry your pain away. Old Mo would not want you to be unhappy over him. He gave you his violin in gratitude for all the happy times he shared with you. This is a very special gift he left you – a Cremonese, made by a great craftsman of northern Italy, it is very old

319

and very valuable. I noticed it on the evening of Merry Mary's ceilidh when the old man let me play it. It has the voice of the angels; under fingers such as yours it will make music such as is in heaven.'

Rachel knew that what Jon was telling her was of great importance, but just then she couldn't fully take it in. Old Mo was dead, he had given her his treasured violin, and that was all that really mattered – the thought, not the value. She handed it to Jon and signalled for him to play. Reverently he placed it under his chin, and drew the bow over the strings. The notes swelled and soared to join the summer song of the birds. Rachel's heart felt like bursting. She was sad, yet happy at the same time, and not even her mother's stern face at the window penetrated her emotions.

Annie's voice was sharp as she came to the door and cried, 'Well now, miss! What is the meaning o' this I'd like to know. Out all night, then comin' home over the moor playin' the fiddle wi' a Jerry as if . . .'

Jon laid a hand on Annie's arm. 'Rachel and Biddy have been sitting all night with old Mo. He died at dawn, and Biddy has just been knocked down by a car. Rachel stayed till the doctor came.'

Annie's hand flew to her mouth. 'Auld Biddy! Oh dear God, no!' She saw the anguish in her daughter's eyes and felt something of her frustration and grief. 'Rachel, 'tis sorry I am about old Mo. I was never happy about you spendin' so much time up by the tinks' camp, but I knew how much the auld de'il meant to you. I'm – sorry I shouted – I would have been angrier still at a lassie who had not the heart nor the courage to bide wi' an auld man in his last breath.' She held out her hand. 'Come you in and sup – you too, Mr Yodel, you have always been kind to my poor dumb lassie and 'tis grateful I am indeed.'

Jon flinched. 'Poor dumb lassie.' Was that how Annie saw her beautiful talented daughter? Rachel was holding her head proudly, and he couldn't tell if the words had made an impression or not. Her mother's expressions were probably commonplace to the girl, but as he sat in with the family and shared their breakfast, he sensed that Rachel was never quite at ease throughout the meal, that she tolerated rather than enjoyed her home life, that when she spread her wings into a wider world she would never be hindered by homesickness. In these respects she was like him. He enjoyed going back occasionally to Germany, but he dreaded going home to Mamma. Rachel adored Rhanna passionately, but had little attachment to a home where no one took any real interest in her life. Her father had done so up to a point, but he was dead now, and she had no one.

Jon glanced over the table at Rachel. The sun was streaming over her, turning her skin to gold, her hair to blue-black satin. Her eyes were shadowed pools, glinting amber where the sun danced into them. She had him! Always she would have him – as long as she needed him.

Chapter Thirteen

No titled lady in the land could have had more affection and attention than was lavished on Biddy over the next few days, but quite unlike the pampered rich, she had no need of wealth or position to further every whim that came into her head. The islanders came in a steady stream bearing delicacies to tempt her appetite and generally to make sure that her time spent in bed would not be weary. While gossip was exchanged in the upstairs bedroom, downstairs in the kitchen the kettle was never off the boil and tea was drunk in great quantities as everything from peat cutting to the price of sugar was discussed with energy. The menfolk sat on the crofter's bench under the window, smoking and adding the odd piece of sage argument to the current topic, but occasionally the voices grew hushed as everyone wondered quietly 'just how bad was auld Biddy'.

Kate came faithfully every day, but other than endless cuppies laced with brandy or whisky, Biddy ate very little. After a few days a dismayed Kate realised that all her culinary efforts were in vain.

'You canny live on whiskified tea!' Kate scolded when yet another meal was rejected, but Biddy put a frail hand on her arm and said, 'Mo ghaoil, my belly has been wi' me for a long time and knows what's best for it – besides,' she said, sinking back on her pillows and sighing deeply, 'there comes a time in a body's life when no amount of food will ever do any good – and my time's come.'

'Away! You've years in you yet, you silly cailleach,' Kate stated cheerfully, but when she turned away from the bed her eyes were sad and her steps heavy as she went downstairs to report the latest news.

If Kate hadn't put a stop to it, the children would have been swarming into the house in their droves to visit the old woman they loved. Instead, Kate allowed them upstairs in ones and twos, and then only for a few minutes at a time. But at Biddy's own request, a little impromptu concert was arranged and Jon, Rachel, Lorn and Lewis arrived to play their fiddles for her. One favourite tune after another filled the bedroom, and very soon her eyes were wet and she had to dab them furtively with a corner of the bedspread.

'Damty grand,' she said in husky appreciation.

Rachel threw back her head to stop her own tears spilling, and found Lewis's hand in hers under cover of the valance. She looked at him quickly, her heart beating very fast, the way it always did lately whenever she saw him or sat beside him. He smiled at her sympathetically and squeezed her hand tighter, and she knew that for the moment sympathy was all that he felt for her. Half the girls on the island were under his charming spell. He went from one to the other like a bee in search of the sweetest nectar, and she knew one day her turn would come.

Jon, sitting with his fiddle on his knee, saw the exchange and was minded afresh that Rachel was growing up. There would be boys – lots of them. And her need for him would grow less and less . . .

His musings were interrupted by Ruth's arrival into the room. Her mother had dispatched her to read the Bible 'for the salvation of Biddy's soul', but Ruth had slipped her notebooks into her pocket, and it was these she proceeded to read. Her face was pink and her voice shaky because she had never been good with an audience, but, as with Lorn and Lewis up by Brodie's Burn, she soon forgot herself, and her sweet voice grew steady.

Everyone in the room was enchanted by her stories and poems. Biddy lay back with a little smile lifting her lips, and closed her eyes in contentment; Lewis once more sought Rachel's hand; Jon looked from the window to the hills and tried to convince himself that Rachel's cheeks were burning because it was stuffy in the room; Lorn gazed at Ruth's bowed golden head and thought about a field full of ripe corn . . .

Ruth's face flushed again as she glanced up and caught him watching her. She closed her books. 'I think Biddy's asleep,' she said softly. 'We'd better go.'

'Asleep nothing.' Biddy's eyes popped open. 'My magazine's on that table; get it for me and read it, Ruth. Your voice is like a burnie purlin' through the heather and I want to hear you readin' your story from your very own lips. It's no' every day I get to hear a writer readin' to me.' So Ruth read *Hebridean Dream*, and half an hour later Biddy really was asleep, lulled by the girl's musical voice.

Everyone looked at each other; something other than the sadness of being by a beloved old lady's sickbed had touched them all, and they were each aware of it. The touching of hands had brought Lewis a step nearer Rachel; the arch of a slender neck and silken strands of hair had stirred something in Lorn's heart that had never been there before; Jon glanced at the four youthful faces surrounding him and felt old at thirty-seven. Life to him was a magical wonderful experience. It made him walk with a spring in his step and a lightness of heart. But the sight of the flush on Rachel's face made some of the magic go out of his life, with the result that his heart felt heavy inside him. Rachel glanced up and saw the sadness in his face, and she smiled, a vibrant radiant smile that told him of the new doors opening in her heart. He nodded and forced himself to smile back. She was so young. She had a right to every happiness that came her way – but he knew she would never find them in Lewis McKenzie, and he hoped she would discover that in time – before she fell too much under Lewis's spell.

When Dodie first heard of the accident he galloped into Biddy's house without any of his usual preliminary and went straight upstairs, his great wellingtons making sucking sounds in the hollows of the well-worn wooden stairs. For him to come straight into a house was unusual; for him to go into a 'leddy's bedroom' was unheard of, but to him the old nurse was not a lady. In his eyes, her standing went far higher than that of any other mortal female known to him, and no title on earth had yet been created for the grumbling, lovable old woman he had known all his life. Dodie had little recall of his own mother – who had died when he was only thirteen, leaving him to fend for himself – and Biddy was the nearest to what he imagined a mother to be. She scolded, nagged, occasionally cuffed him on the ear – but she also conveyed her affection in many ways. When she met him she always gave him a sweetie; when passing her house on his solitary wanderings, he had often been invited in for supper or breakfast. At Christmas she gave him baccy and made him plum pudding, but most wonderful of all, out of everybody in his world, she was the only one who remembered his birthday, and every year, without fail, she presented him with a small reminder of the day.

'I couldny forget the day you were born,' she unfailingly told him. 'Just like a wee squealing piglet you were, wi' ears on you like those on the wally joog in my bedroom.'

Dodie was never offended by these comparisons. In fact, they delighted him. They gave him a feeling of having some sort of roots, and he blushed and smiled, never tiring of hearing such things from the only person who could, like a real mother, give him anecdotes of his babyhood.

When he beheld Biddy in bed, white-faced and

hollow-eyed, her silvery hair brushed back and tied with a blue ribbon, he burst into tears. She appeared to have shrunk, and she looked very small in the big feather bed. But her voice when she scolded him was still as strong as ever. 'Ach, what's wrong wi' you, laddie?' she asked in disgust. 'It's me who's the one should be cryin' – lyin' here waitin' to see when will Lachlan arrive. Come over here this meenit and take this hanky to wipe your eyes.'

He shuffled over, and taking the proffered square of white cotton, proceeded to soak it in seconds. He stood over her bed, a figure of pathos in his thread-bare coat, his stooped shoulders juddering with sobs.

'Ach, laddie,' she said, her voice soft, 'you are a good kind soul, and the Lord knows you were put on this earth for a purpose like the rest o' us. Dry your eyes now and take a sweetie. They're Imperials, your favourites.'

He took the sweet and sucked it loudly, his watery gaze fixed on her tired face. ''Tis sorry I am for greetin',' he sniffed dismally. 'It's just I was feart when I heard you had been knocked down by a motor car. They are dangerous smelly things, and I was aye thinkin' they would stay in the cities and never come to the islands . . . A horse would never knock a body down like that. Even when they are runnin' wild they will make a circle past anybody in their road.'

Biddy nodded in thoughtful agreement. 'Ay, you're right there, Dodie. But times are changin', and there will come a day when the likes o' Todd will no' be kept in business by just horses. Already he's havin' to take in bikes and make fancy gates to make ends meet – ach, these new-fangled ways will no' make for a better world. I'm glad I'll go out of it afore it changes too much.'

The tears sprouted from Dodie's eyes once more. He scrubbed them with his calloused knuckles, and hung his head to hide his shame.

Biddy was growing very tired. She was grateful to the islanders for sparing their time to fill her daytime hours, but she was thankful when night came and she could be alone. Babbie had only been one of many who had offered to stay with her at night, but she had declined all such offers with the reasonable excuse of 'being too weary come night to even hear a mouse fart'.

'Dodie.' She pulled herself up, almost knocking over her teeth in the glass by her elbow. 'Will you stop your blubberin' – or I'll get out this bed and cuff your lug, and you will no' be likin' the sight o' me in my goonie and woolly bedsocks. Now, dry your eyes and listen to me. I want you to do a wee thing for me.'

'Ay, anything at all, Biddy,' he whispered, keeping his head averted just in case she would keep her threat and get out of bed. He knew well that with Biddy anything was possible.

'You like nice things wi' patterns, don't you, laddie?'

'Ay, that I do,' he agreed dismally.

'Well, go over there to the kist and see me over the wee boxie right at the top.'

He did as she bade him, his pale dreaming eyes widening at sight of the wee boxie carved exquisitely in oak and inlaid with mother-of-pearl. The old lady fumbled for her glasses and her eyes grew misty as she touched the relief design of leaves and roses. In a husky far-away voice she murmured, 'My grandfather made this for my fourteenth birthday, the finest jewel box any young lass could wish for – ay, fine I mind him goin' to his wee shed and workin' all the hours God made. It was carved wi' love, for his auld hands were knotted like bits o' driftwood warped by the tide. He died just a fortnight after my birthday, and I have treasured this boxie all my life. But now I'm no' able to give it the care it needs. It has to be polished and kept in the manner it deserves, and you wi' your love o' treasures is just the one to do this for auld Biddy. Take it now and don't be tellin' a soul – you can use it to keep these bits and pieces o' shells and things you are aye gatherin' together.'

Dodie took the box and touched it with reverence, his rough fingers whispering gently over the mother-of-pearl inlay. 'My, my, it's beautiful just,' he said before he was overcome once more with emotion, his Adam's apple working desperately in a bid to keep back the tears. 'I'll be bringing her back to you when you're better able to look after her,' he promised in confusion.

'Ach, no, laddie!' The rebuke was sharp, but the fire had gone out of Biddy's voice. 'I'm giving it to you – as a present. I will never have need of it now.

It's for your birthday when it comes, a special thing to make up for all the years I won't be here to mind your birthday.

'Get away home now, I'm tired o' talkin'. Go you down and tell Mollie to send me up a cuppy.'

But Dodie was beyond speech of any kind. With the tears streaming down his face he laid something on the bed, and loped downstairs and out of the house.

Biddy reached out to the object Dodie had left lying on the counterpane, and as she held it against her bosom, the slow tears filled her eyes and affection for the old eccentric engulfed her. Wherever he went, whatever the occasion, he bestowed his unsophisticated gifts on people, and the uncanny aptness of them had touched many a sore heart. What had prompted him to bring her the thing she had pined for more than any other while lying in bed that hot summer's day, gazing from the window to the heathery hills lying so serenely against the azure sky?

'Oft, oft, have I walked these purpled hills and watched the sun go down.' She murmured the words again that she had tossed aside so scornfully when the American woman had suggested she was delirious. Ah, how often had she walked these dear green hills, sniffing the scents of wildflowers, watching the sun rising and setting, diffusing the sky and sea with breathtaking colours beyond all description. All her life, as a small barefoot girl, and as a black-stockinged old woman, she had freely roamed, revelling in her surroundings even while she grumbled at real or imagined hardships. Now, here she was, too tired even to get up and go to the window to breathe the clean air. She closed her eyes and lifting Dodie's gift to her nostrils she gulped in the scent of the moors. Dodie had made the sachet himself, a crudely sewn piece of muslin stuffed with wild thyme, bell heather, moss, meadowsweet, and an assortment of grasses. 'Ay, you have a fine sensitivity about you, Dodie,' she murmured. 'You might be a poor cratur' to some, but to me you are a child o' God.'

Light steps sounded on the stairs and Babbie came into the room. 'Talking to yourself you daft cailleach?' teased Babbie in greeting, though her bright green eyes noted that the old woman's condition had deteriorated. The young locum had confided in Babbie that he was amazed Biddy had lasted so long. Her pulse was weak and irregular, her respiration laboured, she hadn't eaten for days – yet she was lucid and bright, and Babbie knew that Kate was right when she said, 'She's waitin' to see Lachlan before she goes. I always said she would go when she was ready and no' before.'

'I am just sayin', Dodie and all cratur's like him could teach the rest o' us a lesson. They come into the world innocent and go out o' it the same.'

'He's been to see you then?' Babbie asked, though there was no need for she could detect the vestiges of the old eccentric's particular odour hanging in the air.

'Ay, that he has, he's left his smell but he also left this,' Biddy said, holding up the sachet. 'A wee bit o' the moors sewn into an old bitty curtain – money canny buy what I have here.'

Babbie sat down on the bed to look quizzically at Biddy's face. 'You're a blether – I wonder you have the breath for it. How are you today?'

'Near drawin' my last,' Biddy replied candidly. 'I will never get over the shock o' being knocked down at my very own gate – but it wasny the wifie's fault – it was this de'il here.' Affectionately she rubbed Woody's black head, then with sudden urgency she reached out and took Babbie's arm. 'My lassie, it's up to you now. It will no' be easy. There will be times you will feel like packin' your bags and fleein' away – but you have your man to help you and a fine loon he is too . . .' Her dim eyes twinkled. 'Betimes I forget he's a Jerry at all – he's that like ourselves now. Ay, you have your man to talk to and the best doctor on this God's earth to work alongside.' Her fingers dug into Babbie's arm. 'Is he home yet at all? I want to see him before I go.'

Babbie gathered the old woman into her arms and stroked her hair. Her eyes were wet but her voice steady when she said, 'He'll be home tomorrow and you'll be the first on his list.'

Biddy gave a contented sigh. 'The Lord be thanked, for I don't know how much longer I can hold on. The motor car didny hurt my body, but I'm thinkin' it knocked my auld heart for six. It feels gey shaky, I can tell you.'

Babbie didn't repudiate any of this. To do so would have seemed trite in the face of such courage. Biddy was not afraid of dying, but even so, Babbie could not suppress a sigh of sorrow.

Biddy pushed her away to look long and searchingly at a face that had grown contented over the past few years. The uncertainty of early youth had disappeared; the green, amber-flecked eyes were peaceful; the wide generous mouth bestowed its radiant smile readily. Babbie looked rather weary and sad just now, and Biddy patted her hand. 'You mustny fret for me, lassie, it's your wee shoulders that are going to get the brunt now, and wi' you bein' married, your responsibilities will be even more than mine.' She slid Babbie a sidelong glance. 'I was aye wonderin' – have you never wanted bairnies o' your own?'

Babbie's lips curved. 'You're a nosy cailleach if ever there was one.' Her expression became serious. 'It might sound selfish, but Anton and I always felt content with each other. I know the gossips talk and say it isn't natural, but it's what we want – besides,' she said, and laughed, 'how could I ever be another Biddy McMillan with a wheen of bairnies at my aprons? I'm too busy delivering them to have them. Now, where's your brush and I'll do your hair. You must look your best for all these men who keep sneaking up here to visit you.'

Biddy lay back and closed her eyes as the younger woman worked with her hair. A satisfied smile flitted over her face. 'At least, I got to bring another bairnie

into the world before my number came up. A bonny
wee thing wi' hair black as night. I hear his mother
has given him McMillan as a middle name – ay – I'll
be remembered all right.'

Fergus came with Lachlan the following evening.
Biddy gazed up at tall Fergus and she said dreamily,
'You know what I'm lookin' forward to most of all?
Meeting Mirabelle again. She was a bonny woman
and the finest friend I ever had. My, how she doted
on you and poor Alick – the cratur' – I'll get to see
him, too. You and him were like her very own
bairnies. Mind, the pair o' you were buggers betimes
and sore tried that good woman's heart, but she saw
the good in you and knew how best to bring it out.
You miss your brother, laddie?' she asked gently.

Fergus nodded and said huskily, 'Ay, that I do.
When he was here I took him for granted, and as you
know we didn't always see eye to eye – but – on the
night he died we had more or less called pax and
then . . .'

His voice faltered and she took his big strong hand
in her thin one. 'Weesht, I know fine how you feel,
McKenzie o' the Glen – a grand title that, and it suits
you, laddie. By God, the McKenzies – a stubborn
bunch if ever there was one – wi' tempers like that
bugger Satan himself. But you blow more goodness
than you do fire – especially my wee Shona – aye
was a lovable bairn for all her tantrums – I'd like fine
to see her, so I would.'

Fergus felt his jaw tensing. The realisation that

Biddy was dying hit him like a sledgehammer. He had heard all the gossip about how ill she was but this was the moment of truth: the pallor of her skin, the blue veins showing under the skin of her temples, the purple hue of her lips and hands. She was a part of his life – everyone's lives – a part of Rhanna . . . 'You'll see Shona soon; she'll be home in a few days. She always makes a point of trying to be here when Grant's on leave.'

'She'll be home for my funeral then.' Biddy closed her eyes, and Fergus made to go out of the room, but she stopped him by saying softly, 'The twins, they're good laddies both of them – but Lewis – look to him, Fergus. He's no' strong like his brother. That sounds daft, I know, but there are different kinds o' strength. He'll need a lot o' guidance, but he'll shape up to a good man wi' your help.'

'Ay – I know that, Biddy,' he said, and went quickly downstairs, leaving Lachlan alone in the room.

Lachlan had barely been able to conceal his shock at the change in the old nurse, but he turned from the window and, smiling down at her, managed to say carelessly, 'Disgraceful! I turn my back for five minutes and you get into trouble. Come on, lift your goonie and I'll have a look at you . . .'

But she threw off the suggestion with an impatient grunt. 'Ach, leave me be, you and I know fine it's a waste o' time.' She perched her glasses on the end of her nose and scrutinised his face. It was obvious his much needed holiday had done him good. He was tanned and well-looking; the hollows of his face had filled, and the tired droop had gone from his shoulders. She giggled coyly. 'A peety I hadny been a younger woman – you and me could maybe had one o' they doctor-nurse romances you read about in wimmen's papers – eh?'

He sat down and took her hand, his brown eyes full of the compassion that had made his career as a doctor a unique success. 'You old flirt,' he said huskily. 'Don't you know I've always had a fancy for you? Who could help but love a lady who has given her life to tending others? When God made nurses he set one special mould aside for Biddy McMillan, and when you were created he threw away the design, for there will never be another one to match you. And if that isn't romantic nonsense I'll – I'll eat my stethoscope.' His voice broke and he turned his head quickly.

'Ach, dinna greet for me, laddie.' She tried to sound brusque, but her voice was weak and she fumbled for her hanky. 'See now what you've done?' she scolded shakily. 'I'm greetin' for myself like a daft auld fool. My time has come, Lachlan, and the Lord is waitin' for me – afore the de'il gets to me first!

'Will you do something for me? When I'm in my box at the Hillock, say a few words in the Gaelic in that nice voice o' yours. It was the only thing that kept me awake in Kirk, and, who knows, it might waken me from the dead just when everyone thinks they've got rid o' me. I have asked Mr Gray to do the ceremony. There was a time when I wouldny have gone to the wee hoosie to hear him, but he's changed over the years and is more like one of us now.'

The Rev. Gray had been touched when, on paying a visit to Biddy's bedside, she had said with dignity, 'After I am gone I will be feelin' my mind easier if you would be doing the service. Thon young minister is a fine laddie, but we are not knowing each other well enough yet for him to know the right things to say – and be seein' me out in the Gaelic. You haveny the voice for it, but at least folks will hear you – ay, even to the other side of the island, if you don't mind me sayin' so.'

The Rev. John Gray hadn't minded. In fact, he had been so overwhelmed by the old woman's request that he hadn't been able to say anything for a few moments. It had been one thing to have been accepted by the islanders, but to be singled out in this fashion by one of the most venerable inhabitants was the highest tribute anyone had ever paid him. He was retired now but he and his wife had decided to stay on in the island that had been their home for so long. ('We belong here, Hannah,' he had boomed, 'no sense in starting all over again in some strange place.') He had patted Biddy's hand and, swallowing hard had said, 'My dear Biddy, thank you. It's at times like these I know the work of my life has not been in vain. You are a brave woman to face up to death with such courage, and you can trust me to carry out your wishes.' His stern strong face had relaxed into a smile. 'If I don't do things to your satisfaction you have every right to come back and haunt me.'

Lachlan got up, and, going to the window, gazed

out at the shadowed night hills silhouetted against the midnight-blue sky. It was midsummer and on cloudless nights like this it would never grow truly dark.

'They're bonny, aren't they?' said Biddy softly.

'Ay, mo ghaoil, the hills of summer, so feathery and soft with new green you feel you could go and lay down your head on them.'

Her eyes closed and she quoted on a sigh, '"I to the hills will lift mine eyes . . ."'

Lachlan forced himself to become brisk. 'Phebie wants to come along and spend the night, if you'll let her.'

Biddy held up a blue-veined hand. 'Leave me, laddie. It's kind o' Phebie, but my house is no' my own all day and I'm glad o' night – for a bit peace . . .'

In a few moments Biddy looked to be asleep, and Lachlan went over and tucked her mohair shawl round her shoulders. He stayed for a long moment gazing down at her tired thin face, then with a shake of his head, he went quickly out of the room and tip-toed downstairs to join Fergus. Both men walked silently through Glen Fallan with heavy hearts.

Biddy stirred and shifted Woody from his favourite place in the warm crook of her knees. With trembling hands the old lady threw back the blankets and dragged herself from the bed. She couldn't rest, not yet; there were certain things that had to be done first. Holding onto the furniture, her legs shaking beneath her, she walked slowly to the window and stood looking out over the moors to the glimpse of silver-blue sea beyond. Her eyes took long to focus, and soon became blurred, but she could still see the dark bulk of the mighty hills rising up before her. She smiled, a wistful little half-smile and murmured, '"Soft as the wind blows over your brow there will my feets go freer than now."'

Weakness washed over her. Woody mewed from the bed. 'Ay, I'm comin' back, no mistake about that,' she murmured. Some minutes later she crawled between the sheets, retrieved her 'teeths' from the glass, inserted them, and lay back on the pillows feeling strangely content. Her hand strayed to Woody's head. It was warm and soft. 'Bide a wee, my lamb,' she whispered affectionately. 'It won't be long – not long now . . .'

Next morning, Kirsteen and Babbie found Biddy propped up on her pillows, her silvery hair carefully combed and tied with the blue ribbon. On the breast of her 'goonie' was pinned her silver M.B.E. medal. She had always referred to it as a damty fine brooch to the children who came and requested she take it from its box and pin it on them for a little while. Her hands were clasped over her bosom: grasped in one was the ornately inscribed warrant, in the other was Dodie's sachet of wildflowers. The last breath, the final memory, had been of the moors she had trod for almost eighty-seven years.

Kirsteen went over and gently touched a lock of her snowy hair. 'Goodbye, dear, beautiful old lady. You leave behind a great army of bairnies who will grieve sorely for you in the days and years to come.'

Babbie stood at the foot of the bed gazing at the face of the old nurse who had befriended her, guided her, given Anton and herself a home when first they married. In life Biddy had often looked grumpy and harassed, though a twinkle had never been far from her eyes. Latterly a sweet tranquillity had settled on her features though this was sometimes usurped by fatigue. Now she lay, a gracious, noble figure. Death had swathed her with peace, dignity, and an ethereal quality of grace that could only have sprung from a soul satisfied with a life well spent. Babbie knew she would mourn for Biddy, but gazing upon the calm dear face, she felt an odd peace stealing through her entire being. It was as if the old lady was reaching out beyond the grave and saying to her, 'Don't weep for me, lassie, I was weary and the Lord saw I needed to rest.'

'Look, Kirsteen,' Babbie said, indicating the empty glass at the bedside. 'She put in her teeths for the occasion. She used to say the one thing she dreaded was to die in her sleep without them.'

Kirsteen took out her hanky and blew her nose. 'She always did try to wear them for special occasions, and this was one time she didn't forget to remember.' Stooping she lifted the sleepy cat from Biddy's side. 'She asked the twins to look after Woody for her, and I'm thinking this is one cat who is going to lead the life of a very special lord – it's the least we can do for an old lady who always treated animals like humans – like her bairnies they meant everything in the world to her.'

Chapter Fourteen

If Biddy could have seen the masses of people who came from all over the island and beyond, she would have shook her head and said, 'Ach, it's just a lot o' damty palaver anyways.' But she would have folded her hands over her stomach and smiled rather proudly too, for she had often commented, 'Why can folks no' have their funerals while they're alive and able to see who will turn up? A fine lot o' good it does a dead body no' to be there to count how many friends come to see them off.' But it is doubtful if she could have counted the streams of men, women, and children who crowded into the Kirk and overflowed over the Hillock to listen to the burial ceremony. The flowers ranged from elaborate wreaths to bunches of wildflowers held in the hot grubby hands of the children, and it would have been these that Biddy would have treasured above all others.

Shona and Niall had come home for the funeral, and they stood close together as the coffin was carried from the Kirk to the graveside.

Lachlan began to say in Gaelic the words of the hymn, '"I to the hills will lift mine eyes."' His clear resonant voice carried through the still air. When he was finished there was not a dry eye in the whole gathering.

Niall squeezed Shona's hand as he felt her shoulders trembling. 'I can't help it,' she gulped. 'She was so much a part of Rhanna; she gave so much. I'll never forget how kind and understanding she was to me when you were away at war and I was dreading telling Father I was expecting a baby. She never lectured or went all sour about morals – she just *helped*.'

'I know, my babby.' Niall put his arm round her shoulders and drew her close. 'Rhanna will never be the same without auld Biddy. She helped us all when often there was no one else to turn to. We would like the Biddys of this world to live for ever, but it canny be. Weesht now – and – and give me a loan of your hanky.'

Ruth and Rachel stood close together at the back of the crowd. Morag had been playing the organ for the service inside the Kirk, and it would be some time before she would emerge. Ruth put a comforting arm round Rachel's shoulders. Rachel had taken Biddy's death very badly, blaming herself for it happening. Coming on top of the death of old Mo, it was almost beyond bearing, and she leaned against Ruth gratefully. Through the gleam of tears in her eyes she saw Lewis McKenzie go forward to the graveside with his brother Lorn. Biddy had requested they play a wee tune on the fiddles at the graveside. Rachel had not been able to face it, and Jon had decided it would be more fitting for him to opt out

too and leave it to the twins. Jon watched Rachel's
face as the haunting notes of 'Amazing Grace'
hushed the crowd. Her dark eyes were glazed with
grief. As she listened to the beautiful music her face
turned white, her eyes strayed beyond the branches
of the elms to Lewis standing with his face resting on
the gold wood of his violin, his earth-brown curls
ruffling slightly as a breeze blew up from the sea.
Rachel's eyes were dark with grief, hurt, and naked
yearning. Jon turned away, and some of the feelings
of inadequacy that had plagued him in his early
youth returned with renewed force.

In her white dress Ruth stood out from the black-
clad crowd like a lone snowdrop on bare winter
earth. Not even for this occasion would Morag Ruadh
unbend, and quite a few shocked glances had been
cast at Ruth, though everyone reasoned, 'That
besom, Morag Ruadh! Calls herself a Christian and
doesny even allow her lassie to respect the dead.'
But Ruth didn't feel as badly as she thought she
might. Biddy had seen to that. 'Be wearin' one o' they
bonny white dresses to see me off,' she instructed.
'I'll never know why folks deck themselves out in
thon awful black. They a' look as though they were
worshippin' the de'il! Ay, no doubt that rogue has a
snigger up his black sleeve when folks turn up
wearin' his colours for Christian burials.'

Through the tracery of green on the elm trees Ruth
glimpsed Lorn as he played. Why did she keep
remembering the way he had looked at her in Biddy's
bedroom? A flushed, admiring, furtive look. Their

eyes had met only briefly, but it had been enough for her heart to start fluttering too fast. The leaves swayed in the breeze, and he was lost to her momentarily – only to appear before her gaze with renewed force some seconds later. His hair was lighter than his brother's; a lovely coppery tinge gleamed through the rich earth-brown. Her violet gaze rested on him and stayed there, then quite suddenly he glanced up and seemed to look straight at her. Her heart bounded. He couldn't make her out from that distance of course. It was stupid! But he could, could! Her white dress, her pale hair. She stood out a mile away. A glow warmed her heart – then she saw a movement in front of the Kirk and an unmistakable red head. The glow in her heart vanished and she fingered the white ruffle at her neck nervously.

Grant stood beside Fergus and Kirsteen and looked to where Phebie watched the ceremony with Fiona, who had just arrived the day before. At twenty-two, she was a tall, attractive, assured young woman with lively eyes and an air about her that exuded something of the excitement and wonder of living. She had graduated with honours the year before, and had won a two-year travelling scholarship to study marine biology. Grant had heard Phebie confiding certain things to Kirsteen about her daughter: 'She will never settle down to normal life like other girls of her age.'

'Oh, she's enjoying herself.' Kirsteen had smiled. 'Plenty of time to settle down. At the moment she's playing the field.'

'I know, I know!' Phebie had cried. 'One affair after another, but she never wants to be tied to any of them. She always said she would never marry.'

Grant remembered that too. He couldn't help feeling amused as he recalled her passionate childhood sentiments. 'I'll *never* marry!' she had vehemently and often declared. 'Boys are smelly and noisy. Their minds are as dirty as their habits. All they ever seem to do is pick their noses behind their reading books and try to look up girls' skirts.'

A playful wind lifted Fiona's skirt slightly and moulded it to her hips, which were seductively rounded; her legs were long and very shapely. She turned her head and caught Grant watching her, and her nose went into the air. He reddened. Her opinions of him hadn't altered anyway.

The Rev. Gray began the service. He stood beside the coffin, and as he gazed round at the crowds filling every space he felt a lump rising in his throat. He straightened his shoulders, a fine figure of a man in his robes. Strength was in his face; his thick thatch of white hair was startling against his black cloth. It was a calm day with occasional meek puffs of wind. The sheep bleated from the mist-filled corries of the hills; a dog barked from some distant croft. Mr Gray cleared his throat, and as he began The Lord's Prayer in Gaelic, everyone joined in, murmuring the well-known words in whatever language was best known to them. Mr Gray then conducted a short but sincere service and all the old Gaels present thought how different were his sermons now to the dry theological affairs that had reverberated in the Kirk for so many years. Then, as the coffin was being lowered, Mr Gray began to sing a Gaelic lullaby that had been one of Biddy's favourites. It was so unusual to end a burial service in this manner, that at first the gathering was silent. Then, one by one, every man, woman, and child took up the song and it seemed, as the voices rose heavenwards, that there could have been no more fitting tribute to one who had all her life nursed children on her knee, and crooned lullabies to them in her lilting voice. The song was taken up by those who stood outside the mossy walls of the Kirkyard, and by others even further back, till it seemed the whole of Rhanna was singing in that final moving farewell to Auld Biddy. The tears flowed, for Biddy, for other loved ones gone before, for the uncertainty of life itself. Then the first scatterings of earth were being thrown over the coffin, and everyone was dispersing slowly, as if unwilling to relinquish the feeling of unity that the singing of a Gaelic lullaby had created.

When the graveyard was finally empty, a pathetic stooping figure crept rather than walked over to the fresh grave with its mounds of wreaths and flowers. Dodie had always believed in seeing the departed off in style. Funerals and ceilidhs were the one thing he made the effort to dress up for because he felt it was the least he could do for a departed friend. On this occasion though he was dirty and threadbare. The grey stubble on his face was days old; his eyes

were sunk in his thin face and had a haunted look
about them; the skin on his cheeks was rubbed raw
from endless weepings and wipings. He loomed
over the grave, a vexed lost soul, quite unable to take
the harsh blow of Biddy's death. The tears poured
afresh, a large drip gathered at the end of his nose.
He shuffled his feet and then with an embarrassed
movement reached up and removed his greasy cap
to reveal a downy head of baby-fine white hair.
Twisting the cap in his big workworn hands he
bowed his head and sobbed, 'I'm – sorry I didny
dress up for you, Biddy. I – I've no' been feelin' like
myself since you went. I've looked after your bonny
boxie, she's all polished and standin' at my bedside
where I can be lookin' at her and be mindin' o' you.
Ealasaid had a new bairnie last week, a real bonny
wee calf – you would have liked her, that you would
– I hope you dinna think it cheeky but I've called her
Biddy after you. You're no' a cow, I know, but I felt
I aye wanted to speak your name so dinna be girnin'
about it.' He fumbled under his coat, and withdrawing an untidy wreath of meadowsweet, purple
clover, and white heather, he laid it at the foot of the
grave. 'It will bring you luck up yonder,' he said with
childlike conviction and, turning, he stumbled
blindly out of the Kirkyard.

A week later Lorn walked with Grant, Niall, and
Shona over the hill road to Dodie's cottage. No one
had seen the old eccentric since Biddy's death, and
Lachlan, mindful of him since he had contracted a

stomach ulcer after almost starving himself to death, had said to Niall that morning: 'I'm worried about Dodie. I've a mind he took Biddy's passing very badly. Maybe you and Shona could go along and see if he's all right.'

'I was thinking the same thing myself,' Niall admitted. 'Grant said something about painting the roof of his wee hoosie, so we'll call in at Laigmhor on the way.'

Shona immediately set about filling a basket with foodstuffs from the larder. Slochmhor had been her second home for years now. She was often ashamed of herself for thinking of the lovely rambling old house on the Mull of Kintyre as just 'the house'. She and Niall had lived in it for the past five years, yet she knew she would never think of it as home. Her roots lay on Rhanna, and she knew that one day she would come back to live on the island. She had talked the matter over with Niall and had discovered that he felt as she did. 'Give me a whily to build up some capital, mo ghaoil,' he had told her. 'Then we'll start seriously thinking about moving back to Rhanna. I fancy the idea of being an island vet. Island hopping is one way of making our dreams come true.'

Shona came out of the larder and bumped into Fiona, who eyed the full basket quizzically and enquired eagerly, 'Going for a picnic?'

'Just for a strupak over to Dodie's house.' Fiona's face fell till Shona added, 'We're going to paint the roof of his wee hoosie.'

Next to dabbling in pond life, Fiona enjoyed

dabbling in paint of all kinds, and she said, 'That's different! I could maybe paint some flowers on it instead of that German sign.'

'Come along then,' Shona said, and giggled. 'Might as well make a party of it. We're calling in at Laigmhor for Grant.'

Fiona's bright eyes snapped. 'Dimples McKenzie! No thanks! I'd rather spend my time looking at amoebae through my microscope.'

'Fiona, you're the limit. Why do you and Grant grab one another by the throat every time you meet?'

'Because he's rude, bad-mannered – and – and vulgar!' Fiona snapped then flounced away.

'He called her a cold fish the other day,' little Helen piped up. 'That's why she's mad at him.'

Shona laughed at the sight of her small daughter standing at the kitchen table enveloped in one of Elspeth's aprons, which was liberally sprinkled with flour. The old housekeeper had grown less spicy over the years, and though she could still wield a very able tongue, she had a lot of time and patience to spare for 'wee Ellie' as Helen was affectionately known. Shona looked at her angelic-looking little girl and a memory came of herself learning to make scones under Mirabelle's patient guidance. The child was very like herself at eight years old, though she had also inherited much of Niall's even temper. Shona would have liked more children, but time was passing, she was thirty-three now and still Ellie was an only child. 'We said we would fill the world with our children,' she had said rather sadly to Niall, but he had just answered quietly, 'We will, mo ghaoil, but just now Ellie fills our own little world, and if that's how it was meant for us then it canny be helped.'

'Are you coming with us, Ellie?' Shona asked, hiding a smile as the little girl energetically wielded a rolling pin.

'No, you and Father can go without me for a change.' She glanced up and her golden-brown eyes glinted with devilment. 'I'll let you have a rest from me and I'll torment Elspeth instead.'

'You'll do nothing of the sort, madam,' Elspeth said with asperity. 'Stop rubbing your nose with that floury hand this meenit! No one will want to eat scones covered in germs.'

'Och well. I don't mind. I'll get them all to myself then,' the child returned placidly.

Niall grabbed Shona's hand and they ran outside giggling. 'I'll say one thing for our wee Ellie,' he grinned. 'Unlike her mother she always "keeps the heid" as they say in Glasgow. She must have taken her good nature after me.'

'And her good looks from her mother!' Shona flashed. 'No one could ever accuse her of looking glaikit – not like a daft wee boy I once knew who called me names in the Post Office and was the cause of me getting a good skelping from Mirabelle.'

'Served you right – the best cure for that red-haired temper of yours!'

They arrived at Laigmhor in reminiscent good humour. Fergus came out of the byre, his black eyes lighting at sight of his daughter, who was a picture with her glowing face and her hair the colour of bracken on an autumn day.

'About time you two paid us a visit,' he greeted them. 'Kirsteen was saying only last night you've been neglecting us.'

'We're only here to collect the boys,' Shona explained. 'We thought we should pay Dodie a visit.'

Fergus looked thoughtful. 'Ay, he hasny been around for a time. He'll be taken up with the new calf, but it's as well to make sure he's fine. Grant and Lorn are in the barn, but you'll not get Lewis – he's supposed to be cutting the top field but a fine lot of work he'll get done with Eve at his elbow. Oh I know she's a dab hand around the farm, but lately she's taken to mooning about with her head in the clouds.'

Shona detected a note of annoyance in Fergus's tone, but she kept her counsel. Grant came out of the barn and hailed the visitors with delight. 'Nice of you to stop by once in a while to visit your ageing parents.' He ducked to avoid the swipe Fergus aimed at him and went to rummage in the shed for paint. Soon all four were swinging along the narrow road winding through the moors, waving to the groups of islanders who were up by the peat hags building the slices of turf into mounds to dry in the wind and sun. Except for a few sheep and some Highland cows cudding contentedly in the shade of the house, Dodie's place was deserted with not a single tourist to disturb the stillness.

Grant fetched a rickety chair from the porch, and

climbing onto it he saw that the roof of the wee hoosie was in a poor state of repair, the nails holding the metal tailpiece to the wooden slats rusted through in places. He called down, 'I'm surprised it hasny blown away years ago, there's only one or two good nails holding it down.'

'We'd best repair it before we paint it,' Niall suggested, and went off whistling to look for a hammer.

Lorn went with Grant to rummage through a tiny hut that held a jumble of driftwood and other things hoarded by the old eccentric, who could never bear to return from the shore empty-handed. Nails were obviously low on his list of useful items. A search in the barn and the byre, where Ealasaid was reclining with her new calf, also proved fruitless, and Grant ran a hand through his black curls in disgust. 'The old bugger collects everything *but* nails, as far as I can see. I'm away to look in the house, he's probably got box-loads hidden away in some corner.'

Lorn wasn't listening, he was too taken up with the new calf, and Grant stamped away. He had never been over the threshold of Dodie's house but boldly marched inside to gaze with interest at the dim interior. Ashes spilled from the grate, cobwebs hung from the rafters – more durable-looking than the ancient net curtains draped over the windows. The two car seats from Madam Balfour's abandoned car sat comfortably on either side of the grate. From the ceiling hung a bundle of onions, and Grant smiled, recalling Shona's tales of Mirabelle and her onions, and wondering if the old eccentric had somehow hit on the cure for 'a host o' germs'. Grant forgot about the nails and wandered up the short passageway to the bedroom. On the threshold he paused, mouth agape, hardly able to believe the sight that met his gaze. The room was literally papered with money, Jamaican ten-shilling notes – hundreds of them covering the dingy walls, dozens of them pinned jauntily round the muddy mirror of an aged dressing table. Grant stared in breathless wonder, his black eyes crinkled, and he hugged himself with pure delight. With a fingernail he scraped one of the notes away from the wall and it came off readily, having only been stuck on carelessly with a paste made from flour and water.

'The money from the *Politician*,' Grant breathed. 'God Almighty! The fly old bugger.' Racing outside he called to Lorn.

Shona and Niall had wandered away to look for Dodie but at the sound of Grant's excited voice, they turned quickly and ran over the turf. Soon all four were gazing dumbfounded at the treasure trove. Niall slapped his knee and exploded. 'Well, bugger me! It was always said that some old boy was sitting on a heap of Jamaican money!'

'And fancy it being old Dodie,' Lorn said, his thin face alight at the surprise of the discovery.

Shona's brilliant blue eyes were sparkling, as they had done on another occasion when she and Niall had come to the cottage and seen that Dodie had managed to collect his share of the 'spoils' from

Madam Balfour's car. 'He's the limit, so he is,' she said, giggling. 'But I'm glad he got it instead of the Crown Agents – it's just a pity he can never get to spend any of it.'

Grant's eyes gleamed. 'Oh yes he can –' he started to say but was interrupted by a wail of indignant outrage from Dodie, who had arrived home. All week he had been doing jobs to Burnbreddie in order to gather enough money together to contribute towards the purchase of a headstone for Biddy's grave.

'What are you doing in my house?' he babbled, terror rising in his pale eyes. 'I never stole it! I found it, years ago, comin' in on the tide. I knew it wasny real money so I dried it and stuck it up on my walls to make them look nice.' He sank down on the bed, and burying his face in his hands, began to cry in a storm of abject fear. 'Dinna tell the police! I don't want to go to jail! I would die in jail so I would. I couldny bear never to roam free again, and Ealasaid and my bonny wee Biddy would die too!' He rocked himself back and forth in an agony of stark misgiving. Grant went quickly to sit beside him and put an arm round the shaking shoulders. 'Weesht, weesht, Dodie, nobody's going to tell. We're all glad you found the money and you're wrong – it is real money, and you're going to get to spend it. Dry your eyes and listen to me a minute.'

Dodie drew a greasy sleeve over his face. Through tear-filled eyes he looked at Grant, who was one of his favourite McKenzies. Since the boy had joined the

Merchant Navy he had sent postcards to the old man from all over the world. Erchy's post van stopped regularly at Dodie's cottage, and together they gazed at pictures of 'furrin parts'. The cards were pinned proudly above the fireplace, and on long winter nights Dodie delighted in scrutinising them over and over again, smiling primly at pictures of 'exotic leddies wi' belly buttons', screeching at the haughty expressions on the faces of camels, puzzling as to why 'dark leddies' walked with pots attached to their heads.

'You know I visit places all over the world?' Grant started. 'Well, I could take some of your money away with me and change it for you. Only wee amounts at a time, mind you, but it means every time I come home I would have some money to give you. As long as the Jamaican notes remain legal tender I can go on changing them for you.'

Dodie understood very little of this beyond the fact that Grant could somehow change his bits o' fancy paper into real money. 'My, that would be grand,' he said enthusiastically. 'I could buy lots o' baccy and we could get Biddy a real fine headstone and,' he said, brightening further, 'maybe I could build Ealasaid a new byre.' His eyes roved round the walls and his face fell again. 'But – my bonny walls, they'll no' look the same without these.'

Shona smiled. 'You can buy real wallpaper, Dodie . . .'

'And I'll put it up for you,' Lorn promised rashly. With his interests lying mainly out of doors, he had

Christine Marion Fraser

had little experience of home decorating but the smiles stretching Dodie's lips heightened his resolve.

Niall moved to the door. 'Come on, bairns, we'd better get the painting done before the rain comes.'

Dodie gave a great sigh of contented appreciation. 'I aye said that the doctor and McKenzie o' the Glen had good bairns,' he said, and nodded magnanimously.

Grant's laughing young face became suddenly stern. 'Not a word of this to a soul, Dodie, or we'll all be in jail.'

Outside Grant repeated his warning to the others, but Lorn knew the message was for him. He must not say anything to Lewis who, in his exuberance, often let things slip that had been told to him in confidence. It wasn't lack of loyalty that made him like this, just a love of the limelight, which loosened his tongue often much to his own regret.

'I won't say anything – to anybody.' Lorn's tones were sullen, Lewis was his twin, the bond between them was so strong that a strange telepathy existed between them. They confided everything to each other.

Shona saw his discomfiture and murmured softly, 'Some things are best left unsaid, Lorn – for the sake of other folks.'

Lorn stirred the paint energetically and said nothing. Dodie came galloping up, his arms filled with great sticks of juicy red rhubarb. 'These is for your kindness,' he told them joyfully. 'I washed it in the burnie and I have made wee polkies and filled

358

them wi' sugar. Come you inside and eat it now, a fine treat it is – the best rhubarb on the island – ay,' he said, 'the very best you could get.' He disappeared into the house. The four young people looked at one another; Niall and Shona held their breath, remembering a long ago day of sunlight, of argument and laughter – of Dodie divulging to them the secret of his flourishing rhubarb patch. Niall pulled Shona to him and kissed her burnished hair. The laughter bubbled up and out of them, echoed by Lorn and Grant, who, with paint streaked over their faces, had collapsed against one another in agonies of smothered snorts of mirth.

Part Four

Christmas 1959

Chapter Fifteen

The awakening of Lorn's love for Ruth was like the slow opening of the tender buds of spring. But he wasn't sure if she returned his feelings. Whenever she saw him she seemed nervous, which gave her a remoteness that made him long for her all the more. Sometimes she smiled, a lovely, sweet, uncertain smile. The magic of her smile, the violet of her eyes turning to night, her exquisite stillness, sent pangs of aching hunger gnawing through every nerve in his body – but they seemed unable to find anything to say to each other. None of the things that meant anything. After the usual polite salutations she would walk past him and limp quickly away. Neither of them had matured yet: they hadn't passed beyond adolescent dreams, or the awkwardness of extreme youth and all the agonies of self-doubt that went with it. But she had blossomed over the years in other ways: the plainness of childhood had disappeared gradually, till now there was about her an almost unearthly quality of beauty: her pale silken hair framed an oval face, her slightly turned-up nose was lightly sprinkled with freckles, her skin was exquisitely clear – and her mouth: it was beautifully shaped and oddly sensuous. She was small-boned, and rather too thin, though her breasts were full and firm, curving enticingly under the loose frocks her mother made for her. She had rebelled against having to be continually garbed in white and had had quite a scene over the affair, resisting fiercely the idea that she shouldn't be allowed to express her individuality. But Morag Ruadh had remained tight-lipped, adamant, and shocked at the idea of 'my very own daughter turning on me'. And after a few days of charged silences, of seeing her father and grandparents bearing the brunt of her mother's tongue, Ruth had given in. Nevertheless, she had managed to make it plain that she was a girl with a strong mind and a will of her own, and that it was for her father's sake that she had unbended and not because she went in fear of the Lord.

Ironically, Morag's intention to label her daughter as untouchable only served to heighten her desirability to the opposite sex. Despite her limp she walked with a grace of movement that was oddly rhythmic. To see her wandering along the hillsides on a mist-shrouded morning, clad in her white dress, her pale hair shining, added to the impression that she was a vision who was not quite real. It was also a temptation to the young males of the district to find out for themselves whether she was after all flesh and blood like other girls. But they kept their distance, partly because to do otherwise would be to incur the ungodly wrath of Morag Ruadh, partly because Ruth's shyness was in itself an almost insurmountable barrier, and partly because for any boy to be seen walking with the white virgin would have meant endless teasings and tormentings from young contemporaries.

But Lorn would have cared nothing for the teasing. He longed to walk with Ruth; to hear the sweet singing quality of her voice; to touch her; to find out if she would respond to him; to know if she felt even a little of what he felt for her. But he didn't know how to make the approaches and cursed his lack of self-confidence. Also there were other things to contend with. Only last year he had suffered a setback when he had collapsed while guiding the plough. He remembered the squeezing pains in his chest, the breath forcing itself from his lungs, the terror of not being able to get breath, the stifling panic of slipping gradually into unconsciousness. He had been taken by helicopter to Barra, and from there by plane to Glasgow where he had undergone emergency heart surgery. Dramatic though it had all been, the complication hadn't been a serious one. Lachlan had reassured Kirsteen and Fergus on that point, but Lorn had seen all the old doubts back in his father's eyes. He had forbidden the boy to use the hand plough. 'You'll just have to make do with the tractor,' he had said sternly. 'We'll keep the Clydesdale, though. She can live out her days in the fields, she deserves that much.'

So Lorn had bottled up his frustrations while Lewis strode with Fergus in the fields, shared his manly talk and laughter. More and more Lorn felt shut out and rejected. Everyone except him seemed to be getting on with their lives.

Ruth had become a successful writer, contributing regularly to Scottish magazines. The islanders eagerly devoured her tales and had grown so used to having an author in their midst they no longer went in awe of her, though they were quick to point her out proudly to visiting relatives. Ruth remained unaffected and unspoiled. 'I don't feel different or special,' she confided once to Lorn. 'Just silly when people look at me as if I had horns.' Then she had added with a mischievous smile, 'My ambition is to get a book published. If that happens I might look down my nose at everyone.'

Lewis had become an excellent farmer, though he never let work interfere with fun. Often he came home unsteady and giggling after a night of ceilidhing to recount his latest romantic venture to Lorn. He did everything with a dangerous abandon. When he went out riding he went bareback, galloping his horse at a reckless pace, his blue eyes snapping with exhilaration. When he went swimming he swam further out than anyone else dared. Even while working he had fun, yet no matter how much he tempted Providence he invariably emerged unscathed. Life to him was one great adventure to be enjoyed to the full. He said things that only he could get away with. Girls fell at his feet and made fools of themselves in their efforts to get him to notice them. His manner was charming, witty, outrageous, infectious – and though many an eyebrow was raised at his feckless ways, very few were able to resist his engaging grin.

'He loves people does Lewis McKenzie,' Kate had summed up. 'And there's no' many who canny take to him.'

'Ay, he was born wi' a silver spoon right enough,' Merry Mary had said and frowned slightly. In her opinion ulterior motives lay behind his bland talk and suave manners, her disapproval of him having arisen from the day she discovered that he had collected money from every child on the island after she had very painfully cracked her nose on the handle of her shovel, knocking off her wart in the process. Lewis had been helping her that day and had affected great surprise that the shovel had been left in a particularly slippery part of the vegetable patch. She had felt slightly uneasy as he had tried to hide a triumphant grin even while he fussed over her and marched her off to the doctor's to have the bleeding nose seen to. 'I prefer Lorn myself,' she had continued thoughtfully. 'Quiet he may be, but there's a strength there, ay, that there is. He's truly kind-hearted, too, for all he's suffered. I mind he came to help me in the garden after I hurt my nose thon time, and no' a penny piece would he take for it. His brother never came back – *he* got what he had been waiting for.'

Winter came early to Rhanna that year, with some weeks to go before Christmas. The winds swept in from the Atlantic bringing sheets of freezing rain that seemed to go on perpetually, blotting out the hills and bringing early darkness night after night.

'I hate when it's like this,' Kirsteen sighed one morning, glancing out of the window to the wind-tossed, rain-sodden landscape. 'I wish it would snow instead.'

Fergus got up from the table to stand behind her and nuzzle her ear. She leaned against him, enjoying the strength of his hard body, then with a little self-conscious start she moved out of his reach and ran her hands ruefully through her crisp hair. 'Don't,' she murmured, her fair skin flushing. 'You'll see my white hairs.'

He pulled her to him and kissed the tip of her nose. 'In this light?' he murmured teasingly. 'All I see is a beautiful woman who can still drive me crazy with her feminine wiles – besides, what can be lovelier? Silver threads among the gold.'

'Oh Fergus, don't,' she said uncomfortably, 'that makes me sound like a hundred – and fifty-three is bad enough.'

'Don't be daft,' he said tenderly. 'I still think of you as a girl and always will. Still, it's strange,' he continued thoughtfully. 'How quickly the years pass. I don't feel much older than I did at thirty, and it hits me hard when I realise I'm fifty-nine. Bob was right. I always mind him telling me that at sixty I would be thinking much the same things I did at forty – only then I didn't have a grown-up family, nor was I a grandfather.' He sighed. 'I often think I wasn't cut out to be a father, sometimes I feel I've failed in some way. I mind Murdy Travers telling me to treat my sons the same, but that hasny been easy the way things have turned out. I feel I have to protect Lorn and often wonder if Lewis feels left out.'

She stared at him. 'But – oh, my darling, I know it hasn't been easy. We went over all this some years ago and tortured each other with nasty words – but – you're wrong! I think Lorn is the one who feels shut out. I know you're shielding him because of what happened last year, but he's all right now, Fergus, and quite able to do as much as Lewis around the farm. Oh, don't look like that, darling! Sometimes when you're wrapped up in people you love it's very hard to see things in black and white – oh, look at the time, I must start breakfast.'

Slowly Fergus resumed his seat, his black eyes troubled. Surely – surely Kirsteen was wrong. Lorn couldn't think – mustn't think things like that . . . His thoughts were interrupted as the door opened and a cold blast of air catapulted Bob and the twins inside. Although Bob was in his eighties, he was hale and hearty, wirier and tougher than many a man half his age, though he now walked with a slight stoop and used his shepherd's crook more often to aid him over rough ground.

He now took most of his meals at Laigmhor. Kirsteen couldn't bear to think of him eating solitary makeshift meals in his lonely little cottage on the slopes of Ben Machrie. Folks said he was 'a crafty auld bugger', for it was known that he was quite capable of looking after himself, but Kirsteen shut her ears to the gossip and made the old shepherd welcome. The new arrivals crowded to the sink to have a hasty wash.

'I think old Rosie has a touch of milk fever,' Lewis called over the running water. 'She kicked the pail out of my hand when I touched her udder. It would be grand if Niall was here to see to things like that.'

'Ay,' Fergus responded absently. Lorn sat down opposite and Fergus glanced at his thin young face. 'You're good at things like that, Lorn,' he said, drawing his porridge towards him. 'You'll maybe look at her for me.'

Lorn didn't look up. 'Ay,' was all he said and lifted his spoon. Fergus frowned. Was Kirsteen right after all? Surely not! This boy was the one nearest his heart. They understood one another, had so much in common a telepathy seemed to exist between them. The joy of having such a son was an uncommonly rich and wonderful experience. Murdy's words came to him, 'Never show you have a favourite son'. He never had, by word or deed. Biddy's last words came to him: 'Look to Lewis; with your guidance he will turn out to be a good man.'

Had he in his anxiety to set Lewis's steps in the right direction unwittingly neglected Lorn? Lorn with the inner strength that glowed out of his eyes, who had been born physically frail but fiercely courageous. Had he in his eagerness to protect this fine son of his somehow only succeeded in making him feel cast out? The questions whirled round in confusion in his mind. What was right? God in Heaven, what was the right thing to do in his role as a father? He sucked in his breath and searched his mind for something to say that would be right. With a glance at the rain streaming down the panes he said more harshly than he meant, 'Maybe you'll come with me today, Lorn, and help me to take feed up to the yowes on the hill?'

Lorn, lost in his own deep thoughts, didn't answer, and Fergus, connecting his sullenness with the things Kirsteen had said, felt frustration boiling in him, tensing his jaw, darkening his eyes. Hell! Why did it all have to be so complicated? He was too busy a man to have the patience for all this – and patience had never been one of his strong points.

Lewis dug into his porridge and smiled. 'Don't fret over him, Father, he's just love-sick.' He nudged his brother, who scowled and drew away his arm. 'Never mind,' Lewis continued unruffled. 'The Laird's ceilidh should cheer us all up. A real grand do it will be from all accounts.'

'The Laird's ceilidh?' Kirsteen questioned, puzzled.

'Ay, Matthew was telling us about it in the dairy just now. Burnbreddie is throwing open his doors on Christmas Eve for all his tenants. There's to be a band, a bar, and a buffet table. In other words, a real grand affair, so you'd better think about getting Mother a new dress,' he finished cheekily.

'Things have indeed changed since her leddyship passed on,' Bob observed. 'I hear tell the old house has had its first coat of paint in years. The old lady wouldny allow a thing to be changed – said it all had to be as it was when old Balfour was alive.'

The atmosphere lightened as everyone fell to discussing the latest piece of news. Only Lorn remained silent and as soon as breakfast was over he went upstairs to throw himself on the bed and gaze at the ceiling. He should ask Ruth to the dance. She wouldn't go otherwise, as Dugald wasn't a tenant of the Laird. He had bought his house when he had taken over Merry Mary's shop. Lorn moved restlessly. The ache that had lain dull in his heart for months was growing worse. Was this what love was? A yearning that tore relentlessly at the senses, a burning emptiness that nothing could fill? Sleepless nights, a longing for more and more solitude in which to think – think of her? That shy lovely girl with her grace and sweetness and her uncertain awareness of her feminine power. For she did have power. For all her reserve, for all her shyness she was possessed of a power that overwhelmed him. He had to talk to her more, pluck up the courage to ask her to Burnbreddie's ceilidh – but would that witch of a mother of hers allow her to come?

Lewis bounded into the room but stopped short at sight of his brother. 'Thinking of *her* again? You're all flushed, Lorn my boy. No bloody wonder! Thinking's no use, doing's the thing.' He threw himself onto the edge of the bed. 'How the hell you've managed to wait so long for a girl beats me – no wonder I hear your bedsprings creaking in the night. You wake me up with your tossing and turning. Have you never done it with a girl?' he asked bluntly.

Lorn threw a hand over his eyes. 'Shut up! I'm trying to think.'

'From the look of you, you've succeeded. Why don't you ask Ruth to this dance? Burnbreddie's got some fine haylofts up yonder. I can recommend them.'

'Do you think I should?'

'What? Get Ruth into a hayloft?'

'No, daftie, ask her to the dance?'

'Of course you should. I'm worried about you. It's time you spread your wings a bit – after all, we'll be eighteen in a few days' time. If I get some birthday money, I'm saving it to buy Rachel a really fine birthday present.' He grew serious. 'I'm a bit like you at the moment. I can't get Rachel out of my mind. Funny she's been here all along, yet last time I saw her it was for the first time somehow. What a figure that girl's got! I've sweated over girls before, but Rachel – phew!'

Some days later Lorn and Ruth came face to face in the village. The wind was biting in from the sea and had whipped her skin to roses. 'Lorn, I was hoping to see you,' she greeted him breathlessly, a combination of swift heartbeats and fighting the wind. She rummaged in her pocket and with difficulty withdrew a bulky parcel, which she pushed at him. 'I've been carrying it around for days so it's a wee bit squashed. Happy birthday. I – I knitted it myself, so don't look at it too closely – I'm better with a pen than with knitting needles.'

Wordlessly he took the parcel. For a long tremulous

moment he gazed at her. The wind lifted and tossed her fine golden hair about her face. Her eyes were the colour of the purple-blue clouds racing over the sky, her lips were parted slightly showing her white teeth. For what seemed eternity he gazed at her mouth, then he dropped his eyes and said gruffly, 'Thanks for the present, Ruthie, I'll – I'll have to go now.'

'Ay, me too, I'll – I'll be seeing you.'

They started to walk away from each other though an invisible bond seemed to be tugging at them, slowing their unwilling steps. He stopped. 'Ruthie.'

She whirled round. 'Yes, Lorn.'

'Will you – do you – would you come to Burnbreddie's dance with me?'

Her colour deepened, the answer rushed to her lips though it came out slowly. 'Ay, Lorn, I'd like that.'

They stood apart, staring at one another, eyes bright with longing, then she turned and hurried away, blood pulsing, heart singing, even while she wondered what her mother would say when she asked her permission to attend the dance with Lorn McKenzie.

Lorn rushed home and went straight upstairs to tear open the parcel. It was a scarf, a blue knitted scarf, so long it took ages to pull it from the folds of tissue paper. Inside was a card, which simply said 'From Ruth to Lorn, with love'. With a little whoop of delight he wound the scarf round his neck and surveyed himself in the mirror. She had knitted this for him, especially for him. With her very own hands she had knitted and knitted and knitted – for him. He picked up the card to read it again. The word 'love' leapt out at him and he raised it to his lips to kiss it.

Lewis came in with a rush. He had just returned from Oban. 'It was grand in Oban, though too bad Rachel's in Glasgow now, or we could have met up. Murdy's getting a bit doddery. He keeps losing things and Maggie follows him around like a sheepdog finding all the things he's lost. I laugh all the time when I'm there.' He sat up and said eagerly, 'Wait till I show you what I got for Rachel.' Rummaging in his case he withdrew a flat box out of which he extracted an oyster satin nightdress.

Lorn stared. 'It's a nightdress – and so thin you can see through it.'

Lewis laughed deeply. 'Top marks! Can you picture her in it? I can, and I hope I'll get a chance for a private showing.' He paused. 'What's that you've got twined round your neck?'

'A scarf,' Lorn's tones were defensive. 'A birthday present from Ruthie.' Lewis scrambled up and hugged his brother. 'Well, things are moving at last! Get in there while the going's good – if not, somebody else might beat you to it. The way Ruth looks these days she won't be known as the white virgin for much longer. Too bad you didn't ask me to fetch her something from Oban. Girls love to get presents – and I don't mean things like woolly gloves or scarves that reach to your ankles!'

Lewis chattered on, but Lorn wasn't listening. He was furious with himself. Still, someone else was bound to be making a trip to the mainland before Christmas. He wondered what he could get her. He wouldn't have the nerve to give her a nightdress, only people like Lewis did things like that.

The Laird's invitation had given the villagers something to look forward to. Best clothes were hastily unearthed to be inspected, aired, and repaired. All over the island women sighed over the contents of their wardrobes and dropped broad hints to their menfolk about Christmas gifts. Kirsteen gazed at her collection of dresses in disgust. They were years old and out of date. Normally she never bothered to keep up with changing fashions, but now she longed for something new. With a sigh she got out her best old dress and set about altering it on the little treadle sewing machine Fergus had bought her after the twins were born.

Ruth was in the worst dilemma of all. She didn't want to go to the Burnbreddie dance dressed in the same boring white. She couldn't ask her mother for a new dress. In fact, she couldn't ask for anything till she first asked her mother if she could go to the dance with Lorn, which she kept putting off, knowing the showdown that would surely follow the request. She thought of doing it through her father, but he had been ill recently with flu, and she felt she couldn't burden him with anything else. She was in despair and resigning herself to the fact that she must tell Lorn she couldn't go with him, when Shona, who was home for Christmas, came to her rescue.

'I am hearing Lorn has asked you to the dance,' Shona greeted her. 'What are you wearing?'

'Nothing!' Ruth wailed, her violet eyes dark with unhappiness. 'I haven't asked Mam if I can go yet because she'll only say no.'

Shona's blue eyes snapped. 'Oh, is that so! We'll see about that! It's time you got to enjoy your life. I'm sure if your father knew he would move heaven and hell for you.'

'Och, I know that, Shona, but he's been ill recently and still very weak. He's not able to take trouble at the moment, and Grannie and Granda are over in Barra for a few days so I can't get them to help.'

Shona's nostrils flared. 'Well! You've got me then! Ask me back to your house for a strupak – now.'

Ruth looked at the lovely determined face, the fearless tilt of the auburn head, the fiery sparkle in the wonderful blue eyes – so like Lorn's. 'Will you come home and have a strupak with me, Shona?'

Shona proved a spirited and competent ally. Over tea and scones in the carbolic smelling kitchen she smiled warmly at Morag and said conversationally, 'I was delighted when Lorn told me had asked Ruth to the dance at Burnbreddie. She'll be the belle – no doubt about that. Nothing can be more exciting than a girl's first dance. I mind when Niall took me to mine – oh, it wasn't a grand affair, just a ceilidh in a barn but –'

Morag's cheeks had flamed, and her tones were ominous. 'What's that you say? Lorn taking Ruth to the Burnbreddie dance? It's the first I've heard o' it – of course, I'm the last to hear of her goings on these days. Well, you can tell your brother he needny bother, she won't be going. All thon dancin' and caperin' wi' boys is just a temptation to the de'il, and I made a vow that my lassie would never be tarnished by pleasures that are just excuses to dabble in the unseemly – a vow to the Lord it was and I will no' change my mind now.'

Ruth turned away to hide the tears of frustration and disappointment. 'The Laird has already included her in the guest list,' Shona lied sweetly. 'All the young girls will be going.'

'Well, my Ruth will no' be one o' them!' Morag returned in tight-lipped outrage.

'I'm thinkin' you're wrong there, Morag,' Dugald, white-faced and hollow-eyed, spoke from the rocking chair by the fire. 'I'm the man of this house, and it's time I damned well made you aware of that fact! Ruthie will go to the dance with young McKenzie, and that's final. It's time she started to enjoy her young life.'

The crimson flowed from Morag's face to stain her neck. Her tight lips parted as rage boiled in her, but before she could utter a word Dugald held up his hand and said firmly, 'Don't say it, Morag, you'll only be wasting your breath. Ruthie is going to this dance – and I tell you this – that will only be the start of it. If Lorn wants to take her out anywhere in future, he has my permission. She is, after all, my lassie as well as yours,' he finished softly.

The blood drained from Morag's face, leaving it deathly pale. He was warning her that he knew – knew that she wasn't entirely sure that he was Ruth's father.

'I'll buy the dress myself, Mam,' Ruth's voice came, anxious yet tinged with delight. 'I saved some money from –'

'*No!*' Morag's voice was taut with frustrated temper. 'There will be no new dresses. You can go to this dance, my girl, but you will go in one of your own white frocks!'

'But, Mam –' Ruth began tearfully, but Shona flashed her a triumphant smile.

'Your white dresses are lovely, Ruth, with a bit of alteration . . .'

'I will not alter one single stitch,' Morag stated. 'And that is that! I'm far too busy a woman for any o' that frivolous nonsense.'

'Och, don't worry yourself, Morag,' Shona said, her smile remaining fixed, though she could gladly have torn Morag's hair out by its red roots. 'Kirsteen is a dab hand with her wee sewing machine. Come on, Ruth, we will go and look at your dresses, choose the best one and take it back to Kirsteen – now.'

Dugald turned his face quickly to hide a smile as Shona, her head high, marched Ruth out of the room, leaving Morag standing speechless in the middle of it.

Kirsteen was at first dismayed at the challenge that

had been thrust upon her, but after hearing Shona's account of the scene with Morag she set her lips and went grimly to the task. Removing the long flowing skirt from one of her own evening gowns, she attached it to the bodice of Ruth's dress. To the neck and sleeves she added ruffles of pure white lace, and as a final touch she sewed a row of tiny pearl buttons down the front of the bodice. When Ruth arrived for a fitting she gasped in awe at sight of herself in Kirsteen's wardrobe mirror and whispered, 'How can I ever thank you, Kirsteen?'

'The look on Lorn's face will be thanks enough,' Kirsteen replied, her heart melting as the girl swirled round, sending the long skirt billowing, rejoicing in the fact that the ugly calliper would be hidden from view.

Kirsteen's wish for snow was granted. Three days before Christmas the wind abated and the stars glittered coldly in the night sky. Hoar frost rimed the heather on the hills, the icy grip of winter slowed the burns as icicles gathered. Gradually the fat grey snowclouds rolled over the sea, to be torn apart on the ragged hill peaks, sending snow cascading over the countryside. On Christmas Eve morning Fergus stamped the snow from his boots and, coming into the kitchen, said with a rather sarcastic smile, 'You got your wish, Kirsteen, now would you care to grab a shovel and come and help to dig the ewes out of the drifts? We need every pair of hands.'

At first it seemed fun, working beside Shona and

the men, the former sparkling as she pushed snow-balls down Niall's neck and ran shrieking as he chased her, but by mid-afternoon she was exhausted, and after tea she dozed by the fire in the parlour to wake with a start wondering what time it was. As she dragged herself up to the bedroom she sighed and wondered if all the romance had gone out of her life. Fergus had been sharp with her that morning, and at teatime he had hardly spoken a word. He had murmured some things to Shona that she hadn't been able to catch, and she had felt left out and rather angry at the pair of them.

As she reached the door of her room she wondered if she could possibly make some excuse not to go to the dance. Every bone in her body ached and she felt she could hardly walk, let alone dance. She opened the door to see a warm fire leaping in the grate. On the hearthrug sat the zinc tub piled high with steamy soap bubbles; her fur jacket was laid out on the bed – and beside it lay a gaily wrapped parcel.

Shona put her bright head round the door, her blue eyes full of mischief. 'Father's orders. We all helped to fill it, including Niall, and – I hope you don't mind, but Ellie poured nearly a full bottle of bubble bath in. She says she's going to wait outside the door and watch the bubbles oozing out under the crack!' Shona said, and withdrew before Kirsteen could utter a word.

Without further ado Kirsteen stripped and sank blissfully into the perfumed water, chuckling as bubbles popped under her nose, little drifts of them rising and floating in the draught from the fire. She soaked for fully fifteen minutes till all the tension left her and she emerged to wrap herself in a pink dressing gown, feeling relaxed yet tingling.

'Am I too late to dry your back?' Fergus's deep voice made her jump. The door shut with a little click and he came forward to press himself against her and kiss her. 'Mmm, you smell lovely, I had hoped to catch you in the tub. Too bad we have to go out.'

He smelled of soap and toothpaste. His fingers touched the tips of her breasts and she could easily have forgotten the Burnbreddie dance if he had stood beside her for one more minute. But he moved away, his face rather flushed. He went to the bed, picked up the parcel and handed it to her. 'Merry Christmas, darling, I hope you like it.'

'But we don't open presents till tomorrow.'

'You open this one tonight. I got Burnbreddie's wife to buy it in Oban. You and she are about the same size – anyway – see what you think.'

It was an evening gown of soft blue silk. He zipped her into it and stood behind her, his dark eyes full of love. 'You look beautiful.'

'Oh, Fergus, I feel it, it's just what I needed to boost my morale. If I had known I wouldn't have spent hours altering my old things.' She threw her arms round his neck and kissed him. 'Thank you – for this – and for being my husband.'

Some minutes later she knotted his tie for him. It wasn't often he had occasion to wear one, which was as well because with his one arm he found it a frustrating business to tie a neat knot. He was very handsome in his dark suit and a white shirt that emphasised the mahogany of his skin. Standing before the mirror he said rather jauntily, 'Amazing the difference clothes make. I look rather a distinguished gentleman, don't you think?'

Kirsteen turned from brushing her hair. 'How like Alick you sounded just now. He used to say that, in that light-hearted fashion, just as you did now. He was never like you to look at, but there were little things that marked you out as brothers.'

'Ay,' Fergus said, his tone thoughtful. 'Blood is thicker than water right enough. It's strange how much I miss him, yet look how we used to fight . . .'

From the room at the top of the corridor there came the sound of arguing and laughter. Kirsteen smiled. Lewis would be showing Lorn some last-minute dance steps. In all the excitement of the season Lorn had forgotten that he could barely dance a single step. A few nights ago he had suddenly leapt up from his chair and in a terrified voice had cried, 'I can't dance! I've asked Ruth to this big night out and I can't dance a single one! Bugger it! What the hell will I do?' Lewis had immediately got to his feet. With a deep bow he had intoned in a high voice, 'Please, my lady, will you do me the honour of dancing with me?' To which Lorn had acceded with a gust of laughter. Fergus had said to Kirsteen, 'Come to think of it, I ought to brush up too.' And he had swept her all round the kitchen. Then Niall and

Shona arrived, and they too had joined in the impromptu fun, and it hadn't mattered that the men wore working clothes and the women aprons.

Tonight, however, everything mattered very much to Lorn. He had been nervous all day and several times had been on the point of backing out. His courage embraced everything but social gatherings and on top of it all he had his feelings for Ruth to contend with.

'Those two will never fight like Alick and me,' Fergus said quietly. 'They are so alike in many ways, they share so much.'

'Let's just hope they never fall in love with the same girl – then the trouble will begin,' Kirsteen said. 'Oh, I know Lewis flits about from one to the other, but one day he will really fall in love – like Lorn at this very minute.' She sighed. 'He's so shy – so is Ruth. It won't be easy for them.'

'If they truly love one another it will turn out all right – it did for us.'

'That took years,' she pointed out.

He helped her into the fur jacket and she snuggled against him as he whispered into her ear, 'Ay, but it was worth it. The best things are worth waiting for.'

Chapter Sixteen

Ruth came slowly into the kitchen and stood sparkling-eyed in front of her parents. Dugald drew in his breath; pride brought a lump to his throat: tonight Ruth had grown from an uncertain child into a dazzling young woman. Dugald had given her a tiny pair of pearl earrings for her birthday. These, and a single pink rosebud pinned above her breast, were the only ornamentations she wore, the delicate colour of the rose matching that in her cheeks. She glowed with a radiance that seemed to spread out and touch the bare clinical room with light. He got up and took her hands.

'Ruthie, Shona was right – you will be the belle of the ball – no – more than that, a princess.' He took the mohair stole from her arms and wrapped it round her shoulders. She reached up to kiss his pale cheek then turned a radiant face to her mother and said rather hesitantly, 'Well, Mam?'

Morag cleared her throat and said gruffly, 'Ay, you'll do. You've grown into a bonny young woman – just you mind all the things I've told you and you'll be all right. You had better be going, see no' and keep the McKenzies waiting.'

Over his wife's head Dugald winked at his

daughter and she lowered her face quickly to hide a smile. At the door Morag rather furtively pushed a tiny Bible into her hands. 'Carry this – it will protect you.'

'Where will I keep it, Mam? I don't have a bag.'

Morag flushed and whispered, 'Tuck it into your drawers.' She glanced quickly round as if afraid that someone had overhead the ridiculous suggestion.

Ruth's lips twitched. 'I prefer the words of the Lord to be in my heart, Mam – not in my knickers next to my backside.'

Leaving her mother with her mouth agape, Ruth hurried out into the cold glittering night. A short distance away, parked outside the shop, she saw her father's van. Vehicles of every description were being used to transport people to Burnbreddie, all of them filled to capacity. The Laird had sent out his own cars to bring those whose only hope of getting to the dance would have been by shanks's pony. Everyone had worried that the weather might have prevented them getting over to Nigg, but while the snow had draped itself over hills and fields, the tangy air of the sea had kept the shore roads clear.

Dugald had been determined that for once his daughter would have some freedom, and he had left his van at the shop and given Lorn the keys. Before Ruth reached the vehicle Lorn was out, holding open the passenger door. His heart was beating a tattoo. Lewis had given him a short but uplifting pep talk in the bedroom as they were getting ready. 'Act very cool, even though you feel hot under the collar.

Open doors for her, lead the way, take her wrap, get drinks for her – in fact, behave like a perfect little gentleman. Girls love to feel special, and with a girl like Ruth you'll have to go all out in your efforts. She hasn't got any confidence in herself, you'll have to give her some even though you feel like fainting in the process.' His blue eyes had gleamed. 'It pays in the long run, my lad, believe me.'

Lorn stood by the door, erect and poised while beneath him his legs felt like jelly. On the journey he tried to act very coolly, and succeeded so well that Ruth felt a pang of dismay. This self-assured stranger with the clipped tones wasn't the Lorn she knew. She felt uncomfortable and uncertain, feelings that grew in magnitude as he became silent in his concentration of driving the van over the treacherous cliff road to Nigg. She stole a glance at him. All she could see in the darkness was an anonymous black silhouette sitting straight and rigid behind the wheel. The faint aroma of soap came to her, and her heart quickened further. For the first time in her life she was alone with a boy – and that boy was Lorn McKenzie, whom she loved so much her heart ached with the depth of her emotions. She gazed at the sea swirling and booming restlessly far below. That was how she had felt lately, unable to settle, forever seething inside, unable to find solace in anything, not even her writing. Car lights were behind and in front of them on the normally deserted road, and from the crofts and cottages at Nigg little black dots were scurrying, while a gay little melody drifted from Annack Gow's blackhouse. After a lapse of many years Tam had dared to get his still working again with the help of Graeme Gow and a few others.

The van swerved suddenly as it left the road and made a bumpy path over a lonely moor track. The engine stopped, silence and darkness shrouded them. Lorn's voice came breathlessly, all his composure crumbling away. 'Ruthie – I – before we go up I wanted to give you something – for your birthday and your Christmas combined. I wish I could give you a whole pile of things, but – och – here, take it and open it – it's – it's not much . . .'

The nervous monologue trailed off. He pushed the parcel at her. Briefly their hands touched, flesh burned into flesh, their pulses raced apace, then in confusion she moved away and immersed herself in opening the gift. The cold caress of marble lay heavy in her hands and he said, 'It's a paperweight with a pen sort of attached to it – like an old-fashioned quill, only it isn't. It's a fountain pen. The base is Skye marble, full of lovely colours – greys, greens, and a wee hint of purple, the same colour as your eyes when you're looking very serious.'

'Lorn.' Her voice was low, melodious. 'I can't see it – but it's beautiful.'

They laughed at the silly remark, then without conscious thought their hands entwined. He drew her towards him. The scent of roses filled his nostrils, her nearness made his senses whirl. Briefly he touched her soft hair with his lips. They both trembled, each feeling the tremors of the other. For an eternal moment they remained apart, lips close but not touching then with a soft little moan his mouth moulded to hers and all the longing and misery of endless days and nights melted into obscurity.

The kiss was fleeting, inexperienced, tender, but it was only the beginning of dreams, a warm sweet promise of greater things to come.

'I suppose we'd better go.' His lilting voice was shaky.

'Ay,' she said softly, unwilling to relinquish the intimate lovely experience of being alone with him. She had looked forward to the dance, now she knew she had only savoured the anticipation of being in his company. It would have been enough for her to spend the whole evening with him in her father's draughty van and her heart sank a little as they drove up to Burnbreddie House. Light flooded the silvered lawns, people laughed as they held each other upright on the slippery road.

The interior of the house had lost its gloomy look. The walls were bright with new paint, modern furniture had replaced the monstrous overstuffed sofas, in the hall a great log fire crackled up the chimney.

'Stay beside me, please,' Ruth whispered as they went inside to be swallowed up in an atmosphere of laughter and chinking glasses. In the background a band played soft music. Lorn's own composure was fast failing him but somehow he managed to carry out Lewis's advice. The Laird and his charming wife Rena were the perfect hosts, welcoming and smiling, making the guests feel relaxed and at home. The

Rhanna folk were used to homely ceilidhs but this was a much grander occasion, and an unnatural politeness prevailed. But nothing could dampen their spirits for long. Tam's eyes gleamed at sight of the bar set up in a corner of the room. Behind it presided his son, Angus. Tam rubbed his hands together and spoke to the Laird in his most polite tones, 'Is this no' terrible weather just? I will just go and have a wee dram to warm up my blood.' He winked confidingly. 'I am no' as young as I was and Kate would have me comin' out tonight without my combinations. Ay, ay – women,' he ended sadly.

Kate yanked him away. 'You liar, Tam McKinnon! It would take a hacksaw to cut you out these damt drawers o' yours. You sew yourself into them in September and never a chink o' air gets in till summer comes!'

Lorn squeezed Ruth's hand and they giggled. Rena spotted them and led them further inside, her warm smile lighting her face. 'How charming you look tonight, Ruth. Your dress is lovely. You're a very lucky young man, Lorn.'

Everyone else was also thinking how radiant Ruth looked that evening. 'A bonny, bonny lass,' Mollie murmured to Todd. 'I doubt it's the first time I've seen her alone at a gathering.'

Todd chuckled. 'Ay, thanks to our Shona. I hear tell she left Morag wi' no' a leg to stand on, and Morag's mouth dropped so wide you could have used it as a goal at a shinty match.'

The young men gaped openly at Ruth and some

of the happiness left her when she heard the whispers. 'Would you look at the white virgin,' and, 'In that dress she's more like the virgin bride. By God, I wouldny mind a first night wi' her.'

Lorn's fists bunched at his sides, and Ruth's face flamed. But she was with Lorn. As long as he stayed by her side she would be all right. He was so handsome that evening with his earth-brown curls shining under the lights. His face was filling out a little and he looked very tall in his dark suit. His hand was warm in hers. He was making her feel like a desirable young girl instead of plain little Ruth Donaldson whom young men avoided like the plague. There was a strength in him that made her feel safe – yet, he was like her – shy, afraid of crowds . . .

The first polite exchanges over with, the islanders became less constrained. Some of them were taking to the floor, awkwardly to begin with, but as the uisge-beatha warmed the blood, and the band struck up well-known Strathspeys and reels, the room became filled with swirling dresses and swinging kilts.

Lorn felt himself growing hot with unease. He couldn't possibly lead Ruth onto the floor; the few steps he had learned from Lewis sank to the pit of his mind and refused to re-surface.

He gave Ruth's arm a little squeeze. 'Go and sit down over yonder, Ruthie. I'll – I'll be with you in a wee minute.'

She glanced at him hesitantly but limped away to sit unobtrusively on a large antique settle with a high back. Lewis came over to Lorn, a frown darkening his brow. 'What the hell's wrong with you now? You've got the lass, now make the most of it. Get over there and dance with her.'

'I can't.'

Lewis deftly lifted a glass of whisky from a passing tray. 'Here, drink this, it will do you good. While you're at it, do I have your permission to ask Ruth to dance?'

'Ay, away you go, tell her I'll be with her in a whily.'

He fingered the glass of whisky. He seldom drank, only at weddings, funerals and Hogmanay, and then only in moderation. He watched his brother going up to Ruth, saw relief replacing the apprehension she had felt. With a decisive movement he raised the glass to his lips and downed the contents in one gulp. It gripped at his throat before it burned into his belly, but he felt himself steadying. Shona waved to him, his mother raised a sparkling face and smiled at him. She looked like a girl in the swirling blue dress. His father was straight and ruggedly handsome in his good suit. It didn't matter that it was slightly outdated. When folk looked at Fergus McKenzie they saw the man, not the wrappings. Lorn recalled his mother telling him that at one time Fergus had been so shy of crowds he had seldom gone to ceilidhs – but now his silvered dark head was proudly tilted as he swept Kirsteen round the room. Lorn straightened his shoulders. Maybe when he was older he would grow more confident but maturity was far away yet for him – he had to find his courage now . . . Ruth was dancing beautifully in Lewis's arms, forgetting her limp, forgetting her nerves. Her hair was like spun gold under the lights, she was no longer a vision but a lovely desirable young girl . . . Lorn heard snatches of a conversation some boys were having: 'I wonder who will be the first to get the white virgin.'

'Ach, it'll be Lewis, he has a way wi' the lassies.'

'Never mind the McKenzie lads. I might have a try at her myself.'

Lorn swung round but the boys had moved over to several giggling young maidens who had arrived on the scene. Then Shona came marching over to speak sternly to her young brother. 'What's this, Lorn McKenzie? Lewis dancing with Ruth? I though she was *your* partner.'

'Go on, man,' Niall urged. 'Once you're on the floor it doesn't matter if you have three left feet. Look at Tam and the others. They canny dance two right steps but they're still enjoying themselves.'

They whirled away. The dancers were really warming up with the Laird and his wife 'hooching' as loud as anyone. The laughter began to get through to Lorn, excitement surged in his veins – one more drink and he would be ready for anything. Angus McKinnon grinned at him. 'A dram or a beer, son?'

'A dram – a big one.'

'Coming up, I'll make it a treble seeing it's you.'

Lewis was strangely aware of Ruth's femininity as he held her slender waist and felt the heat of her body. Her head came only to his shoulder, the fragrance of roses filled his nostrils – but it wasn't Ruth he wanted. His eyes continually strayed over her head to the door.

Ruth sensed his inattentiveness and some of her confidence left her. She had forgotten her limp, forgotten the earlier remarks directed at her. Lewis was cool, assured, she felt herself floating in his arms like thistledown. He had paid her flattering compliments, whispered silly things in her ear that made her laugh – but now his restlessness came to her. She looked round for Lorn and an odd feeling of foreboding filled her heart when she spotted him over at the bar drinking, his dark head thrown back as he laughed with Angus. Misery engulfed her. Was he drinking to give himself courage to dance with a lame girl – a white virgin – a virgin bride? She stumbled as the dance came to an end. Lewis put a steadying hand under her arm and was leading her back to her seat when a buzz went round the room. Rachel was standing under one of the archways. She had just arrived and if she had meant to make an entrance she was certainly succeeding. She was sensational-looking in a long rich red evening gown with a low-cut front. A sheen of blue lay over the silken black of her hair, which was swept over one ear and pinned with a diamanté clasp. She moved across the room, a statuesque figure, her tilted head and slow measured step suggesting supreme self-confidence. The sensuous sway of her hips caused women as well as men to turn and stare.

'A Jezebel if ever there was one,' Elspeth said to Behag, who tightened her lips and shook her head in extreme disapproval.

Jon, who had been watching the door as anxiously as Lewis, started to walk towards Rachel, but Lewis was there first, taking her hand, leading her away. But Rachel had spotted Ruth, and with a seductive sidelong glance at Lewis, she broke away and went to greet her friend who received her with quiet pleasure. Physically they were completely opposite. Rachel was the picture of elegance in her red gown: her golden skin glowed, the dark eyes smouldered with life, her lovely body taunted every young red-blooded male in the room. Ruth, however, with her pale hair and milky skin, was a startling comparison. In her flowing white dress she looked fragile and vulnerable; her feminine appeal was subtle, faintly suppressed, yet there was about her small-boned body a faint sybaritic quality that was strangely, movingly sweet, ensnared as it was in a young woman who was still a child in so many ways. She and Rachel not only looked different, they lived in different worlds. Rachel had moved into a sphere of sophistication, her sights set firmly on a career as a solo violinist; Ruth was able to pursue her writing yet still remain on Rhanna. In every way she was a girl of the islands, yet the friendship, nurtured in the two from childhood, had never wavered. Though Rachel's chosen career had taken her away from Rhanna, she was at heart the same free spirit who had roamed barefoot over the moors and bays, and she was always glad to be home. In a mixture of vocal and sign language the two exchanged news and gossip and commented eagerly on one another's dresses.

'Dance with me, Rachel.' Lewis's hand was on her arm, holding it in an urgent grip. With a provocative smile lifting her mouth, she allowed him to sweep her away. Her body was pliant in his arms, moulding to each of his movements. He said nothing, he couldn't, he was too conscious of her mouth, the exciting sway of her limbs, the enticing swell of her breasts.

The other girls watched and none of them liked Rachel McKinnon that evening. She had never been one of them; she had always been remote, untamed, cool, passionate – different from 'normal' girls. To some degree Ruth came into this category as well, but unlike Rachel she wasn't considered a threat, a competitor in the ring of eligible females. No one could imagine Ruth tempting Lewis into her arms; the looks that had been cast at her earlier had been merely amused. Lewis had taken pity on her, that was all – but it wasn't pity that flushed his face now, nor was the brilliance in his blue eyes the result of too much drinking. And so his entourage of female admirers and conquests past and present, glowered long and hard at the oblivious Rachel.

Lorn had witnessed the exchanges through a blur. His head was swimming and he felt sick. He knew he shouldn't have gulped down that last drink so quickly. He watched Ruth limping back to her

corner, dejection slowing her steps. Perhaps if he
went to sit by her, explained to her that he couldn't
dance, had never danced, she would understand and
be content just to sit and talk . . . The lights merged
and swam; the room turned upside down. Teasing
remarks came to him but barely penetrated the fuzz
in his head. A group of boys sniggered as he swayed
past, and some of the older men came forward to
take his arm, but he shook them off and made his
unsteady way up a long dim corridor to a side door,
which he wrenched open.

The cold night air washed over him, the sweat
dried on his body, making him shiver. Falling to his
knees in the snow he was violently sick and in the
midst of his misery, he hated himself: Ruth would
never forgive him; she would think him a drunken
coward. He felt degraded, cheated and ill, but above
all he ached with humiliation and self-loathing.

Lewis danced Rachel to the side of the hall. She
looked cool, but her heart was racing madly. How
often she had dreamed of a night like this – music,
dancing, laughter, the arms of Lewis Fraser McKenzie
enfolding her, holding her close.

Without a word Lewis took her hand, and they
slipped away. He had often been to Burnbreddie
with his father and knew the lay-out well. He led her
through the silent corridors to a room well away from
the main hall. This was the Laird's study, an untidy,
comfortable den with worn leather armchairs and a
huge oak desk. A connecting door led to another

room, full of cubbyholes, a filing cabinet, and a plush velvet sofa scattered with plump chenille cushions, and it was into this room that Lewis led Rachel and bolted the door after them. She didn't draw back, nor was she shocked at the boldness of the venture. Like him she was a daredevil; convention had never cluttered her life. He went forward to switch on a shaded wall light, then turned to her. Her lustrous eyes were dark with laughter – and something else: passion, smouldering, beckoning to him, taunting him. He came to stand by her. His eyes, a startling blue in his flushed handsome face, travelled over her face to her body, lingering on the curving swell of her breasts. The mellow light spread over her, deepening her dress to blood-red, her skin to golden-rose. He gazed at the arch of her throat, the graceful curve of her shoulders, then he focused again on her mouth: the red parted lips, the pearly teeth, the pink tip of her tongue showing between them. Slowly he bent and kissed the hollow of her throat, his lips laying a trail of fire up to her mouth. Over and over their mouths met in swift, breathless kisses that made them tremble.

'I got you a present, Rachel.' His voice was hoarse with desire, and with shaking hands he took the small parcel from his pocket and gave it to her.

She tormented him by slowly peeling off the wrapping paper. She smiled at sight of the nightdress and teased him by holding it against herself, moulding it to the curves of her body. With one hand she propped it against her shoulders, with the other she traced the shape of it – over her belly, her waist.

He could contain himself no longer; roughly he pulled her to him and claimed her lips, pushing them apart, his tongue probing, searching for hers.

She was in the arms of an expert lover, but she wasn't afraid; she had gained plenty of experience with men over the last year or two and knew how to handle them. She knew that playing the field was a dangerous game, and even at the height of desire one half of her always remained alert, aware of the price she might have to pay if she allowed herself to relax completely. She wanted Lewis – for a very long time she had wanted him, and she wouldn't rest till she had experienced the delights that she knew an affair with him would bring. She would take it all, and she would take it now, because later – later she had to give her all to her music and she would have no time to spare for the Lewis McKenzies of the world – except perhaps – occasionally . . .

His hands were on her thighs, pulling her in ever closer to him. With a little shiver of anticipation she heard the slow unzipping of her dress. Together they sank onto the couch. He was moving, lost, groaning with pleasure. She wanted him to go on, never to stop; she was burning, beating, pulsing with the need for him . . . With a supreme effort of willpower she tore herself free and began to pull her dress over her shoulders. She was trembling, panting, fumbling behind her back for her zip. It stuck. Darting to the door she threw open the bolt, wrenched the door open, went through, shut it, and with her back to it found the zip and began pulling it up. She heard him scrambling up, cursing her, and a triumphant smile lifted the corners of her lovely mouth. For years Lewis McKenzie had made her wait – now it was his turn. Just for a little while would she make him sweat it out – her legs trembled again – for a very little while. She began to run, through the corridors, tidying herself as she went. Lewis pulled open the door of the cubby room. Little bitch! Cruel, flaunting little bitch! He gritted his teeth, rage replacing passion. Snatching up the nightdress from the floor he was about to tear it apart but stopped. No! By God, no! Damned if he would ruin the thing. He had bought it for her and he meant to see it draped round that lovely body of hers if it was the last thing he did. His head was pounding as hard as his heart, and he passed a hand over his hot brow. Fresh air, he needed fresh air, had to cool down.

Stuffing the scrap of oyster satin into his pocket he went up a short passageway to a side door, opened it – and found Lorn sitting on the steps. His skin was clammy, he was shivering uncontrollably and he smelled of vomit. 'Lorn! God Almighty!' Lewis cried. 'What happened?'

'Nothing,' Lorn whispered miserably. 'I took a few drinks, came out here – and was sick.'

'How long ago?'

'I don't know – about an hour – I couldn't go back in.'

Lewis hoisted his brother to his feet and put a shoulder under his armpit. 'Hold on,' he ordered. 'I'll get you home. I'll take Lachlan's car. I'll explain when I bring it back; he won't mind.'

'What – about Ruthie?'

'Ach, I'll take her home later. Oh, don't worry, I'm no' going to steal her – I've had enough of lassies for one night – now hold on and shut up.'

Jon watched Rachel's departure also and his brown eyes were dull. He felt foolish and angry with himself. It wasn't right for him to feel this way about a young girl . . . Yes! Dammit! It was right! Love could never be wrong and he would go on loving, caring, protecting this beautiful child as long as there was breath in him. He was also concerned for her. He knew she'd had boys before, that was natural; but her time with Lewis McKenzie had come, and somehow he knew it was what she had waited for. He knew that their affair would be a tempestuous one. Anton came over and touched his arm, his keen blue eyes full of understanding as he said, 'My friend, you love her very much, I watch you and I feel your pain. Am I not right?'

Jon flushed and nodded and Anton went on softly, 'She will come to you in the end, Jon. You and she were made for each other . . .' Jon opened his mouth to protest but Anton held up his hand. 'Ah yes, it is so. Age makes no difference with love to bridge the years. She is very young, and she is sowing the wild oats. Rachel is a very clever girl – she is sowing them quickly, because she knows that her kind of ambition will take all her concentration. There will be no time later for frivolous love affairs then – and that is when you must step in and be ready to take over.'

Babbie came over, lovely that evening in a green dress that matched her eyes. 'You haven't danced with me tonight, Jon Jodl. Why don't you ask me now?'

Jon shook his head, his thoughts were with Rachel and he couldn't bring himself to enter into the jollity of an evening where everyone in the gay whirling crowd seemed to have a partner. 'Thank you, Babbie, you are very kind, but I think I will go and keep company with the little maiden sitting over there in the corner. Like me she seems not to have a partner, and she looks as if she would like to curl up and die.'

Anton and Babbie watched him walking away. The latter took her husband's arm and murmured, 'Poor Jon, I hope he finds a happiness as great as ours. He's so nice and deserves only the best.'

'He will get it, liebling.' Anton gazed into her eyes and smiled. 'Take it from a great philosopher. Jon will have his wish; all he needs is patience and understanding.'

Ruth watched Jon approaching. She liked this kindly German who had integrated so well with the community. He had done a lot for it, but mostly he encouraged the island children to take an interest in music. He had succeeded so well that many had discovered hidden talents under his guidance. She knew he was in love with Rachel. From the beginning he had devoted himself to her unstintingly – he had encouraged her ambitions, had gone to endless trouble to help her fulfil her dreams – and now – like her, he was tortured by a love that seemed out of reach. She stood up, and when she spoke she sounded slightly breathless. 'Jon, are you enjoying yourself?'

He reddened again and smiled wistfully. 'Not very much, jungfräulich.'

'Then – will you take me home please? My father's van is outside – I – I don't feel very well.'

He put a steadying hand under her elbow, the trembling of her delicate young body came to him. 'I will be honoured to accompany you home, jungfräulich. Take my arm and we will walk to the archway there – no one will see us slipping away – they are all too busy enjoying themselves.'

It was later than usual when Ruth came into the kitchen next morning. Her parents were seated at the table and Morag raised her head to say somewhat sharply, 'You're late at table, Ruth. What happened last night to make you oversleep?'

'Nothing happened, Mam.' Ruth's voice was flat and lifeless. 'I'm still a virgin, if that's what you mean.' Ignoring her mother's shocked gasp she went on, her voice rising a little, 'There's not a lad in the whole of Rhanna who would dance with the white virgin for fear of being laughed at. That's what they call me behind my back, only last night it was worse – they called me the virgin bride instead. You've got what you always wanted, Mam, an untarnished daughter.

You've labelled me, you've made folks laugh behind my back and call me names, you always tried to make me believe that boys were dirty-minded and wicked – and now you've got a daughter who will one day be known as the virgin spinster.' At the door to the hall she turned, 'I've told a lie – someone did dance with me – Lewis McKenzie – because he felt sorry for me.' Her face was very pale as she went out of the kitchen, her limp more pronounced than it had been for years.

Dugald looked at his wife with contempt. When he spoke his voice was tightly controlled. 'Satisfied? You've used the innocence of that lovely young life to ease the burden of your own ungodly guilt. I saw bitterness in her just now, Morag, for the first time I saw bitterness and it was an ugly expression to see in my Ruthie's face.' He stood up, tall, over-thin, white with anger and sadness. 'I'm going up to her. You pray a lot to the Lord to save your soul, but you might remember that your family have souls too. I think the time has come for you to pray for us as well – if it isn't too late to mend the damage you have done.'

After a sleepless night, passing solitary hours thinking about Ruth, Lorn decided he must go to her and explain the reasons for his behaviour at the dance, and soon after breakfast he went over to Morag's cottage to ask to see Ruth. But Morag was outraged by his request.

'You leave my lassie be,' she told him through tight

lips. 'A fine mess we are all in because of you! What kind of laddie are you anyway? Asking a lass to a ceilidh, then creeping away to a corner to drink yourself stupid. Oh, ay, folks are talking right enough, news of that sort travels fast.'

'Ay, you're right enough there.' Lorn's voice was ominously quiet. 'Folks do talk. Has it ever occurred to you that folk might be talking about you? Or do you think you're so saintly there's nothing that anyone can find bad to say about you!'

Morag's face flamed red. 'How dare you speak to me like that you – you McKenzie upstart!'

'I dare because it's true – just as I've dared to come here this morning and ask to see Ruthie. I just want to explain something to her.'

Morag thought about Ruth upstairs in tears, and a fresh upsurge of guilt made her angrier still. 'Indeed you will not. You've done enough damage to be going on with. Fancy her coming home here and laying all the blame on me!'

'All the blame is with you!' Lorn couldn't help himself shouting. 'And I didn't get drunk last night because – oh – what's the use of trying to explain anything to you! You never hear anything for all the brimstone bunging up your lugs!'

Morag let out a yell of outrage and slammed the door. Turning, Lorn walked away, his shoulders stooped with dejection.

The next day he heard that Ruth's father had taken her for an indefinite period to Coll where he had relatives. Immediately Lorn went to get the address from Isabel, but she and Jim Jim were not yet home from their holiday in Barra. He thought about going to see Totie Little of Portvoynachan, whom he suspected was more than just a good friend of Dugald's, but Totie too had 'gone away for a whily', leaving the Post Office in charge of Jemima Sugden, a retired teacher of the area. Lorn was in a daze of despair. Just a few days ago he had been sublimely happy – now he didn't know where to turn. And there was no one he could find who would help him.

Part Five

1960

Chapter Seventeen

Rachel made an excuse to extend her Christmas holidays, and she and Lewis ran wild together, like children. They ran and played through the virgin tracts of snow on the moors, danced close together at the ceilidhs, walked hand in hand along the wide, windswept bays. They looked like beautiful children with the fresh bloom of youth on their cheeks, immaturity allowing them to indulge in the kind of things they might never do again with the onset of adult sobriety. But the passions that consumed them belonged to a man and a woman, and when childish things were done with they fell into each other's arms, eager for the pleasures of love. It seemed they could never tire of one another. He couldn't get enough of her silken body pressed against his – the sight of her long-legged, firm-breasted young body sent him crazy with desire – and they had to force themselves not to be seen touching in public places. Though Annie had always allowed her daughter to run free, though her own morals had often been dirty linen to be mulled over by the gossips, she had an inbuilt sense of propriety, which had been passed to Rachel. Oh, she was going with Lewis McKenzie all right, but she was careful to give the impression that, to her, he was just another boy. So while Behag, Elspeth, and others who came into the category of nosy cailleachs, tightened their lips and talked among themselves of sinful flaunting, the rest of the population looked and saw just a lass and a lad having a bit of a fling. But soon after the New Year Rachel went away, and Lewis seemed to retreat into himself. He had changed since his eighteenth birthday: he had laughed less, and had become moody and irritable. Everyone put it down to the affair over Rachel, but Lachlan, to whom Lewis went complaining of headaches, knew better. On questioning the boy Lachlan discovered he was suffering other symptoms as well.

'I get dizzy a lot,' Lewis told him off-handedly, 'and sometimes I can't get things into focus – and I'm getting as grumpy as old Behag,' he finished with a grin that didn't entirely hide his anxiety.

Lachlan bent over his desk, keeping his voice even as he said, 'Too much wine, women and song, you young rascal. Right, we'll arrange for you to have a thorough check-up. I'll give you some painkillers just now, and make the arrangements to get you over to Glasgow for some tests . . .'

'*Glasgow!* Och, c'mon now, Doctor!' burst out Lewis, his face going pale. 'It surely isn't serious enough for that!'

Lachlan's smile was warm, reassuring. 'Heads are funny parts of the anatomy, Lewis. It could be you're just needing glasses – it could be a thousand and one things – but I have to be sure, and I don't have the facilities here to carry out the necessary tests. I'll get a letter away to Glasgow and let your parents know . . .'

'*No!*' Lewis exploded violently. 'I couldn't bear Mother worrying over me and wondering about getting over to Glasgow to see me.'

'The tests will only take a day or two,' Lachlan said patiently.

Lewis looked him straight in the eye. 'On the other hand they might take ages.' He shook his head. 'No, Lachlan, I'm old enough now to do things for myself. I'll make up some excuse to be away from home for a while. If – if everything is all right I will have saved a lot of fuss, and unless I need specs, no one need be any the wiser.'

Kirsteen and Fergus had no inkling that Lewis was ill, they only knew that both their sons were becoming increasingly difficult to live with.

'Hell, Kirsteen, what are we going to do with them?' Fergus appealed one day in bewilderment. 'I thought it was bad enough when Shona was going through all this, but I didn't expect it with boys! They moon about like sick puppies and it's impossible to talk to either of them!'

Kirsteen sighed. 'Darling, darling, I know. We mustn't forget that we mooned about, too, when we were in a tangle over each other. I wonder if we were as difficult to live with. I want to help, but they just turn away as if they had been scalded. Lorn is impossible – and Lewis –' She frowned. 'Lewis is behaving very strangely – out of character. He's so bad-tempered and moody. It seemed to start before Christmas and has got worse and worse. Maybe it's the real thing with Rachel. Thank goodness Grant isn't here to bother us with the affairs of *his* heart – I couldn't take three of them moping about.'

Rachel was gone only two weeks when Lewis announced his intention of going to Glasgow to stay with Andrew McKinnon, a great friend of his, who had gone to the city to find work. 'It will only be for a week or so,' Lewis told his parents. 'I'll write.'

But the week stretched to a month, and Kate nodded her head sorrowfully. 'The laddie has got it bad this time. Fancy following Rachel to Glasgow – mind, who can blame him? Though she's my own granddaughter I have to admit she's a bonny bonny lassie – she has that tempting look about her men canny resist.' She pushed out her ample bosom. 'I had it myself in my day, but for all Tam noticed I might have been born wi' my head screwed back to front and my bosoms where my bum is!'

When Lewis returned, neither Fergus nor Kirsteen could get much out of him beyond the fact that Glasgow was busier but the same as ever it was.

'Did you see Rachel at all?' Kirsteen persisted, her blue eyes glinting with exasperation.

Lewis grunted and refused to expand on the subject.

Fergus glowered in puzzlement at the son who, from the start, had laughed at life. The boy had always eaten like a healthy young horse, now he toyed with his food, his face was thinner, he'd had his hair cropped in Glasgow and somehow the boy had left him, leaving in his place a stranger whom Fergus didn't know. 'Are you well enough?' he asked sharply.

Lewis's head jerked up, the blue eyes flashed. 'Of course I am – at least I was till I came home and you all started poking and prying into my affairs. Och – why can't you leave me be!' he said and angrily scrunched back his chair and stomped away out of the house to walk moodily through Glen Fallan.

Lorn pushed back his chair also, and moved to follow his brother, catching up with him by Murdy's house, where quite a little crowd were gathered. Then Andrew McKinnon stepped onto the road and hailed Lewis with delight. 'Lewis McKenzie, you young bugger! It seems years since I saw you. I heard you were in Glasgow and you never even came to see me. I could have shown you the town!'

Lewis's face reddened and he groaned, 'Oh, no.'

The crowd were staring at him. Murdy spat at the ground and murmured in an aside to his wife, 'Stayin' wi' Andrew indeed! The young stallion must have had a fine time to himself wi' that Rachel! Stayin' wi' her more like!'

Lewis clenched his fists. 'You can't get away with *anything* in a place like this. They all want to know your business, and by God! They make it their business to find out where you've been, what you've been doing! Christ Almighty!' he exploded. 'You can't even fart in this place but they all hear the bloody explosion!'

Despite himself, Lorn sniggered, and Lewis looked at him and laughed also, especially when a peacefully grazing cow lifted its head at his cries of protest and, as if on cue, lifted its tail and released a might ripple of wind.

'God! Did you hear that!' Murdy bellowed. 'It minded me of old Shelagh farting in kirk when the minister was bawling out thon awful sermons in our lugs!'

Lorn clapped his hand over his mouth and both boys erupted into laughter. 'I tell you what,' Lorn said, throwing an arm over his brother's shoulders, 'let's go back and get the horses out. A good ride over the sands might help us to get things into perspective. We're a miserable pair of buggers at the moment, and are making Father and Mother the same . . .'

They arrived back at Laigmhor with rosy cheeks and were in time to see Erchy whistling up the cobbled yard to the kitchen door. He popped his head round. 'Telegram. I'm thinkin' I will be waiting for an answer and watch your faces while I have a cuppy.'

Kirsteen had turned slightly pale. Telegrams weren't always the harbingers of good tidings. 'Is – is it happy news, Erchy?'

Erchy grinned and spooned generous amounts of sugar into his tea. 'Good, I'm thinkin'. Ay, damty good right enough.'

Kirsteen tore open the envelope. The words leapt out at her: 'Got married last week. Home in a few days. Grant.' She gasped and slowly read the news aloud.

'Where did it come from?' Fergus asked as the colour mounted in Kirsteen's face.

'Here, take it,' she said faintly and handed over the scrap of paper with shaking fingers.

'Country of origin, Kingston, Jamaica,' Fergus said. 'Well, bugger me! He's done it at last!'

Erchy slapped his knee and beamed widely. 'Ay, he was aye a one for surprises was young Grant.' His smile widened. 'It might be there's more to come – maybe he married one o' they native girls wi' the belly buttons he's always sendin' to auld Dodie.'

Lorn and Lewis came in to hear the tail end of this, and the latter picked up the telegram, his eyes crinkling, while Erchy indulged in further fancies. Everyone stared at him blankly for a few moments before they erupted into gales of laughter. Then Kirsteen went rushing over to Slochmhor with the news.

Phebie wiped floury hands on her apron and hugged Kirsteen delightedly.

'Does he say exactly when he'll be home?' Lachlan asked with a smile.

'No! That's just it!' wailed Kirsteen. 'It's obvious he's taking leave and flying back from Jamaica with his new wife. Och, I could kill him that I could! We must have a ceilidh and the house is a boorach! The only double bed in the house is in our room – we'll have to give them that. Fergus and me will just have to move another bed into Grant's old room because

Shona and Niall will want to come home for the reception – unless of course you put them up here. I hope she won't be one of those very sophisticated types . . . Erchy thinks she might be a West Indian girl, and knowing Grant I wouldn't put it past him! Oh, they're beautiful girls and I'm not in the least prejudiced, but can you imagine what the cailleachs will say! I've got absolutely nothing to wear either – nothing that's suitable that is. I wonder if it should be a formal gathering – oh, I wish I knew what she was like . . .' She paused.

Phebie had fallen into Lachlan's arms. The pair of them were helpless with laughter. 'You should hear yourself, mo ghaoil,' Lachlan gasped. 'You sound like an old gramophone record with the needle stuck!'

Phebie wiped her eyes. 'I tell you this – if that besom Fiona ever decides to get married I'll no' be working myself into a state over some laddie I've never met – ay – even supposing he was the future king of Britain and ate herring with a gold fork! Now, you calm yourself this minute. Am I not here to help you get the house in order? By the time we're finished it will be fit for a princess, and we might no' consider her good enough to set foot over the doorstep.'

Lachlan's mask of jollity fell as he watched Kirsteen going down the path. Only that morning he had received Lewis's reports from the hospital – to the effect that the boy had a deep-seated brain tumour, which was inoperable. He had sat, white-faced,

staring at the words, unable to believe the evidence
of his eyes. He was so shocked that Phebie, coming
into the surgery, had glanced at the papers on his
desk and gone quickly to get him some whisky. He
had buried his face into her soft breasts and whispered helplessly, 'How am I going to tell him, Phebie?
How? How?'

She had cradled him gently, her heart brimful of
love for this dear husband of hers on whose
shoulders so many burdens had been heaped over
the years. 'I know how you must feel,' she had
murmured. 'Dear God! I can't believe it myself! It
might be better if he didn't know – if you just told
Kirsteen and Fergus.'

'No, no.' He shook his head as if to clear it. 'He
made me promise not to mention anything. As far as
everyone knew he was away in Glasgow for a jaunt.
He'll have to be told, Phebie, but he won't want a
fuss. I've a feeling he'll make me promise not to tell
another soul. He's funny about illness; even as a wee
lad he hated to be near sickness. I mind once he
turned and ran from the room when Lorn had a bad
turn. No, he'll carry this alone; it will be easier for
him than sharing it with those whose faces will
remind him of it every waking day. I – I'll tell him in
the morning.'

She put her hands on his shoulders. 'God be with
you, Lachy; yours has been a difficult role but you've
never shirked any of it.'

He took her in his arms and kissed her. 'Only
because you have stood by my side all these years.

417

I wouldn't have got by without you – and now you're going to be called upon to be very strong indeed, mo ghaoil. If Lewis reacts the way I think he will, you will be called upon to put on the greatest act of your life for the benefit of the McKenzies.'

Next morning Lachlan walked over the fields of Laigmhor. The frosty air was fragrant with the scent of newly turned earth. Lewis was driving the tractor that pulled the plough. He was alone as Lachlan had guessed he might be.

At sight of the doctor walking along by the edge of the field Lewis's blue eyes darkened. Something was wrong. Lachlan wouldn't have come up here to talk to him if everything had been all right. Lewis shivered as the cold hand of fear clawed into his stomach. He jumped down from the tractor, and as he went to meet Lachlan he recalled his horrible time in hospital: the hellish apprehension; the bewilderment of never knowing what was going to happen next, bewilderment that turned to fear as days stretched into weeks and no one would tell him why he was being kept in, just the rather distant smiles and the stock phrases: 'Patience, young man, these things take time,' or: 'Won't be long now, lad, just another day or two.' Once Lewis had cried out, 'What things? What takes time? I want to know! It's *my* bloody head!'

Which outburst had sent ripples of shock through the hospital staff, who treated Lewis rather coldly for the remainder of his stay.

How different was Lachlan with his warmth, his

humanity – how different was a man who walked over the soil to personally talk to a boy who was so apprehensive his voice shook as he said, 'You've got the results of the tests, Lachlan, and if they had been good you would have had no call to come here and tell me.'

Lachlan's face was drawn, his brown eyes full of a terrible despair as he looked straight into the boy's eyes. 'Ay, you're right, Lewis, the news isn't good. I had a mind to tell your mother and father first – but I didn't think you'd want that.'

Lewis sank onto the bank. He shook his head and stared at his hands. 'No, whatever it is they mustny find out – tell me, Lachlan, and tell me quickly.'

When Lachlan's soft pleasant voice finally halted there was silence. Then Lewis burst into tears that rasped harshly in his throat, and shook his head from side to side in an agony of disbelief before he buried his face in his hands. Lachlan gathered him into his arms, saying nothing, letting the tears flow. When the boy was finally quiet Lachlan said firmly, 'We're going to fight this thing, Lewis. I'll arrange for you to have treatment . . .'

'No, no, Lachlan,' Lewis said, drawing away, his eyes full of a desperate pleading. 'I don't want to go through months of hell lying in some hospital only to die anyway. I hate hospital – being surrounded by sick people. Just leave things be. All I ask is that you won't say a word to anybody – promise – not one word – please.'

Lachlan drew in his breath. 'Ay, if that's what you want, Lewis.'

419

'It's what I want – by the way – I almost forgot to ask – how long?'

'Six months – a year perhaps – with treatment it could –'

'Lachlan – will you – could you go now? I want very much to be alone for a while.'

Lachlan got up and began to walk over the tracts of rich brown earth, his steps heavy.

'Lachlan.'

Lachlan spun round. 'Ay, son?'

'You won't let me suffer – will you?'

'No, I won't let you suffer, Lewis, I'll do everything in my power to help you.' He walked quickly away, aware of nothing but the pain of unshed tears and the sight of a young boy sitting alone in the fields knowing that soon he was going to die.

Lewis was thankful for the diversion that Grant's news had brought. He was able to be quiet without anyone noticing or asking questions. For the next few days Laigmhor was such a hive of activity that Fergus groaned at the disruption of normal routine, and old Bob grew so disgusted at being told continually to wipe his feet and watch where he put his pipe ash that he took a huff and stamped off to the peaceful disorder of his own little cottage. The news had soon spread and old Joe, who had just celebrated his 100th birthday, and who had received a telegram from the Queen to mark the occasion, shook his snowy head and chortled. To him Grant was still a boy, not long removed from golden childhood days when he had spent fascinating hours in the old sailor's company, listening to his tales of the sea. 'Fancy, that lad married,' he murmured, 'I wouldny be surprised if he brings back a beautiful mermaid . . .' His sea-green eyes were faraway. 'Did I ever tell you about the one I saw sitting on the rocks near Mingulay?' he said, and the small boy to whom he addressed the question shook his head and listened avidly to the unfolding of a tale that had been told to numerous children before him.

Some days later the McKenzies walked with the McLachlans down to the harbour to await the boat. The whole of Portcull had somehow contrived to be there too, and as the steamer pushed into the pier, everyday tasks were abandoned and all eyes were focused on the gangplank.

'She'll maybe be wearin' one o' they grass skirt things,' Tam said, 'though she'll no' be wearin' it long in this wind.'

His cronies chuckled with delight, but Ranald scratched his head with his paint brush and said in disgust, 'Ach, you're thinkin' o' the lassies from they South Sea Islands. The Jamaicans wear clothes the same as you and me.'

'Hairy jerseys and trousers?' Todd said. 'Ach no, young Grant was aye a one for legs. This lassie will no' be wearin' the trowser – mark my words.'

Shona and Niall came running down the gangplank with Ellie, now a tall leggy twelve-year-old, leading the way. She rushed at Fergus and he cuddled her to him and put out his arm to take Shona to him as well. 'It's nice to see familiar faces,' he said rather nervously. 'Go and buck Kirsteen up, will you? She's badly needing some female support.'

Shona's eyes twinkled. 'Och, Father, there's absolutely nothing to worry about, I can assure you . . .'

Kirsteen darted over, her fair skin stained with crimson. 'They're coming,' she gulped, 'I can see Grant . . . Oh, God. I hope she'll like her in-laws . . .' Her eyes widened. 'I'm a mother-in-law – I never thought of that . . .'

A black curly head bobbed among the crowd, next to it was a sleek brown one, and Fergus mouthed to Kirsteen, 'Hold on tight, darling, we're about to meet our new daughter-in-law.'

A gasp went up as Grant came into full view. Hanging on his arm was Fiona, tall and elegant in a smart, well-cut blue jacket, red polo neck jumper, and immaculate navy-blue trousers. Her glowing face was a deep golden brown and for a moment everyone wondered if she was a native lass dressed in the trowser, or that wittrock Fiona McLachlan flaunting the laws o' decency.

'Fiona.' Phebie was so surprised she could hardly say the name.

A smile curved Lachlan's mouth. 'It would just be like the thing if –' Fiona threw herself at him, smothering the rest of the sentence. Kirsteen was caught up in the embrace of her eldest son.

'Your wife,' she gasped. 'Where is she?'

Grant extricated Fiona from her father's arms and drew her forward.

'Right here. Meet Mrs McKenzie.'

'But – you two loathe the sight of each other!' Phebie cried, her round face both delighted and bewildered.

'Ach, we were just bairns then,' Fiona said, laughing. 'We had to travel halfway round the world before we discovered it was love. I was in the Caribbean studying its marine life when who should pop up but Dimples McKenzie.'

Grant hugged her to him and kissed her fringe of shining hair. 'The moment I saw my wee Robin again I realised why I'd never married any of the beautiful girls who had queued up for years . . .' He looked around at the rugged slopes of Sgurr nan Ruadh etched against the sky. 'One day we might build a love nest here and hatch out a whole clutch of wee robins with dimples. Now let's go, before Behag chokes on all those flies she's catching!'

Later that evening, when all the gossip was exhausted, Grant found himself alone with the twins and he ruffled Lorn's curls affectionately. 'To think I used to carry you on my shoulders,' he teased. 'If yours grow any wider you'll be carrying me.'

'Me too,' Lewis said, flopping rather wearily onto a chair. Grant looked at him, surprised anew at the change in this once dashing brother of his. 'You've grown thinner, Lewis my lad,' he observed with a frown. 'I've been hearing about this affair between you and Rachel. Don't let it get you down so badly. It might just be infatuation . . .'

Lewis jumped up, a dark flush spreading over his face. 'I might have known the gossips would be at it! I thought *you* at least would have had more sense not to believe all you hear.' He banged out of the room and Lorn spread his hands ruefully. 'You've touched on a sore spot. He's not long back from Glasgow but won't say what happened between him and Rachel. He's like a bear with a sore head.'

'Och well, he'll get over it, he's just growing up. Come on – upstairs, I've got presents for the pair of you. They might cheer you up.'

The next morning Dodie almost fell on his back when Erchy arrived at his door bearing an invitation to the reception that was to be held at Laigmhor that evening. 'My, my,' Dodie said, his voice husky as his big fingers caressed the silver-gilt edging on the card. 'I have never had the likes in my life.'

'Well see you have a bath and wear your best bib and tucker,' Erchy instructed severely.

'I will do no such thing,' Dodie intoned primly. 'I'll be wearin' a suit, my very best, bibs is only for babies.'

Dodie was thrilled. He loved and respected all the McKenzies, but none more so than Grant, who had been the means of bringing a few riches to his life. Many of his ambitions had been fulfilled. Ealasaid had had a roomy byre built for her; the interior of the cottage was gay with bright wallpaper and paint;

at the head of Biddy's grave sat a very unusual stone straight from the Rhanna shores, and inscribed on it in Gaelic were the words, 'Fàilte don Nèamh, Dodie', which, when translated, meant 'Welcome to Heaven'.

'What way are you puttin' that!' Tam had scoffed when first he saw it. 'It's the Lord will welcome her to heaven. You canny very well welcome her to yonder place from down here. You're daft, man!'

'Ach, it's you who's daft,' Dodie returned with asperity. 'Biddy knows fine what I mean, an' that's more than can be said for the likes o' you. I'm no' up there to welcome her so I can best do it from down here. Anyways, Biddy aye said heaven was all around us, so if she's as much down here as she is up there she will be havin' two heavens to keep her going.'

The reception relaxed the atmosphere at Laigmhor. The young couple radiated so much happiness everyone was touched by it, even the twins forgetting themselves in the festivities that went on for several nights. Because Grant had reached the status of Second Mate at this stage in his career, it meant that he could take his wife with him on his voyages, though Fiona had some very decided plans of her own for the future. But it was enough that at the moment they could be together, and they were both glowing with happiness as they stood at the rails of the boat waving farewell to the crowd on the pier. Lewis had taken his big brother aside at the last moment to apologise for his sullen behaviour.

'Ach, think nothing of it,' Grant had said. 'Girls do that to people; Fiona did it to me plenty.'

'When will you be back?'

'Hard to say, a few months anyway. Maybe longer.'

Lewis had taken his hand then and had squeezed it very hard. 'Goodbye then, I hope you'll both be very very happy.'

His voice had been very husky and Grant had looked at him keenly. 'Hey, c'mon now – things will come all right in the end, they always do.'

Lewis had nodded. 'Ay,' was all he had said before turning on his heel and walking quickly away.

Rachel came home briefly at Easter. Lewis arranged to meet her at the harbour, and together they walked along the rocky finger of Port Rum Point. She was different; he sensed it immediately. And she didn't look at him. She was barefooted, and as they walked she stopped every so often to curl her toes into the wet sands. He was reminded of the gypsy-like Rachel of childhood, running barefoot over moor and shore, her long brown legs carrying her swiftly to favourite haunts. Lewis found himself pining for those days again, all the carefree days of early youth when the whole world was his, when he had moulded life to suit his whims. Now he could command nothing – nothing. It was over between them, he knew even before she turned at the head of the Point to look at him. She gazed for a long time at this tall handsome young McKenzie, and her heart died a little inside her. She knew him so well – his strengths, his weaknesses. She would always love him, but there was no place in her life for passionate young men; she had to have stability and she would never find that in him.

He took her hands and murmured, 'Rachel, I've waited so long.'

His blue eyes were so miserable, she drew in her breath. This wasn't Lewis McKenzie, laughing, carefree Lewis who had chased girls since he was in short trousers . . .

'I've missed you so,' he went on huskily. 'You mean the world to me – no, don't move away from me, look at me . . .' She put a finger to his lips and stepped back, and he knew then what it was he had seen in Rachel a long long time ago: a strength of will that bordered on ruthlessness. She had always known where she was going, and would allow nobody to stand in the way of her ambitions – she could – and she would – turn her back on love, the kind of love that might hinder her chances of a brilliant career.

She turned her head to look back along the rocky shoreline. He followed her gaze and saw a figure sitting some distance away gazing thoughtfully into the water. 'Jon,' he said softly. 'It's him, isn't it? You're going to marry Jon?' She kept her face averted as she nodded her head. 'But he's old enough to be your father!' he cried so vehemently that Jon raised his head. Lewis paused and stared at her. 'That's what you want, isn't it? What you've always wanted since

Dokie Joe died on the *Magpie*.' Rachel turned her restless gaze towards the great glistening needles of the Sgor Creags. Her throat constricted and she nodded. He bunched his fists. 'What about me, Rachel? I need you, just now I need you very much.'

She looked at him steadily; his body was tight with hurt . . . Yet she saw no anger in him. Somewhere at the back of her mind she thought that rather odd. He was so easily moved to laughter, passion, anger – now there was none and she felt uneasy.

His shoulders sagged suddenly. 'Let me kiss you – one more time.'

His voice was soft, gentle, and she knew if she succumbed to his request she might never have the will to walk away from him. Briefly she touched his arm, and he made to take her hand, but she evaded him and began to run, back along the length of the Point – to Jon, who stood up at her approach and held out his arms.

Jon had seen that her eyes were too bright. She stopped a short distance from him and, leaning against a rock, closed her eyes so that he couldn't see what was in them. His thin arms enclosed her, protective and safe – so safe, she knew she would always find comfort in the gentle haven of his arms. She didn't want to look back at that strong young figure standing alone at the tip of Port Rum Point, but something made her want to look and look – for ever. To remember the wild, fiery passion of youthful love, the bittersweet ecstasy of living through a time she had always known could not last.

She would never know again such untamed joy, such burning, consuming desire – such laughter. Her memories of Lewis would be wonderful, yet always they would be tinged with poignancy. Somewhere, sometime, she would look back on her exquisite experiences with him – and she would cry. Love with Jon would be gentle and good; she would never betray him for other men – she had had her times of carefree love. Jon had understood that, and he had waited – so patiently and devotedly he had waited.

Rachel turned her back on Lewis and looked up at Jon, at his dear honest face; at the steady brown eyes; at the little beard flecked with grey. She had grown to love him dearly, he had taught her so much, and they shared so much. A sob caught in her throat. She took Jon's hand and made him run till they got to the harbour. She didn't look back again . . .

Anton and Babbie were thrilled at the news. With the exception of her mother, Rachel hadn't let Jon tell anybody else till she had first broken it to Lewis. Anton came in from the fields, his blue eyes glowing in his face at sight of Jon with his arm round Rachel's slender waist. 'I knew things would work out for you,' he laughed. 'My Babbie sometimes laughs at my philosophies, but I am quite often correct. We must celebrate . . .' He went to a cupboard and withdrew a bottle of whisky, which he held up to the light. 'You see, I now have the customs of the islands – we will drink a dram together.' He drew Babbie to him and kissed her red curls. 'If you find happiness like ours you will be rich indeed. Is that not so, liebling?'

'Ay, indeed, it is so,' Babbie agreed softly, her fingers curling over his hand. Whenever she saw him stripped to the waist like this, the mark of his scar standing out from the surrounding tanned skin, she was minded afresh of the day she had first seen him lying deathly pale on the scrubbed white table at Slochmhor, and, as always, her love for him flooded her heart and she wanted to take his fair head in her hands and kiss it where the sun had bleached it almost white.

She looked at the tall stunning girl by Jon's side, wondering if such a beauty would be faithful to a man so many years her senior. Rachel lacked speech, but with her kind of looks, that would never be such a great obstacle. Men would ogle her wherever she went: she exuded a magnetism that was definitely sexual; she was a very physical sort of girl – yet there was also about her an aura that was spiritual, a rare sensitive depth in her great burning eyes . . . Babbie went to fetch the glasses and she saw Rachel's hand go up to reverently touch Jon's little beard, her long fingers staying there for a moment before they moved up to trace the outline of his mouth. Babbie smiled to herself. It was going to be all right for Jon. Rachel would love him, and love him well – she would, in time, forget Lewis McKenzie.

As the toasts were being made, Jon drew Rachel's head towards his lips and kissed the raven curls. 'I feel I must be the luckiest man in the whole world.

I have here the perfect girl. With her there will be peace; I will hear only music – no nagging – no scolding. My poor little Papa was deafened by Mamma's voice booming in his ears telling him all the things he should and shouldn't do.'

Babbie smiled impishly. 'Rachel might not be able to nag you, but she could turn instead to hitting you – what will you do then, Jon Jodl?'

'I will have no option but to turn the tables and start nagging till she doesn't hit me any more.'

Everyone laughed, the glasses chinked. Rachel held onto Jon's hand and looked forward to the excitement of going to Germany to meet his mother. They were leaving on the morning boat. If she won the travelling scholarship she was working for, there would be a lot of excitement ahead. But all that was in the future, and at the moment she and Jon would take one step at a time . . . For a minute her mind strayed to Lewis, the rapture, the laughter – an indefinable sadness made her shiver . . . She gave herself a little shake and forced herself away from the past. She must look forward to a future filled with music, with the tender, undemanding love of Jon, the man who would never hinder her, but who would help her in all the years of their lives together.

Chapter Eighteen

Lewis walked slowly up to the headland of Burg. It was June, the mist of rain that swept over the cliffs was soft and warm. The clouds were breaking apart to reveal patches of cornflower-blue sky; a ray of sun spilled over a fat fluffy cloud and beat warmly on the green springy turf of the headland. He had recently returned from a two-week stay at the Travers'. Since Rachel's going he hadn't been able to settle to anything. Fergus had been patient but now it was beginning to wear thin. 'You'll earn your keep around here, my lad,' he had warned that morning. 'You can't go gallivanting off when it comes up your hump!'

Lewis dug his hands into his pockets and stared moodily down to the wide curve of Burg Bay, which lay north of the rock-strewn shores of Port Rum Point. He made his way down a rutted sheep track, kicking stones as he went, feeling a sensation of giddiness washing over him as he paused to gaze down at the rock pools far below. 'Lewis, you'll have to eat more.' His mother's familiar plea rang in his ears. 'If you keep on pining like this you'll make yourself ill. Do you think Rachel is pining for you? You must forget, Lewis, you must.'

He couldn't eat, he couldn't do any of the things that had once made his life so sweet. Even Lorn couldn't reach him these days – yet, they were so close, they always would be. On the evening of his return from the Travers' they had raced to the big barn to measure themselves on the growing posts. Lorn had only an inch to go now before he caught up . . . They had laughed; it had been like old times; yet he knew Lorn's jollity was forced, that his mind was on Ruth. He had changed: he had started going out more, to ceilidhs, with girls; his shell of shyness appeared at last to have cracked. It was as if they had reversed roles, and he was as Lorn had once been – intense, introverted, thoughtful. Lorn was doing all the things Lewis had once loved – yet Lewis felt it wasn't real somehow, that Lorn was forcing himself, rebelling against the image of his true self – trying to forget . . . Now Lorn, too, had gone away. He seldom left the island but just three days ago he had gone away on the steamer to spend a holiday with Shona and Niall on the Mull of Kintyre.

Lewis reached the beach and saw a movement on the rocks near the water, the glint of a golden head . . . Ruth sat hugging her knees, lost in thought. She heard nothing till Lewis was just a few yards away, then she started and lifted her head. At first she thought the tall boy with the thin haunted face was Lorn, and her heart began to race. She had seen this same boy last night. She had looked from her window and had spotted him walking along the harbour with Eve Patterson. They had been talking

with their heads close together and she had drawn
her head back behind the curtains, pain and hurt
catching at her throat. He had forgotten her so easily
– so very very easily. She had been gone for just over
five months, yet for all he cared she might never have
returned. She couldn't forget that evening on the
moors, the sweet nearness of him, the innocent
tenderness of that first beautiful kiss . . .

She started to her feet. 'Lorn.' The name was a
mere breath on her lips – but then she saw it wasn't
Lorn, it was Lewis – a vastly changed Lewis from the
boy she remembered. His blue eyes were pain-
racked; the hollows in his cheeks belonged to
someone who was ill . . . Could love do that to a boy
like Lewis? Break a heart that once had brimmed over
with the love of life? . . . Yes! Yes! Love could do that
to anyone – anyone. Her father had only come back
from Coll because she had been so unhappy there;
she had wanted to come back to Rhanna to be near
Lorn.

Lewis came over and stood looking down at her
for a long time before he said quietly, 'It's nice to see
you back, Ruth. You look thin though, your holiday
over on Coll doesn't seem to have done you much
good.'

'No – I – I wanted to come back.'

'Lorn isn't here. He went away to Kintyre a few
days back.'

'Oh!' she stammered out. So it hadn't been Lorn
she had seen last night; it had been Lewis. She felt
relief even as sadness drowned her. She had come

back to see Lorn and he wasn't here. She couldn't bring herself to ask how long he would be gone, and there was silence. The sea bubbled to the shore, lapping the sands, swaying the fronds of seaweed back and forth.

Lewis sat down on a rock and picked up a shell, turning it over in his fingers. 'You shouldn't spend so much time alone, Ruth.'

'You were coming down here to be alone,' she pointed out.

'Ay, ay, you're right, I was.'

'Did you hear my father has bought a boat? He's giving up the shop and going to start lobster fishing. I'll be able to spend a lot of time with him in the evenings.'

'He did it for you, mo ghaoil.'

'And for health reasons too –' Her voice faltered and her eyes grew dark. 'Ach, you're right, he did it for me, but I think he'll be glad to get away from the shop. When the summer is over I might take over the shop myself – I like to keep busy.'

'To stop yourself thinking about Lorn?'

She flushed and bit her lip. 'Ay, that's right, Lewis.' She gazed at him steadily. 'You've changed, Lewis; you never used to take the time to analyse people – Lorn was the one who did that.'

He stared at the shell, a terrible dejection stooping his shoulders. 'Things change, Ruth,' he said at last, wearily. 'Folk change – circumstances, I suppose.' He got up and held out his hand. 'Will you walk with me, Ruth?'

She hesitated but only fractionally. She placed her hand in his. The strong brown fingers curled over hers. It felt rather strange to be walking over the beach with Lewis McKenzie, but it was oddly comforting to be with someone who understood how she was feeling.

After that day they met regularly. Often they walked to the wide sweeping sands of Aosdana Bay, the setting for so many of her father's tales. She recounted the days of her childhood to Lewis, telling him of the magical hours spent with her father. Quietly he listened to her musical voice talking about the legends of the Hebrides, and peace stole into his heart. Once he was at the bay before her. He was standing by the water's edge gazing far out to sea. He looked very lonely, and her heart went out to him. She went further up the shore to sit on the creels that lay piled against a sturdy stone boatshed. It belonged to an eccentric old man known as Hector the Boat. Every waking day of his life was spent either pottering with boats in the shed or fishing for lobsters out on the Sound. He was mending his pots and he peered at Ruth from lowered brows, smiling his one-toothed beguiling smile, his eyes crinkling in his rosy face. 'Will you be havin' a clappy doo wi' me, lassie?' he asked, indicating a driftwood fire on which sat a can filled to the brim with large mussels. Hector liked his mussels fresh from the shore, edging the shells apart with his tobacco knife and scooping out the contents, which he slithered down his throat with great enjoyment.

'No, thank you, Hector,' Ruth said and smiled. 'But – would you let Lewis and me have one of your boats for a whily? We'll collect some nice big clappy doos for you when the tide goes out.'

Hector acceded readily and Ruth ran to Lewis. Without a word she led him over to a small rowing boat tied up in a sheltered part of the bay. Together they pushed off and very soon they were bobbing peacefully in the translucent green water of Aosdana Bay. It was very calm and Lewis stopped rowing and let the boat drift gently on the wavelets.

'Talk to me.' Ruth's voice was low. 'Get it all out of your heart – it might help.'

She was surprised to see the glint of tears in the blue eyes of Lewis McKenzie. 'Could I, Ruth?' he asked huskily. 'Could I tell you everything? I have to tell someone or I think I might go mad.'

'I'll listen, Lewis, I'm a very good listener.'

Once he had opened up his heart it seemed as if he would never stop. There, out on the calm clear waters of Aosdana Bay he unburdened his mind and heart of things that had troubled it for a very long time. Ruth felt some of his pain washing into her. As the sea sighs over the sands and leaves behind that which it doesn't want, so Lewis left with her the unfettered debris of his mind. The lilting voice that was so like Lorn's flowed through her soul, and something of the terrible despair that was in him was left behind in her, and she knew it would never entirely leave her. When finally he stopped talking and there was only the sigh of the sea and the hush of the breeze, she buried her head in her arms and cried as if her heart would break. He stared at her bowed head. Her hair was like the sun, so bright it dazzled his eyes. Putting out a finger he gently stroked the silken strands and murmured, 'Sweet Ruth! And could you go with me? My helpmate in the woods to be . . .'

She raised her head to gaze at him wonderingly. 'But that's . . .'

He nodded. 'Wordsworth, the very mannie. It's Lorn's book but lately I've taken to reading a lot of things I never looked at before. That verse was meant for you, but the whole poem is more like Rachel – and myself really.'

'A slighted child, at her own will, went wandering over dale and hill, In thoughtless freedom bold,' Ruth quoted.

'Ay, that is very like Rachel. She always needed freedom, she would die without it.'

The boat rocked as he came closer. She gazed into his eyes – so blue, like Lorn's. Lorn and Lewis, they were so alike, they were of the same mould. She closed her eyes and felt the warm lips of Lewis McKenzie on hers. It was a fleeting kiss, very tender and gentle. 'You're a very sweet girl, Ruth, so very sweet.' The next kiss was longer, more demanding. She allowed herself to melt into his arms. A dew of tears lay on her lashes; she felt weak with love – for Lorn – weak with sadness – for Lewis. The two emotions mixed and merged and in the end she didn't know if she was crying for two boys who looked the same, who laughed and talked the same – or if she was crying for herself, for her own heartache.

The days of June slipped past. Every morning and evening Ruth went with her father to the lobster pots and almost every afternoon she met Lewis by Aosdana Bay. Morag Ruadh saw little of her daughter that summer of her nineteenth year, but she didn't worry unduly. Very often Dugald went out in the morning and stayed away all day, and Morag imagined that Ruth was with him. She didn't question him on the matter, and for the first time in her life Ruth knew unbounded freedom.

Fergus and Kirsteen didn't mind Lewis going off in the afternoons because he made up for it working hard around the farm morning and evening. He seemed to be happier; he had stopped snapping and going off in the huff, and Fergus said with a fervent sigh, 'Thank the Lord! We might get a bit of peace about the place now.'

'Ay, we might,' agreed Kirsteen, though inwardly she sighed. Rumours were beginning to circulate about Ruth and Lewis, and she dreaded to think what would happen when Lorn came home and found the gossip to be true.

On a hot day in midsummer Lewis met Ruth at Aosdana Bay. It was deserted. Hector the Boat was off fishing, and Ruth was very conscious of the solitude. With Hector around her meetings with Lewis seemed innocent and safe. He was wearing a blue shirt that day, a blue that matched his eyes, his earth-brown curls glinted chestnut in the sun – so like Lorn's. He was standing very close and she could see the pulse beating in his neck – the pulse of his life. Something tugged at her throat. He caught her and kissed her hair. It was warm and smelled of sunshine.

'Ruth, you're so sweet,' he whispered. 'I want to say so much to you. These last weeks I don't know how I would have lived without you – oh Ruth – mo ghaoil –' His lips came down on hers. He buried his face in her neck and nuzzled her ears. She felt the world turning upside down – if only this was Lorn . . . if only she didn't feel such sadness . . .

'Ruth,' his voice came again, slightly breathless in her ear. 'Let me love you, please please my darling little girl, I love you –' He put a finger over her lips. 'It's true, Ruth, I've never said that to any girl before – not even Rachel. I thought what I felt for her was love – now I know it was infatuation. I love you, Ruth, I really love you.'

'*No!*' She broke away from him and put her hands over her eyes to shut out the sight of his handsome young face – so young . . . She couldn't let pity for him engulf her . . . Even as she tortured herself, even as conflicting emotions whirled in her mind, she felt Lewis's arm around her waist leading her to Hector's boathouse. She stumbled, but Lewis held her tighter.

The shed was cool after the heat. It smelled of peat smoke and tar; cobwebs patterned the window panes; the sound of the sea ebbed and grew; ebbed and grew. Abruptly Lewis pulled her to him and kissed her throat, her eyes, her hot cheeks. She couldn't respond to him – she wouldn't. It wasn't right! It wasn't, it wasn't . . . His lips were warm, firm yet gentle, but she sensed his mounting passion. She didn't know how to kiss back – she didn't want to . . . His tongue met hers and something rose up inside her, commanding her tongue to meet and merge, meet and merge with his . . .

In a panic she pulled herself out of his arms. 'Please, I'll have to go,' she whispered. 'Don't – you mustn't make me feel I have to do this! It isn't fair, Lewis! You know it isn't fair!'

He was removing his shirt, pressing his naked body to hers. 'Weesht, weesht,' he soothed. 'Relax my dear little Ruth, relax . . .'

Her breasts tingled suddenly. He was touching her, doing things to her body that made her draw in her breath . . . Why, why was she caught up like this – caught between Lorn and Lewis? 'Lorn.' She murmured the name but Lewis was beyond hearing anything. He was fumbling with the buttons of her white dress, moving it down over her shoulders, pulling the sleeves down over her arms. Her throat grew tight. She tried to pull away from him but he was all at once strong yet gentle. With one hand he kept a tight grip of her arm; with the other he held up the dress to look at it almost reverently. It dazzled white in the sun streaming through the grubby windows.

'Pure, so pure,' he murmured beneath his breath before he tossed the garment onto a chair where it lay in crumpled folds. He turned his blue gaze on her; it was dazed, faraway. She was afraid now, her fear clawing inside her belly like a living thing, and with a sob she struggled in his embrace but his hands were grasping her shoulders, forcing her back – back . . .

'Ruth.' Her name on his lips was beautiful. 'You must give me this. I have no one now but you – only you.'

Her mind went numb. She had no recollection of him pushing her down onto the narrow bunk . . . She thought of her calliper – how ugly – how ugly – he mustn't be allowed to see . . .

Her breasts were in his hands, the skin of them milky white, the nipples like small pink rosebuds – so pure – so young. He bent his head to kiss them; a dew of sweat gleamed on his brow . . .

Briefly she saw sun, slanting, spilling its rays over his bronzed naked shoulders – and then there was no light, only his lips on hers, his body moving, his shoulders rippling beneath her fingers, his long lean legs pushing hers apart . . .

Pain ripped through her. She cried out once, then forgot the pain. He was murmuring her name over and over, stroking her hair, gently, so gently carrying her into oblivion. As the song of the sea swells and surges so she was swept along on waves of wanting – needing . . .

She forgot where she was, who she was with. This was Lorn loving her, wanting her – taking her . . . The sea rang in her ears, her heart pounded; once more she said the name: 'Lorn.'

She opened her eyes and saw not Lorn but Lewis, awash with passion, taking her – taking away her virginity . . . She clenched her fist against her mouth to stop from screaming out – his body was so tense the muscles were standing out. He quivered and cried out, then he fell against her, still saying her name, stroking her hair, kissing her lips . . . and she felt nothing – nothing except shame, and guilt so deep and raw it was like a knife turning inside her. Her hands fell away from his shoulders, her eyes were the colour of night, black with hatred of herself and what she had done. Crimson flooded her cheeks, her fingers clutched the blankets. Turning her golden head away from him she felt the tears falling slowly over her cheeks.

'I don't love you,' she sobbed. 'I hate myself. How can I ever face Lorn again? Everything is finished . . . finished – Now there is nothing . . .'

'No, don't say that, Ruth!' he cried then in a voice so low she barely heard it. 'Please, please don't say that. I couldn't bear it if you left me now.'

But she wasn't listening, all she could say over and over was, 'I hate myself, I hate myself, and Lorn will hate me too.'

He lay down beside her and took her in his arms. She didn't resist but lay passively against him while he soothed her as if she was a little girl. Eventually, when she had stopped crying and just lay staring unseeingly towards the window he said urgently, 'Promise you'll see me again, Ruth. You're the only one in the whole wide world who can help me. Don't let me face my future alone. Promise me; promise, Ruth.'

'I promise,' she said dully. Suddenly he was angry and he shook her slightly, as if trying to force her out of the torpor into which she had sunk. 'Ruth, look at me! Don't hate me! I couldn't bear it if I thought you hated me!'

She brought her eyes from the window and gazed into his tormented face. Her hand came up and she stroked the damp brown hair from his brow. 'I don't hate you, Lewis, I've never hated you. I like you – very, very much – and – I won't leave you.'

Lorn returned with Shona, Niall and Ellie at the end of July. Shona was so highly excited about something she could hardly wait till she got inside the doors of Laigmhor before she burst out, 'We're coming home, Father. Next spring! We've got enough capital saved to take a gamble. We'll buy a motor launch and Niall can go hopping about the islands. Ellie will be at school in Oban by then, so I'll have plenty of spare time on my hands. I thought maybe I could help Babbie out. She could be doing with it, so she could. While we're here this summer we'll start looking for a house . . .'

'You don't have to look very far!' Fergus's deep voice was full of joy. 'Biddy's cottage is still free. It will do you till you find something more suitable. Shona, mo ghaoil –' His voice had grown husky. 'To think it's nineteen years since you left Rhanna! And now you're coming back. I canny believe it – you'll have to give me some time to take it in. My mind is a bit fuddled these days – old age creeping in.'

Everyone laughed and began talking at once. Lorn grabbed Lewis's arm, and together they walked across the cobbled yard to the big barn. Lorn was tall and broad, his face had filled out considerably, and there was hardly any need for them to go to the growing posts to find out that the difference between them was barely half an inch.

'Hell!' Lorn was delighted. 'I'm six feet one and a half inches! Me! Skinny wee Lorn McKenzie!' He threw himself down on a bundle of hay and looked up at the cobwebby roof. 'It's grand to be back! I didn't want to stay away so long, but Niall was so busy I began going with him on his rounds and was able to help him quite a bit – especially with the cows and horses. When he and Shona come back here to stay I might get to go with Niall now and again. Father won't miss me, he'll have you; he always trusted you more than me to do all the heavy stuff . . .' He sat up, his blue eyes brilliant. 'I did a lot of thinking when I was away, and I've decided – no more of this moping around to see if things are going to work out between Ruthie and me! I'm going to make them work! I'm going to see her – tonight! I heard tell she was down at Mara Òran Bay . . .' He stopped suddenly and peered into his brother's face. 'What the hell's ailing you? You've hardly said a word since we got back. You're not still mooning around after Rachel, are you? I should have thought you would have got somebody else by now.'

Lewis was very pale. He was unable to meet his brother's eyes as he said, 'Ach, I'm fine! I just thought you and me could have spent this evening together. Ruth won't be back from the lobsters till late.'

'To hell with time!' laughed Lorn carelessly. 'I've let enough of it pass in misery. I'm going to see Ruthie, and I'm going tonight.'

Lewis turned away. He couldn't bear to see the eager shining hope in his brother's eyes, and he couldn't bring himself to take away that hope by voicing the things that had happened between him and Ruth.

The Sound of Rhanna was a sheet of purpled silver when Lorn finally came whistling down through Glen Fallan and walked along the cliffs above Mara Òran Bay. One or two fishermen were hauling their boats up onto the sand and Lorn went to give a helping hand.

'Is Ruthie back yet at all?' he asked of Fingal McLeod, who had sat down on a rock to unscrew his peg leg and swig at the hip flask contained therein. Fingal shook his head, 'Na, na, lad, but she'll no' be long. Look there she and her father are now,' he said, holding out the flask. 'Will you have a swallock? Warms the blood after the sun goes down.'

Lorn was about to refuse, remembering that it was the devil's brew that had caused the misunderstanding between him and Ruth in the first place, but his earlier confidence was seeping away a little and he thanked Fingal and took a swallow from the flask.

Fingal then got up and went away over the sands, his wooden leg leaving a thin winding trail behind him. The beach was deserted now and Lorn waited, his heart in his mouth as he watched the black little blob that was Dugald's boat coming closer. The sound of it scrunching on the shingle was like thunder in Lorn's ears. Ruth's back was to him as she helped her father drag the boat up above the tide line. Some distance away Lorn remained immobile, savouring yet dreading the confrontation. Ruth turned suddenly and saw him. Her heartbeat rushed in her ears and she almost fainted. Although Lorn was several yards away she could see his eyes quite clearly; they were a keen blue in his bronzed face. She felt he could see into her very soul, read her very mind. She felt soiled in his sight, degraded beyond all measure. She had waited for this moment, longed for it; now it was here and it was too late . . . too late . . .

'Ruthie, can I speak to you?' His voice was soft, breathless with hope and longing, his hands outstretched in appeal. 'We've both been very silly but – well – will you let me explain?'

'No, Lorn, go away, I don't want to see you.' It was her voice but it seemed to come from another self, a being filled with self-loathing. Anger was the only way she could bear to turn her back on him, and her voice was harsh with it.

Disbelief filled his eyes, that and a hurt so deep she knew if she went on looking at him she would cry aloud in her anguish. 'I'm sorry, Ruthie.' His voice was flat, dead. 'I was foolish enough to think you might feel a little of what I feel for you – I can see now I was wrong.' He stumbled up the beach, hardly able to see where he was going for the mist of tears that blinded him.

Dugald turned a troubled face to his daughter. 'What was that all about, Ruthie?' he asked with a frown. 'I thought you were more than fond of young Lorn. If I'm no' mistaking he was the reason we left Coll to come back here.'

She watched the tall, beloved figure of Lorn McKenzie walking away from her, out of her life – perhaps for ever. He would never lower himself to speak to her again. The McKenzie pride was in him. She could never face him and feel clean in his presence again – now now. The beautiful thing that had been between them was over almost before the buds of their love had ripened. They would remain like that, eternally unfurled, never to blossom forth into glorious flower.

She closed her eyes and swayed. Her father's voice came again from a very long distance: 'Ruthie! Are you all right?' She forced herself to answer normally. 'Ay, Father, I'm right enough. Come you home now, Mam will be waiting with the supper and if we're late she'll punish us by saying Grace after Grace before we can get a bite to eat.'

It was strange, on a small island like Rhanna, where gossip and talk abounded, that more than three weeks were to elapse before Lorn found out the reasons for Ruth's rejection of him. Lewis had taken to meeting her in the evenings, and Lorn assumed that his brother had got over Rachel and was starting to lead again a normal life. Lorn himself had rarely gone out since that fateful meeting with Ruth, but after tea one evening Fergus asked him to go over to Rumhor with a message. He was driving the trap back over the cliff road, and paused for a moment to look down on the wide sweeping curve of Aosdana Bay. Two people were walking hand in hand over the sands, a boy and a girl. Every so often they stopped and the boy bent his dark head to kiss the girl, whose hair shone golden in the light. Lorn's heart pounded and he felt light-headed. Lewis and Ruth! He didn't want to believe the evidence of his eyes, and for quite some minutes he stared in disbelief at the couple far below. Hurt filled his heart till it felt like bursting. So, that was why Ruth hadn't wanted to talk to him or have anything more to do with him! Lewis had found someone else all right! In his restless seeking after pleasure Lewis had turned to the very girl whom Lorn felt was his alone, who in time, Lorn knew, would come to him, and with whom the lovely thing that had been growing would blossom anew. With a strangled little sob he urged the pony forward and drove it back to Laigmhor at a reckless pace. Anger had replaced hurt, a fury so intense it blinded him. He would have it out with Lewis! By God! He would kill him for this! How could he? How could he do this to his own twin brother?

He made some excuse to remain out of doors and waited in the shadow of the barn for his brother's return. He had to wait for a long time, long enough for his anger to simmer steadily till it was at boiling point by the time he saw Lewis turn in at the field gate and come slowly along.

Lewis was looking neither to the right nor left of him. His eyes were on the rutted road, his steps were slow and seemed to drag. When Lorn jumped out into his path he started, but his eyes were strange, out of focus, as if he wasn't seeing properly.

Lorn's fists bunched. 'So! The wanderer has returned!' he ground out menacingly. 'You and Ruth must have had a lot to talk about – or did you have other things on your mind! The kind of things that have filled it since you had your first lusty roll in the grass with Mary Anderson!'

Lewis had gone very pale. He backed away from the dark-faced tower of revengeful wrath who blocked his way. He looked confused and passed a hand over his eyes as he muttered, 'Lorn, calm down, for God's sake, calm down. I'm sorry you had to find out this way about Ruth and me. Keep her out of it though. It wasn't her doing, it was mine. Just something that happened . . .'

'Too bloody true!' Lorn exploded. 'The way things always just happen for you. The minute I turn my back you're off with the one girl who means anything to me! You could have had your pick, but that isn't good enough for hot pants McKenzie! Oh no! The grass on the other side – eh, Lewis? Is that it! Finish with one and go after even tastier fruits! Oh, you had to have the first sampling, didn't you? Quite a challenge! To be the first! The first with everything!' he laughed bitterly. 'Well, there's a first time for everything; even I can see that though I was too blind and stupid to see what was going on under my very nose! We've never fought before, but the time has come for that too. I'm going to beat the living bloody daylights out of you. Get them up!' His fists were up in front of his face, his blue eyes were wild, his nostrils aflare in his chalky white face.

'Och, c'mon, little brother,' Lewis's voice was uneasy. 'Try to see reason. All you ever did was gawp at Ruth – at least I make her feel like the lovely girl she is . . .'

Lorn went berserk then. With a roar he rushed at his brother and punched him to the ground. Lorn hopped around him as he staggered to his feet then landed him another blow that sent him flying onto the grass verge.

The cows chomped peacefully nearby; the grinding of their teeth and Lorn's rasping breaths the only sounds in the world. Lewis lay in the grass, stunned and bruised, shaking his head, drawing a hand across the blood welling from a split lip. Grabbing at tufts of grass he got up once more but staggered and fell, sprawling his full length on the rut of grass growing in the middle of the track. Lorn fumed. He clenched and unclenched his fists.

'Playing possum!' he sneered. 'Get up! Get up, you coward, and fight back!'

Lewis did get up, so quickly that Lorn was taken aback as he watched his brother half-running, half-falling towards the stables. Lorn began to run to the stables also, but was almost sent flying as his brother raced past on his horse, riding it without saddle or bridle, urging it on over the fields in the direction of Portvoynachan. Lorn raced into the stables and, leaping onto Dusk's broad back, he kicked in his heels and the horse took off at a gallop. Away in front was Lewis, a fleeing dot on the horizon. Lorn goaded his horse faster and faster till he was within shouting distance of his brother. 'Come back! Come back, you coward!' he roared. Lewis was making for the cliff road to Portvoynachan. The ground flew by beneath his horse's thudding hooves, the drumming of them mingling with those of Dusk, the air reeling with the abuse Lorn was hurling. The air rang with his accusations, the ringing of hooves. Lumps of turf flew; the fields and moors became a brown and green blur. Lewis's horse bucked as he was guided towards the crumbling cliff paths, its eyes rolled in bloodshot fear as sods of grass and sand disintegrated under his hooves. But now they were on the beach. All was smooth and wide and clear. The sea frothed over the shell sands, rattling the tiny pebbles. Both horses thundered over the bay – Aosdana Bay – where the sea was pink and turquoise and great rocks rose like sentinels out of the water. Lewis's horse was running smoothly and faltered only slightly as his rider suddenly pitched from his back onto the rocks fringing the bay. There was a sickening thud as the dark head struck a spear of basalt.

Fifty yards away, Lorn couldn't believe the sight

that he had just witnessed. He pulled on his horse's mane and, jumping down, ran as he had never run in his life before to drop on his knees by his brother's side. The rock had torn a gaping gash in Lewis's head; the blood was flowing swiftly, matting Lewis's hair into red-brown tufts; his eyes were brilliant in his white face.

The sounds of Lewis's world came to him clearly. The bleating of the sheep rose up from the machair that lay between the north slopes and the shoreless sea to the north, ascending as the smoke of peat fires to the rosy vault of the heavens. It was a fluffy cloud evening, soft cirrus clouds floated over the emerald-green of the clifftops far above. Over the wide white sands the sea glistened, capturing in its vast reaches the blues, greens, and purples of an opal. The great mountains beyond the bay cast their purple-blue shadows on the still waters of inlets and bays that stretched as far as the eye could see. The fishing boats were coming home, their sails red in the fiery eye of the sinking sun. The tangible sense of life was all around, exquisite, timeless as time itself yet so swift in its passing it was almost a mockery. Lewis saw it all, a beauty that was partly physical, partly spiritual. Here he had walked, here he had talked – here he had loved – with Ruth. His lips were very white and trembled slightly. A little smile hovered and he whispered, 'Look, Lorn, a fluffy cloud night . . .' His hand came up and his finger pointed. 'See – up yonder – a face – with a little beard . . . I think – it must be the face – of God.'

Lorn's senses reeled; he felt as if he was gazing down a long long tunnel and at the end of it was the face of the brother he loved with his very soul. It was the face of Lewis – yet it was *his* face. He felt the tunnel whirling, spinning, round and round till Lewis's face was his and his face was Lewis's. Was this what it was like being born? A long tunnel, a vortex; pain; choking. Birth, death, birth, death. Lewis had come first into the world and he would be the first to go out of it – or would he? Lorn felt himself spinning through endless space, of time and tears yet to come, of grief blacker than space, of – emptiness . . . Lewis couldn't go – they were part of each other.

'Why did you fall? Why did you fall!' he heard himself crying. 'There was no reason, no reason . . .' His voice reverberated against the cliffs and then there was silence.

'Lorn,' Lewis's ghost of a whisper came from a long way off. Lorn spun back through the vortex, back to his own life, back to the white face of his dying brother whose head was cradled on his knee. The blood was seeping through his trousers – Lewis's blood? Or his? It was warm – warm and red . . . He whimpered and bit his lip. Strong, he had to be strong.

'Ay, what is it, Lewis?' His voice spoke the words automatically.

'I'm frightened, take me and hold me – the way I used to hold you in the sea.'

Lorn lay down on the sands and entwined his brother in his arms. Lewis smiled. 'Babies – we're both just big babies . . . Lorn, listen. Ruth – she loves you – I meant nothing to her – it was always you . . .'

'Shut up! Don't talk,' Lorn said fiercely.

'Why not – not much time left – for blethering –'
His eyes grew big and wide. For eternal moments
everything that was life was there in the blue brilliance of Lewis's eyes before they grew dull and
heavy, like blinds shutting out the light of day. 'Is –
is it dark?' he whispered in panic.

Lorn gazed at the vast red ball in the heavens shed-
ding blinding sheets of flame over the sea. 'Ay, Lewis,
it's dark,' he murmured.

'Then – I'm still – alive . . .' The words came out
in a sigh, his eyes closed, and he grew still and heavy
in his brother's arms.

Lorn never knew how long he sat there with his
dead brother cradled to his breast, but the sun had
long gone and the sea was dark when he finally came
out of the deep trance into which he had sunk. The
horses had wandered to the patches of machair
among the dunes and were contentedly nibbling the
sweet clovers. Lewis's arms were still where he had
placed them in his dying moments, round Lorn's
waist. Lorn never wanted to tear himself away from
that last brotherly embrace, but the loneliness and
grief were engulfing him; gently he eased himself
away and stood for a few seconds gazing down at
Lewis's body lying beside a rock pool in which was
reflected the last remnants of gold from the evening
sky; then he turned and ran. He had no memory of
jumping onto his horse and riding over the cliffs to
Laigmhor, of bursting into the kitchen to cry out in

deepest anguish, 'I've killed Lewis, I've killed him, I've killed him!' The world went black then and spun mercifully away from him and he didn't hear his mother's agonised cries of protest, nor was he aware of Niall and his father carrying him upstairs between them.

Many miles away Rachel sat staring before her as one witnessing a dark and terrible dream unfolding before her strangely faraway eyes. More than half an hour ago she had experienced a cold eerie sensation washing over her as a vision of Lewis erupted into her mind. It wasn't the same Lewis who had loved her with such passion, but a hollow-eyed boy, pale as death, white lips moving, eyes dark with a terrible fear of being forced to travel to some unknown place far far away from the life he had so loved – it was the same feeling she had had when her father died, and Rachel shuddered and knew that Lewis McKenzie, the boy who was with her wherever she went, whatever she did, was no more of the earth.

Ruth wandered alone in the gloaming, not aware of distance or of time, and as she walked through the cool green valleys of the hills her troubled soul became calm, and she knew what she had to do. Lewis's funeral was now two days in the past. Only snatches of it remained fixed in Ruth's mind: the pale stunned faces of Lewis's family; Lorn, a shadow without control of himself, relying implicitly on others to guide his steps, his dry dull eyes telling of grief locked away, unable to relieve his agony in the healing balm of tears. Rachel had been there too. No one had told her of the tragedy, but she had been there just the same. She and Ruth had stood by one of the big elm trees at the top of the Hillock, watching the ceremony, neither of them speaking till it was all over. Then Ruth had turned to her friend and had said, "Tis glad I am you came, Rachel, but you're a bit late to give Lewis the help he needed. He turned to me for that and somehow everything went wrong. I'm sure you will be happy though – you will go far with Jon at your side.' Her voice had been very quiet, and Rachel had flushed and turned her face away. For the first time there had been reproach in Ruth's voice and Rachel could hardly bear that. How could she explain? How could she tell Ruth that she could never have forsaken her music for the love of a mercurial boy like Lewis? She turned her dark expressive gaze on Ruth, begging for understanding, asking for a return of the simple unquestioning faith they had shared for so long. She took Ruth's hand and held it very tightly, and for a long, long time they gazed at one another, both of them knowing that the lovely innocent years of childhood were finally done with. They had been so close as children; theirs had been a rare friendship, one filled with simple trust. Now an even greater understanding had to grow between them, and it had its first stirrings then, with the holding of hands, the dark deep pleas for forgiveness that were there in Rachel's eyes. Ruth felt self-reproach searing through her. It was wrong of her to blame Rachel; she hadn't

known that Lewis was dying. Even if she had stayed
with him she couldn't have saved him – nothing –
no one could have done that. For a moment she was
tempted to tell the other girl about Lewis, but the idea
left her as quickly as it had come. She had sworn to
Lewis that she would tell no one of his illness – that
she wouldn't utter a single word about it till all the
pain and grief of his death had departed from the
lives of those who had loved him most. His death
had been put down to an accident, and Ruth believed
this to be the case also. She wanted to believe it. He
had told her that he wasn't going to wait till his
condition had deteriorated to the stage where he
would be lying in bed with those he loved best
watching him dying. He had meant to take his own
life but Ruth knew he would never have deliberately
done such a thing in front of his twin brother. She
guessed he had taken one of his giddy spells and
simply fallen off his horse. Some of his most
profound words came back to her, so clearly she
heard the lilt of his voice, the note of pleading. 'After
I'm dead, Ruth, I want you to wait a whily before you
tell my family I had a brain tumour. Mother would
go mad thinking of all the things she should have
done for me. Seven or eight months should see them
over the shock of losing me. I want them to know
why I was such a grumpy bugger all this time, but
not right away. I am going to ask Lachlan to wait
also, to hold his tongue till a few months after I am
dead and gone – though of course I won't tell him
how I plan to go. It's a lot to ask of you, Ruth, but

do this for me – a dying wish if you like.'

There in the graveyard, Ruth had had no inkling of the quarrel that had taken place between Lewis and his brother or she would most certainly have run to Lorn and spilled out her heart to him. Instead, she had put her arms round Rachel and held her close. Raven curls had touched those of palest gold, and each of them had felt a great sadness for days gone, never to return.

Ruth's heart had felt numb. One day Rachel would go away, far away to foreign places, while she – she hadn't known then what she was going to do. She had stepped out of her friend's arms. 'I won't see you for a whily, Rachel, I'm going away, I don't know where yet – but I'm going away . . .'

Ruth stood amidst the heather and closed her eyes. She wished she was more like Rachel, able to turn her back on the kind of love that seemed to bring more heartache than joy – but she wasn't like Rachel. When she married it would be for love . . . Would she ever marry for that? She remembered running up to Lorn after the ceremony, taking his arm and saying quickly, 'I'm sorry – dearest Lorn – I'm sorry I've hurt you so – if only you knew . . . I hope one day you will understand . . .' He had stared at her dazedly as if he was seeing her from a very far distance. His earth-brown curls had been chestnut in a glint of watery sun breaking through the clouds, his eyes, for all their sadness, so intensely blue she could hardly tear her eyes away from them as for a brief moment they focused on her face. His lips had moved and he had whispered, 'Ruthie, it's you – it's you, Ruthie.'

'Ay, Lorn, it's me,' she had said, nodding, her voice so choked by tears she could hardly get the words out. His hand had come up to take hers, but she had stumbled away from him, away out of the Kirkyard to walk unseeingly past the schoolhouse and along the shore to the clinical confines of home.

Now as she stood on the brow of the hill, watching the sun go down behind the corries, she knew that she had to get away, away from Rhanna and all it meant. Yesterday she had met Shona, her auburn hair tossing in the wind, her blue eyes full of compassion as she said, 'If you want somewhere to be at peace for a whily, you are welcome to stay with Niall and me in Kintyre. Sometimes it helps to get away, Ruth. It helped me once when my heart was as troubled as yours is now.'

The words rang in Ruth's ears as she walked homewards through the darkening night. Her father was in the kitchen and she went to him, and putting her arms round him, said quietly, 'I'm going away, Father, just for a whily. Shona has asked me to go and stay with her and Niall. They're going away on the morning boat and I'm going with them. Don't tell anyone where I am, not even Mam; I must be free of everything till I get myself sorted out. Och, I hate leaving you, I love you, Father – I'll – I'll write. I'll send my letters to the shop and you can maybe answer them when you have the time.'

He seemed to expect the news because he held her at arm's length and his grey steady eyes were full of understanding as he said huskily, 'I'll miss you, my babby, but I think you're very wise. Don't give up your writing – whatever else you do don't give up your writing.'

She didn't answer. Going to her bedroom she hastily packed a small case and the first thing she put into it was the marble paperweight given to her by Lorn on a far off night when the world had been full of laughter, life, and the first tender stirrings of love.

Very early next morning Ruth came downstairs dressed in a neat navy-blue suit and a violet blouse that matched her eyes. She had bought the clothes from a mail-order catalogue whilst she was on Coll, and had smuggled them away, never knowing when she would get the chance to wear them. Now her chance had come.

Her mother was at the fire, pounding vigorously at the porridge, but at the opening of the door she turned her red head and the sight that met her eyes made the blood drain from her face. 'Where are you going, my girl?' she said in a flat monotone. 'And why are you dressed like that? Where is your white frock?'

'I left it upstairs, Mam.' Ruth's voice was calm, though her heart was beating so fast she felt she would faint. This confrontation with her mother was what she had dreaded more than any other. The thought of it had kept her awake all night, yet now she felt a great sense of relief coming on top of her apprehension, and her dark purple gaze never wavered from her mother's face.

Morag's hand tightened on the wooden spoon till

her knuckles were white. 'So, you've sinned in the eyes o' the Lord,' she gritted. 'Everything I told you, all the things I warned you against – you never heeded a word – no' a single word . . .' Her voice began to rise: 'You wanton, brazen wee hussy that you are! You're no better than that Jezebel, Rachel McKinnon! I warned you, I warned you about her, but did you listen? No, oh no! She contaminated you wi' her flirting and caperin' around wi' boys of all kinds. Tell me, tell me, girl, was it that Lorn McKenzie? Was it?'

'No, Mam, it wasn't Lorn.' Ruth wasn't frightened any more, her heart was as steady as her voice.

'Then who was it, girl? *Who was it!*'

Ruth's eyes were big and bright and beautiful as she answered, almost triumphantly, 'It was Lewis McKenzie, Mam, and he's dead so there is no' a thing in the whole world you can do about it.'

Turning round she kissed the white head of Dugald who had been standing close behind her all the time she was speaking, then, lifting her case, she walked across the carbolic-smelling floor, slipped unhurriedly out into the clean air of morning, and walked with her head high towards the steamer tied up in Portcull harbour.

Part Six

Autumn 1960

Chapter Nineteen

Kirsteen walked slowly upstairs and into her bedroom. Going to the dresser she pulled it open and took out the big family Bible that lay there. The pages fell open at the book of Job. Here lay the papery-brown fragments of the two rosebuds Fergus had plucked on the night their twin sons were born. How long ago it seemed – yet how near – the joy, the pain, the laughter – the uncertainty of those early days when Lorn's life had hung in the balance – the later uncertainty when he had undergone one operation, one crisis after another. Now he was big and well and strong – physically. Mentally he was ill. Since the death of his brother he had retreated into a world where nothing, no one could reach.

Everything that had meant anything in his life had gone out of it – first Lewis, then Ruth . . . Kirsteen lowered her head and a tear fell onto the withered roses pressed between the pages. The sounds of the late September evening came through the open window – the barking of the sheepdogs, the lowing of the cattle from the byre. A calf had been born that morning, new life, just as it had been at Laigmhor the night her twin sons were born . . .

Fergus came up behind her and pressed his lips

against her hair. He knew how her heart ached, the same deep pain lay heavy in his own heart – yet – he knew they had to go on – that life had to go on. Shona would be coming back to Rhanna the following spring, back to stay after more than nineteen years' absence. He couldn't help looking forward to her coming home, was unable to stop the little surge of joy that lifted his spirits every time he thought about it. He couldn't help but feel a small stab of hope on this sweet evening in autumn when the air was filled with the scent of peat smoke, and the golden leaves that littered the cobbled yard were frisking in the breeze. Yet, he couldn't shut out the sadness either nor help but feel something of Kirsteen's pain. He put his strong right arm around her waist and whispered in her ear, 'You must try not to feel so sad, my darling, it's not easy I know but you'll have to try.'

She shook her head. 'I know, but I can't help it. I'm sad for Lewis, for life – the beauty of it, the passing of it. Perhaps I cry for it all, all the remembrances – Mirabelle – Biddy – Alick – so many people who lived and loved and died. I might be crying because I am growing a bit nearer death myself. Oh – not yet! But it's nearer today than it was yesterday. Ay, I think I cry for that – and . . .' she turned and buried her face into the warm flesh of his neck, 'I cry for you too, my dearest, dearest love – just because I love you so much and don't know what I would ever do if anything happened to you.'

He drew her in close to him, conveying some of

his strength to her as he soothed her tenderly. 'Weesht, weesht now, my darling, you mustny think such things. We have many years together yet – we'll live till we're a hundred – if the Lord spares us, of course.'

She smiled and gave a watery sniff. 'Of course we will, how could I ever think we might only live to be ninety-nine?' She leaned against him. 'Oh, if only Lorn could find some happiness, I think then I might begin to live a wee bit myself.'

'Anybody at home?' Lachlan's deep voice came from below. He was sitting in the inglenook in the kitchen when they came down, his fine, sensitive face full of something that neither Fergus nor Kirsteen could define, a muted excitement mingled with a slight apprehension. Although he was past sixty he had never lost his boyish look. His hair, though slightly threaded with grey, was in the main still dark and thick. 'Sit you both down,' he instructed in his quiet pleasant voice. 'But before you do I think it might be a good idea if you fetched us a dram, Fergus. What I have to tell you might hurt and upset you – on the other hand it might take some of the weight from your hearts and help you to understand better the last few months of Lewis's life.' He smiled ruefully. 'It will lift a burden from my own mind, too. Ay, and poor Phebie's as well . . .' He hesitated. 'Actually the things I am about to tell you were meant to keep a whily longer, but I got a letter from Ruth this morning that changed my mind.'

'From Ruth?'

'Ay, as you know she's staying with Shona and Niall, and seemingly they got a letter from you to the effect that Lorn was eating out his heart, not only with grief but with guilt. I had no idea he blamed himself for Lewis's accident.'

'Neither did we until last week!' Kirsteen cried. 'On the night Lewis – died – Lorn came racing home here shouting that he had killed Lewis. We knew it was just shock, of course, and he never said any more on the subject. Then last week it all came spilling out. He and Lewis had had a dreadful fight. Lorn chased him over the shore and – Lewis fell off his horse. Lorn thinks that somehow he is to blame!'

'Ay, they did fight – about Ruth – as you've probably guessed,' Lachlan said gently. 'Ruth had no idea of this. Like everyone else she assumed the boys were joyriding on the beach when the accident happened. Shona confided certain things in your letter to Ruth, who immediately contacted me . . . You see, with the exception of Phebie and myself, Ruth was the only other person who knew the truth about Lewis.'

'What truth?' Fergus asked harshly.

'I'll explain – where is Lorn by the way?'

'Out in the stables with the horses,' Kirsteen said rather wonderingly. 'He spends a lot of time in there nowadays.'

'Ay, well best to leave him where he is just now. I want to talk to you both first.'

And talk he did. The hands of the clock crept round, but not one of them noticed the passage of

time. It was almost midnight when Lachlan finally sat
back, his brown eyes full of compassion as he looked
at the two people sitting close together on the settle.
Kirsteen was staring at her hands lying on her lap,
Fergus's arm was round her, holding her very tightly.
Finally she looked up, her blue eyes misted with
tears as she whispered, 'Our laddie was a wild, wild
devil in his day. Times were he was so fickle I could
fine have skelped some sense into him but – oh God!
He died a man, Lachlan, a fine young man with a
brave brave heart.'

'Ay, he did that, Kirsteen,' Lachlan agreed softly.
Reaching inside the breast pocket of his jacket he
withdrew a bulky package. 'This is for Lorn – would
one of you give it to him? The sooner the better.'

Fergus stood up. His eyes were very misty as he
said huskily, 'I'll take it to him now – and –' he held
out his hand to grip Lachlan's firmly, 'thank you,
Lachlan, for everything. You and Phebie are more
than friends of this family – you're part of us.'

He went quickly outside to the stables. They were
warm and steamy and smelled of hay. Lorn was
sitting in a corner, close by the big Clydesdale Myrtle,
whom he loved fiercely. He was polishing her
harness, talking to her quietly. He spent many of his
free hours in the stables, grooming the horses,
cleaning the stalls, tiring himself out so that by the
time he crept up to bed, often in the small hours of
morning, he was too tired to think – to remember.
He didn't look up as Fergus came in, but went on
rubbing at the harness, which was already shining

from previous care lavished upon it. Fergus's shadow danced in the light from the lantern hanging from a beam. He held out the package, his eyes black with love and compassion for this haunted son of his who had blamed himself for his brother's death and who had lived neither in the land of the living nor of the dead for five long, weary weeks. 'This is for you,' he said softly, 'from Lewis.'

Lorn did look up then, his blue eyes wary, his voice harsh as he cried out, 'What do you mean – from Lewis?'

'Just what I say. Read it and read it well, son. I'll leave you in peace, for peace is what you need now, and I hope the things that Lewis has to tell you will bring you peace of mind in full measure,' Fergus said and went out, closing the door softly behind him.

For fully five tremulous minutes Lorn stared at the brown paper package on top of the golden bale of hay, then with a little cry he snatched it up and withdrew the contents, a large diary bound in red leather and a letter. He laid the letter to one side and ran trembling fingers over the gold-edged pages of the book. He had given it to Lewis last Christmas – the Christmas of 1959 – the day after that terrible evening of the Burnbreddie dance. His heart was beating very fast as he opened the diary. The first few pages were blank but just after the end of February 1960 the writings began, Lewis's large untidy scrawl filling the pages, and as Lorn read he heard the echo of his brother's voice inside his head so that even as he was reading the words it was as if Lewis was reading them out, keeping him company there in the stables with Myrtle and Dusk and the ponies peacefully lying in their stalls. Lorn settled himself back among the hay, and as he read the message, written to him alone, it was as if he and Lewis were the only two people alive in the whole of the quiet night world.

3rd March 1960
Lorn, by the time you get this I will be up in the great blue yonder. I don't think I will go to hell. I haven't been an angel but I haven't committed any great crimes, either. I have a brain tumour. Lachlan told me it was perhaps there when I was born but only started to become active recently. So I didn't escape after all. At first it was just bad headaches, which got worse. And then I went to Lachlan. I am not afraid – I am terrified! From the time I knew what death was all about it scared the breeks off me. Maybe some inbuilt instinct warned me that my time on earth was to be short. I don't know. All I know is I've been in hell since I found out, and I've put those I love most in hell with me. I wouldn't let Lachlan tell any of you. Mother and Father will suffer enough when it is over and done with, so why make them suffer now. I have been to Glasgow and had tests done and the doctors told Lachlan the tumour was inoperable. That is why I went away. Not to see Rachel, but to go to hospital. It was gey lonely there, I can tell you, and the longest month I ever spent. I'm going to enjoy the time left to me. I'll have a bonny time and to hell with tomorrow. I'm tired

now, my head hurts a lot and I see things double. I'll speak to you again later.

April 1960
The spring is coming in and I've never been so aware of life as I am now. Lachlan wanted me to go to Glasgow for treatment, but I wasn't having it. I don't want to prolong the agony. Lachlan gives me painkillers. He and Phebie are wonderful. Have you ever noticed Lachlan's eyes when he knows you're feeling pretty damned sick and there's nothing much he can do to help? Of course you have, little brother, you've know illness since you were born. I'm not good at describing things, but Lachlan has God in his eyes.

These last few weeks I've been running wild. There's so much I want to do. If I sit still I begin to think and I get scared so I get up and go. I wander up to Brodie's Burn a lot and I remember the day we met Ruth up there. It helps just to sit and think about her tales of the past. I used to hate dwelling in the past, now it's all I ever want – I don't want to think of the future. As well as being sick in the head (don't laugh) I'm pretty sick at heart just now. I've got Rachel on the brain! She grows in there and, like the tumour she won't go away. Funny how girls can do that to men. I've had a lot of girls in my time. They meant nothing, I never felt for them the way I feel for Rachel. She's different, like a wild rose blowing in the wind, so beautiful I shiver whenever I think of her smooth golden skin and those big dark eyes of hers. That doesn't sound like me, eh? For the first time I feel there's more to all this love business than just a quick roll in the hay.

Rachel has told me she's going to marry Jon. I can't believe it! Yet – I can. He can be trusted; he's like her father. I think that's what she needs, a father figure. Rachel has got a strength in her that's a wee bit eerie at times. She knows where she's going, what she wants from life; and she'll get it, too. I looked into her eyes today and an odd shiver went through me. The old ones are right. Rachel has the power. Whatever it is, she's got it.

May 1960

I watched you today, Lorn, and saw myself. You've grown, little brother. I won't be able to call you that much longer. You're getting stronger and I'm getting weaker. You deserve it, you skinny wee rabbit! (You can't hit me where I'm going.)

I watch Father and Mother too. I've taken to watching people. Mother is beautiful, more from inside now she's getting older. Yet, in some ways, she always seems young. Father is getting older too, it shows in his hair and the crinkles round his eyes – but that's all. His back is straight, he's hard and strong as an ox. In a way I'm glad I won't see them growing really old, they'll always be as they are now. I can't imagine Mother a wee old woman or Father a grey auld bodach. I'm smiling writing this, so you smile too – go on – smile, you bugger! The time for weeping is over. I'm thinking now of how I love our parents. Mother is a very easy person to love but my love for our father isn't so easy to explain. I've respected him all my life and there have been times when I have felt really close to him but never like you and him. He understands you because you're two of a kind, but I think I always worried him a wee bit. He's a hard man to live up to – not because he's ever been a Holy Wullie, God forbid! He's got a lot of ideals, though, and I think I was born without a single one. He's a dour, stubborn bugger – like you – but I love you both. Shona's a lot like the pair of you – stubborn as a mule's arse but there's a wonderful sunny side to her nature. She must have taken that after her own mother. She's always known I was a coward about death and sickness but she always had a lot of understanding for me. Many's the time I've blessed having a big sister like her. Grant's the happy-go-lucky one of the family – a bit like me but with more sense of responsibility. Maybe I should have gone round the world like him, but then I would have missed everything that's here on Rhanna. I've loved every minute of my life here and I thank God for letting me be born on a Hebridean island – here I can breathe and be as free as the wind – I'm talking about God now, thinking about Him in a way I never did before. Ruth has helped me there. Somehow, through all the hellfire and thunder dinned into her ears since she was born, she's managed to extract the truth from her Bible and to see God. She told me there was a time when she hated God, but the years have opened up her eyes to the truth and beauty behind it all – and now I'm going to sleep. Tomorrow I will write more – tonight my head hurts and I'm seeing everything double – even you lying in your bed snoring. I'm writing this by the light of a torch and it's strange to be writing to you when you're here beside me in the room.

It's June now. You're away staying with Shona and Niall and I miss you, little brother, always I miss you when we're apart. I walked over to Burg and met Ruth. She thought I was you at first. I saw the hope in those lovely eyes of hers then it faded when she realised it was me. She came back from Coll because she couldn't stand to be away from you only to find you had gone. You're a daft pair of buggers! All this beating about the bush because of a stupid mis-understanding. I told her the reason you got drunk at the Burnbreddie dance and she got quite angry about it. She says all you had to do was tell her you couldn't dance. She doesn't much like dancing either, and would have been quite happy just talking to you all night.

I've been meeting Ruth a lot over at Aosdana Bay. Today we got out one of Hector's boats and I poured out my soul to her. She cried for me and I kissed her. Ruth is like sunshine. Her hair smells of it. When she talks about you her eyes grow dreamy and go really purple, the colour of the heather hills in autumn. Her

voice is like music. I could listen to her all day. The
sound of her voice is like a burn tinkling over the
stones on the moor. She called me Lorn when I
kissed her the second time. Fancy the blow to my
ego! Girls have always fallen at my feet now this wee
lassie with the big dreamy eyes feels me kissing her
and imagines I'm you!

Weeks have passed. I know now why you love Ruth.
She's truly good. I've grown to love the innocence
of this sweet shy girl with her lovely face. I love all
her moods, her sadness, her joys. I feel a strange sort
of rapture just being in her company. She's so
different from Rachel. Rachel always gave out a sense
of great power; Ruth is fragile and vulnerable. I feel
I want to protect her, to keep her safe, yet she has
an inner strength that is like yours. She's stronger
than me. She's been my crutch these last weeks.
When she knows I'm in pain she takes my head in
her hands and soothes me. I knew Rachel wouldn't
feel pity, that's why I never told her about myself,
and to have her feel sorry for me would have been
more than I could stand. Yet, even if she had known
she would still have turned from me. She started off
life with a show of toughness, time and events hardened her till her toughness became genuine. Ruth
has no shell, she is laid bare to all the hurt the world
can give her. Her only defence is shyness – yet, when
she has to defend people she loves she's like a
tigress. Mind what she did to Canty Tam when he
sneered at Rachel? Well she did the same thing to me

one day when I said you were soft. I was being jealous of all the talking she did about you and she turned on me like a wild cat and sent me off licking my wounds.

It's midsummer now and Hector has gone off for his annual holiday to Mull. Today I made love to Ruth. I know you will curl up inside reading this but don't hate me or feel anger against Ruth. She thought I was you, she called me Lorn and she cried and hated herself. I thought she wasn't going to see me again. She's all I've got now, the only person in the whole world who can help me in my last days here on earth. Whatever you do, don't blame Ruth for what happened. She's torn between her love for you and her sorrow for me – because that's all she really feels for me. I love her in a way I've never loved any girl before. I've never felt tenderness for any other girl, but that is what I feel for Ruth, tenderness. It's a good job I'm not going to be around for very much longer because I would have fought you tooth and nail for Ruth even though it would have been useless. She loves you and no one else. I only have her for a little while; you will have her for the rest of your life. Ruth has made me live even while I'm dying, so don't waste time holding grudges, just remember that in my last days Ruth comforted me, gave me light when there was darkness. Little brother of mine, I love you. You may ask yourself how can I say such a thing when guilt is tearing me in two and I know I can't go on seeing Ruth much longer for fear you will find out. But I can't say I don't love you just because we both love the same girl. That would be daft. You're my brother, my twin, you're me really and I'm you and all this is getting so complicated I'm laying down my pen. You're coming home tomorrow and I don't know how I'm going to face you, so I'm taking the coward's way out. I'll start seeing Ruth in the evenings so as not to arouse too many suspicions. I can't let go of Ruth – not yet.

12th August 1960
I'm feeling really bad today. I get dizzy a lot. When I'm supposed to be working I just sit up in the fields, seeing two of everything. I can't enjoy any of the things I love. I can't see to read now and it's getting more difficult to keep on writing in this diary. When I'm out riding I feel like falling off, everything just goes round in circles. I think that's how I'll go out. I'll take one of the horses and just pitch over the cliffs. I tell you this, I'm not waiting for this thing to kill me, I'm going to kill it first! After all, I'm a McKenzie and we're a family who don't like anything to get the better of us!

24th August 1960
How beautiful is this small island world of ours. I am aware of every blade of grass, every whisper of life in the forests and moors. The sky is so wide, I feel a great sense of freedom and space – as if I could spread my wings and fly like the birds. Just lately I have felt a strange peace coming over me, an accept-

ance of that which is to come. It might sound daft coming from me, but I'm not afraid of death any more. The folk of our island are beautiful, especially the old ones. They have got wisdom and contentment in their eyes. With a few exceptions the people of Rhanna are a serene lot.

I am going over to see Lachlan later this morning and I am taking this diary with me. I will ask him to give it to you eight months after I am gone and at the same time to explain to Mother and Father why I was such a dour, moody bugger to live with this year. I am going to see Ruth tonight and will make her promise not to say a word till the time is up. Why eight months? Well, I'm a bit in the dark when it comes to people's feelings on grief. I never wanted to know any of those things and always used to turn away from them. When I was in hospital there was a chap there who had not long lost his wife. I asked him how long it took to get over it. He said he never had, that you never do get over losing someone you love and that eight months passed before he could think of her without crying. Around that time he also felt that he wanted to start living again, to go forward, not dwell in the past. I mind too when Rachel lost her father it was April and for months after I used to shiver when I looked at her. She wore the same clothes as usual, yet I felt as if a thick black blanket was covering her. Round about Christmas that year I felt as if the blanket was growing thinner, letting Rachel shine out again. I'm a daft bugger but these are the only incidents I have to go on, so eight months it is. It won't be easy for Lachlan and Ruth but I have to make them see I'm doing it for my family – you will have gotten over losing me by then and better able to take all this. I know you'll miss me, of all the charmers who ever lived I think I must be about the nicest! With one exception, my wee brother, Lorn Lachlan McKenzie – my better half! Thanks for being my brother, I couldn't have had a better one. Don't think you're getting rid of me though. I'll be keeping my beady eye on you – sort of watching over you like a guardian angel. (I like the idea of that! I'll have wings like the birds and be able to fly.)

Have a grand life. On fluffy cloud days look up and remember me – who knows – you might see my face up there watching you, so be careful when you go rolling in the heather with Ruth. (On the other hand don't be too fussy, I might pick up a few hints.) By the time you get this you and Ruth might be married. If so, be happy and good in a naughty kind of way. (I always found being too good the most boring thing on earth.) Mo Beannachd leat, daonnan.

Lorn closed the book with a soft little snap. Lewis had died on the evening of August 24th 1960. For a moment it all came back, the horror, the grief, the heartrending pain. These last words, from Lewis to him, were the final thoughts, the final goodbyes. Then the ending of the diary came to him: Mo Beannachd leat, daonnan, the Gaelic for 'My blessings be with you always'.

The words rang in his head like a benediction, a prayer. Lewis had spoken, not from the grave but from life, all the eager thrusting force that had been in him, even to the end of his short young life. The experiences of his last months had been crammed into a few pages, yet they were so beautiful; wistful, yet so filled with every kind of emotion he had been like an atom, spreading outwards in the universe to embrace it and hold it to himself as if to savour all the wonder of creation. Lorn shivered and felt a thread of some of that wonder weaving its way into him till he felt like laughing and crying at the same time. A tear rolled slowly down his face to be followed by another. Faster and faster they fell, the first tears he had cried since his brother's going. His strong young body shook with a storm of weeping, and when it was finally over, when the great shuddering sobs had finally ceased, he felt as if a balm had been poured over his soul. Myrtle turned and nuzzled his neck with her velvety nose, and getting up he buried his face into her mane and said aloud, 'Thank you, thank you, big brother, you have set me free, I'm free now because I know the truth – and I don't hurt any more . . .'

His eyes fell on the letter lying on the bale of hay. The one word written on the envelope leapt out at him. That hand, he knew it, so well he knew it. 'Lorn' was all it said but it was enough for him to know who had written it, for had he not, over and over, looked at that very name inscribed into a birthday card given to him by Ruth to mark his eighteenth year? With trembling fingers he slit open the envelope and sank down against Myrtle to devour the letter with hungry eyes.

26th September
1960

Dearest Lorn,

I am sending this to Lachlan to ask him to give it to you along with Lewis's diary. You shouldn't have found out any of this for some months yet, but when I found out you blamed yourself for Lewis's accident I couldn't bear it and wrote to Lachlan. As it is, it has been a long and weary few weeks, and I'm glad the waiting is over and you at last know the truth. There is so much I want to say to you, so much you have to understand before you can even begin to forgive me. I don't know if you ever can. I have done things, so many things that have been hurtful and wrong but that were the only things I could do to give Lewis comfort when he needed it most. Often I remember and I hate myself. Lying in bed at night I cry thinking of you, your pain and your hurt. I want you in my arms, to have and to hold, and my body aches with loneliness. I miss so many people, my darling father, my friends on Rhanna – but most of all I miss you, my darling Lorn, and long to see you again.

Shona and Niall have been so kind to me, I will never forget how they helped me when I needed help most. They are like a pair of excited bairns at the moment and talk constantly about going home. They can't wait to get back to Rhanna.

I don't have many plans for my future. I tried to start writing a book, but it was no use. I kept seeing your face on every blank page so I have put my pen aside for a while and have taken instead to daydreaming. I might go back to my aunt in Coll, but wherever I go, remember this – every minute, every hour, every day of my life, I think of you.

Ruthie.

Lorn crushed the letter to his breast and sank down against Myrtle's soft flanks. The stable was peaceful and he had so very much to think about. He didn't go back to the house that night.

Fergus and Kirsteen slept fitfully. Like Lorn they had a lot of new thoughts that jumbled around in their heads before they began to settle into some sort of order. But just before dawn Kirsteen finally fell into an exhausted sleep. Fergus looked at her, the hands thrown over the pillow, the lock of crisp hair falling over her brow. She looked like a child in her repose, and, leaning over, he kissed her silvered hair gently then got up out of bed to get quickly dressed. It was a glorious autumn morning; the peat smoke was rising from the chimneys of Portcull; the fishing boats were sailing out of the harbour; the subdued clatter of milk churns came from the dairy. By the side of the road some distance away Dodie was sitting on a tiny stool by Ealasaid's flank, his big fingers gently extracting the milk for his breakfast. Fergus breathed deeply. It was the start of another day, a beautiful new day filled with all the promise of new life, new beginnings, new hope. He walked towards the fragrant fields; the rich smell of newly turned earth was strong in the air and he looked up. There on the golden horizon was silhouetted the figure of Lorn lifting the kale, in front of him plodded the noble sturdy form of Myrtle, the magnificent Clydesdale. Fergus swallowed the tears in his throat. 'This is my son,' he thought proudly. 'Against all the odds he has become a farmer and a true son of the soil.'

He heard himself calling, 'Lorn! Lorn!'

Lorn looked up, his blue eyes fixed on the beloved man who was his father. A great swelling joy exploded inside him. He began to run towards the lower fields, stumbling, falling in his haste, but someone seemed to be at his elbow, urging him on, helping him up. Lewis! Of course it was Lewis! Death could never rob him of the brother who had shared his life from the moment of conception. They were of the same flesh, the same heart beating – the same spirit. Lewis would go on living in him. As the years passed people would look at him and know what Lewis would have looked like that day – that tomorrow – that forever. They had both loved the same people – the same girl – perhaps one day Ruthie would come back to Rhanna – back to a love that could never forget her. If she didn't he would go to her – by God he would!

'I'm coming, Father!' he cried, the tears pouring unheeded out of his eyes. His heart was beating, pulsing, bounding with a joy he felt could never be exceeded – but it could – it could! One day it would – with Ruthie!

Fergus watched his son running swift and sure over the dew-wet fields. He saw him trip and almost fall, but in seconds he was steady again, his feet flying swiftly.

'Lorn,' whispered Fergus, the lump in his throat fading as tears dissolved it away. The boy reached him and pulled up short, shy for a moment, then he was in his father's strong embrace, the deep sure thudding of the beloved heart filled his ears. Fergus looked up and Lorn followed his gaze. Ruth was coming over the fields from Brodie's Burn, her slim body dressed in palest green, which blended harmoniously with the grasses.

'She must have come home on last night's steamer,' Fergus said softly.

Joy and hope accelerated Lorn's heartbeats; his eyes were filled with so much love they were luminous in their expression. Ruth spotted him, and her steps faltered, slowed. Lorn left his father's side and began to run, conscious of every ray of light, every sparkle in the diamond-like dew drops misting the fields. The dazzle in them found reflection on the teardrops poised on his lower lashes. Ruth had begun to run also, her hair a golden halo, now against the green of the grass, now against the deep blue sky. She was a vision of sweet and lovely girlhood with hardly a trace of a limp to hamper her graceful movements.

Kirsteen came out of the house and walked towards Fergus, hesitantly at first. Then she saw his powerful, dark face lifted up, transformed with the light of inner joy. She ran to him and he held out his strong right arm to take her in his embrace. Her gaze followed his and a little sob caught in her throat as she stood there with the man she loved, watching the two young people meeting and embracing on the brow of the silvered fields. The sun burst over the lower shoulder of Ben Machrie, morning broke in all its golden glory bathing the moors, brushing amber over the ethereal purpled peaks of the hills of Rhanna.